YPSILANTI DISTRICT LIE

7101 9100 080 568

D0098296

GOOD EVENING MR. & MRS. AMERICA, AND ALL THE SHIPS AT SEA

Fiction
Bausch
NOV 01 1996

GOOD EVENING MR. & MRS. AMERICA, AND ALL THE SHIPS AT SEA

 RICHARD BAUSCH

Ypsilanti District Library
229 W. Michigan Ave.
Ypsilanti, MI 48197

HarperCollins*Publishers*

GOOD EVENING MR. & MRS. AMERICA, AND ALL THE SHIPS AT SEA.
Copyright © 1996 by Richard Bausch. All rights reserved. Printed in the
United States of America. No part of this book may be used or repro-
duced in any manner whatsoever without written permission except in the
case of brief quotations embodied in critical articles and reviews. For
information address HarperCollins Publishers, Inc., 10 East 53rd Street,
New York, NY 10022.

HarperCollins books may be purchased for educational, business, or sales
promotional use. For information please write: Special Markets
Department, HarperCollins Publishers, Inc., 10 East 53rd Street, New
York, NY 10022.

Designed by Nancy Singer

Library of Congress Cataloging-in-Publication Data

Bausch, Richard.
    Good evening Mr. & Mrs. America, and all the ships at sea : a novel /
Richard Bausch. — 1st ed.
       p.   cm.
    ISBN 0-06-017332-7
    I. Title.
PS3552.A846G66   1996
813' .54—dc20   96-19624

96 97 98 99 00 ❖/HC 10 9 8 7 6 5 4 3 2

Suzie

It is the duty of old men to lie to the young.

—Thornton Wilder, *The Eighth Day*

The places that we have known belong now only to the little world of space on which we map them for our own convenience . . . remembrance of a particular form is but regret for a particular moment; and houses, roads, avenues are as fugitive, alas, as the years.

—Marcel Proust, *Swann's Way*

Acknowledgments

Thanks to Alan Cheuse for suggesting this book to me while riding through Washington, D.C., during the inaugural parties in January 1993, and for providing me with the title.

Thanks also to Robert Jones, for fighting.

Author's Note

This is a work of fiction. I made up everything except the facts and the politics, which everybody knows are of little importance.

*T*he other students still enrolled in the D'Allessandro School for Broadcasting in the fall of 1964 had heavy responsibilities and worries, and were making sacrifices to come to school. Lately it had seemed to Walter Marshall as if there were some general discouragement these students were all stoically enduring to continue acquiring their training, though Mr. D'Allessandro himself was always cheerful, and went about his business in the usual meaningless hurry. He had a big ring of keys attached to the belt, and each evening he opened his office with a great jingling of the keys and breathless protestations about how pressed for time he was. Everything he did, every aspect of the school's operations, took place in the same hectic rush.

The building that housed the school was old—it had been erected during the presidency of Andrew Jackson—and occasionally the lights flickered or went out, as though something in the heart of the structure had failed momentarily. There were holes in the plaster of the ceilings in the corridors, and some of the wainscoting had come away from the walls of the rooms; The radiator pipes made an awful pounding noise in cold weather, when they worked at all. And if the building itself was dilapidated, the school's equipment was not much better—several student desks were falling apart; some of the switches on the electronic console in the sound booth were broken; there were sheets of baffling dangling from the ceiling in the studio; only one of the phones worked. Mr. D'Allessandro had cut down on the electricity as much as possible, and was economizing in other ways: When the toilet in the men's bathroom broke, instead of calling a plumber he had fashioned a small cardboard sign for the one good bathroom: OCCUPIED (the U was closed at the top, so it looked as if it said OCCOPIED); because the radiator in his office was unpredictable and worked on its own undiscoverable schedule, he could be found some winter evenings sitting at his desk wearing a coat.

In the middle of all these homely concessions to frugality, Walter Marshall felt more than a little guilty: His tuition had been paid for out of an inheritance from his father; and just as it was becoming clear to his classmates that he had the best prospects for landing a job after graduation—he was already spending some Saturday mornings taping sixty-second commercials in English to be run during a South American public affairs program on Sunday afternoons—he had let it be known that he was no longer interested in broadcasting as a career.

So while the others struggled to meet their payments and to fulfill the responsibilities that were weighing them down—and while Mr. D'Allessandro himself seemed more harried and threadbare than ever—Marshall was coasting through only in order that the money already spent would not be wasted.

Aside from Albert Waple, who had been friendly from the first days, the other students had begun keeping a certain distance. There was never any unpleasantness—but in fact they now possessed more shared experience to talk about, since together they had also begun to arrive at the painful conclusion that the resources they were spending on this training might as well have been spent on something else.

There was Ricky Dalmas, who at twenty-two was only three years older than Marshall, but who already had a wife and two children. During the days, he worked in an auto shop behind the parts counter, and barely made enough money to pay his rent. Of course he could not afford payments on a car. School nights, his wife packed sandwiches for his evening meal, and sent him trudging through the weather to school. Often, he had part of a sandwich with him to eat during the break, and when he did not have anything, he watched the others eat their candy bars and snack crackers. No one offered him anything, because he always refused and always seemed vaguely affronted by the offer. He kept an unlighted pipe in his mouth a lot of the time, bringing it out and holding it up as if to savor its aroma before he spoke. This was a nervous gesture, unconscious as a blink, and it was rendered all the more awkward by the fact that you could see him striving to be the sort of person who held a pipe a certain way—a man pondering troubles, the complexities of existence. Each night he wore the same dark green sport coat with patches on the sleeves, and his hair always dangled over his forehead, black, straight, and with a sheen like polish. At times the dark forelock looked exactly like that of Adolf Hitler in the photographs, but no one ever mentioned this. The pipe had a chip in its stem, and he had a chipped tooth, and it was difficult not to connect the two, somehow, as though there had been some kind of collision in his past having to do with the pipe. He had not finished high school, and was now having some trouble with the required work. His best hope for the future, according to Mr. D'Allessandro himself, was to find a job selling advertising time or something. That was as near as he would ever get to a real job in broadcasting, and Mr. D'Allessandro had been straight with him about it. He would never work the microphones, because his voice was too high-pitched, his ear for where emphasis ought to fall too weak. "There's no way to fake a tin ear," Mr. D'Allessandro told him.

Yet each night, as part of the second-year training schedule, Dalmas was required to read out some advertising copy, which—as was nearly always immediately evident—he had taken the trouble to write himself.

You know, death is always inconvenient, but to make it even more convenient, try Gausson's Funeral Home on West Pike Street in Landover Heights. That's Gausson's Funeral Home, the place to bring your family and friends during moments of grief . . .

There was Joe Baker, thirty-one years old, a civil servant now, though until the year before last he had been an elementary school teacher, in Alabama. He had been with the National Guard there during the riots three summers ago. "They had me guarding a church in Montgomery," he told Marshall in the first minutes of their acquaintance. "After the Freedom Riders came in and this mob went after them. That was a world of hurt. A bunch got away from the mob and gathered in this old church. A lot of the famous ones, too. I mean the whole boatload of Civil Rightsers—King himself was in there—making speeches and singing. It was something. Didn't know if anybody'd get out alive, least of all me. I believe in integration, too. I do. You know why? I think it's good for business. A lot of Southerners do. Even the ones raising all the hell. Like the bus-company owners. That's the most ridiculous thing in the world. Everybody knows they need the Negro's business—can't survive without it. And here they are insisting on this back of the bus shit. For the sake of form. All knee-jerk shit, you see? They're afraid to look at it differently. And then everybody's afraid of the crowd." He was also married, with three daughters, one of whom occasionally came with him to class. She looked nothing like her father, and he teased that this was one of God's mercies to the country. Baker was heavy-jowled, and pug-nosed, and wore a flattop haircut that showed the crown of his scalp. His mouth was crowded with teeth, especially on the bottom row, and they made his jaw stick out. The starched white shirt he always wore was invariably rolled up at the sleeves, showing powerful, almost hairless forearms. He possessed a good radio voice, but could not distinguish the tones needed—again, a problem of emphasis. When he spoke into the microphone, you could hear authority and confidence, but there was no music in it; it sounded flat, almost machine spoken—which was not at all the way he sounded simply talking. His ambition was to work his way up to sports announcer.

Only auto accident I ever had, it was summer, I was going slow in traffic, bumper to bumper, and I saw this beautiful girl—this vision, you know?—come walking out of a bank over on H Street. I couldn't take my eyes off her, and—bang!—I hit the guy in front of me.

I'm—what—eighteen years old, scared shitless, and out of the car this old, old man comes, all bent over with a cane. He walks slow, back to the window of my car, leans in and without quite looking at me says, "That's all right, son. I saw her, too." Then he turns around and walks back to his car and gets in, and that's just the way I want to be when I'm eighty-five . . .

There was Martin Alvarez, whose uncle worked at the FCC, and who claimed to have important connections there. Even these, he seemed to be saying at times, would do him no good. He was twenty-eight or twenty-nine, unmarried, and it was hard to know much else about him, since he never wanted to come out with the other students after classes and he seldom talked about himself. Big-shouldered and dark and round-faced, he spoke with an accent that made the others wonder why he was not the one doing advertisements for South American Radio. One of his eyes had a white fleck of something in it, and when he looked at you, with his white smile and his enthusiasm, the fleck made you think of helpless children in dire circumstances.

My favorite guy een show business ess thees guy Bert Pahks. Mos' talented guy I have ever seen, mun. No sheet. I saw him perform at thees club las' year, almos' keel me, mun . . .

The one woman in the class, Mrs. Gordon, had a very rich— even an attractive—voice and some ability to hit the right notes, but she had problems with certain words. At a point early in the course of study, she had announced to the others that there were words she simply would not say in any context, as a matter of principle—she did not use them in her daily affairs if she could help it, and she certainly would not use them, no matter the pressure or the cost, on the public airwaves. She was adamant about this, for personal reasons. She would not say the word "i-n-t-e-r-c-o-u-r-s-e," she said, spelling it out very slowly as if intending to deprive the letters of their meaning when in proximity with each other, or the words "s-e-x," "b-r-e-a-s-t," "l-o-v-e-r," or any word implying the name of a body part or function, including "k-i-d-n-e-y" function. She was not old—she might have been only a dozen years Marshall's senior—

but she dressed and behaved as though she were. She came to class in severe suits and dresses, with high white collars and long sleeves, even during the hot, airless days of late June, and her hair was always tied up in a bun at the back of her head, then wrapped tight in a white hairnet. Marshall had supposed that the grounds for the restrictions she placed on language were religious.

They were not.

One evening, quite out of the blue, she expressed in the strongest way her conviction that God did not exist. Marshall had said something about Kennedy's funeral, how Cardinal Cushing had called for the angels to greet him, and how there had been something oddly emotionless about the old man's voice. "It's all a lot of baloney," Mrs. Gordon broke in. "A terrible lie. Something to keep people happy until they carry them away in the box." Her voice was nearly shrill. The others stared at her. "I didn't mean to interrupt," she said to Marshall, nervously touching her collar and looking down. You could see the effort it took to restore her demeanor.

In the evenings, just before class, her husband dropped her off, and was always waiting to pick her up when class was over. Marshall had watched her get into the car, and lean over to kiss the husband on the cheek, the husband concentrating on getting into the flow of traffic; and as the car moved off, the two of them stared straight ahead.

When Mrs. Gordon read copy, she did so in soft tones that were somehow motherly and caressive; even, in an odd way, alluring: If you did not look at her, you would have sworn that she was a much older, much more comfortable and confident woman.

This evening, ladies and gentlemen, we will be listening to the incomparable music of Wolfgang Amadeus Mozart . . .

Finally, there was Albert Waple. Tall, thin, sad-looking, ugly and angular, Albert had rough, strong, long-fingered hands, lean arms, and pipe-thin legs, like all the old caricatures one saw of Abraham Lincoln, and he had told Marshall when they first knew each other that his close friends called him Abe. "I think it's in honor of my good qualities, as well as appearance," he said with a knowing smile. "You can call me that, too, if you want. Because I bet we'll be friends." He was twenty-two, severely myopic, and engaged to be married to the young woman who had taught him to read Braille. He could not wear glasses because the lenses were not made that could help him see any better, and, in fact, his doctors had told him that in a few years what little sight he did have would leave him. He wanted to be ready for the experience, and learning to read Braille was a way of doing that. He had thick, ash-blond hair, which usually stood straight up off the top of his head, as if he had just been aroused from a night's sleep; and if it was true that he could not drive a car, nor do many of the things people around him could do, he behaved always as though he were quite content to be where he was, doing whatever he happened to be doing. He could read only in direct, bright light, with the book almost touching his nose, yet he read a lot. It gave him terrible headaches, and caused cramps in his neck and back, and still he pursued it with the calm pitted happy resolute stubbornness of someone who appreciates a thing wholly, without the slightest doubt about its value. When reading, he looked like a man examining the smallest minutia, searching for some moving thing on the page; but of course he was attending to the words, the sounds that language made, saying the lines quietly to himself, and it was this whispering that had made him think he might make a career in radio. He liked the music of the words when they were arranged well, read aloud, and he read copy with a good, easy flair, a friendly sort of confiding simplicity.

His eyes were so deep set that his face seemed caved in on either side of his nose, and when he wasn't reading, he tended to gaze off, a look of patient acceptance on his face—he was someone to whom the whole of the rest of the world was a bad blur of colors and shapes, and he did not seem to mind this at all. Often, he had his copy done in Braille, now, speaking in his soft, amiable, small voice about the trouble in Alabama, or Laos, or Vietnam. He might as well have been some kindly stammering person on the telephone. And no matter how often Mr. D'Allessandro corrected him, talking about objectivity and distance, the detached, professional voice of radio news, he always took it quite seriously and patiently, and then went on in the same way, unable to be other than what he was.

Let's see, what do we have here—oh, yes, Jimmy Hoffa, president of the teamsters union, has been found guilty of jury tampering—that's from a trial in sixty-two, I believe. He's been sentenced to eight years imprisonment and a ten-thousand-dollar fine. He's still liable for conviction in another case, where he's charged with fraud and conspiracy, too.

Marshall imagined that this offhand style might start a trend, and that Albert would be famous one day, sitting on *The Tonight Show* with the new, younger guy, the former game-show host, talking with fondness about the old radio-school days, when Mr. D'Allessandro tried to get him to sound like everyone else. . . .

Regarding Marshall's own future, broadcasting was now the farthest thing from his mind. He had other, loftier, ideas, having calculated that in the year 1988 he would be forty-three—John F. Kennedy's exact age when Kennedy had assumed the office of president. (It was difficult not to see significance in the fact that 1988 would be a presidential election year, too.) Since Kennedy's assassination, he had dreamed about politics—"the honorable profession" Kennedy had called it—and had entertained hopes of following in the dead president's footsteps. He felt something like a sense of mission about it, wanting to serve the people, as Kennedy had set out to do, although he had not given much thought to what the people actually might need in the way of service: Freedom, Opportunity, and Peace, of course . . . and jobs . . . less crime . . . and Medicare . . . and fully integrated schools, buses, and lunch counters. Integration generally. For real. An end to the nuclear threat. And security from the monolithic Communist plot to achieve world domination. He supposed that more definite ideas would come to him as he progressed. He considered that he was a patriot; he had recently described himself as an idealist without illusions, using the martyred president's phrase, though again he was not certain about the meaning of the phrase as it might actually apply to him. What he knew for certain was that he desired the chance to risk everything for his country.

And when 1988 did roll around, if he was a politician, perhaps he would be in a position to run. . . .

He told no one about his plan, of course—not really. Well, he had spoken of it to Alice Kane, the young woman who worked the mailroom with him at the Census Bureau, on Twelfth Street. When he came to the job, the summer before President Kennedy's assassination, Alice was already there, working in another department. He'd met her in the cafeteria. They had been seeing each other for a few months now, "just friends" she said to everyone else, including her father, who ran the Washington bureau of the news for CBS. The fact was that there were a number of young girls in the building who liked Marshall's company, and troubled to spend time with him in the dead hour after lunch on summer afternoons. He was what they called cute, among themselves: He had a way of paying such deep attention to them; they felt almost revered in his presence. Moreover, he was naturally rather funny; he could imitate the gestures and voices of others with startling accuracy—he did Dick Nixon especially well, and the speech about retiring from politics after California had the temerity to elect Pat Brown over him the year before last—and he told stories, mostly having to do with various embarrassments he had experienced while in school, all of which amused and diverted them and made them laugh. He understood in a visceral, unspoken way that to these young women, if he was lovable, he was also not a serious candidate for love-life, as they called it to his face more than once, and he was usually happy enough to play to their idea of him as the harmless young clown. This was the role he played with all the women he knew, including the German girl he saw two nights a week at the D'Allessandro School. With Alice, though, there had been a shift toward something more substantial; they had been taking lunch hours together, and on the days he didn't have school, she rode the same bus with him into Arlington. They had talked about more important matters, like the future, his future. It was becoming clear that she looked upon him less frivolously than the others. As a person to tell serious things to, she was the logical choice (for instance, she was the one to whom he had described himself as an idealist without illusions). Four years older than he was, and better informed about certain things concerning world news, she seemed to admire his intelligence, his finer qualities—an obvious tenderness of heart, the high-minded sentiments, the will to improve himself. He had read *War and Peace*, for instance (it was an abridged version, but he had bought the paperbacks of the full edition, translated by Rosemary Edmonds, and he was several chapters into the first volume). Though Alice often teased him about the age difference, she had a way of seeming to hang on his every word. Once, in a strangely dolorous mood, she talked about what others might think of her, going around like this with a nineteen-year-old. This murmured confidence seemed to imply an invitation for him to reciprocate. And so he had mentioned, casually, but concentrating intensely on her face, that he was thinking of pursuing the presidency.

"The presidency," she said. "The presidency of what?"

"The—the United States," he said.

"Really? You?"

"Sure," he said through a small gulp. "Why not?"

"You're too sensitive. And blunt. And you don't have any money. I mean, being interested in politics is one thing—but gosh."

He had read somewhere that people thought Robert Kennedy was blunt. "It doesn't always take money," he said.

"It helps."

"What do you mean, 'blunt'?"

"Blunt. Blunt. As in, you don't have a lot of subtlety."

This did not sound good. He felt odd, having to pick through these thoughts while she watched him. He felt quite stupid doing it.

"I'd have an easier time believing you were going to be a painter," she said.

He was abruptly pleased. "I'm color-blind," he told her.

"You draw good pictures."

True—though he had no feeling for it at all, nor the slightest desire to pursue it. "I'm not interested in art," he said. "Not to do, anyway, like a career."

"Well, politics might be fun. I'm involved in some politics, you might say. I've been working for Civil Rights. We both live in what is still a segregated state, you know. Even though it's against the law now. Do you believe in Civil Rights?"

"I do," he said. "Very much."

She was staring off. "Running for president." She turned to him. "Stranger things have happened, I guess. Actually, now that I think of it, I'd have pictured you as an actor, or a comedian, like—I don't know, the driving instructor guy, Newhart."

"Politics," he said.

As her eyes began to show belief in what he could one day do, he could not help feeling vaguely proprietary toward her. Perhaps it was just a matter of having one's mind made up, but somehow the sense of his own excellent future made him expansive, almost self-assured. She seemed to think it was inevitable, going on about his strong principles and sharp intellect, his good sense of humor, the things he could bring to the profession. Clearly, she was impressed with him. He liked talking to her, sounding the depths of her admiration, and she was not afraid to advise him, either. According to Alice, he was spinning his wheels going to radio school; he should start college immediately. Her father had never attended such a school. And before becoming an important producer of news he had worked in several places as an announcer. He had a strong college education, and that was the important thing these days, though some of the men he worked with hadn't gone beyond twelfth grade. There was a night school in the same building as the D'Allessandro School of Broadcasting, she said; she herself had attended the school two years ago. She had flunked out, because she could not get through the French or the math. (Courses designed to thin the ranks. They didn't want you to finish college if you weren't really up to it.) But he would do well at the night college, an intelligent, well-read young man like him, and then he could transfer his grades and go to a real school and get a degree. Just as her father had done. All a young man needed was a little push.

"Right, Walter?"

"I don't even need the push," he told her. "I'm way ahead of you." Perhaps he could use radio work to help put himself through college.

"If you get good enough grades," Alice Kane told him, "you can get a scholarship. My father got a scholarship his second year."

"There's some money," he said. "A small inheritance."

"Really? Your father?"

"Yes," he said. "It's a little money."

"You never said anything."

"It's not much," he said.

This afternoon, a rainy Monday in early October, she approached him at work and invited herself along to his evening of radio school. Earlier in the day, at lunch, they had run into Mr. D'Allessandro, who, when Marshall introduced Alice and mentioned in passing who her father was, became quite solicitous, asking Alice to come visit the radio school any time, wondering if she might want to come tonight, though any night was fine, any night would be quite all right for a person of her background.

"Well, and actually I do know something about it, of course," she said now. "I've been in real stations and watched how they operate. And Mr. D'Allessandro did say tonight would be good, too, didn't he? I've been wanting to, anyway. What do you think?"

Marshall sought vainly for something to say.

"I was always curious about it when I was going to the night college. Is it all right? Or I could just go on over there myself—see you there, or something."

"No, we'll go," he said.

The truth was, he liked the hours between the end of work and the beginning of school precisely because it was time to be alone, completely free of the requirements of his mother or Alice, or anyone else. He could spend the whole two hours imagining himself years older, a different man, established, someone with the power to do good things. He could look at the streets of Washington, D.C., conjuring up how it might change in the time it would take him to get where he hoped he would go. Or he could happen upon the German girl at her studies, and perhaps she would feel like talking to him. Her name was Natalie, and the sight of her took his breath away.

"Won't we have fun?" Alice broke in, a little doubtful, apparently seeing that he had drifted far from her.

"It's pretty miserable out," he managed.

"Gloomy weather always makes me feel sort of giddy inside," she said. "I don't think I know why, actually."

Actually. That was her word. It came out with an automatic flourish in her talk, like a form of punctuation. "Actually, I've been intending to try night school again myself."

He liked her, and had even found himself thinking about her

when he was alone. There was something warm and welcoming in her dark eyes, and she had a strong sense of the ridiculous; she could make him laugh. She was very short and slight—the kind of girl who, as his mother had put it, was blessed with nice features, and would be pretty if she could only gain some weight. (His mother inclined to a sort of scary detachment about the way people looked or behaved: About the young man himself, she had said, "You're not what I'd call extremely good-looking—you're no movie star—but you're nice and tall, and you'll have rugged features when you get old enough. Also, you have good, broad shoulders and a nice-shaped head, so you shouldn't let your hair grow. For that, you need to fill out around the face. Your face is too thin." She said all this while gazing at his hair, which for some months he had been trying to comb like Kennedy's. He couldn't get it to behave; it was too curly, too wiry. "You do need to get wider in the face," his mother told him. "And you will. Don't worry, you will.")

Now, Alice Kane said, "Maybe it's just that I think people are silly to let their feelings be influenced by the weather. It's like deciding there's something the matter with a person if she's twenty-three and not married yet."

"I usually don't even notice the weather," said Marshall.

"Did you hear what I just said, Walter?"

"Well, I don't let the weather affect me," he said.

"No. Usually you've got your head buried in a book. I think you ought to breeze through college."

Here was her bright admiration again. A grown woman.

"You really don't mind if I come with you to the school, then?"

"It's a long walk, too."

"I used to go to the night college there, remember? I flunked three courses, actually. I didn't finish *Beowulf* and I couldn't get past the verb 'to be' in French. And then college math. My God. I guess I should've done the French in high school, like everybody else. I walked into that room and everybody was speaking the language. I felt like saying—Hey, look, folks, if you can already speak frog, why are you taking frog 101?"

"You said that?"

"I *felt* like saying it. I didn't say anything. My father's always called them frogs, and I thought of saying something. But I sat there like a lump while they talked, and wondered if I shouldn't get a passport or something—ask to speak to the American ambassador."

"And you want to sit through an evening of radio school?"

"I thought it might be nice. See what they do. Anyway, I've been doing some sitting through things lately, if you know what I mean."

He did not know what she meant.

She gave his shoulder a light punch with her fist. "Taking part in sit-ins, silly."

"Really?" He was fascinated.

She smiled. "Well, we live in the old Confederacy." She sighed, and seemed to consider. "Actually, there's this place in Maryland, of all places. I went there with my family to eat crabs when I was little. It's in Pope's Creek. A sign on the door, big as life. 'White Only.' The sign's not there anymore, but the practice sure is."

"I went there as a kid," he said. "I remember it was—yeah, white only. I remember."

"Well, see?"

"There's a law now, though. They're not still—"

"Of course they are."

"But—what about the law?"

"You're sheltered."

"No," he said. Though of course it was true.

"Anyway, we'll have fun tonight," she said.

"You sure you won't be bored?"

"I've always been taught that boredom is a personal failure. Look, if you don't want me along, just say so. I'm a big girl." She spoke briskly, with a clipped something in her voice. "I mean, we've been going around together and I don't know what you do when you go to radio school, and Mr. D'Allessandro seemed so interested to have me come visit, and I thought I'd take him up on it, that's all. It's a chance to spend part of the evening together. Don't you want me along?"

"Of course I do," he said. "I want you to have fun, though."

She patted his arm, smiling. "I'll suffer through it."

The week before, Joe Baker had brought his wife in—a big, sorrowful-looking, soft-featured woman with mournful, watery blue eyes, who seemed to be trying to melt back into the elements that had produced her. There was a strange, withdrawing, shying-away quality to her actions, and she wouldn't meet anyone's gaze. Baker was cheery and talkative, and kept his arm around her through most of the evening, but the skin under his eyes took on an ashen, shadowed hue as he smiled, attending to everyone's expression. His face shone, as if he had put on some polish and buffed it for the occasion.

"I met Fanny in Alabama," he said. "Didn't I, honey?"

She nodded.

"I was in the guard."

"That's right," she said.

"Fanny was living with her mother in Montgomery, but she's from Boston."

"Yes," Fanny said.

"I like Boston," Marshall said.

"You been to Boston?" Baker asked.

"No. I think it's a good place. I follow the Red Sox."

"You'd like it," said Fanny.

"I went to school in Montgomery," Baker said, "and did most of my growing up there. Pretty town. Or it used to be. But I hated it."

Marshall couldn't help noticing that Baker's wife kept wringing her doughy-looking hands in her heavy lap, staring down. And Baker went on talking, a man with a deep dread of silences, pauses. There was something mortified about both of them, really, as if they had been caught out in the open in each other's company.

"Fanny liked Montgomery," Baker went on. "She'd go back tomorrow. Whole town's coming apart, and there's mobs in the streets, and she wants to live there."

"No one cares what I want," Fanny said in a small voice, still looking at her hands.

"That's right, my love," said Baker, smiling broadly, as if the whole conversation had been a joke.

The feeling, all that long evening, had been one of acute embarrassment.

Now, briefly, Marshall saw himself as being like Baker someday, trying to talk over any hesitation while others looked at Alice Kane and wondered. Oddly, he saw himself married to her; it was years later and he had come to whatever this was that Baker and his wife had come to, and all the others understood, in spite of everything he tried, that this was not what he had planned.

He was ashamed of himself for having such ungenerous thoughts.

At five-fifteen, they left work together and walked in a warm mist up Pennsylvania Avenue, toward the Treasury Department, the White House, and Lafayette Park.

"Back during the war," he said, "there were soldiers on the roofs of all these buildings."

"No kidding," she said without interest. "What were they doing?"

"Watching for German planes. My father was one of the soldiers. He had a guard post up on top of the Treasury Building."

"What a funny image—a man guarding all that money."

"He wasn't guarding the money."

"I bet they all made jokes about it, though."

"I suppose it's possible," Marshall said.

"I'd like to have heard him talk about it."

"We only talked about it once. He came back here when he was—when he knew he didn't have long. You know. His heart was giving out on him."

She said nothing.

"The whole time I was growing up I thought I should feel some anger against him for leaving us," Walter Marshall said. "I was too young, and couldn't really remember much about him. And so it wasn't there—wasn't in me—to be angry with him. There were pictures, but you can't really take anything from a picture. A picture really isn't worth anything when you don't remember the face. And there were times when I wished I had him around, you know, but it never got to be something I was mad at. It was just what had happened to us all, I guess. And I guess my mother had something to do with that. Her attitude about it, I mean. Then, when he came here, somehow it was like he was this old friend of hers. I liked him, and—but I felt sorry for him, too, and couldn't quite believe that's who he was. My father. We came here, you know. He stood there by that statue and told me about how things were during the war. He said this was always his favorite part of the city when he lived here."

"It's so sad," she said. "Trying to make up for everything before you go."

"He was—peaceful about it," said Marshall, remembering how strange it felt to stand in that place with the old man, someone he had never known, this very courtly, heart-weak gentleman with the unsteady, tottering walk and the broken smile. The only image of him that the boy had carried with him out of childhood was a blur: someone in a dark green fatigue jacket—army issue, circa 1940—making a trail through drifting snow around a big, rotund, bearlike snowman, everything gauzy-looking in the swirl of flakes, the shape of his father there, hands in the pockets of the green jacket, a pipe jutting from his mouth trailing smoke, leading several neighborhood children and Marshall in some game lost to memory now—some improvisation that had arrived in the happy blush of an unexpected gift: a snow day, a nature-enforced holiday from school and work—counting steps, slogging through the trodden snow, circling the enormous, still figure with the red woolen cap on its featureless round head. No matter how hard he tried, Marshall could not see the face of the man in the dark green jacket—only the jacket, and the skinny legs, the boots, the faces of the other children, whose names he had forgotten long ago. It was as if the face were obscured by the roiling mist of snow, still falling, still sifting down in the wind.

"It's so sad," Alice said.

"What?"

"Your father. Stop daydreaming."

"He didn't—didn't seem to want a lot more than he'd had," Marshall said.

"Why haven't you ever told me this?" she demanded. "That the two of you came here. We've been on this street before. Don't you think about it every time you come by here?"

"Sure I do."

"And you never thought to tell me about it? You're so phlegmatic about some things."

He didn't know the word, and he didn't want her to know he didn't know it. He raised one eyebrow, as if to accept this description of himself, and kept silent.

This was a long walk, and normally provided him with opportunities to explore and to watch people, or to wander into the drugstores, to browse among the magazines and paperback books in their metal racks. It was amazing how completely people looked through you in the streets of a large city. You could walk among them like an invisible guest from another world, observing everyone. He thought of mentioning something about this, but she began talking about the election, how there was no danger that Goldwater would actually be elected president. Marshall quickened his pace, crossing Fifteenth Street, and she hurried along at his side, talking. "My father gets so mad at me because I make jokes about the name—a person can't help his name, I guess." She sang, "Every time I pee, I see, Goldwater," and then laughed. "Actually I liked that thing he said in his acceptance speech at the convention—that stuff about moderation and extremism something and something—it was an interesting way to look at it—"

"Moderation in the pursuit of justice is no virtue, extremism in the defense of liberty is no vice," Marshall said.

"You have the best memory of anyone I know."

He felt as though he were probably quite extraordinary. Along with being phlegmatic. He couldn't wait to get to his dictionary, at home.

"I don't know how anybody can remember anything," she said. "I certainly can't."

The sidewalk was crowded, and the whoosh and rush of cars sounded all around them. He was attuned to everything. At the beginning of himself. It felt that way sometimes, and it was a pleasant feeling. He was an aggregate of possibility. He walked along, watching the fluid, moving world around him. Lights made shimmery ponds of reflection in the road surface and shone in the windows of passing cars. A black limousine with big tailfins went speeding by, and Alice wondered aloud if it was Johnson. No, Johnson was in New England, campaigning.

Decorations girded the tops of the streetlamps lining F Street— little cones of white light, suggesting the shape of Christmas trees.

Through the efforts of the new First Lady, there had been money appropriated for renovations on the street, and the decorations were part of a recent ceremony. The city would probably leave the decorations there, now, through the holidays. Beyond the newly paved street, far off in the waning afternoon, a siren wailed. They went on up Fifteenth and over to Lafayette Park, past stacks of wooden planks that in early January would be used to begin building bleachers for someone's inaugural parade. In the park, all the trees were heavy with the mist, the green washing out of them, and there was a gloomy, abandoned look to the patches of leaf-littered grass. The statues seemed to rise out of the dark in their striving, radiant with mist. She had taken hold of his arm, talking about the needlelike rain, and the lights along F Street, her father, who always made such a big fuss every year. Wouldn't it be nice, she said, to arrange a double date: Marshall and Alice, with Marshall's mother and Alice's father. "Don't you think so?"

"My mother wouldn't go on a blind date," Marshall told her. "And your father doesn't like me."

"How can you say that? You only met him once."

As they were leaving the park, a man approached them, wearing a signboard. "Hey, kid," he said. "Wait—where you going?" He took hold of Marshall's sleeve. "You think this is a democracy, kid? Do you? This is not a democracy." The signboard said US OUT OF UN. There were more words below this, but they were unreadable, washing out in the rain. "What's your name, kid? I seen you coming through here before, hunh? What's your name?"

"What's yours?" Marshall said. "I've seen *you* here before, too. I come through here every Monday and Wednesday."

"My name is Walter Winchell. I never seen you before."

"You're not Walter Winchell."

"Bet me." The man held out his hand.

Marshall looked at him. "That's my name, too."

"Walter Winchell?"

"No, my name is Walter."

"Don't bullshit me, kid." The man turned to Alice. "Excuse the language, miss."

"That is really my name," Marshall said. "Would you like to see my driver's license?"

The man regarded him, as if to gauge his level of seriousness. Then he nodded. "Yeah. Why not."

"His name is Walter," Alice said. "I can vouch for him."

"Lemme see it," said the man.

"First, admit you're not Walter Winchell," Alice said.

The man frowned. "I can't help what somebody else's name is, sweetie. I'm not the radio guy." He turned to Marshall. "Now let me see what you got."

Marshall produced the license, and held it up for the man to see. The man took his wrist, held the license closer to his face, turning so that it would catch the light of a streetlamp. Marshall turned with him. It was as if they were moving slowly through the steps of a dance.

"I can't—" the man said. "I can't make it out—"

"It says 'Walter,'" Marshall said. "See?"

The man said, "Where? Come over here in the light." He pulled Marshall with him to the corner, directly under the lamp. He still held the young man's wrist, and he stared at the license. "I can't read it—the glare on the plastic. Can you get it out of the plastic?"

Marshall tried to pull the card out of its slip. His hands were getting wet.

"Here," the man said. "Let me."

Marshall handed it to him. The man tried for a moment to remove the little card, then held the whole thing up to the light again. "You got anything else with your name on it?"

"It's right there," Marshall said. "What's the matter with your eyes?"

The man suddenly thrust it at him. "Agh. I'll take your word for it. I can't read it in this light."

"It says 'Walter,'" the young man said, putting it back in his wallet.

"Okay," the man said. "What do you want, a medal? You reckonize me. And maybe I reckonize you, too. So what. There's no money in your wallet."

"Do you want money?" Marshall asked him. "Is there something I can do? I'd like to help you."

"Shit," the man said, turning away. "Kid's crazy."

"Do you want some money?" Marshall asked him, trying to reach under his raincoat.

The man took him by the arms. "Look, I don't want your money. Leave it where it is. All right?" He patted Marshall's shoulders and stepped back, almost danced back, bowing and shaking his head. "Jesus."

Marshall let Alice pull him along, looking back at the man, who kept watching him, then turned and seemed to hurry out of sight.

"My God, what're you thinking of when you pull this stuff?" Alice said.

"I'm thinking of giving to the poor," he told her.

She said, "Saint Francis in Italian pointy-toed shoes."

"Well, isn't that what we're all supposed to do?"

"The Bible doesn't say anything about giving to people with signboards on, I know it. I've read enough of it to know that."

They crossed H Street and made their way toward Eighteenth. Cars and buses were lined up at a stoplight, and the two of them hurried across. In the headlights, you could see how hard it was misting.

"Want to eat at Wheaton's?" she asked. "I always used to stop at Wheaton's."

"On Eighteenth. Me, too. I mean, I do now."

"The one just down from Saint Matt's."

Marshall said, "I don't call it that."

"I didn't think I was being disrespectful," she said.

"No," he said. "It's fine."

"You got quiet. What's wrong?"

"Nothing," he told her.

"Okay," she said simply. They went on in silence for a time. And then she began talking about the folk craze—the Kingston Trio, whom she had seen in concert, and the Modern Folk Quartet, and Bob Dylan, which she pronounced Dye-lan. Dye-lan and Joan Baez were going together, and she had a music magazine, *Folkworld*, that showed them sitting next to each other in a circle of people, at some gathering in Carmel. Young people were doing dramatic things all over the country, and she said the knowledge of that filled her with an ache, a desire to get on with things. "We're going to do a sit-in down in Pope's Creek this week sometime," she said. "It hasn't been decided yet."

"I don't like the Beatles," Marshall told her. "All they have is that mop hair. They don't have any real talent. I don't understand what all the fuss is about."

"Do you like Dye-lan?"

"I don't really know that much about him. He wrote that Peter, Paul and Mary song. Isn't it pronounced like the guy in *Gunsmoke*?"

"No, it's Dye-lan, I'm sure. Because he writes about death a lot. You should hear him sing. He sounds like a ninety-year-old man, and he's only my age."

"I like Peter, Paul and Mary. The Kingston Trio. And Judy Collins."

They went on, up Eighteenth Street. In the shop windows, there were photographs of Kennedy. Some were still draped in black cloth, or in the folds of the American flag, or red-white-and-blue crepe. They were mostly candid shots—Kennedy concentrating on something, writing, staring off, listening, a young man burdened with the cares of office. Public places all across the country were being named for him, and merchants sold recordings of his speeches, books about his life—his heroism, his wit, his pain, his courage.

"Time is such a funny thing," Alice said. "It feels like he lived forever ago, doesn't it?"

"I saw him once," Marshall told her. "On a lunch hour. Summer before last. His hair was so reddish with the sun on it. It surprised me. I remember being surprised by the redness in it. I've been reading his speeches."

"The way you read. It amazes me that you got bad grades."

"I read fast, too," he said.

"Kennedy could read more than a thousand words a minute."

"I'm like that," he hurried to say.

"I've never thought you seemed like the type to be in radio."

"What type is that?" he said.

"Oh, sort of talky—you know. With a big voice. Like my dad. Some of the people he brings over. "

"I had a teacher tell me I should be in radio," he said. "When I was in the eleventh grade. My mother works with him now. Mr. Atwater."

"Well," she said. "Radio's not for you."

"I've decided that," he said.

"Right. You're going to be president."

"It's a little early to talk about *that*." He was very pleased.

"I told you my dad met Kennedy a couple times. He has friends who knew Kennedy pretty well. One interviewed Kennedy on TV, with Cronkite and the others."

"My father went to school with Mitchell Brightman," he told her.

"That's him," Alice said, delighted. "That's the one."

At Wheaton's they hesitated. The counter was crowded and noisy, and a man near the door was smoking a thick, black cigar that Alice said took her breath away. In the harsh light of the drug-store entrance, Marshall saw the small hairs growing at the corners of her lips. He looked away. They were going to have to wait a few minutes for a seat.

"I think I'm going to have an ice cream sundae," he said.

"You and sundaes. Didn't you have one for lunch yesterday?"

"I can't remember."

She had begun to speak before he was finished. "One day I'd like to talk to your mother about your diet."

"I don't think you'd get very far," he said.

"I still say she and my father would like each other."

"Maybe I'll have chili," he said, wanting to change the subject.

Alice breathed, then turned to the man with the cigar, a coffee-colored older man with a darker place on the side of his face and a red patch in his very close-cropped, wiry hair. "Would you please put that out, sir? It's choking me."

"No," the man said, all good nature.

"It's so strong."

He smiled and shook his head. "I didn't send for you. And I ain't keeping you here, either, Missy."

Marshall felt as if he should say something to defend her, but then the moment passed. Alice started into the store, and he followed, glancing back at the man with the cigar, who still smiled, blowing smoke.

"Some people," she said. "I don't feel very good, now."

There were no seats at the counter. This part of the store smelled of perfume and wet clothes and the cooking meat on the griddle. Faintly, there came the odor of the cigar. Two women got up from the counter and lifted full shopping bags, moving away.

"Well?" Walter asked. "Shall we stay or go?"

Alice moved to the counter, sat down, and, removing her light raincoat, draped it across her lap. He left his on, taking his own seat, and tried to get the waiter's attention. The waiter was pouring coffee for a customer at the other end of the counter. Two men were arguing over a typed page one of them held.

"It's specious," the one man said. He had gray hair at his temples, and wore wire-framed glasses and a three-piece blue suit with a darker blue tie. "It's specious," he said again.

Marshall made a mental note to look up the word, along with "phlegmatic," and to be alert for the chance to use both of them in context. The man in the brown suit was an egghead, no doubt. At work, there was a man who had been to Harvard, and the mailroom employees called him an egghead. His hair was also graying at the temples, as if knowledge caused the physical change. The mailroom employees uttered the word with something bordering on disdain, and yet Marshall had read in separate places that Franklin Roosevelt and Adlai Stevenson were eggheads; he had seen it used in descriptions of Kennedy, as well, and he was certain that it was meant in those contexts to suggest sophistication and intellectual prowess. No picture of Roosevelt showed gray hair at the temples, and of course the whole idea was insane. Marshall wondered at his own ability to wander far afield, and to spend himself on such meaningless mental junk.

Alice shifted in her seat. "I'm starving."

"You just said you weren't hungry."

"I did?" She frowned. "I didn't mean to hurt your feelings back there."

"When?" he said.

"Saying 'Saint Matt's,' like that. I should be more careful."

"It didn't hurt my feelings."

"As you know, I'm not anything," she said. "Actually, my father's sort of agnostic. I mean, he believes God exists but he doesn't think about it at all. It's like that, sort of. So we never went to any churches, and I'm deprived. What's it like to be something?"

He didn't know how to answer. He shrugged, turned and signaled the waiter again, without success. Opposite them, in the mirror, his own ill-defined features looked back, a boy's skinny face. A face that still wouldn't produce enough whiskers to require him to shave, though he shaved anyway, three times a week. He saw Alice watching him.

"You go to church every Sunday," she said. "I think I'd like that."

"I used to go every day," he told her.

"Every *day*?"

"Almost. I missed sometimes in the week. But not much. I'd say a prayer that I'd wake up in time, and I did every morning, just at the right time. I didn't always get up, though. If it was especially bad out, I'd go back to sleep. I thought I was going to seminary, you know. I'm sure I told you that."

"Lots of times. I know you're very devout."

Somehow, this made him feel awkward; he was too much aware of his own coloring. She sat there, staring at him.

"A priest," she said.

"Well," he said. "That's over, now."

"I like church," she said. "I wouldn't mind being a Catholic. I think it might be fun. I think I'd really like the confession part."

"It makes you feel cleansed," he said.

"I love to hear you talk about it. You must go all the time."

"Not so much," he said. "Pretty much." The light seemed too bright.

"And you went from the priesthood to politics."

"Maybe," he said. "Politics, maybe." How strange to have it all said out that way.

She looked at her own reflection in the mirror. "I read somewhere that every Catholic boy thinks about the priesthood at one time or another. Do you think Kennedy ever thought about the priesthood?"

"I haven't seen anything—"

"I know who *did* think about it, though—a political figure of the twentieth century who was the leader of a whole country who thought very seriously about the priesthood when he was a young man."

Marshall nodded. "Okay."

"Can you guess?"

He shook his head.

"Hitler."

He said, "Well, I'm sure there were others, too."

"Yeah," she said. "Mussolini."

The waiter came to take their orders. He stood in front of them, holding his pad and waiting—a balding, heavyset man with a tattoo of a falcon on one arm.

"Oh," she said. "Let me see. I'll have a cup of chili with onions and crackers, and the pork chops, with a baked potato, and a salad. And these chicken wings. Am I going too fast?"

The waiter looked at her with drowsy eyes. "Salad—" he said.

"And milk. And coffee. Oh, and sour cream and butter on the potato."

"And you?" he said to Marshall.

"I'd just like a chocolate sundae."

"You're really going to do it." Alice was pleased. "Me, too, then. Drop everything I said and just give me that, too."

The waiter glared at her.

"Chocolate sundae," she said. "Sorry."

He moved off.

"So Mitch Brightman knew your father and he knows mine. Small world."

"They were a couple years apart in school."

"Small world," she repeated.

"What's he like?" Marshall said.

"Brightman?" she paused, thinking. "Brightman's—he's—I don't know. Actually, I've seen him lots around the house. You ought to be able to imitate him pretty easily, Walter. Have you ever tried?"

"His manner isn't extreme enough," Walter said. "I can do Walter Cronkite, though."

"Let me hear you."

"What so-ert of a dayy was it," he said. "A day like all days . . ."

She laughed. "It's close. I like it."

"Brightman's voice is too deep," he said.

She thought a moment. "I know him pretty well, actually. He's stayed over a few times when he's had a snootful. He drinks a lot, you know. Dad covers for him sometimes. Once, not too long ago, he drank a whole bottle of I.W. Harper before lunch on a Sunday. I know this because he came to our house for dinner that night. The woman he was with told my dad what he'd had to drink already, and she asked us to go easy on the drinks. My dad gave him watered-down bourbon all evening, and I guess he didn't notice it, but when they left he tucked a fifth of my dad's whiskey under his coat. My dad missed it the next afternoon, and thought maybe he'd lost his memory or something, and then Brightman's lady called to thank us for the dinner and apologized for the theft of the bottle."

"He never looks like a drinker on television," Marshall said.

"It's kind of a secret. He can go for periods, you know, without having anything, and then he goes on these—I can't remember what my father calls them. But they all have to watch out for the signs. Actually, he's only tolerable when he's sober. He gets so vain and conceited when he's had too much. You never saw anything like him. You can be talking to him, and he can be drunk as a skunk, and you wouldn't notice it. Except he turns into such a vain person. Much worse than when he's himself, although my father says he's really only himself—his true self—when he *is* drunk. It gets so he won't let anyone leave the room while he's talking—not even to the bathroom. You should hear my dad on the subject of Mitchell Brightman. And, actually, the two of them are friends, too. They've known each other for years and years. They both worked with the *Person to Person* guy."

"Edward R. Murrow?" Marshall said.

"That was the team—Patrick Kane, Mitchell Brightman, and Murrow."

They watched the waiter making the sundaes.

"So tell me," she said. "How complicated is it to convert? Suppose a person wanted to convert?"

"You take instruction," he said.

She thought this over. "You mean, like somebody who wants to be a citizen?"

"Right," he said.

"And I'd have to have a sponsor."

"Maybe, I don't know."

"Well, the person who converted me, wouldn't that person be my sponsor?"

He nodded.

"And you're still very religious."

He felt the same rush of chagrin. At the other end of the counter, a very beautiful woman leaned close to an older man, talking fast, tapping the end of her cigarette into the ashtray at her elbow.

"Actually, you know, I have to admit it," Alice went on. "I've never really thought much about being Catholic. I bet it's wonderful. The lady who raised me, Minnie, she's Baptist by birth, but I've never really seen her go to church. She's religious, though. It's in her talk."

"And she doesn't go to church?"

"She goes. I've just never been there."

He thought she would say more, so he waited.

"Minnie," she said. "The big colored lady who was leaving that night you came home with me."

"She raised you?"

"Nothing but. Only mother I can ever remember. I used to love the smell of her. She always had the nicest smell—sweet, like something just baked, or like fresh-picked flowers. I used to love to sit in her big lap and go to sleep while she read to me."

They were quiet for a time. Alice seemed to be replaying in her mind the memory of being read to.

"Anyway," she said, "I used to want to be Jewish because of the holidays—you know, back when I was in high school. A hundred fifty years ago."

When Marshall looked into the mirror and saw Alice's thin, high-cheeked, staring face, he felt exposed, as though all the others at the counter were watching the two of them. It came to him that over the past few weeks he had done most of the talking, and that the talk had been about himself. He was briefly ashamed of this, and sought in his mind for some way of making up for it.

"Your mother died before you were old enough to remember," he said.

"That's the fact."

"And your father never remarried?"

"Nope. He got close a few times. To tell you the truth, I don't think he likes women very much. He seems much more comfortable around other men. I mean—he's not queer or anything. Just—I don't know. Masculine. He likes hunting and fishing—all that stuff."

"I saw." Marshall meant the trophies all around the house where Alice lived.

She cleared her throat, then looked at him. "A person has to convert, doesn't she. If she marries a Catholic."

"Not necessarily," he said. "My mother's father was a Lutheran."

"Really."

"A practicing Lutheran sort of person," he said, smiling at her.

"No kidding."

She sat back, her hands on the counter. Then she rested one elbow on it, looking around, biting the cuticle of one thumbnail. "What do you think made you want to be a priest? Was it just being a Catholic boy, like Hitler and Mussolini? Well, not exactly them, of course. I just meant not being cut out for it and thinking you are."

He shrugged. There was something too defining about the question. It unnerved him.

"Boy, Hitler wasn't cut out for it, was he?"

Marshall shook his head. He thought she was talking too loud.

"What did your mother say about it all? I guess a Catholic mother would love to have a priest in the family."

"She didn't say much—listen, could we talk about something else?"

The waiter set the two sundaes before them.

"I'm sorry," Alice said. "I didn't mean to pry."

"Don't apologize," Marshall said and realized that he had sounded more brusque than he'd meant to. "There's nothing to apologize about."

"Of course there is." She took a mouthful of the ice cream.

"No," he said.

She wiped her lips. "That man's awful cigar."

The man with the cigar was standing at the book rack, just to her right. The rack squealed as he turned it. He blew more smoke.

"Do you want to move?" Marshall said.

She seemed not to have heard this. She took another spoonful of the ice cream, then looked at him in the mirror and gave a little, pained smile. A moment later, she said, "My father's holding this silly party for me—it's silly. I'm going to be twenty-four, you see, which is, I guess, the cut-off point in his little mind. Anyway, he wants you to come, too. He's having some of the people he knows at CBS over. And I guess he's hoping I'll fall in love with one of them." She laughed. "I don't suppose you'd feel like coming to it. Actually, I'm fairly sure Mitchell Brightman will be there."

She had spoken this last as though it would be an enticement to him. The fact that it *was* rankled him. "When?" he said, and then filled his mouth with ice cream.

"This coming Friday."

The color in her cheeks, and the small, crooked smile on her face made him concentrate on the ice cream.

"I mean, you've never met these people, I know. And I know it's late notice. That's the way Dad does things. I know he makes you nervous. But you could talk to some of these people about Kennedy, I'll bet."

He had met Mr. Kane once, perhaps a month ago, having accepted an invitation from Alice to accompany her home for coffee after the two of them had been to see *The Guns of Navarone*, in town. The old man was large and imposing, with a clean, bald pate and dark, gray-tinged hair over his ears and around the back of his head. His face had the appearance of having been pulled over his nose, the end of which covered the line of his lips. Aside from a certain slant of the eyes, Alice looked nothing like him. To the young man he had been pleasant enough, but rather distant, finally, and he had driven him home without uttering a word—twenty minutes of the low hum of the radio, with Marshall issuing polite directions.

"I don't think your father likes me very much."

"Oh, that's silly," she said. "He didn't know I was bringing anybody home that time. That's all."

"Yes, but—he didn't seem to take to me later, either."

"Well, he's shy."

"He goes around with people like Edward R. Murrow and Mitchell Brightman, and he's shy?"

"It's true. He is shy. And he doesn't dislike you, either. You notice he didn't stay around when we were sitting in the living room. If he didn't like you, he would've stayed right there with us instead of going upstairs. He wouldn't have trusted you with me." She sighed, and tapped her spoon once against the lip of the bowl.

"Actually, I'm dreading this party. Maybe I'll miss it—just say thanks, no thanks and go out and see a movie. Have you seen *My Fair Lady*?"

"Not yet."

"I haven't, either."

In the awkward silence that followed, he decided to try one more time, gently, to dissuade her from coming to the school with him. "Listen," he said. "There's really not much going on tonight. I'm not even up tonight."

"Up. What's that mean—up?"

"We practice being on the air. We do all the jobs there are in a normal radio station. But it doesn't go anywhere. It's just rehearsing, sort of. And I'm not up tonight. I'm just supposed to sit in the booth and watch."

Her face brightened. "Great. Then let's go see it."

"See what?"

"The movie."

He was momentarily at a loss.

"*My Fair Lady*."

"Oh, that—no, I really have to go to class."

She gave him an uncomprehending look.

"I just meant—you know, there's really nothing for you to see."

"Nothing—"

"There wouldn't be anything happening, you know. Just me sitting in the booth and watching a lot of dials."

She nodded, with that small smile, then gathered the coat on her lap, as if she had received a chill. "This is a lot of ice cream, actually."

"If there was something going on," Marshall said, "it'd be different . . ."

She'd taken a big bite of the sundae, and a dollop of the whipped cream dropped onto her chin. "Whoops," she said, her mouth full.

To his horror, he saw tears in her eyes. "Here," he said, reaching for a napkin.

"Oh, no—really." She caught the ice cream with the palm of her hand, looking from one end of the counter to the other, then she took the napkin he held out. "Messy." Her voice broke.

"They taste too good to worry about the mess," he offered.

"I really shouldn't have it," she managed. "Too much sugar."

"Anyway," he said. "I hope you don't mind this boring night at the school."

"Oh, well, actually—it turns out—I really should be going home. It's silly for me—"

"Aren't you going to finish your sundae?" he said.

She touched his wrist. "You finish it."

"I won't be able to."

She had stood, she was putting her coat on, in a hurry now.

"I'll walk you to the bus stop," Marshall said, standing, wishing he'd kept his mouth shut in the first place. "Come on, let me walk you there."

"Don't be silly," said Alice. "It's only on the corner—at K Street."

"No, really—I want to."

"I don't want you to," she said, looking into her purse. "Please." She pulled a hanky out and brushed her eyes. "Something's stinging me—that awful man smoking that cigar."

"Alice," he said. "Listen—you know—I don't even know what 'phlegmatic' means."

She gave him another uncomprehending look. "What?"

"Let me—" He reached for her arm. But then she started away from him. "Alice—"

"I have to go," she said. "That's easy to understand, isn't it?"

"Alice," he heard himself say, "don't, please."

She paused, stared.

"I—there's something I've been meaning to say . . ." He had, in fact, been deciding over the past few days that he wanted to clarify things between them. He had liked the sense that he was having an effect on her—but this: He hadn't imagined she could be hurt by any of it.

"Yes?" she said.

"I've been at such loose ends," he told her.

She said, "I know."

The pained look in her eyes, the clear anticipation of bad news, stopped his breath. He looked down, shifted his weight, trying to organize his thoughts. There were flattened cigarette butts on the floor. And he *had* known how she felt about him, he had basked in it.

"I think I know," she said, "what you're trying to say. You're trying to say you don't want to see me anymore."

"No," he said quickly. "That's not it. God, how can you say that?"

"It's not?"

"No," he said, and felt as though he had lied.

"Oh, Walter."

He looked at her—the wet, bottomlessly dark eyes.

"Walter, are you—oh, please. Say it."

"I can't." He was short of breath.

"Is it because you're afraid I'll say no?"

He nodded out of a kind of stupified reflex.

"I won't say no, Walter." Her eyes were filled with tears.

"Will you marry me?" he heard himself say. The words sounded like something he had mouthed in a game somewhere, a long time ago. It was only the next thing to say under these circumstances. He felt like a little, little boy, standing there under her suddenly happy gaze.

"Walter," she said. "Yes, I will."

"I mean it," he told her, unable to believe himself, but feeling now as though this was the right thing to do. Somewhere in him there blossomed a sense of what an adventure it would be, to be grown enough to have a wife.

"Oh, darling." She walked into his arms.

He held her, looking at the man with the cigar, who had turned, and regarded them with interest, still blowing smoke. Marshall thought the smoke was making him dizzy, too, now. "I didn't mean anything—didn't mean to hurt your feelings," he said in her ear. "I just—I didn't want you to be bored."

She stepped back the length of her arms and looked at him. "How could you think I'd be bored? We'd be together. It would be the nearest thing to heaven. Have you seen *An Affair to Remember*?"

He wanted to ask her to be quiet. "No," he said. He couldn't catch his breath.

"That's what this feels like to me."

It was coming down on him again that he had actually proposed to her. Somehow, he had caused this woman to fall in love with him, and even as his nerves shook, even as a part of him refused to believe it was possible, he determined to go through with everything. "I hope you'll forgive me," he stammered, having lost the thread of the conversation. She was going on about the movie—Cary Grant and Deborah Kerr. She stopped herself at last, and looked at him with a shy turn of her head.

"Honey, do you mind if I don't go with you tonight? I want to go home and tell my father."

Honey.

The word dropped into him like something heavy dropped into a pool of standing water. "Of course," he said. "That's—that would be fine." In fact, he had never wanted more passionately to be alone. He thought of trying to find a way to tell his mother, everyone else he knew. If he were going to go through with it, everyone would have to know.

"Oh," she said, still holding his hands. "And did you really ask me to marry you?"

He nodded, wishing she would stop making such a fuss.

She leaned up to kiss him.

"Not here," Marshall said.

"You're shaking. Look at your hands."

He held them out in front of him.

"That's so sweet. It's going to be just fine, darling." She threw her arms around him.

"All these people," he said.

"I don't care," said Alice. "I don't. I'm so happy. Oh, this is the closest thing to heaven."

"I feel—me, too." His voice caught on the last word, and it came out falsetto.

She laughed softly. "You look like you've just had the fright of your life."

"It's that cigar smoke," he said for lack of anything else to blame it on.

She touched his face. "I love you."

"Yes," he said. "I—I'm the same. I feel the same."

"I can't eat another bite."

"No."

"You, too?"

"Right," he said.

"When will we do it?" she asked.

He said, "Do it?" His heart jumped.

"Get married."

"Oh—as soon as I can get a good job, I guess."

"No," she said. "You have to go on to college, like we planned."

"You want to wait until after I finish college?" He felt a moment's relief from the increasing pressure inside his backbone.

"Oh, no," she said. "I don't want to wait that long."

"Right," he managed.

"Do you?" she asked.

"Do I what?" he said. Then, "Oh, that—no."

"I'd like to help you get through school."

"Right."

"Well," she said. "What about after you finish radio school, this June?"

"Okay. Sure."

"A June wedding."

"Right."

"Would that be nice?"

"Wonderful," he said.

She gazed at him. "That's why you were so agitated all evening—you were trying to get up the nerve to ask me."

He nodded, utterly hopeless now. He would have agreed to anything.

"You sweetie."

"Not really," he said.

"And listen, I want you to know something. I'll convert. I'll be Catholic so fast it'll make your head swim."

This struck him as an uncannily accurate and discomfiting description of his present condition. And there was this cramp, high up in his back.

She kissed him on the side of the face. "I know you have to go to school. I'm going to go home and set my father on his ear. Sure you don't mind?"

"I'm sure," he said.

After a pause, she said, "You must want to spend a little time alone, too. I mean that's perfectly understandable." Then she murmured, almost to herself, "Alice Kane Marshall. I like the sound of it."

"I can't eat any more," he told her.

"Oh, who can eat?"

"If you two would get out of my way, *I* could," said the man with the cigar.

Alice said it was like being in a movie. Marshall reached into his pants pocket for his money, and found nothing. He tried the other pockets, and he went through the pockets of his coat. "My money. I had two twenty-dollar bills."

She took his coat and looked through it. There was something motherly about the way she looked at him, turning the coat in her hands. "Nothing."

He turned and bent down to look under the stool and along the floor.

"Walter Winchell," Alice said. "He must've stolen it off you."

He dug down in the pockets of his pants again, and looked in his wallet. There was the driver's license, with smudges on it.

"Walter Winchell, the crazy with the signboard," she said.

"The money was in my pocket under my coat."

"Here," Alice said, shaking her head, reaching into her purse.

Briefly, it was as though they were already married—had been married a long time and she was vaguely impatient and unhappy with him. She gave him a ten and six ones, and put a five on the counter. "You wanted to help the poor, and I guess you did that, all right."

"It's gone," he said.

She smiled. "You're something." Her new confidence had changed her, and he didn't know how to behave under its influence. He put his coat on and she was already buttoning it.

"Let me," he said.

"Stand still," she told him. And when she had accomplished her self-appointed task, she patted his chest. "There."

Out in the street, she said, "You haven't ever really kissed me."

"No," he said. "Right."

She seemed to puff up with something. It was as if her face abruptly expanded. "Walter, are you just going to stand there and say 'right' over and over?"

He was feeling the cramp now in his lower abdomen. She reached up to kiss him on the mouth, a bumbling embrace. She stood on her toes, and moved her head from side to side, her thin arms tight around his neck. After what seemed a long time, she stepped back, becoming several inches shorter in the instant of dropping down to her heels. "I love you," she said. In the unreal light her face looked stained. "See you tomorrow."

"Tomorrow," he told her. "Yes."

He watched as she made her quick way through the throng of people on the sidewalk, instinctively understanding that this was expected. Occasionally, she turned and waved to him, going away. He waved back.

He had not meant to act selfishly, or foolishly.

The mist was turning into rain. He looked down toward K Street for a moment, but she was gone, and it was done. He, Walter Marshall, four months shy of being twenty years old, frightened and alone and worried, the victim of a pickpocket, standing in the wet street with money given to him by this young woman, was completely unable to imagine how it could have happened that along with everything else, he was now engaged to be married.

The young man had imagined his own future, over the past year—down to the wife he'd have. His wife, the probable First Lady, would look something like Natalie Bowman, the girl at school. No, that was not the truth (how easy it was to lie to oneself!)—the truth was that the probable First Lady in his day-dreams *was* Natalie Bowman. He had spent time with her waiting for classes to begin, and they had talked, mostly about the weather outside the window of the library—the end-of-summer heat, the cooler, late afternoons of September, the days growing incremen-tally shorter. On occasion, he had clowned for her and made her laugh. She spoke with the slightest trace of an accent, now and then pronouncing the letter *w* with a "v" sound, and sometimes she let words drop from her speech, minor lapses that charmed him and brought his attention to the wonderful shape of her mouth, the way her deep green eyes changed when she smiled or laughed. To her, he was an amusing boy, a pretty prize for someone younger. He had filled hours at work planning things to tell her that she might find funny, working through what he would do to amuse her, keep her sitting with him in the little library room. It seemed that there was always something about to pull her away from him, something drawing her on, associations he could never fathom. There was an air of mystery about her, as though she were somehow marking time, waiting for some element of her present existence to release her. An aspect of her attention was always elsewhere, and there were moments when she seemed rather gloomily distracted. When he could make her laugh, could break the spell, he felt strong and capable, felt privileged, in a way, though she never spoke about her moods, and seemed at times merely to accept his talk as though it were the natural and predictable outcome of his proximity. He didn't care. He might have accepted much less to be allowed to remain in her presence. Her tall, lithe figure and her dark, aristocratic features reminded him of Jackie Kennedy, and she was Catholic, too. It had been easy enough visualizing his first lady as being that very girl, that dreamy, complicated girl.

On some school nights, walking past the shopwindows with their mannequins in all the poses of self-assurance and grace, he had let his fancy roam over the great possibilities, going so far as rehearsing the phrases of what might one day be an inaugural address. It was a way of idly passing the time, though he was serious about it, too, and often caught himself hoping the world wouldn't change too much before he could get there and deliver his speech.

My fellow world citizens, ask not what we can do for any one country but what together we can do as a country for the whole world.

Mrs. Alice Kane Marshall.

The sound of it was all wrong, wasn't it? Walking in the rain toward school, he tried to picture her as a wife, and could only see Jackie moving gracefully through the rooms of the White House, as she had in the television special about the history and the refurbishing that she had been engaged in. Alice Marshall, First Lady. It was absurd. He wasn't even old enough to vote yet, and there was something sinful—wasn't there?—about this kind of daydreaming. The whole thing made him queasy.

He walked along the street in the increasing rain, reasoning with himself: Alice was older, and knew the way things were; he would never intentionally hurt her feelings, and she must know that, too. If he ever did get to be president, he would reward her hugely. He would tell the whole world what a good friend she'd been, since the early days . . .

Except that he was engaged to be married to her. He was going to marry her.

He went on up Eighteenth Street. The streetlamps sent their glow up into the heavy sky, showing the mist, the moving tag ends of clouds. In the window of a clothing store there was a photograph of Kennedy from the side; he was sitting at a polished desk with a window behind him, writing something, his face careworn and intent. Marshall looked at the gray cloth of his suit, the striped shirt cuffs coming out of the sleeves. "This blazing talent," Stevenson had called him. Kennedy. In 1956, during the televising of the Democratic Convention, Marshall had seen him for the first time, standing at the podium behind a dense thicket of microphones while the thousands cheered. The boy, then eleven years old, had asked his mother who the man with the funny hair was. "That's John F. Kennedy," she had said. "He's going to be president some day." Such a handsome man. Marshall had to suppress the wish that time might hurry. It would be good to get beyond the present. He felt caught in it. Briefly, he saw his own flag-draped casket borne by a horse-drawn caisson down Pennsylvania, all the leaders of the world in tow. Perhaps the flag would be the flag of the United Nations.

My fellow citizens of the world . . .

"Oh, stop it," he said aloud.

The quality of light behind him changed with the headlights of a passing car, and the ghost of his own reflection became visible in the glass, just at Kennedy's shoulder. He could not understand what Alice, or anyone else, for that matter, could possibly find attractive about that skinny face. It's familiarity made him move away from the window. He had a vision of himself standing in an open place with someone, his grown son. He saw himself opening a door, and Alice waiting on the other side, with children.

Oh, Walter. I'm going to go home and set my father on his ear . . .

He walked on, trying to will the images out of himself.

The radio-school classes didn't start until six-thirty, and occasionally he stopped for a while at Saint Matthew's. Though it was raining and the walk took him half a block out of his way, he headed there tonight. One of the priests had been a friend of his mother's in her high school days, and was sometimes in the church on weekday evenings. Father Soberg knew of Marshall's once yearning for the priesthood, and had talked with him about seminary life, about the religious books the boy was still reading— *The Spiritual Exercises of St. Ignatius Loyola*; the meditations of St. Francis de Sales; the *Summa Theologica* of St. Thomas Aquinas; all of Fulton J. Sheen; some of Thomas Merton; even a little de Chardin. The priest had taken an interest in the young man, had given him some of the books.

Now Marshall, pressing forward through the rain, wondered if Father Soberg would be in the church, and if it would be possible to tell the priest what had just happened. The rain was coming in a downpour, swept by gusts of wind. Saint Matthew's Cathedral looked medieval, standing so tall in its little section of Rhode Island Avenue, a prodigious stone shadow on the wide glow of the raining city sky. He hurried up its marble steps, thinking as usual of the procession of famous people coming down in the chilly sun of that terrible Monday almost a year ago. Kennedy's funeral. Everybody important in the whole world, it seemed. Movie actors and the leaders of countries, ex-presidents and royalty, princes of the Church. They had all stood on these very steps, and the navy band had played the song about those in peril on the sea.

He opened the heavy wooden door and entered.

Inside, it was warm, and there was the hum of the city all around, as if it came from the recesses of the high arches in the vaulted ceiling. The church was empty. He approached the communion rail and the votive candles, the first pew. Alice would never understand something like this. Here, close to the altar, one could breathe the tallow smell of the burning candles, and when the air stirred, it carried some suspirant redolence of the stone in the walls and the riblike supporting arches. The shadows clinging to those high spaces above the altar seemed to be attending to him. When he knelt down, the wooden kneeler creaked with his weight. There was an accepting quality here, in the silence, with its small stirrings of air and its icons gazing out of the gloom in their placid, finished sanctity.

He could calm down, and decide how to proceed.

The first thing, he knew, was that the feelings and the welfare of another human being were at stake. Someone he liked, whose affections he had sought. No, there wasn't anything for it. If Alice wanted to get married, he would get married. Besides, somewhere far beneath the scared sense that he had begun something catastrophic he was still receiving that glimmer of an alluring aspect of the idea—its novelty. The strange, breathless thrill it had given him when she called him darling. Well, it had been like a thrill, hadn't it? It had been like riding down a steep incline at tremendous speed.

He folded his hands, bowed his head, trying to think about praying. But he couldn't keep his eyes closed. At the front of the church, the crucifix cast its long shadow across the altar. It was almost life-sized, but was not, he knew, a true representation of Christ's execution. He knew that to show the truth—to give the actual historical representation—would be far more terrible.

He had recently read a book by a French doctor named Barbet who had studied the physical effects of crucifixion, using experiments with fresh cadavers. The doctor proved that if the nails had been driven into the center of the palm, as depicted in most statues, the body's weight would have torn the flesh in the hand, bringing the nail out between the fingers and defeating the purpose of the execution. The book was filled with photographs and diagrams describing the experiments the doctor had used to make an accurate description of what Christ must have physically suffered at Calvary. And Walter Marshall, having read the book, was aware that the nails—the jagged, dull-edged, primitive spikes of Rome—had been driven through each wrist, just at what is called the median nerve, which, when frayed, as a sharp point pushing through the metacarpal bones would fray it, caused unbearable pain throughout the entire body. Horrible pain all over, and never mind the thorns piercing the circumference of the head, the whip across the back, the hunger, the slow bleeding, the blows of the guards, the nail wounds themselves, the awful cramping of the diaphragm in the chest, causing the inability to breathe out, necessitating that the victim push up on the nails in the feet in order to reach a straightened posture and therefore end the cramping and be able to exhale and gain more air, gain more of whatever is left of life—the sight of the world, light, even in humiliation, exhaustion, and agony.

He could get married. It was a small thing.

He looked at the sorrowful face on the cross and tried not to think beyond that, tried to see into the spirit of the icon.

they have numbered all my bones

Sometimes, kneeling here thinking of Christ's suffering, knowing the terrible reality of it and inwardly offering himself up to suffer, too, he had experienced a heightening of his senses. It was as though something washed over him inside, waves of velvet on all the inner surfaces. He had striven to divorce himself from this sensation, for fear of growing too attached to the feeling itself as pleasure, as something to be enjoyed *with*, and *in*, the body rather than as the simple, haphazard element of his continuing devotion to the will and majesty of God.

It was all so complicated.

Tonight, he experienced no stirrings of spiritual ecstasy. Tonight, he felt the smallest measure of distance between himself and the anguished shape on the cross. He said an act of contrition, having to repeat it several times, because, again, his mind kept wandering away.

Lord, if I have sinned, please help get me out of it.

He bowed his head, trying once more to concentrate. Everything was racing, and perhaps he had a fever, was coming down with something. He saw Alice in his mind, that look of painful anticipation on her face, and then he was looking at the shape of Natalie, as she stretched out in the window seat of the D'Allessandro School's library.

Stop it. Lord, please.

For a few seconds, he was aware of the stirring on the other side of the church without quite attending to it. Father Soberg had walked in, looking hurried and vaguely disgruntled, barely genuflecting as he walked across the central aisle, in front of the sacrament. The priest lighted a votive candle, and stood before it, praying for a time, then went back across the aisle, again barely genuflecting. As he started down the side aisle, he saw Marshall and stopped, frowning, apparently trying to decide about him. Marshall bowed his head, but now the other moved toward him, stepped into the pew, and walked up to him.

"Aren't you running a little late, Walter?"

"A little," the young man said. "Not really. It doesn't start till six-thirty."

"Did you want to see me?" Father Soberg was in his mid-forties—with dark, close-cut hair and a shadow of stubble on his bony cheeks. He had large, flat-fingered hands, and his squarish face looked more stern than he ever was. There was something almost angry about his features, the dark brows set in a perpetual frowning arc. He had been out in the rain, too.

"If you have something to do," Marshall said.

"I've just been doing what I had to do." Father Soberg sat down, but in the posture of someone who is about to get up and leave. "Everything's fine. You looked troubled—and really like you don't want to be bothered. That's why I hesitated."

"I'm fine."

"Your face is pale as death," said Father Soberg. "Are you ill?"

"I don't think so, Father."

"How's your mother."

"She's okay—she doesn't like the job at the high school as much—now that I'm not there."

"You tell her I ask after her, don't you?"

"Yes, Father."

"Good lad. Well, you're all right, then?"

"I'm engaged to be married," Marshall said suddenly. It had come out of him with the force of a cough.

Father Soberg smiled, tilted his head to one side. "When did this happen?"

"Just now," said Marshall. His voice croaked oddly. He repeated it. "Just now."

"You seem rather astounded," Father Soberg said. "It happens every day, son. Though I will say you're a little young."

"I know," said Marshall with more emphasis than he had intended.

"Do I know the girl?"

He shook his head.

"Well, it's a big decision. Bound to make a man nervous."

"Yes, Father."

"Is she Catholic?"

"She says she'll convert." The young man heard the discouragement in his own voice.

"Don't you want her to?"

"I don't know."

"I don't mean to press it. I'm sorry."

"No, it's all right," Marshall said. "Really."

"I'm sure she's a wonderful girl."

"Yes, Father."

"Well, there you are." The priest touched his shoulder, looking into the dimness at the back of the church. "You know I'm being transferred."

"You're being transferred?"

"Your mother didn't—" Father Soberg seemed puzzled. "Well, it's to this—Vietnam place. South, of course. A city called Saigon, in South Vietnam. One year, with the mission there. Mostly to help close it down. Then I don't know where I'll be."

"South Vietnam," Marshall said.

"Yes, I know. And we just bombed them in the north." Father Soberg looked down, and sighed. "Well. Say hello to your mother for me. And congratulations."

"Thanks, Father."

He moved to the side aisle again and on to the heavy doors leading out into the street. Marshall watched him go. The door closed slowly, and soon the church was quiet again. Except that everything in the place seemed reduced to its essential properties: stone and paint, wood and steel, plaster and glass. Even the crucifix: The face of the crucified Christ looked merely dyspeptic and irritable, a badly rendered human face on a statue supported by steel wires bolted to the rafters. Walter Marshall closed his eyes and tried to pray.

Somewhere, in the books he had been poring over, he had read that the journey of a soul toward perfection was a journey away from distractions.

At the enclosed bus stand on Eighteenth Street and L, Albert Waple stood, his textbook held up to his face, reading. When Marshall approached, the other peered out at him.

"Why're you standing here, Albert? Aren't you coming to class?"

"Sure," Albert said, still squinting. "You look different. I recognized you, but you do look different."

"I don't know how," said Marshall.

"It's not the clothes." Albert was studying him.

Marshall resisted the sensation of annoyance. "Do I look pale?"

"Ah. It's the hair."

He felt caught out. "No," he said.

"Yep," said Albert. "You've done something. Did you get it cut?"

"No."

"You're combing it different, then."

"I've been combing it this way for a long time. Since before I met you."

Albert stepped closer. "Maybe it's the light."

"Look, could we get off the subject of my hair?"

"Are you sensitive about it?"

"Why would I be sensitive about it? It's hair."

Albert seemed genuinely puzzled. "I wouldn't know."

"Come on, Albert."

"No, I just thought you looked different tonight."

"Do I look pale?"

Albert studied him. "No more than usual."

"Maybe I do need a haircut." Marshall tried to seem as careless and as uninterested as possible.

"You know, it looks like somebody—reminds me of somebody—if it wasn't so blond."

"What're you doing at the bus stop, anyway?"

"Waiting for the bus."

"You're not coming to class?"

"I have a surprise," Albert said.

"Okay." Marshall waited. After a few moments, it became clear that the other had started reading again. "Well, what?" Marshall said.

Albert peered at him. "I'm sorry?"

"What's the surprise?"

"It wouldn't be a surprise if I told you."

"It's a surprise for me?"

"Yep."

"I've got a surprise for you, too."

"Okay," Albert said. "You go first."

"I'm getting married. Alice and me." The words seemed empty. Albert stared.

"Well?"

"That's great," said Albert. "You and Alice."

Marshall looked down the street at the headlights of cars stopped at the red light across from where Connecticut Avenue and Eighteenth Street crossed. From the bus stop you could see most of the length of Eighteenth, with its hotel fronts and shops and movie theaters and bars. The lights seemed about to dissolve in the rain. Albert stood there smiling, with that look of myopic calm that was always dimly embarrassing.

"Well, you're getting married, aren't you? Is it so strange for me to do the same?"

"No, I said—it's great. Don't mind me. I've always been slow on the uptake."

"I don't know why you should act so funny about it."

"It's wonderful," Albert said. "Who's acting funny?"

"Nobody," Marshall said. "Maybe it's just me."

"When did you ask her?"

Marshall looked down the street again. "Tonight—a half hour ago."

"That's great," his friend said. "We can have a celebration."

"I don't know," said Marshall. "Maybe another time."

"No time like the present—because, remember, I have a surprise for you." Albert shifted a little, shaking his head. "I can't keep it a secret anymore. Guess who's coming on the bus?"

"Who?"

"Emma." He nodded proudly.

"Emma."

Now his deep eyes seemed to narrow, as though something had flown at him from the night outside the booth.

"Oh, Emma," Marshall said.

"I told you one day she'd do it. Her aunt Patty put her on the bus in Alexandria an hour ago. The bus driver has instructions to let her off at this stop."

"That's great," Marshall said, staring off at the traffic again. "That's wonderful."

"It's not every blind girl who'll make a trip like that, just to meet her fiancé's friend."

"I guess not," Marshall said.

They were quiet. Albert watched the street, squinting in the light.

"Just to meet me," said Marshall. "That's something."

"So you have to make a big deal out of it," Albert said. "Okay?"

"Well—it is a big deal."

"Not that she couldn't do it every day, you know. Emma's no shrinking violet."

"I can't wait to meet her, Albert."

Albert said, "I'm so happy tonight. What a happy night."

"You always seem happy," Marshall told him.

Albert was thinking of something else. "I had to work real hard getting her aunt Patty to allow this. Emma's only eighteen—and Aunt Patty—well, it's hard to let go. I had such a bad time figuring out how I was going to tell her that Emma and I wanted to get married."

Marshall waited for him to tell the story. But Albert merely went back to his book, his face disappearing into it.

"How did you?" Marshall asked.

"How'd I what?"

This happened a lot. "Tell Aunt Patty that you and Emma were going to get married."

"Oh," Albert said, laughing. "I didn't."

"You mean you haven't told her yet?"

"Emma told her. We walked into the room and Emma said, 'Aunt Patty, Albert wants to talk to you about something.' And I saw Aunt Patty turn her face toward me—couldn't see her eyes, of course. Just the shape. So there I am, and I open my big stupid mouth to tell her, and nothing comes out. A complete utter nothing from nowhere nohow, no way. I couldn't even draw a breath. And then Emma told her."

"What happened?"

"Aunt Patty broke out in hives."

Marshall smiled at him.

"She's a funny lady. Whenever she's really happy or really sad, she breaks out in hives."

"She was happy," Marshall said.

Albert shook his head. "No." It sounded almost like a question. "I wouldn't say she was happy."

"But she's happy now."

"No."

They were quiet.

"Emma's young, you know. And Aunt Patty can see."

Marshall was puzzled by this, and Albert must have sensed it.

"I can still see, too," he said. "I know what happens to the mirror every time I look into it. I don't make the best scenery in the world."

"Scenery isn't everything," Marshall said, disliking the sense as he spoke that his words were automatic, not really felt.

"You're a good friend," Albert told him.

They had known each other since the first week of radio school, a year ago in September, because for a time, before Albert had taken his small room in town, they had been passengers on the same bus home to Virginia. Albert liked to tell people things about himself, and he did so with such great faith in the kindness with which it would be received that one quickly felt protective of him, and wanted not to disappoint him or make him feel, even by a slip of the tongue, that this sentimental assumption was mistaken. Marshall had never asked him home, and seldom called him at his own place—they had met only three or four times outside school, in fact, several times for lunch with Alice—and yet when Marshall arrived each school night, Albert was always there, always behaving without any tentativeness at all, as though they were the best of friends. Marshall liked him while half-consciously entertaining a curious sense of superiority to him—feeling himself in possession of a worldliness the other lacked. Albert trusted people too much, and Marshall had seen the looks on the faces of strangers those nights on the bus to Arlington.

He had told Marshall in the first minutes they knew each other that Emma was blind from birth, that her father had been killed in the war, at Anzio, and she had lost her mother before she was two years old. And that she had been Albert's teacher when he set out to learn how to read Braille. They had fallen in love, he said, in a matter of seconds. Then he smiled and asked if Marshall minded a little exaggeration now and then. "Anyway," he'd said. "We fell in love and I asked her to marry me after the second lesson. Does that seem too soon?"

"It's fast," Marshall had told him.

"No," Albert had said, picking at his own long, acne-scarred face, "it's definite."

Albert liked to make jokes at his own expense, but he was proud of his ability to be decisive. It was a quality he tried to cultivate in himself.

"I'd like to wait with you," Marshall said now. "But I have to do some research in the school library. I'm doing commercials from 1945, remember, for the history of broadcasting."

"Oh." Albert appeared crestfallen. His features registered all his emotions with a strange exaggeration. "I thought we might cut out of class after the first hour and go get a sandwich or something."

"I'm sorry," Marshall said. "I really can't."

"I won't stand in the way of progress," said Albert, quickly regaining his cheerfulness.

The truth was that while Marshall did have work to do—he had been asked by the Spanish radio announcer to write a commercial for an office supply company, and there was indeed research for the class in the history of broadcasting to do—it was nothing that couldn't wait. He wanted to get to the school the half hour early to see Natalie, who usually waited in the library for classes to start. For the minute it took him to make his excuse to Albert, he had forgotten Alice altogether.

Remembering her brought a small whimper up out of the back of his throat.

"What?" Albert said.

"I didn't say anything."

"Well," Albert said. "I've got some reading to do, too." He waved, then turned and put the book back up to the tip of his nose.

"'Bye," Marshall said.

Albert looked up. His visage was almost crowlike—that long nose and the deeply recessed eyes. "We'll come get you."

Marshall waved at him and went on, and when he had gone a few paces he stopped and turned. There his friend was—a tall, stooped, shadowy figure in the light of the booth, the mist trailing down out of the falling darkness.

Lately each evening, just as he approached the school, having allowed himself as little thought of Natalie as possible, he would look up to see her in the window of the library. If she saw him, she might wave. Usually, she was reading a book, studying. And sometimes she wasn't there at all. Sometimes, it was as though the building were haunted with her.

Tonight, though, she was sitting in the window overlooking the street. Seeing her, his heart lifted, and then sank.

He would be a married man by June.

As he went up the front steps, he was aware that she could see him from where she sat. He bounded up the stairs and lost his footing near the top, barking his knee on the concrete. This, he knew, was the just punishment of God. Managing to stand up, and to seem in charge of himself, he made his way onto the stone porch. The pain made his eyes water. When he glanced at the window, she lifted one slender hand to wave at him.

The foyer of the school was always dim—a long, thin strip of fading linoleum down the middle of it, entering a narrow hallway with bare gray walls and tall doorways to classrooms on either side. The hall ended at a closed white-painted door that, as far as he knew, no one ever entered or came from. To the right of the foyer was a narrow wooden stairway, painted a glossy dark green, creaking with age, at the top of which was the metal-framed entrance to the D'Allessandro School for Broadcasting, with its letters painted in red on the glass doors. The broadcasting school and the downstairs night college were both owned and operated by Mr. D'Allessandro and his wife, with Mrs. D'Allessandro primarily responsible for the night college, though Mr. D'Allessandro also taught a course there in the etymology of words (now and then he talked about this class, and about the euphony of language when utilized by the right voice, the voice that understood what the notes were and struck the right ones). To the left of the foyer was the night college's general office—a small room, with a desk and telephone for the secretary, walls with the framed diplomas of Mr. and Mrs. D'Allessandro, and glass-framed photographs of both of them with various important people (Mr. D'Allessandro had done broadcasting for the Voice of America during Eisenhower's first term, and there were pictures of him shaking hands with John Foster Dulles and Averell Harriman to prove it). To the left of this room was the arched entryway of the small library, whose tall, leaded window looked out onto the street.

Walter Marshall stalled for a minute, pretending to look at the photographs, then tried to amble into the library, hoping his face would not show the strain of what the pain in his knee was doing to him. The broadcasting school's books were all along one wall, opposite literature and history and social science, which, such as it was, made up the rest of the collection. The room itself wasn't much larger than a private parlor, really, and indeed it was furnished that way—there were sofas and easy chairs placed in the corners, an oak table and chairs at the center.

Marshall sat at the table and opened one of the books, a history of broadcasting. He looked over at Natalie and smiled. Always, he had felt the necessity of waiting for her to make the first move to talk. She rose and walked over to him. There was a bronze cast to her lovely skin, and the healthy protein shine of her black hair made her look Polynesian. "How are you this evening, Walter?"

"Fine," he said.

"You look worn out." She touched his forehead. "The weather is so bad. You look like you have a little fever." Her hand dropped to her side. "Well, I have to memorize some poetry. And I'd rather talk to you."

"I love poetry," he said.

"I know, you told me that."

"I did," he said. "I guess I did."

She smiled. "Sometimes, you know, I think maybe I make you nervous." Her soft eyes were the color of a clear, early spring sky.

"Oh—no." The last word came out in that terrible falsetto. He faked a cough, cleared his throat. "This weather—my sinuses."

"Now you joke vith me." She sat down at his side. "We are making too much noise in the library, I think. Good thing there's no one else around to scold us. They all vent out in the rain before you came."

He looked at the doorway of the room, and then at her again. "No one," he said.

"Tell me something funny, Walter. You seem upset."

"No," he said.

"You don't seem so happy. Tell me a joke, maybe."

"I don't know any new ones," he said.

"Oh, there must be something. Be funny. I'm lonely for a laugh."

"I can't think of anything. I'm sorry. It's hard when you ask for it like that."

"Don't be glum," she said. "Does the rainy day make you glum?"

"Rainy days make me feel all—rainy and watery," he said.

She smiled. "There, that wasn't so hard."

"It wasn't funny, either."

"Too bad," she said. Then she sighed. "It gets dark too early in the winter, but we have talked about that, I guess. We must be running out of talk."

"There's lots to say," he told her. "The day's tilting—you notice how light it is in the mornings?"

"It's starting so qvick. The early dark."

"I always hated it," he said.

"I don't like it, either." She stood. "Now we're both depressed."

He gazed at her and felt that the smile on his face wasn't enough. "I always feel good when I'm with you," he said.

She laughed. "Oh, boy. Now, you make me feel ashamed for my bad mood about the dark. I take it all back." She paused a moment, looked beyond him at the open door. "Well, anyway. Good luck with your schoolvork." Then she turned and went back to the window seat, where she opened her book and seemed to concentrate. He paged through his own book. On one of the pages was a picture of Alice's father, Patrick Kane, cigarette dangling from the corner of his mouth, standing in a gray space with Edward R. Murrow. Marshall saw the hand of God in it. His knee throbbed, reminding him. Natalie lounged quietly in the window seat, the lovely ankle of one leg under the thigh of the other. She held a big volume of Shakespeare on her lap, and seemed perfectly content the way beautiful women can sometimes be, as if quite aware of their own exquisiteness and quite at home with it, too. Certainly she was aware of the effect she was having on him. He tried hard to apply himself to the book, and after a few distracted moments he heard Albert coming in with his fiancée, Albert's high-pitched voice gently coaxing, reassuring. "This way."

Marshall heard them enter the room behind him. They settled into one of the sofas. He did not turn around. For some reason, there had to be an element of drama in this moment, since he was about to meet a person he had never met before. He stared at the book, at the picture of Alice's father, with his small eyes and heavy jowls.

Albert spoke to his fiancée. "Walter has such powers of concentration, you know."

"This is a nice room, isn't it? I can smell the lovely books."

Marshall felt awful, but couldn't raise the will to lift his head just yet.

In the window seat, Natalie turned a page, sighed, then closed the book, rose, and walked breezily out of the room. "Good-bye," she said. Marshall allowed himself a glance at her, and this was the opening Albert needed.

"Walter?" he said. "Here she is. Fresh in from Alexandria on the bus."

Marshall turned, and with a kind of automatic impulse, feigned surprise. "Oh, hi."

Emma was a young, squarely set woman with pale, faintly mottled skin and the look of a girl whose appearance is a matter for someone other than herself to consider. Her fine, sandy-colored hair was braided and pinned close to her head, and her eyes were clouded, turned so deeply in on themselves that one's first impulse was to look away. She was holding dark glasses in one thin white hand, and he realized that she'd removed the glasses because she was being introduced to him. "Albert speaks so highly of you," she said, smiling.

"How nice to meet you," said Marshall, trying not to think about Natalie.

It came to him like all the badness of high school that Albert and his fiancée were not very handsome people physically, and something in Natalie's so-well-inhabited beauty made him feel caught out, as though being with these two people might have somehow lessened his chances. He stood, and remembered Alice again. For a moment, he couldn't find his voice. "Let's go on upstairs."

"Don't let us bother you," Albert said. "We'll sit right here and wait for you."

"I'm finished."

"May I shake your hand?" Emma said, reaching.

Marshall took it. Her palm was cool. She let her fingers glide over his fingers and up to his wrist. Then she took hold again and shook.

"Nice," she said. "I can tell you're a nice person."

No.

"And he's joining the ranks of the snared," Albert said.

"Albert, don't put it like that."

"Oh, but we love being snared," Albert said. "Just try throwing us back."

Marshall ushered them out and along the corridor to the stairs. Albert then led the way up, holding Emma's hand.

Upstairs, beyond the aluminum and glass doors with the words THE D'ALLESSANDRO SCHOOL FOR BROADCASTING painted on them, sitting on stools in the light of the studio, with its acoustically baffled walls and its little sound booth crowded with equipment, were the other members of Mr. D'Allessandro's radio school, class of 1965. This evening, they were all sitting quietly together, as if waiting for something or someone. This was supposed to be Martin Alvarez's night in the sound booth, and it was Baker's night to read the news and commercials. No one had done anything toward getting ready.

"I'm glad you're—all—here," Albert said, peering at them. "I wanted you to meet Emma."

"Hello," Emma said, removing her coat. Albert took it from her.

Alvarez stood and gently put his hand in hers. "Ees bery nice to meet you. We have some trouble."

"Trouble?"

"What's wrong?" Albert said. "The console break down?" He smiled, turning.

Marshall saw the expression on Alvarez's face. He looked at the others. "What is it?" he said.

Baker spoke. "Mr. D'Allessandro is in the hospital. They think it's his heart."

"My God," said Emma, taking hold of Albert's arm. "Oh, my God."

"Take it easy," Albert said. Then, turning to Baker. "Do they know how bad?"

"Just that they took him in this afternoon around five," said Baker. "We don't know much more. We're waiting for Mrs. D'Allessandro to call. She seemed pretty calm. But you never know with these things."

Marshall stared at him.

"She said to wait. She asked us to wait here."

Ricky Dalmas stood away from his stool, bringing the pipe with the chip out of the stem from his mouth. "I'm the one who answered the phone," he said. "Heart trouble. But Mrs. D'Allessandro didn't seem distraught."

"I talked to her," Baker said. "She seemed pretty calm."

They were all quiet, then. Outside, someone leaned on a car horn. The sound came to them like a kind of insistence on the part of the city, and now, far off, there were sirens. Marshall went to the sound booth and looked in. Here was Mr. D'Allessandro's coffee cup in its place on the small table.

"I think he was at home when it happened," Baker said.

"What'll we do if he can't come back to the school?" Ricky Dalmas wanted to know. "I need to get a job in radio. I need this degree."

"We won't get our money back," said Mrs. Gordon. "That's for sure."

"Everything'll work out all right," Albert said, picking at his cheek, not looking at any of them. Emma had not let go of his arm. Her face was white as the walls.

"My father had a heart attack ten years ago," Ricky Dalmas said. "And he's still around. He drinks a lot, too." It was clear from the expression on his face that he hadn't meant to add this.

No one else seemed to have heard him, anyway. Marshall averted his eyes. The others were all deep in their own thoughts. After a few moments, Baker said, "Well, maybe we ought to go on and start with the night's schedule."

"I don't think so," said Mrs. Gordon.

"You want to just sit here?"

"Mrs. D'Allessandro asked us to wait, and we're waiting."

"What're we waiting for, though?"

"When she calls, we'll know, I guess."

"You think this is the end of the school?"

"Eet's not the end of nothing," Alvarez said. "The money ees spent."

"They'll have to get someone else," said Mrs. Gordon.

"Who'll they get?" Marshall asked.

Dalmas, sucking on the pipe, looked at him. And Baker said, "Let's just wait and see what happens."

They waited. Emma coughed, then cleared her throat. "I—I need to sit down."

"Honey," Albert said. "Don't assume the worst. It could be perfectly all right."

She turned to him, holding tight.

"Be easy," he told her. Then he faced the others. "I didn't introduce Emma to the rest of you."

"Oh, Albert," said Emma. "Nobody feels like that now. Please."

"This is Emma," he said, guiding her toward Mrs. Gordon, who stood and reached for Emma's hands. For a little space, it was as though they had all gathered for a social occasion. Emma was introduced around, and Albert made a joke at his own expense concerning his worries about being a clumsy oaf married to the strict little Miss Em. Gradually, then, they all grew quiet, waiting for the phone to ring, or for someone to arrive.

Emma had taken a seat near the door, and Marshall saw that she kept wringing her hands. Albert stood at her side, gently patting her shoulder.

"Today," Ricky Dalmas said, "I told my wife something like this would happen. I did. I said, 'You watch, just as I'm starting to get better, Mr. D'Allessandro will have a heart attack and the school will close.'"

No one answered him.

"I've got some sort of sixth sense."

"It's a coincidence," said Mrs. Gordon. "That's all."

"Oh, yeah? When Kennedy was shot—same thing. I was working in the office and the phone rang, right? And this girl I was with said, 'I wonder what that is,' and I said, 'Probably the president's been shot.' I knew it, right? It's some extrasensory thing, like that TV show."

"I was sitting in a barber's chair," Baker said. "Over on Twelfth Street."

"I was at work," Marshall said.

"I was in Braille school," Emma said, still clinging to Albert's arm. "And it came over the intercom."

"We were driving to Missouri," said Mrs. Gordon. "For Thanksgiving. It was broadcast over the car radio. My husband was so upset we had to stop. We were both very upset."

"What about you?" Baker said to Alvarez.

"Mun, I was home asleep with the flu."

Baker looked at Marshall. "You?"

"At work," Marshall said. "I saw him in a parade in the summer—some foreign dignitary was visiting."

Albert said, "It's like we're all fixed in our own times and places. I know where all of you were at a certain hour of a given day on earth. My father said it was that way with Roosevelt. When Roosevelt died."

"Where were you?" Marshall asked him.

"When Roosevelt died?"

"No—"

"Just kidding, Walter. I was at work. The stockroom at the AFL-CIO, across from the White House. Same place I work now, really, except I've moved up to the seventh floor, to janitorial. When I went home that night, the bells—church bells—"

"I know," Marshall said, interrupting him. "It was raining, and they were tolling all over town. This slow tolling. And nobody talking—not on the streets and not in the buses. It was quiet as a funeral everywhere."

"The only sound," Albert said, "was the rain, and the car tires in the wet streets, and those bells going off every ten seconds or so."

"Yes."

They all paused, as though listening for the bells.

"Anybody want something to drink?" Baker asked abruptly.

"I'll go," said Marshall, thinking, in spite of himself and all his best intentions, of Natalie.

"Walter and I will go," Albert said. Then he leaned down and murmured something to Emma. Marshall couldn't make it out. He heard, "Sure?"

Emma nodded.

"Who wants what?" Albert asked.

Baker wrote the orders down on a piece of school stationery, and Albert took it from him, along with the money people had put in. "Let's go," he said to Marshall.

Marshall led the way down. As the two of them moved past the library door, he saw that Natalie was in the window seat again, but instead of reading, she was gazing—longingly, he thought—out at the street.

"Hey," Marshall said to her. "Want something to drink?"

"No," she said without quite looking back. "Thank you."

"What're you looking for? There's a lot of drippy, watery people out there."

"Nothing," she said almost impatiently through a smile. "Thanks anyway."

"What's wrong?" Albert wanted to know.

Marshall moved quickly out of the doorway. "Nothing's wrong."

They descended to the basement of the building, where Albert paused under the one ceiling light and tried to read what Baker had written.

Marshall took the list from him. "Here, I'll do it."

"Poor Emma," Albert said. "What a night to bring her here."

"She got so white," Marshall said.

Albert nodded, sadly, the one hand up to his face. "It scares her pretty bad. I've been trying to get her to stop worrying all the time."

"It's probably going to be okay." Marshall wanted to change the subject. He put the coins in the machine, and as each bottle dropped into the pan, Albert retrieved it, bending low, groaning like an old man. On the way back upstairs, they saw that the night college was going ahead with the evening's work as though nothing were amiss. Perhaps they didn't even know about Mr. D'Allessandro.

At the glass doors, Baker stood. "Mrs. D'Allessandro wants to talk to you, Walter."

"Me?"

In the studio, the others were all standing, and Albert passed the drinks around. Emma felt her way to his side and held one arm. "It's okay," he said, low.

Marshall stepped into the sound booth, thinking he would be talking on the phone, but Mrs. D'Allessandro herself was sitting there at the console, the phone handset held tightly to her ear. She was a big, platinum-blonde woman with a slightly puffy, ruddy face—the face of someone with an appetite for rich food and wine, whose features have not yet been ruined by these indulgences; it was somehow not the face of someone in distress. She signaled for Marshall to close the door, then turned away slightly.

She said into the phone, "That's correct."

Her accent was like that of the new English groups. Liverpool. She had met her husband in London, during the war, and had come to America with him when the war ended. She was an American citizen now, taught history and English literature in the night college, and administered the schedules and classes from the office off the foyer downstairs. She said "All right" into the phone, nodding. She hadn't looked at Marshall, but held one hand up as if to ask for patience. "I know. I'll have the information sent to you." She put the handset back in its cradle and turned to him. "Somebody asking about the radio school, believe it or not—I shouldn't have picked up. But there's nobody in the office." Folding her hands in her lap, she took a second to study him. On the other side of the glass, he saw Dalmas talking to Albert while Baker and Mrs. Gordon looked on. Emma still held on to Albert's arm, standing close, the side of her face against his chest, as though she were listening for his heartbeat.

Mrs. D'Allessandro sighed. "Nice lot, aren't they?"

"Yes," said Marshall.

"They can't hear us, then?"

"No, ma'am. Not unless you put that switch on." He pointed to the small red button on the console.

"Well, we shan't push that one, shall we?" She smiled, took a breath, and sat up. "I—that is, we—have a favor to ask of you."

Marshall waited.

"Don't stare like that. It makes me nervous."

"Yes, ma'am." He was unaware that he had been staring.

"Do you know that your irises don't reach the bottom lids of your eyes?"

"No, ma'am." He looked at the ghost reflection of himself in the glass, superimposed over the faces of Albert and Emma. Albert smiled.

"It's very disconcerting to look into eyes like that," Mrs. D'Allessandro went on.

"I didn't mean to stare," Marshall told her.

"My husband has informed me that you—that he ran into you and your lady friend earlier today."

"Yes, ma'am."

"Yes, well—he wants to talk to you about it." She cleared her throat, then pulled the edge of her dress down over her knees. "That is, he would like very much to discuss something with you. Tonight, if at all possible."

"Is he—going to be all right?"

She waved this away. "Oh, unquestionably—a little problem. We were worried about his heart. He has a history. It's nothing—nothing to worry about at all. But he is in hospital. As a precaution. And he—wondered if I couldn't bring you round to see him. I could drive you home afterward. I mean, I'd be happy to do that, if you needed me to."

"What about the others?" Marshall asked.

"Yes, well, what about them? They'll have to forgo class tonight."

"He—he just wants to see me?"

"You're—Walter Marshall, are you?"

"Yes, ma'am."

"Well, that's it, then. Those are my instructions." She stood. "Now, if you don't mind, I'll just step out and tell these people that we'll have to dispense with classes for tonight. I should've said so over the phone, but I wasn't thinking very clearly. Oh, and, I don't think Mr. D'Allessandro wants the others to know about this, um, meeting."

"Yes, ma'am."

She frowned, staring. She seemed for a moment to be considering something about his appearance. "I don't recall when I've met a more polite young man." Now she smiled. "Makes me feel rather like an old person. You don't see me as old, then?"

He shook his head.

"I'm only forty-three."

"Yes, ma'am."

"Does it strike you as odd that I'd tell my age so blithely?"

"No."

She gave forth a small laugh. "Nothing surprises anyone these days, I suppose." Then she opened the door to the studio and began to tell the others about canceling the night's class. Albert moved across the room to where Marshall stood, and Emma moved with him. "Well, I guess we can go celebrate."

"I can't," Marshall told him.

Albert said nothing for a moment.

"I'd love to, Albert. But I just can't tonight."

Albert indicated Emma with a slight nod of his head. "Maybe it's for the best. She's pretty upset."

"It wasn't a heart attack," Marshall said to her.

She moved to stand even closer to Albert, who shook his head and seemed to want to say more. But it was a moment before he spoke. "It's not the specific thing," he said. "You see. It's—you understand."

"Yes," Marshall said, not understanding at all.

"So I'll see you on Wednesday?"

"Wednesday, yes."

"We'll have to have a double date," Emma said in a shaky voice.

"That would be nice."

The others were filing out. Albert took a step toward the door and then looked over his shoulder at Marshall. "You coming? We'll walk you to the bus stop."

"Actually—I've got some work to do. In—in the library," Marshall told him.

Albert nodded, all good nature and credulity. "Oh, sure. Well, congratulations again."

"Thanks."

"Congratulations," Emma said.

They went out and down the stairs, and Emma called good-bye again from the door. Albert turned to look back, squinted into the light, smiling, and then went on out. Mrs. D'Allessandro stood next to Marshall on the landing, and when the door finally closed, she said, "I know that must've been a bit awkward for you."

He said nothing.

She was putting her coat on, tying a scarf around her neck. He buttoned his own coat. "Ready?" she said.

"Yes, ma'am."

"If you don't mind my asking, what were they congratulating you about?"

"Oh," Marshall said, with a start. "That—I—I'm engaged to be married."

"To this—Alice, I take it?"

"Yes, ma'am."

"How nice for everyone," she said. "That's very good news."

"Yes, m—" His voice quavered and caught again. He cleared his throat and tried once more. "Yes, ma'am."

She started down the stairs. "Positively the most polite boy," she said. "We should have you copied."

She drove erratically, gripping the wheel with both hands, appearing to strain in order to keep sitting upright, using the wheel as support. He looked out at the wet street, and every other car seemed to veer at them before gliding by, some of them with horns blaring. There were several near misses. When Mrs. D'Allessandro stopped at a light, she pressed the brake in one steady motion until it locked, and they pitched forward on the seat. The car skidded a few yards, and she struggled to get it straight. Marshall found it necessary to put both hands on the dashboard. They had come to a stop in the middle of an intersection.

"Bloody rain," she said.

Another car swung past, barely missing the passenger-side door. Marshall let out a small shout of alarm.

"Excuse me," she said, grinding the gears. "We'll be off in a moment."

He nodded, then remembered to say, "Yes, ma'am."

"You needn't call me 'ma'am.' And, in fact, I wish you wouldn't."

"Yes, m . . ." he began.

She turned to him and seemed about to say more. But then she sighed and looked out at the glimmering street. "Can't get over those eyes of yours."

The light changed, and they jerked forward. She hit the brakes again and brought the heel of her hand against the horn. "Bloody American drivers."

Marshall hadn't seen the other car this time. He had closed his eyes, facing away from her, as though looking out the passenger-side window.

"I'll never understand it," she said. "Brutal country. It infects people. They come here as normal as pie and in five minutes they're ready to kill. I never should've left England."

In other circumstances, he might've thought to say something patriotic. But he was giving all his attention to the road. The car had eased forward, and was gathering speed. "I always try to make the next light," she said, speeding up. There were cars entering the street from both sides, and apparently she didn't see them, or was simply ignoring them. He couldn't help crossing his arms in front of his face.

"Perfectly awful," she said.

Horns sounded and then receded. He sat up and looked out the back window, at the confusion of lights. When he looked at Mrs. D'Allessandro again, she had her round shoulders hunched, someone forging ahead, eyes narrowed, hands tight on the wheel, mouth partly open as if she were facing into a strong wind.

They went through another intersection, horns blaring from both sides. And at the next intersection they skidded to a stop just as the light turned green.

"I wish they'd bloody well make up their minds," Mrs. D'Allessandro said.

They went sailing through a pair of slowing trucks. Marshall read the words "Dry Cleaning" on the side of one far too close. He sat up and held his breath, one hand on the dash.

"Are you nervous?" she said.

"No, ma'am." He'd actually made a croaking sound this time. He did not try to repeat the words, but only looked at her and smiled.

"Nervous," she said.

They went on, through the rain and the traffic lights, the busy intersections, the shifting lanes, the veering shapes of the backs of cars. Marshall held tight, his weight pressed against the back of the seat.

At last, the hospital came into view—they barreled past the signs and into the parking lot, the right-side wheels rolling over the curb and severely jostling the inside of the car. He hit his head on the ceiling. Mrs. D'Allessandro pulled into a parking space without slowing down, and then stopped with the suddenness of emergency. They skidded again, and bumped the curb.

"There," she said, turning the ignition off.

Marshall rubbed the top of his head. There was a welt starting.

"Are you hurt?" She took his face between her hands and stared at him. "Are you dizzy?"

"No. My head."

"You're fine." She let go of him. "Do you have a hairbrush? You look a bit disheveled. Here." She combed her fingers through his hair, then took his chin and regarded him. "Best we can do, I suppose."

They got out of the car. He saw scratches in the finish and several dents in the fenders. It was not an old car. "Does Mr. D'Allessandro usually do the driving?" he asked.

She seemed incredulous that he could ask such a question. "He doesn't have a license to drive. He let it lapse five years ago."

Marshall couldn't help thinking about Mr. D'Allessandro's heart trouble. He made his way around to join her on the sidewalk. She waited, her purse held in front of her with both hands.

"No," she said. "I do all the driving. When there's any driving to do. There's less than three thousand miles on this car."

He looked at it again. A Ford Falcon. The name seemed absurdly diminished by the battered look of the fenders.

They crossed the lot in the tall, misting shadow of the building. As they reached the glass doors leading inside, she took his arm and stopped him. "Is that man following us?"

Marshall turned to look. A figure was moving across the lot, a few feet from the road, a man holding a briefcase, a newspaper under his arm. The man moved along amid the parked cars, paused at one, and began digging in his coat pockets.

"I thought I saw him watching us," Mrs. D'Allessandro said.

"I don't think so," Marshall told her.

She still held on to his arm. "You're a good young man," she said. "We're going to trust you. We're going to put ourselves in your hands."

He nodded automatically, meaning to say that he understood her words. But he did not understand, and as she led him into the building, he paused to say so.

"That's what this meeting's about," she said.

Chapter

4

 r. D'Allessandro was in a room on the seventh floor.
In the bed next to his, a man lay, heavily asleep,
mouth open, head thrown back, legs spread wide, as
though he had fallen over from a standing position after being hit
on the chin. His snores were audible all the way out to the nurses'
station. "Can you believe it?" Mr. D'Allessandro said over the
noise. "I've even tried turning him on his side. I've asked the nurse
to pull the curtain at least, but nobody hears what you say."

Mrs. D'Allessandro pulled the curtain around the other bed,
and then they all listened for a time. The snoring went on, and
grew even louder—one would have been hard pressed to believe
that it was a human sound.

"Isn't it incredible?" D'Allessandro said to his wife. "That's
what I've been dealing with all afternoon and evening. Incredible."

"Poor boy," she said.

"I can't hear you."

She indicated Marshall with a nod of her head.

In the next instant, with a suddenness that made them pause,
the snoring stopped, then continued in a minor key, a little less
loud.

Mrs. D'Allessandro nodded toward Marshall again.

"Yes," her husband said with a shrugging motion, as if he were throwing a weight off his shoulders. "I see you brought our young friend along."

"Your perception is unfailing as usual, dear."

He held out a bony hand for Marshall to shake. D'Allessandro was twelve years older than his wife, yet there was about his face a tight quality, as though the skin had been stretched and polished. His mouth was turned down, and when he smiled, one's first help- less impression was that he had grimaced with some sudden pang— it usually took a second to realize that he was pleased—and his watery eyes had a way of shifting from you even as they took you in. "So, young sir. Did Mrs. D'Allessandro talk to you—"

"I didn't tell him anything," said his wife.

He looked at her and then seemed to grimace. He was now supporting himself on one elbow. He drew a sudden breath, and paused, staring at Marshall. "You know I have very good hopes for you." His voice when he meant to be especially emphatic took on a whispery overly dramatic quality that always made Marshall want to glance away. He almost did so now. Mr. D'Allessandro went on. "I think you're one of the better students we've had here, and, frankly, I'd be very surprised if you didn't land a good job very soon after you graduate."

This was something he had already said more than once. The young man nodded at him, then turned his attention to Mrs. D'Allessandro, who sighed, moved restlessly to the foot of the bed, and sat down.

"Noise getting to you?" her husband asked without looking at her.

In the next bed, the snoring went on, the same toneless hum, as if the patient, even in his unconscious state, were in contention for an audience.

"I'm not bothered by the noise, Lawrence."

"You looked a bit distracted, dear."

"Get on with it, why don't you."

"I was about to." He reached out and put his thin, cool hand on Marshall's wrist, then took it away. "My gastric distress isn't quite what it seems, lad."

Mrs. D'Allessandro cleared her throat abruptly. "I told them it was your heart."

Again, D'Allessandro answered without looking at her. His eyes were on Marshall, and they narrowed the smallest increment. "I thought we agreed it would be an ulcer, dear."

"Heart seemed easier at the time," she said.

"It's not what we agreed on, though."

"That hardly matters now."

"Still, it constitutes a deviation from the agreed-upon plan." He spoke through his teeth.

"Please, proceed with it, Lawrence."

"You see," D'Allessandro said, grimacing for real this time, and never taking his eyes off the young man, "I have stomach trouble that is not exactly of the ulcer variety, like our snoring friend here."

Marshall was unable to decide what to do with his own facial expressions—whether concern was called for, or the polite smile of being in humor with the other man, or a frown of sympathy. There was a light in D'Allessandro's eyes, as if he had just told a joke, though presently the grimace-smile returned, and his wife shifted her weight impatiently at the foot of the bed. The snoring seemed to be growing louder—such a series of fluting and bellowing drafts of air that they stopped and listened again, for a moment.

When it lessened, Mr. D'Allessandro shook his head, and then sat up, arranging his pillows behind him. "Crank the bed up a little," he said to Marshall.

"Here," said Mrs. D'Allessandro, rising. She wound the crank with a competent speed that looked a little like temper. When he was satisfied, her husband said, "That's better," arranging the blankets across his lap. He was sitting almost straight up. She returned to the foot of the bed.

He smiled, or grimaced, at Marshall. "My stomach is hurt from a blow, you see."

Marshall did not see, and it must've shown in his expression.

"Someone hit me there. Hard."

"Oh, Lawrence," Mrs. D'Allessandro said. "For mercy's sake, do get on with it, will you?"

"There's a way of going about these things, Esther."

She said nothing. He moved in the bed, arranging himself,

smoothing the blanket over his legs, frowning with pain. Then he cleared his throat, and coughed. Marshall thought of rooms where people died, watching as Mrs. D'Allessandro brought a little slide puzzle out of her purse and began furiously trying to work it. The incongruity of this, along with the mounting sense of catastrophe in the room, made him consider trying to extricate himself. But he was curious, too. And now Mr. D'Allessandro turned to him and started talking about the ageless appeal of speed, of swiftness, of competition—racing men, racing women, racing horses, racing dogs, racing cars—and of trying to predict and capitalize on the results of such contests. His dear father and both of his dear uncles, may they rest in peace, had worked around the horses, had spent the best part of their lives at the track. He had grown up among them, and oh, that was the life a boy ought to lead—being around horses and horsemen, walking the animals, feeding them and grooming them, and being there for the sights and sounds and excitements of the race; being five years old and standing between shouting men at trackside, seeing a flashing confusion of thundering hooves go by, kicking up the raked, red dirt and shaking the whole world, it seemed; and how good it was to stand in the raised, dry dust of the race, the fine, floating dust that gathered in clouds on the summer breezes, and mixed with the smell of the horses. He made it clear that he was drawing from fond memory, the clearest and best recollection, the kind that made your heart stir again.

His wife kept working the little puzzle, clicking the pieces into place with a strange, distracted efficiency.

"Well, young man," Mr. D'Allessandro said, "do you—do you see what I mean?"

Marshall nodded, though he did not see at all.

"The point of all this," Mr. D'Allessandro went on, grimacing or smiling, "is that one must try to enjoy these things without diminishing one's, shall we say, resources. In short, lad, I'm afraid I've let the love of these things wrest from me my ability to discipline myself. And the result is that I've incurred some few problems of arrearage."

"Oh, God," Mrs. D'Allessandro said without looking up from her puzzle. "Micawber."

Her husband said, "My wife is English." Then he paused,

sighed, and seemed to collect himself. "There are some gentlemen I owe money to, you see, a—rather a lot of it, I'm afraid. And they're not—ah, particularly interested in the hows and wherefores of the matter. No. They want their money without reference to the hows and wherefores. And since I can't take blood from a stone—well, you get the picture. I gave them a large payment, see. A lot of what I owe them, and it's put me in a sort of a bind vis-à-vis the school."

"Vis—" Marshall began. He had just seen the phrase in print somewhere.

"The school," Mr. D'Allessandro said. "Yes. I'm afraid if something isn't done I won't be able to continue for the rest of the—the school year, you see. Next term. And because of these, er, these very insistent gentlemen—well, it's a bit—it's actually imperative that I receive another term's tuitions, and even that I increase their number. Which, my young friend, is where you come in."

Mrs. D'Allessandro opened her purse and looked into it, then shut it again. She cleared her throat, set her hands together, with the little puzzle in the middle, and rested her elbows on the purse in her lap, staring at Marshall.

Mr. D'Allessandro addressed the young man. "We wondered if you'd be willing to help us out."

"Sure," said Marshall, wanting, as always, to please.

"What we thought," Mr. D'Allessandro said, putting his hands carefully together over his chest, "was that if we could bring someone well known to the school, to give a talk—maybe spend the evening. You see? Someone—er, famous, who'd do it for nothing—for a favor, let us say."

They were both watching him now. "I see," he said.

"Well?"

He nodded. He could think of nothing else to do.

"Your nice lady friend," Mrs. D'Allessandro said.

"Alice Kane," Marshall told her, and the sinking sensation came back.

"Kane. There, yes," said Mr. D'Allessandro. "You—you introduced me to her."

"Yes, sir."

"Oh," he said quickly. "You shouldn't address me as 'sir.' I consider that we're all on the same footing here."

"All on the same footing," said his wife with a surprisingly jovial laugh. "Except you, Lawrence, who happen to be flat on your back with a possible ruptured spleen." She grew serious again, turning the little puzzle in her hand. "Bruises and lacerations in the chestal area and abdomen." She paused. "My darling."

Marshall looked from one to the other of them.

"As you can plainly see, I'm not flat on my back, as you put it," D'Allessandro said. "Dear."

She made a huffing sound in the back of her throat, but said nothing.

"What we hoped," D'Allessandro went on with an air of at last getting down to business, "is that you might approach your lady friend about her very influential father. See if he might be willing to give us the favor of—the company of anyone he might prevail upon, you see, in order for us to put together a program that might draw a few extra students for the spring. It has to be a big name, though. Like—well, like on the Edward R. Murrow level. Someone of that ilk."

Marshall sat with his hands on his thighs, nodding.

"You—you think you might help us out?" D'Allessandro said. "I'm afraid I haven't done a very good job of"—he looked at his wife briefly—"explaining things. The truth is, it's a bit in the area of a desperate situation—but we did have Averell Harriman once, for a graduation speech. Well, he agreed to do it, and then the whole thing fell through."

"Do you want to tell him why?" she said.

"That won't be necessary. Love."

"It's such a lovely story, though. And I'll bet young Mr. Marshall would like to hear another gambling story."

"I wouldn't call it a gambling story, Esther."

She leaned toward the young man. "The school will be forced to close its doors at the end of this term." She spoke crisply.

"That's unfortunately a possibility," said her husband with an air of resignation.

She opened her purse and dropped the little plastic puzzle in. Snapping the purse shut, she put it on the floor at her feet, straightened and touched her hair lightly, then folded her hands on one knee, regarding Marshall with a calm, measuring expression.

"If we could get five or six new students by spring," her husband said. "I've just signed someone on to start immediately, in fact. A young fellow who will help us on another score. The—with the way we appear to the—the—well, let us say the surrounding environs. But that's another thing. What I thought was that along with a slight increase in the present tuition—this program I was thinking about. You see, we might get a temporary permit to broadcast in the area—a onetime deal. With a famous name—somebody your young lady friend's father might get for us, see—we'd be able to do that. And we could make it a night of public affairs, or some such thing. While advertising what we do so well. We could talk about the profession of newscaster. There we are. A—a symposium."

"Or maybe something in honor of our martyred president," Mrs. D'Allessandro said.

"There. Now that's a wonderful idea, Esther."

"Why, thank you," Esther said. And, after another little pause, "Darling."

Marshall had the unnerving impression that the two of them had been through all this before, and that this brainstorming was a performance, for his benefit. But then Mr. D'Allessandro looked at him with such apparently innocent hope in his moist green eyes, and with that complicated smile on his face. They were both waiting for him to respond. And as though to contribute to the increasing sense of expectancy in the room, the other patient abruptly stopped snoring.

"Do you want me to bring Alice here?" Marshall asked, feeling, in the heavy silence, as though he should whisper.

"Bring her here?" Mrs. D'Allessandro said, also whispering. "To the hospital?"

Mr. D'Allessandro seemed alarmed at the prospect. "Oh, no, I wouldn't want to bother her that much. No, no indeed. I was thinking you might prevail upon her yourself."

After a pause, in which the young man continued to nod, though he was still confused, Esther D'Allessandro said, "We want you to ask her for us."

"Yes, ma'am."

"Then you'll do it?" her husband said.

Marshall was still nodding at him.

"Marvelous. Esther, I feel the tide is going to change."

"We'll see," Esther said, rising, bending to retrieve her purse. "Now you should rest that spleen."

"Ha ha," said her husband mirthlessly. "I feel better already." He turned to Marshall and offered his thin hand again. "My young friend," he said, "bless you."

"Yes, sir."

The snoring started up once more, so loud that it required them to pitch their voices nearly at the level of a shout.

"You'll report back tomorrow?" Mr. D'Allessandro said.

"Tomorrow?"

A shadow seemed to cross his face. He sat forward. "We need an answer very soon."

"I'll try," said Marshall.

"What?"

"I'll try."

"There's the spirit." D'Allessandro settled back on his pillows, and clasped his hands behind his head. "A young man of definite talent and ability," he said to his wife. "I knew we could count on him."

"Rest," Mrs. D'Allessandro told him, then turned and ushered Marshall out of the room. She closed the door, and left him standing out in the corridor for a moment. There was a window above the water fountain a few feet away, and he looked at his reflection in it, put his hands in the side pockets of his coat, and thought of being president. Then he pushed the hair across his forehead, and patted it down. Mrs. D'Allessandro came out of the room and took him by the arm. "The thing about my husband is his unlimited capacity for hope."

"Yes, ma'am."

"I don't give this much of a chance for working. And the trouble is, it was his damned hopefulness that got us in this trouble in the first place. That's what a bet always is, young man, whether anyone admits it or not. Naked, childlike hope. I've gone along with it all this time, like a fool."

They went down in the elevator, the two of them doubled in the shining metal doors, and when they stepped out into the lobby, a man in a gray overcoat blocked their path. He was small in the way a miniature terrier is small—nothing at all out of proportion; a full-length photograph, without anything to compare him against, would give utterly no clue as to his actual size: One could easily be convinced that he was six feet tall. Under the bright light of the downstairs lobby of the hospital, moving to confront Mrs. D'Allessandro, his fingers closing on the cloth of her sleeve as he pulled her aside to talk, he seemed not quite real. A toy man, with toy hands and toy feet, wearing a toy overcoat, a toy hat atop the toy head. The face was aquiline, with sharp lines in the cheeks and on either side of the mouth, running down into the neck. "I don't understand," said Mrs. D'Allessandro with an edge of distress, pulling from his grasp.

Out of reflex, Marshall stepped forward, and the little man put his hands in the pockets of his overcoat and smiled, showing a perfect row of small, white teeth.

"Please wait for me outside," Mrs. D'Allessandro said. It wasn't immediately clear to whom she was speaking.

"This your son?" the toy man wanted to know, still smiling.

"He's a—friend."

"Tough?"

No one said anything.

The little man hadn't taken his eyes from Marshall. He was still smiling, and his voice when he spoke was almost friendly. "How tough are you, kid?"

"It's not what you think," Mrs. D'Allessandro said to him. "This boy can help us get what we need. Do you understand? Your boss gets what he wants." She turned to Marshall. "Please. I asked for you to wait for me outside."

The little man stepped forward and offered his hand to Marshall. The hand was very warm, the grip surprisingly strong. It hurt, and Marshall quickly pulled his own hand away. "Name's Marcus," the man said. "Nice to make your acquaintance, kid. So tell me, you got a rich aunt or something?"

"Please," said Mrs. D'Allessandro. "We're working it all out. He said we could have a couple of weeks."

"So he did," the little man said, smiling. "So you do."

"Then I don't understand."

He turned to her. "Mr. Brace just wanted to demonstrate his

continuing interest. I'm to serve as a gentle reminder of that interest. Accruing daily, of course."

"We're aware of everything," she said through her teeth. "How dare he do this."

"You're *aware*," said the little man, still smiling. "That will be a mar-vu-lous boost to Mr. Brace's confidence." He stepped back and tipped his hat. "Mar-vu-lous, yes. Good day to you both." Then he gave an exaggerated bow, looking for that instant like a dressed-up boy at a party, bending with a sweeping motion of the hand that held the hat. "I'll probably see you tomorrow, of course. Mr. Brace likes to keep reminding his clients of their obligations."

"We don't need reminding. You might remind Mr. Brace—if that's what he wants to call himself—that Lawrence is not one of his ordinary clients. He's not going to run off or anything."

The little man had started away, and only called back over his shoulder, "Nevertheless."

They watched him go out through the revolving door and on down the street.

Mrs. D'Allessandro held her purse tight, with both hands, and did not move for a moment. Marshall thought of touching her arm, offering his support—he thought she might topple over. At length she seemed to come to herself, and she stared at him as though surprised to find him there. "I have to go," she said. "There are things I have to do. I don't think—I suppose I could take you back to the school."

"I can take the bus home," Marshall told her.

"Yes," she said, distracted. "The bus."

"If you could drop me on K Street."

"Of course." She started out, then stopped, turned around, and headed for the bank of elevators. "I should tell him—" She stopped again. Marshall waited a few feet behind her. She whirled suddenly and faced him, her small hands gripping the closed purse. "You will help us?"

"I certainly will," Marshall offered, though, in fact, he had no idea how he would begin to be of any real help. He wanted to tell her that Alice's father was really rather stern and frightening, and he did not know how he would ever find the words to ask him what Mr. D'Allessandro wanted asked.

"Bless you," Mrs. D'Allessandro was saying. "Come on. We have to hurry. I'm supposed to be somewhere by eight o'clock. Lawrence isn't the only one scheming to find money."

They hurried out to the car. Getting in, and sitting there while she wrestled with her coat and then worked to get her timing right on the clutch, Marshall felt weirdly close to her, as though they had lived through years together.

"What're you staring at?" she said as the car jerked backward and stalled.

"I'm sorry," he said. "I wasn't . . . "

She struggled with the gearshift, and there was a loud grinding. "You think I'm old," she said, looking back, then turning to work the gearshift once more. "It's natural. But listen, I have my whole life in front of me, just like you."

"Yes, ma'am," Marshall said.

"And stop calling me 'ma'am.'" She had gotten them moving along the street, and began to pick up speed. The surfaces before them reflected light, all in motion, colors bleeding into each other from the rain and mist. "Tell me how to get to K Street," she said.

He wasn't sure, and she must have read his hesitation that way.

"Well, it has to be in this direction," she said, turning into the stream of traffic.

It took them awhile to find it, and through it all she kept veering in and out of lanes, nearly missing several collisions. At one point, she turned down a one-way street, and in order to correct herself, abruptly spun the wheel to the left, bumped the car up onto the sidewalk, scattering a group of startled pedestrians, then backed down into the road and headed in the appointed direction.

Finally, they pulled onto K Street, and she stopped. "Can you meet me at the school tomorrow afternoon at five?"

"Yes," he managed. But it seemed important to add, "I don't know if I can have an answer for you that soon."

"Please try." She gestured for him to get out.

He did so.

"Don't forget," she said, lurching away as he shut the door.

He watched her drive on, jerking, nearly stalling, to I Street, where she went left with a smoothness that seemed to contradict everything that had gone before. When, a moment or two later, he heard squealing brakes, he believed he knew the cause.

It was past nine o'clock, and the street was quiet. He let the first bus go by, and then, on an impulse, walked up Eighteenth Street to the school. The upstairs windows were dark. He sat alone in the little library, not quite admitting to himself what he was waiting and hoping for while others moved past the doorway, going in and out. Two women stood on the stone stairs of the entrance and talked about Christmas shopping. Natalie was nowhere to be seen, and no one else came to the library. He turned the pages of a magazine and stayed where he was, ashamed of himself. He had given no thought to what he might have said, or to what might have happened had she been there.

Natalie, I've been wanting to talk to you because you're the one I really want to marry. You'd make such a beautiful First Lady . . .

"God," he said aloud, "cut it out." He stirred, checked to be certain that he hadn't been heard by anyone. The building seemed empty.

In the street door, on his way out, he ran into Natalie. She was hurrying up the stairs to get out of the rain. She wore a white scarf that made her skin look darker. She looked at him and smiled. It was raining hard again, a torrent, sheets of it sweeping across the street. She stood waiting, seemed almost unaware of him, and he remained where he was.

"Miserable weather," he said.

She nodded. She had folded her arms and was staring out with a look of consternation on her face.

"Are you waiting for a ride?" he asked.

She hadn't heard him. She sighed, unfolded her arms, and thrust her hands into the pockets of the coat. She was almost as tall as Marshall.

He repeated the question.

"No, Walter," she said. "I was walking home."

"You live near here?"

She nodded. "I'm getting out of the rain."

"I thought you forgot something, maybe."

"No. I just took a job."

"You were coming from somewhere else."

She seemed bemused by this. She only glanced at him as she spoke. "I was down the street. I have a new job."

"Did you memorize the Shakespeare?"

"Shakespeare, yes. A sonnet."

"I love Shakespeare," Marshall told her.

"So you said." She looked out at the rain.

"Has something upset you?" he said.

Again, it was as though she hadn't heard him.

"Natalie?"

"Yes, I hear you, Walter."

"I've been reading some Shakespeare, too," he said.

She looked at him and seemed to consider, then shrugged. "I vould like to read him better. I have trouble with his word choices. It's a langwege problem."

He nodded. He was running out of things to say. This meeting was oddly disjointed, and he supposed it had to do with the fact that it was removed from the usual context, sitting in the library or standing by the vending machines in the basement.

The rain had let up, and she reached her hand out to test it.

"Want to go get some coffee or something?" he said.

"I'm sorry, Walter—no. I haf to go now." She was already stepping away from him. "'Bye."

"Wait," he said. "I'll walk you."

She headed in the opposite direction from where he needed to go to catch his bus. He walked along at her side, trying to keep his mind absolutely blank. They had gone about two blocks when she stopped, and extended one slender hand. "You are so kind."

"You know me," he said. "Saint Walter."

She shook her head, smiling at him. "You shouldn't make fun. You are nicer than some men. You don't need to have heroes."

"I guess that makes me your hero," he said, trying for a lighter tone. "Gee, tanks," he added, in the accent of Jackie Gleason doing Joe the bartender.

"You don't understand me, Walter."

"I tought I did, tho, lady."

"I'm serious."

"Yes," he said. "I was just trying to be funny. You wanted me to be funny earlier—"

"I'm sorry. Forgive me."

The rain picked up a little. He took her hand, and felt as though something important had taken place. "Are you all right?" he said. It seemed to him that all their previous talk, everything he had ever said to her, had been at a level of frivolous chatter, and that now something more might be said.

"Such a kind, gentle boy," she said. "A sveet man you vill be. Don't change."

"I won't." He had spoken too quickly, realizing that she had made a boy of him with this last. "I'm a man now," he said.

She let go of his hand. "Yes. I know. Well, good night." She turned from him, and walked up the sidewalk to the entrance. He looked at the building—a tall, flat-roofed row house not unlike the D'Allessandro School in appearance. Most of the windows were dark. Rain ran down the dingy surfaces. She went on inside, and she did not look back. The tall door at the front of the building squeaked as she opened it, and squeaked as she shut it, moving out of the small light in the foyer. For a few moments, he remained where he was, gazing at the many windows, with dark green sills and panes, some blocked with curtains, and some with figurines or flowers in them. One lighted window shone on the top floor, as if this were a beacon for wanderers in the inclement city streets. When a window on the second floor filled with light, he stood back a step, not wanting her to look out and see him still standing there.

But he couldn't bring himself to leave right away, in the vain hope that she might decide to come back out and speak to him. For some obscure reason, it would be all right for her to find him here if she walked back out of the building. But she was nowhere, and the light in the window went out. Even so, it was a few moments before he started back down to K Street, and the late bus.

In 1964, the buses that rode to the Virginia side of the river were all old pre–World War II models, with small windows and no air-conditioning. From the front they looked angry, with their low-browed windshields and metal grillwork. Two of them waiting side by side at a light looked like scowling cousins, irritated by having to be seen in such nearness to each other. In cold weather, they were seldom warm enough, and the air inside them was often redolent of exhaust fumes. They rattled and clattered over the uneven streets like wagons full of loose metal. Walter Marshall liked the sound, and he liked the rickety feel of them, which fed somehow the sense of the world as being a place with its own old life, the life he was now entering: It would only have charmed him more had they been ramshackle stagecoaches rumbling over dirt roads.

His bus took him down the Whitehurst Freeway, built out over a soft bend of the Potomac, along tall brick facades and a thousand factory windows, past the sign that read, THE OBJECTIONABLE ODORS YOU MAY NOTICE IN THE AREA DO NOT EMANATE FROM THIS PLANT, and on to Key Bridge, with its view of the river glistening with rain, the reflected lights of the city crowding to its banks.

The rain had increased, and the clouds were trailing their ragged ends along the tops of the trees that lined Route 50. It looked like the low sky was breaking into feathery pieces. At a corner of the road, just past the Marriott in Rosslyn, was a field of grass and flowers that he had once described to his mother as being the place he would think of, the one place he would hold most clearly in his mind if it turned out that, like his father and grandfather and great-grandfather, he ended up fighting for his country. He never failed to look for the field, even in the dark. And when it was shrouded in night, as it was now, he took comfort from it anyway, knowing it was there beyond his pale, shimmery reflection in the window. The contemplation of it never failed to give him a warm sense of patriotic duty fulfilled, as though he had already been to war and done brave things to preserve the spot in its pristine beauty.

At his stop in Arlington, a small booth for passengers stood at the curb, and his mother waited for him there. It distressed him to see this, since she never came to meet him unless she felt blue, and had begun to worry—as only she could worry. Sometimes he had inklings of what it must be to have her mind, with its steady stream of frightful images. Whenever he took the car out and she heard sirens, no matter how far away, she believed immediately, with grisly pictures in her mind, that the sirens were responding to the fatal accident involving her son. If he had gone for a walk and was late coming home, and forgot to call her, she imagined the circumstances in which he had been abducted, beaten, shot, or stabbed. In her own terrible and helpless imaginings, Mrs. Marshall had lost her one son many times: through illnesses of every stripe and kind, through madness, through accident or negligence, hers or his own; he had fallen down stairs, walked in front of speeding trucks, been hit by a train, crushed by a downed aircraft, and trampled by panicked crowds in the street. He had tripped and plummeted into deep holes, wandered into the exposed end of a live power line; he had been burned, or exploded, or maimed, or crushed. Storms had taken him, lightning had struck him, tornados had touched down on the spot where he walked. These images came to her unbidden, in a flash of panic, and once the thought occurred to her, she could not unthink it, nor bring herself to behave other than as though it were true. There had been night phone calls to hospitals, to the police, to the offices of newspapers, to friends and relatives. Several times the young man had come home to find her sitting up with someone—a sleepy cousin or a stranger in the employ of the city—frantically unscrolling her dream of the latest catastrophe that had befallen him.

Her tendency to worry in this morbid way increased whenever she had been putting cordials in her tea, and since his father's sorrowing, valedictory visit two years ago, the occasions on which she felt the need to have the cordial tea, as she called it, had arisen more often than he liked to contemplate, hoping as he did that it would change with time. The cordials came in fancy bottles, and had odd, foreign-sounding names—Galliano; Kahlua; Grand Marnier; crème de menthe; crème de cacao; Amaretto; Drambuie. They were the polite, sweet drinks one took in tiny glasses. Except that Loretta Marshall liked pouring them into tea, and some evenings she drank tea till bedtime.

Tonight, she had looked out and seen the rain, and decided the roads must be getting slick. She had not quite gotten to the point of mentally assigning him to some disaster, but she had come out to wait for him. He got off the bus and she greeted him with a motherly kiss on the cheek. "Button your coat," she said, already doing it for him, fussing with him as Alice had done. "It's so chilly."

"Let me," he said.

She slapped his hand away, smiling. "I've got it."

He allowed himself to be buttoned up, standing in full view of the other passengers, as the bus pulled away from the curb.

"So," she said. "How was night school?"

At the same time, he had said, "How was work?"

And she answered, "Some dumb new kid scraped himself with a culture needle in the biology lab. It broke the skin, and Mr. Judd had the ambulance and everything. Poor boy was scared out of his mind. They were growing staph germs in the culture, though. So they took precautions. Gave him a couple of shots and soaked the cut in iodine. Mr. Atwater was gone all afternoon. And that was my life today."

"He didn't come over tonight?" Marshall asked.

"He had a meeting with the PTA."

Clark Atwater was the principal of the high school, and sometimes taught a course in social studies. Marshall's mother was his secretary, and lunched with him occasionally at the school, since Marshall had graduated. Now and again she went out with him. Recently, they had gone to see *Hello, Dolly!*—Mr. Atwater had a friend who worked in the box office at the National Theater, and could get tickets for almost nothing. They had come home singing the title song, a little tipsy from the experience, if not from the wine they had drunk at dinner.

"Hel-lo, L'retta," Mr. Atwater sang, waving at the passing cars in the street. "Well, Hel-lo, L'retta."

The young man took her arm as they walked across the street, and along it to the apartment-house entrance. There was the slightest unsteadiness in her step. The building was an old, box-shaped structure three stories high and a city block wide, with a sagging canopy over the main entrance, and a wobbly looking fire escape winding down from a complicated tangle of iron and neon at the level of the roof. It was made of multicolored brick, but in large patches on this side the brick had faded to one ashen shade. Some of the windows were blocked with air conditioners. Others were open. You had the sense, gazing at it, that if another building were close enough, there would surely be laundry strewn across the spaces, from window to window and fire escape to fire escape. The apartment itself was on the third floor, up two flights of steps just to the left of the main entrance. A bank of mailboxes stood to the right as you entered. Marshall's mother always paused to look in hers each time she passed through, no matter what time of day or night. The same affliction that caused her to imagine catastrophic events each day for her son also caused her to check for mail each time she passed through the foyer. Marshall had recently understood this, and was astute enough to recognize some slight taint of it in himself: It was simply that an aspect of her imagination, whenever it was engaged, provided her, always, with an attendant belief. The remotest fancied possibility produced behavior—perhaps someone passing along the street in the fifteen minutes she had been gone to wait for him at the bus stop, at almost ten o'clock at night, had put some message to her in the mailbox. The thought, no matter how fleeting, no matter how absurdly unlikely, brought forth the conviction, and she could not walk past the box without looking in. "Nothing," she said.

They went on up to the apartment. Marshall, who had been buzzing with worry about what he had been through with the D'Allessandros—and thinking about the walk with Natalie to her apartment building—experienced a disheartening moment of remembering that this was a night in which he had momentous news. He did not know quite how he would put it, and soon he was wondering if it might be better to wait until the clear light of day, when the cordials would have worn off. His mother walked on through to the lighted kitchen, where she liked to sit. A bottle of crème de menthe stood on the small table, with a smoking cigarette in an ashtray full of butt ends, and a box of tea bags. The cigarette had burned down almost to the filter. "I could've started a fire," she said, crushing it out, lighting another. "Want some mint tea?"

"No, thanks," Marshall said. "Think I'll go on to bed."

She put the cigarette down in the ashtray where the other had been, then took her jacket off and hung it over the back of the chair. She was wearing jeans, and a dark blue sweater, and she looked boyish—the jeans accentuated her thin bones. Her short, cropped hair had strands of white in it. Sitting down, she took up the cigarette and puffed on it, then talked the smoke out, leaning her elbow on the back of the chair so that the cigarette was at the level of her ear. The smoke made a grayish, moving wreath around her head. "Well, now," she said, "why don't you tell me about this party I'm supposed to go to."

He sat down across from her, unable, for the moment, to say much of anything.

"This is the skinny little girl you've been going around with at work?" she said. "Alice?"

"Yes, ma'am."

"A nice girl. She called around seven o'clock, all excited."

He could only manage a small, breathed "Yes." He was convinced that Alice had told her everything, even as he almost choked with incredulousness that she could have done so.

"Said she's having this birthday party," his mother went on. "Or her father's having it, is that it?"

Marshall couldn't speak.

"Well?"

He nodded again, watching her smoke the cigarette. "What else did she say?" he ventured.

"She said you told her you'd try to get me to come, and she wanted to put her own vote in. She really used the word 'vote,' Walter."

This seemed an odd thing to fix on. It threw him off. "What's wrong with that?" he asked.

She shrugged. "Just sounded strange. Are we voting on something?"

Once more, he was unable to find a word to utter in response.

"What is it, son?" His mother reached over and touched his cheek. "You feel okay?"

"Fine," he said. "Fine." Then, "Did Alice—did she say anything else?"

"I had the feeling that she wanted to—why?"

"Oh, no reason."

"What's the matter, Walter? Tell me."

The only thing he could find the strength to say was, "I had my pocket picked tonight. Guy took forty dollars. A pickpocket."

"My God." She stood and took his face in her hands. "Are you all right? Did he hurt you?"

"It was a pickpocket," he said. "I didn't even feel it. And I would've given it to him, too, that's the thing. All he had to do was ask, and maybe he didn't even have to do that. I'd have given him whatever he needed. And he stole it. Can you believe that?"

"You've got to stay away from people in the city," she said, sitting back down. "Don't talk to anyone, and don't look at anyone, either. Eye contact can be a bad thing in the city. He might've really hurt you."

"I told you I didn't even feel it happen," he said. "We were talking—"

"You *actually talked* to him?"

"How do you think he got close enough to pick my pocket?"

"What were you talking about?"

"Nothing," he said. "It was silly. We were arguing about—names—"

"I tell you not to talk to anyone and here you are having an argument with a criminal? God," she said, communing with her own anxiety. "How could you be talking to a criminal?"

He explained as best he could, then took his eyes from her and looked at his hands. There was so much more to tell her.

"You're sure you're okay?"

"I'm fine," he said, deciding that everything else could wait. "I'm tired." He feigned a yawn. "I think I'll go to bed."

"It's a little early for you, isn't it?"

"I'll read," he said.

"Don't you want to be with me?" She pretended to pout.

He leaned over and kissed her cool forehead. "If you want me to stay up, I will."

"Clark says we're too close. He says it'll ruin you."

"Mr. Atwater doesn't know enough about us to make a comment like that."

"Well, I think sometimes—I know I've kept too close a watch on you."

He kissed her forehead again. In the morning, she would remember that he had not told her about Alice.

"I'm going to bed myself." She yawned, stretching her arms toward the ceiling.

Into this casual sleepiness, he said, "I think I'm getting married."

Briefly, her yawn froze, so that she simply looked at him agape, her arms still stretched high. She brought them to the table and started to rise, but then she sat back down. Her hands were holding the edge of the table, as if to support herself.

"Alice," he said. "I—I asked her tonight."

"You had a busy night. You got mugged and you got engaged."

"It wasn't a mugging."

She seemed to be going over everything to herself. Her lips moved, but she said nothing.

"Alice gave me the money to get home," he said.

"Is this going to be soon? Getting married?"

"Not too soon."

Now her fingers were moving in a pattern on the tabletop. "And in your mind, son, how soon is too soon?"

"Oh," he said, unable to keep himself from mumbling. "Next—June, maybe."

"June?"

He nodded.

"That's not too soon?"

He couldn't say anything.

"June."

"I think so."

His mother stared at him. "Well," she said. "You should get some sleep. I can tell it's been a rough day. Anyway, it's been a *busy* day."

"Sometime around June," he said. "We didn't really settle on a—a time." He felt foolish, again, as though he were a child playing at being adult. He stood there.

"Are you all right, son?"

"I'm fine. I saw Father Soberg."

"How is he?"

"He asked that I remember him to you."

"I hope you told him hello for me."

"How come you didn't tell me he was going overseas?"

"Oh, that," she said. "I guess I forgot. I don't like to think about this war—or whatever it is. They never got around to declaring Korea a war, either. And a lot of boys died."

"He seemed okay about it."

"Well, then I'm glad for him."

There was something artificial about this last exchange. It caused him to take a step toward the other room.

"Good night," she said.

He walked over and kissed her cheek, then went back to his room. Closing the door, he leaned against it and waited a few seconds, listening for her movements. He couldn't really hear anything. She coughed. There was the small sound of dishes being moved about in the kitchen. Finally, she walked past his door, toward her own room, and soon she was in the bathroom cleaning her teeth. He turned around in the narrow, carpeted space between his bed and the door and breathed a long sigh—not a sigh of relief. He felt no relaxing of the muscles of his chest and lower jaw. His mother's acceptance of the idea of his getting married had made the whole thing seem somehow accomplished. It was really going to happen. All his nerves were jumping.

When he looked at his room, it seemed the room of a boy: On the wall, along with the crucifix and the picture of Jesus revealing his sacred heart, hung photographs of Ted Williams and Mickey Mantle, Willie Mays and Hank Aaron, and a bright red-and-gold pennant from his high school. The dresser top was crowded with things: a thick deck of baseball cards, several model airplanes, a paint-by-numbers set, a stack of comic books. Dirty clothes were strewn across the foot of the unmade bed. Only the night table provided any sense of maturity: books by Fulton Sheen and Thomas Merton stood in a row along with *The Spiritual Exercises of Saint Ignatius Loyola*, *The Summa Theologica*, Edwin O'Connor's *The Edge of Sadness*, the unexpurgated edition of *War and Peace* alongside the abridged version, two anthologies of poetry, a collection of the speeches of JFK—and, of course, Dr. Barbet's book on Calvary. Above this was a map of Washington with radial circles in bright red, distances from ground zero in a nuclear attack. He and his mother were in the shock and heat part of the second circle. He had bought the map in a Drug Fair shortly after the missile crisis.

He picked up *A Doctor Looks at Calvary*, ran the palm of his hand over the cover, looked at the title page, and then put it back again.

Everything was so orderly in the pages of a book.

He got himself ready for bed, knowing he wouldn't sleep for the fluttering in his stomach. Lying down, folding his hands across his chest, he said his prayers and waited to fall off. Brief dreams of marriage, of trouble with shadowy figures, of boylike men in suits that looked too big for them, of Alice in odd incarnations—one had her wearing a police uniform, directing traffic—kept him stirring. It was impossible to concentrate on the prayers. Then his mother was banging on the wall.

"What?" he said, sitting upright, trying to see.

"Do you want me to go to this party? I mean, is that your vote, too?"

"Oh," he said. "Right. Yes. My vote."

"That's such an odd way to put it. Isn't it?"

"She's nervous," he said.

"I'm not criticizing her."

"No, I know," he said.

"Okay, then. I will. I'll go to the party."

He lay back down.

"Do you think they'll have cordials?"

"I don't know." He was sitting up again. He listened for her.

"Good night," she said.

"Good night." He settled back and began the long wait for sleep.

Chapter

5

That awful Friday in November, almost a year ago, when the news was official, the president was dead, he had walked up to Saint Matthew's with Alice and another girl, a friend of hers who was visiting from Chicago. It seemed that the thing to do was get to a church, and so they had gone to the cathedral, walking through the slow, quiet rain and the widely separated tolling of the bells, and at Saint Matthew's they had knelt in a back pew, the three of them in that big, empty expanse of shadows and empty rows and wavering votive candles. At the front of the church, a lone man knelt, a brown presence—brown hair, brown suit, light brown raincoat draped over the communion rail. He sniffled, and the sound rose into the high, dark, hollow, central nave. Then he stood, a tall, balding-at-the-crown, barrel-chested man, and turned from them, gathering his coat, sniffling. Abruptly, he cried out, "Why?" his sobbing voice repeating in the heights above him. "Why?" he cried again. And then again, "Why?" He kept shouting into his own echo, lurching heavily, almost staggering, to the back of the church. "Why?" he demanded. "Why?" Finally, he pushed the doors open and was gone, off into the tolling darkness, still sobbing.

Marshall, having witnessed this from his place, kneeling between the two girls in the second-to-last pew, put his face in his hands and began to cry. He had a cold. He had been nursing a sore throat, a runny nose, a cough. His nose was dripping, the air passages closing off as he wept, and Alice's friend turned to him, offering a handkerchief. He took it and blew his nose with it, since at the moment that was his most pressing need. He had thought she meant for him to do this. He folded the handkerchief, then, and tried to return it to her, not quite thinking clearly—the knowledge that she would not want it now coming to him in precisely the moment that she said, "You keep it," holding her hands, fingers together, palms toward him, as if to help push the thing back in his direction.

"Thank you," he murmured.

And they had said, really, nothing else to each other. Alice and she were going to the airport, where the friend was to board a plane to go home.

That weekend, Marshall and his mother spent long hours in front of the television set. There were stark pictures of the arrival of the casket from Dallas—men lowering it from the back of a truck, Jackie and Bobby Kennedy stepping down from there and moving through the crowd of suited men to the waiting hearse, Jackie with bloodstains all over her leg, her face drawn and pale and stunned—and there were reports from the scenes in Dallas as Lee Oswald was brought out into the light, handcuffed, with a swollen left eye, surrounded by shouting policemen and television people.

Did you kill the president?

No, I've not been charged with that. In fact, nobody has said that to me yet. The first thing I heard about it is when the newspaper reporters in the hall, axed me that question . . .

These scenes were talked about and analyzed, and replayed, and then there were biographical films about the president. The film narrators talked about his determination, and the fact that he was in pain most of his adult life. They showed clips from his news conferences, and played back his inaugural address. And then there was Vice President Johnson, standing with his wife in the glare of camera lights on the airport tarmac, speaking slowly in his Southern accent into a bank of microphones:

> *This is a sad tam . . . for awl people. We have suffered a loss . . . which cannot be weighed . . . for me, it is a deep, pers'nal tragedeh . . . I know the world shares . . . the sorruh . . . that Mrs. Kennedeh and her fam'ly bear. I will . . . do my best. That is awl . . . I can do. I ask your help . . . and God's.*

The cameras showed every stage of the casket's progression to the White House, that Saturday morning, and then the former presidents and the members of Congress and the dignitaries from around the world filing in to pay their respects. It rained all day, and for a while a satellite hookup showed a memorial service being held in England, at Westminster Abbey. And then Sunday morning, after Mass, Marshall and his mother came back to the apartment to find that Oswald had been shot. The television newspeople showed it several times, once in slow motion, and they talked about how the unthinkable had become reality, how the nightmare only seemed to be getting worse. This was played against the images of people crying in the streets as the cortege made its slow progress down Pennsylvania Avenue to the Capitol. The young man and his mother numbly watched it all, and said very little to each other. When Jackie walked to the casket with Caroline, and kissed it for the last time, the two of them wept together. And on that sunny, cold Monday, when the actual funeral Mass took place, they watched and prayed with the others on television. Jackie knelt to take communion, and there was a strange solace in seeing it.

"That poor girl," Marshall's mother said.

As the procession moved through the streets and on toward Arlington Cemetery, she made tea, and poured Drambuie into it. She asked Marshall if he would like some. "You're only eighteen, I know. But these are special circumstances."

"Yes," he told her. "I will have some."

She made it for him, and measured out the Drambuie with a teaspoon. They drank it quietly, watching the ceremony at the grave site, and when the planes flew over, Marshall went outside to watch them come roaring overhead in the wide, white-streaked blue, making their long turn back to the north. Watching them, he couldn't help feeling that everything would be different now, that some chance had been lost forever. He went inside and had more of the tea and Drambuie, sitting in the living room with the television and the voices of newsmen murmuring through the ritual. When it was over, he and his mother had a small meal of sandwiches, still drinking the tea. They sat across from each other at the kitchen table. By now she had stopped measuring the cordial and was pouring it into his tea in the same quantities as she poured it into her own. He noticed this, of course, but said nothing. He was beginning to feel the alcohol, and he liked the sensation. She made another pot of tea, and they sipped it with the Drambuie. The sun had gone down, and for a time they sat in the increasing dark, talking.

Or, rather, she talked. She told him about being a little girl during the Depression, in rural Virginia, and about meeting his father, fresh off a ship in Norfolk, handsome and gregarious, proud of his navy uniform and his war record. He had done brave things in the war, she said, and it hadn't finally mattered in the way he was allowed to live his life. She said this, and then she seemed to decide against saying more. The young man pressed her, hungry for any detail about his father. "There's no need," she said. "It's done with. You and I did all right. We got along." She had never blamed the old man for leaving, because things would have been worse if he had stayed.

When it was almost too dark to see, she got up and turned on the ceiling light, and together they did the few dishes.

"You're a good man," she said to him. "To stay in all weekend with me."

He kissed the side of her face.

"Let's have one more cup of tea."

"Okay."

They sat at the table again, quietly sipping the hot tea. Marshall noticed that his eyes stung from all the television.

"I still don't believe it," his mother said.

After a pause, he told her about the walk up to Saint Matthew's in the rain, the way the bells kept tolling, and how quiet the people in the streets were. He went on to describe the scene at Saint Matthew's, the huge silence with its small echoes of their movements, the sobbing man, the way his anguished question reverberated in the spaces above them, and how after the man had left, their own emotions had taken over. Then he told about using Alice's friend's handkerchief to blow his nose. "She'll be telling that years from now," he said. "How this guy blew his nose into a handkerchief she'd offered so he could wipe his eyes, and how he tried to give the thing to her when he was through. That's what she'll remember. Me with my runny nose." His mother stared at him for a moment, and then she laughed. He was startled, but he began laughing, too, as she continued. They went on helplessly, almost feverishly, for what seemed a long time.

"I don't know," she said. "I'm sorry, I couldn't help it. The thought of you trying to give it back to her. I shouldn't be laughing."

"No," Marshall said. "It is funny. I can't believe I did it."

They had gotten control of themselves, they were breathing, wiping their eyes. She lighted a cigarette, and sighed the smoke.

"I still can't believe it. Even after all that pomp and ceremony."

"What did you think of Cardinal Cushing?" Marshall asked her.

"I didn't think of him." She laughed. "I mean—I'm sorry." And she laughed again.

"No," Marshall said. "Isn't his delivery strange?"

She kept laughing, and so he broke into an imitation of the cardinal's odd intonations. "May the—aw—angels, deah Jack—aw—lead ye-ew—aw—into pa-ra-doise. May the—aw—saints—aw greet ye-eew at yoah co-a-ming."

His mother put her head down on her folded arms, laughing.

"Isn't that it, though?" Marshall said. "I don't mean any disrespect."

She tried to speak to him and went on laughing, and so, because he had the ability to, he repeated it. "May the—aw—angels, deah Jack—aw—lead ye-ew—"

"Stop it," she said. "Please. You sound just like him." She got up and went into the bathroom and closed the door. He heard her coughing and trying to breathe.

"Are you all right?" he said.

She opened the door and came out, holding a cloth rag to her mouth. Her eyes were glazed over with tears, and at last she took his arm and said, "You've got to be careful making me laugh that hard. I'm afraid for my heart."

"I'm sorry," he said.

"I wonder where you get it." She coughed. "Ah. Oh, Lord. I feel guilty laughing at a time like this, but you sounded so much like him. Where do you get that ability from? I don't have it, and your father certainly didn't—"

"I shouldn't've done it," he said.

"No," said his mother. "We needed it. Don't you apologize."

He had gone to bed that night with the Drambuie swimming in his blood, and the stark, black-and-white images of the weekend running through his mind. He was sleepy enough, but was a little afraid to try, given the dizziness he felt. In those moments just before he drifted off, he saw again the footage of the dead president's inaugural address—

Let the word go forth, from this time and place, to friend and foe alike, that the torch has been passed to a new generation of Americans.

And this was when the idea came to him—part of a wavering dream in half sleep, but registering somewhere deep, amid all the terrible pictures of those four excruciating days—that he, Walter Marshall, might pick up the torch.

"You told her about us?" Alice said. "And she didn't react?"

"Well, she reacted."

"Tell me everything she said."

"She didn't have a lot to say."

"Then she didn't react."

"I don't know how you mean 'react.' She heard me. I could tell that it got through to her what I was saying."

"But you don't remember what she said."

"What could she say? I told her about it, and that was that."

"Was she happy for you?"

"I think so, sure."

"Did she say she was happy?"

"Alice, I just told you, she didn't have a lot to say."

"She hates it," Alice said. "She hates the whole idea. She threw a fit and you don't know how to tell me."

"She did not throw a fit. Anyway, she's not the type of person who throws fits."

"Then she brooded. She got quiet and wouldn't talk to you."

"No," he said.

"But she was upset, wasn't she?"

They were in the mailroom, next to the collating machine, a series of paper trays on a long steel bar that ran with a noisy clatter of metal and sucking of air and shuffling of paper. Above them was a large, many-paned window, and the crossed patterns of elongated shade gave the area a barred look, as though they were the inmates of a cell. Because Marshall's supervisor, Mr. Wolfschmidt, was seated at the desk nearby, they were speaking in low tones while Marshall put more paper in the machine.

"Well?" Alice said. "Tell me."

He looked at her, at the small lines of worry and distress in her face, and thought about how she was older than he. "What about you?" he said. "What did your father say?"

This seemed to stop her.

"I bet *he* threw a fit."

"Then your mother *did* throw a fit."

"She did not." He had said this too loud.

Mr. Wolfschmidt looked up from his desk, then leaned toward them slightly, lowering his glasses to look over the frame of them at Alice. "Something you need, young lady?" he said.

"No, sir," Alice said.

"Move along, then," he said, waving her away. "Shoo."

She looked at Marshall. "See you at lunch?"

He nodded.

"We'll talk," she said.

He remembered what he had to ask of her, and his smile felt forced. He tried to mean it. She smiled back, reached over, and patted his hand. As she had when she had first stepped into the room and faced him, she touched the tips of her fingers to her lips and blew a kiss at him.

There was a scary fluttering in his stomach. He started the machine and it made its loud gear-cranking, whir and hiss. For a few seconds he lost himself in the sound. He began taking the collated pages out of the last tray, and when Wolfschmidt approached, crossing through the barred shadows from the window, the movement startled him into a small shout. Mr. Wolfschmidt pushed the button on the machine, cutting it off, and stood gazing at him, his heavy, dark-haired arms folded. "Girlfriend?"

Since Wolfschmidt had rarely spoken to him beyond the simple one-word commands necessary to the smooth operation of the mailroom, Marshall was too surprised to answer right away.

"This girl—you and she are friendly."

He nodded.

Mr. Wolfschmidt smiled. "Boy meets girl," he said, unfolding his arms and making a small pantomime motion, as though he held a bowl in one palm and were stirring liquid in it with the index finger of the other hand.

"Yes, sir." Marshall smiled back.

"Boy meets girl, romance and flowers, *ja*?"

He nodded again.

"*Ja*," Wolfschmidt said, and suddenly, "I thought so. You will please carry on your love affair outside this office." He continued standing there regarding the young man as if there were something amusing, or even heartening, about him. The tone of his voice was sour and unfriendly, though. "You understand me?"

"Yes, sir," Marshall said.

"Very good. We should not be wasting time with such things during working hours, should we?"

He gave what he supposed was the required nod of acquiescence.

"She is a very good-looking young girl, you think?"

Again, he nodded. This was the longest conversation he had yet had with the man—except the first one, when he had been hired.

"You like all the girls, *ja*?"

"Yes, sir."

"And they like you. I see you with them in the lunch hour."

In fact, Marshall had made them all laugh, imitating Mr.

Wolfschmidt's voice and accent, acting out the sale of a tank to an Englishman.

"They like you, *ja*?"

"Sir?" he said.

"And you like them. I see you watching them, when they come down the hall, outside there." Mr. Wolfschmidt pointed to the doorway. "You like to look at them?"

Marshall felt the need to deny this. "No," he said.

"You *don't* like looking? You are punishing yourself, then."

He couldn't answer. It seemed to him that the older man had perceived something about his makeup. His mother had recently said that he must learn to stop punishing himself. "I don't look *that* way," he got out. "The way *you* mean."

"Oh? And what way is that? Now suddenly it's a sin to appreciate God's creation? Now who's got the dirty mind, here? You? Me? Somebody else?"

He was silent.

"No harm in looking, *ja*?"

"No, sir."

"But you must concentrate on your work, too. Is this not so?"

"I'll—concentrate," Marshall said.

Wolfschmidt reached over and pushed the button on the machine, and with a high-pitched gasp of air it sprang to life. "See that you do," he said, an amused expression on his blocklike face.

Wolfschmidt, as everyone who worked for him knew soon enough, had been born and raised in Germany, his family having come to America in the mid-thirties, when his father, an architect of national repute, had decided that the Nazi party was not going to be the salvation of the German people after all. Wolfschmidt Sr. brought his wife and son to live in Washington, and still lived there, within a few blocks of the bureau. Occasionally he visited the mailroom—a diminutive, hawk-nosed, white-haired gentleman with fierce, ice-colored eyes and bushy white brows. Wolfschmidt Jr. bustled around this very fragile-looking gentleman who did not quite come up to his shoulders, and seemed happy to see him, though it was painfully clear that his life as the manager of a mailroom was a fact about which there had been some conflict: The old gentleman never failed to be grumpy and abrupt, with that attitude people take when convinced that their children are wasting valuable time. After each visit, Mr. Wolfschmidt was bad-tempered for days.

"Life will be so much better for everyone if the work is done to satisfaction," he said now, turning away from Marshall. It was a saying he liked to use—probably taken from the angry little father.

For some reason, all this made the young man feel lonely and depressed. He spent the rest of the morning in a kind of fog, watching Wolfschmidt out of the corner of his eye, trying to concentrate on his work, and thinking of Alice and her wedding plans.

Lunch hour, he walked with her across the street and up the block to the little sandwich shop where they had run into Mr. D'Allessandro—an L-shaped room, with a window at one end, looking out onto the street. They sat in the window end and watched the passersby. The day was sunny and clear, with a strong, warm, southerly wind that kicked up dust and grime from the gutters. Men clutching their hats rushed through a storm of leaves, paper scraps, and blown dirt.

"I missed my bus and had to drive today, and I'm glad I did," Alice said, watching the dust kick up out of the gutters. "It's going to be so miserably warm."

"It's just the wind. When the wind dies down, it's not so bad."

"Hey," Alice said. "You haven't even kissed me hello." She closed her eyes and leaned toward him, puckering.

Embarrassed, he met her halfway.

When their lips touched, she opened her eyes and looked at him. "You're looking."

"No I wasn't."

"Well, it wasn't much of a kiss."

"This is a public place," he told her. "We're sitting in a window."

"People kiss all the time in public, now. I think it's neat."

"Alice," he said. But he was at a loss.

"It's the religion," she said. "Isn't it?"

This irked him. "No."

"Do you love me?" The look on her face softened him, and made him sorry.

"Of course," he said.

"You do, don't you?"

"I just said—" He stopped, looked at the room. "I said I do. Jeez, Alice. Are you teasing me?"

"I'm dead serious," she said with a half smile.

"Well, I love you, okay?" The words leaving his lips had the quality of recited lines.

"I can't help it," she told him. "Actually, I'm a little insecure."

"It's fine, really. I know the feeling."

"Your mother's not happy about us, though."

"I said she's fine. Really. What about your father?"

"Oh, he's—fine."

"You told him."

"First thing."

"And he didn't react?"

She smiled. "You sound like me, now."

"My mother's coming to your party," he said.

Alice smiled. "Then everything's set."

"I have to ask you something."

The waiter came—a tall, skinny boy with long sideburns and an overbite. They ordered chicken sandwiches and Cokes and watched him write it all down laboriously in a little spiral note-book. When he had gone, Alice turned to the window and rested her chin on her palms. "It's such a beautiful day from this side of the glass."

She seemed to her fiancé to be posing for him. He said, "If it weren't so windy."

"I said, 'on this side of the glass.'"

"I heard you."

"Actually, I love the wind." This was said with a great dramatic tossing of her hair.

He couldn't look at her. He studied the backs of his hands on the table.

"Don't you?"

"I never thought about it that way," he said. "One way or the other. Wind. You know, it's never been a big subject of talk around our house. During the last tornado, we forgot to even mention it because of the Bengal tigers in the foyer."

"Don't be sarcastic, Walter."

"I was trying to be funny."

On the sidewalk before them a man stopped and put one hand to his face. Apparently, a speck of something had blown into his eye. Another man paused to help him, and they moved off slowly. Marshall carefully folded his napkin, feeling as though this little tableau had been a kind of comment from the world concerning what she had said about the wind.

"On *The Tonight Show*, last night, Johnny Carson danced with Pearl Bailey."

"I didn't see it," Marshall said.

"They did a duet, actually. A love song. Really sweet and friendly and kidding, you know. It made me think about the way things could be if only people would stop and think. I mean, here's this colored woman, you know, teasing and being affectionate with this white guy on national TV. You—you see what I mean? It wasn't as if there had ever been anything like a store or a restaurant where she wouldn't be welcome because of the color of her skin. I mean, who could think not to welcome Pearl Bailey? And they looked like such good friends. Why can't the rest of the country take the hint?"

"They probably are."

"We have some decisions to make," she said after a pause.

He waited. She seemed content to sit, watching the street. It was as though she wanted to give him time to think. But then he wondered if she expected him to respond in some way. He cleared his throat and murmured, "Yes."

She said, "What?"

"I said 'Yes.'"

"Oh." She stared out the window again. The street was empty, with a stripe of shade moving in it, some cloud being hauled across the hot sky by the wind.

"We have to decide," she said.

He said, "I have to ask you something."

They had spoken at almost the same instant, and they laughed nervously.

"You first," she said.

He hesitated. Before he could explain, the waiter was putting their sandwiches down.

"It's about your mother, isn't it?" Alice said. "She wants me to convert."

"No," he said. "That's not it."

"You told her I would, though, didn't you?"

He couldn't remember if he had. He said, "It's not about that."

"Actually, my father has a problem with it."

"He does?"

She nodded, biting into her sandwich. "Turns out he doesn't like your church much."

"My church—" Marshall looked at her.

"I didn't know he was such an anti-Papist," she said.

"Papist?" He had never heard the word, though he felt the sense of recognizing it as she spoke it.

She nodded.

"He doesn't like church—"

"Not just any church," she interrupted him. "*Your* church." She took a bite of the sandwich, and thought a moment. "Actually, it's not that he doesn't like Catholics, especially. He has trouble with the institution. You'll be fine." She went on eating, holding the sandwich with both hands. He saw that her fingernails were painted a soft pink, and that she had stained the edge of her Coke glass with lipstick. He felt a sudden wave of disbelief, watching her tuck a piece of chicken into her mouth. It was as though he had just awakened, somehow, from a dream of life, and found himself here, with this strange young woman, this woman he did not know. "It's simply a matter of getting used to the idea of me belonging to the institution," she went on, talking through her chewing. "He's really very happy for us. You'll see."

He took a bite of his sandwich, though his appetite was gone.

"Where are you?" she said, staring dreamily at him.

"Pardon?" he said.

She smiled, and put her sandwich down. There was a way she had of doing things like this, a certain fastidiousness of motion, as though the sandwich were a delicate mechanism with explosive charges embedded in it. "Tell me what you're thinking," she said. A tiny bit of chicken had lodged between her front teeth. He ran his tongue over his own teeth, and tried to concentrate on his sandwich. "Well?" she said.

"I have to ask you something," he managed.

Folding her hands under her chin, she regarded him, and when he couldn't speak right away, reached over and touched his cheek. "Do I make you nervous, now?"

"No," he said, unable to keep himself from recoiling.

If she noticed this, she gave no sign of it. "Ask me anything," she said, withdrawing her hand. "I'm all yours."

It took most of the rest of the lunch hour to make clear what the D'Allessandros wanted. This was not from any complexity in the request itself, of course, but merely that Marshall had difficulty saying it all out in plain words. Because he hesitated, she jumped to conclusions, heading everything in the wrong direction, requiring more clarification, and more hesitating. First, she assumed that Mr. D'Allessandro wanted to hold the wedding at his school, and she went off on a tangent about what a fine thing that would be, perhaps in conjunction with Marshall's graduation. Then she supposed Mr. D'Allessandro had advised Marshall concerning getting married, and had even advised against it, so soon after high school. She said she knew there would be objections from all sides on that score, because she was older, and this would cause some people to feel the moral constraint of their opinions.

It took more than a few moments to make her understand that the request had nothing to do with them as a newly engaged couple.

When what he wanted was at last understood, she seemed rather puzzled as to what had been so difficult. "I don't see the problem."

"I'm supposed to get your father to ask somebody big to come to the school."

"So?"

"Someone like Edward R. Murrow."

"Yes?"

Marshall was unable to respond to this.

"Well, really, Walter. Do you think he'd refuse you? Now?"

He couldn't keep the exasperation out of his voice. "I don't know."

"You're going to be his son-in-law."

This had the effect of making him cramp up in his lower abdomen. "Excuse me," he said, rather too loudly. "I'll be right back."

"What's the matter?" she said.

He couldn't pause to answer her, but made his way, hurrying, to the men's room. There, in that close, little, ammonia-smelling space, the feeling subsided. He washed his face, then stood quietly, trying to calm himself. His hair had come down across his forehead, and for a time he tried to set it back so that it would look like Kennedy's. An instant later, he was assailed with a sense of himself as being rather ridiculous. He ran both hands through his hair, trying to make it go the way it seemed to want to. Nothing seemed quite right, and he was becoming aware of the time. In the one stall a man coughed deeply, then made an elaborate series of noises clearing his throat. Marshall saw the shoes, brown shoes with scuff marks on them, below the level of the stall, and something in his soul turned on the image, as if he had been shown a picture of some future version of himself—this hawking man with scuffed, dull-brown shoes, in a stall in the rest room of a sandwich shop in the city. The man blew his nose, coughed again, and spat.

Outside, Alice had eaten the rest of her sandwich. She sat with her arms folded under her breasts, gazing at the street. "I know just the person for you," she said.

Marshall waited for her to go on.

"Mitch Brightman."

"I thought you said he has a drinking problem."

"He likes to do this sort of thing, though. And he's not so bad that he can't put on a good show."

"Your father wouldn't mind asking him?"

"You can ask him yourself," Alice said brightly. "This weekend."

On the way back to the office, she held his hand and swung it between them. The warm wind gusted, and even so, a chill went through him. He allowed himself to be guided along the sidewalk. "Who do you want to invite to the wedding?" she said.

"I don't know."

She stopped. "Is everything all right? You seem so depressed. Are you sure it's all right with your mother?"

"I'm not depressed," he said.

"You seem unhappy. Look, you shouldn't worry about my dad, Walter. You'll see."

He forced a smile. And he reminded himself that he had asked this girl to be his wife. He imagined what it might be like, coming home to her. He could not even see himself kissing her, for some reason, though he was quick to recall that such thoughts were occasions of sin. He attempted to clear his mind, to head off the impure thought.

"Well." She started walking again, still holding his hand. "What about your friends at school?"

"There's just Albert," he said. "I don't think any of the others would come."

"Why not?"

"I don't know any of them that well."

"What about friends from high school?"

"They're all off at college. And none of them took the trouble to stay in touch with me."

"You sound bitter."

"No," he said.

"So—Albert's it?"

"Albert's the only friend of mine you'd want at your party." But then he remembered Emma. "Well, and there's his fiancée."

"Albert's getting married, too?" This excited her. She let go of his hand and walked a few paces ahead, trying to contain herself. When she turned, she had clasped her hands under her chin again, and then she threw them wide. "I love it. When can I meet her?"

He didn't know, and yet to say this seemed somehow inappropriate. He simply stood there and weathered her excitement. She had walked back to him, and was resting her wrists on his shoulders.

"Don't you see how perfect it is, Walter? I wondered about poor Albert, and felt so bad for him in a way—so nice and kindly, and with all those physical problems, and it turns out even Albert's got somebody. Oh, I feel good about this. I think we were meant to be happy, don't you?"

There were others in the street, and cars had come to a stop on the corner where they stood, with Alice turning slowly now and talking about how happy for Albert she was. "I liked him right from the start. Let's have them come to the party, too. Will you see Albert today?"

"I'll see him tomorrow night, at class, I guess."

"You have to call him and invite him before something else gets in their way. Call him as soon as we get back."

The light changed. He didn't remember coming up to it. They crossed the street in the blustery heat, and she took his hand once more. As they reached the enclosed entrance of the building, she turned to him and, throwing her arms around his neck, kissed him on the mouth. He thought of hell, the vivid slides the nuns had shown in religion class on Saturday mornings, and the voice that had said, "Listen to the cries of the damned as they fall into the pit," and you heard the screams, and then the little bell dinged for the next slide.

She let go and looked at him. "Do you ever French kiss?"

"I did once," he said.

"Did you like it?"

His blood moved. "I can't discuss it," he said.

She nodded. "The religion, huh."

He pushed past her and went inside, and she followed.

"I understand, honey."

"Okay," he said.

"You're not mad at me?"

"No."

He walked to the bank of elevators and pushed the button and then thought of being on the elevator alone with her. "Maybe I'll walk up," he said. "It's just the fourth floor for me."

"Walter, it's all right, you know. We're engaged."

"I know," he told her. "But can't we talk about this some other time? I have to go to work now."

"I understand," she said. "Really."

The elevator opened.

"I'll walk up," he said. "It's only four flights."

"Don't be ridiculous." She got on and turned, waiting for him.

He got on, too.

When the doors closed she put her arms around his neck again and, before he could do anything about it, was kissing him, moving her hips against his and squeezing tight, so that the bones of her wrists seemed about to cut off the blood flow at the back of his neck. He had his hands flat against her back, and when the little bell sounded, he patted her shoulders and tried to step away. She laughed. "You're so cute when you're nervous," she said. "I'll see you at four-thirty."

"I have to go up to the school and see Mrs. D'Allessandro about Mitchell Brightman. Like we discussed."

She touched his cheek. "Anyone would think you were avoiding me, Walter. I'll wait until tomorrow. Maybe I'll drive to work again, so we won't have to worry about the buses home. But call me tonight. And don't forget to call Albert." The doors closed on her.

He breathed, looked into the dull metal of the doors and tried to arrange himself, then made his way down the thin corridor, at the end of which Mr. Wolfschmidt waited, arms folded, a sardonic little smile creasing his face.

Chapter

6

urid appeals to sexual appetite were everywhere. They seemed to glare at him from every source and surface: the covers of books and magazines, billboards, radio, television (the Sardo bath commercial was the worst, with its naked and beautiful woman luxuriating in suds, running her slender, soapy hands over her perfect arms, just managing, therefore, to shield her breasts). He was continually being ambushed. Sometimes it seemed that the only safe place for him was the confessional, in his side of the booth, with the muffled sound of the other person's confession coming through the closed panel, and the dim shape of the crucifix in the dark.

Through his senior year of high school, when he had thought he was going to study for the priesthood, he had gone to confession twice a week, and to Mass and communion almost every day. It was somehow more than piety. He had a purpose, which felt practical enough: According to the catechism, and to the books he had been reading, all the sacraments yielded grace, and grace was nourishment; it provided one with the strength to resist the allure and glamour, the sheer magnetism, of sin. And for Walter Marshall, there was really only one sin, one offense of heaven that he was always trying to fortify himself against: the sin of lust. The immense tide of impure thoughts and desires that seemed always about to engulf him. The huge interior rush of blood-deep yearning that continually afflicted him. For years now, he had been in a constant battle to keep from thinking about sex every waking minute. And what was worse, the temptation followed him into sleep. It wound itself through his sometimes terrifyingly pleasurable dreams, and sought to remind him of its presence in every daily transaction—his curiosity was boundless, as was his mind's feverish capacity to present him with voluptuous images and morbid temptations.

In the days before he had read the works of Thomas Merton and others, it seemed to him that the rest of the commandments were easy. In his innocence, he had seldom given them a thought: It took no effort at all to refrain from using the Lord's name; to keep from bearing false witness, or killing anyone, or adoring another God, or stealing what did not belong to him. These matters seemed settled by something in his nature: It was just not in him to do harm to anyone or anything. But the very fact of sex made him weak. It had gotten so bad that, sitting in the front pew of the church during Mass, he had even had thoughts about the nuns, their rounded hips under the black cloth of the habits, those womanly bodies, their folds and secrets, their very difference from him. These thoughts went through him before he could quite manage to unthink them, and though he worked very hard not to indulge himself (for he knew that would be the sin), each one left its residue in his heart, as though every impulse were only part of a heavy chain whose slow forging would eventually pull him down.

The city was humming with sensual heat. Women walked by him in their colors, and he tried not to look at any of them. Alice had gotten his senses going today. He was out of breath with his own heart's blood. He caught himself supposing that one benefit of marrying Alice would be that, after the honeymoon, this constant pressure would be gone at last.

Mrs. D'Allessandro was waiting in the library. She stood at the window that overlooked the street and watched him climb the stairs. Inside the building there was a perceptible difference in the light.

Everything was a shade dimmer, and he saw that the office was empty, the desk lamp turned off. He found Mrs. D'Allessandro sitting at the center table in the little book-lined room, her hands folded before her on the polished surface. She watched him enter but did not move. On the table before her was part of a submarine sandwich in a fold of white paper.

"Well?" she said.

"I spoke to her. We're supposed to see Mitchell Brightman this week."

"Not Edward R. Murrow?"

"I don't think so. She said Mitchell Brightman would be perfect. He does this sort of thing."

A voice came from the chair in the corner of the room, behind Marshall. "And what sort of thing is that?"

It was the little toy man. Marshall couldn't keep from emitting a small whimper, seeing him there.

The toy man seemed not to have noticed. "Is this *the* Mitchell Brightman?"

"Yes, sir."

"What sort of thing does Mr. Brightman do when he's not on television?"

"We made a payment," Mrs. D'Allessandro said, almost sweetly. "A large payment. We're getting everything in order. What more does Terrence want?"

"I'm supposed to make a report," the little man said. "That's all I know."

Marshall listened while she began to talk about the forum, and raising tuition; the idea of charging admission, and of getting permission to actually broadcast the evening to the local area. She did not move from her place at the table, but the toy man got up, walked across the room to the windows, and looked out at the street. His dark blue suit was a bit loose in the sleeves. Mrs. D'Allessandro kept her hands folded tightly on the edge of the table so that she looked like someone saying grace before eating the big sandwich that was there. She went on about the plans for Mitchell Brightman's visit to the D'Allessandro School. Although all the details were not yet worked out, something concerning President Kennedy would be the focus of the evening, which couldn't fail to elicit a large interest from the community. Brightman had known the president personally, and been close to him during some of the more famous passages, and that alone made him a very good draw. The event simply could not fail to have the desired effect.

The little man turned at the window, his hands in his pockets, and leaned against the frame, perfectly relaxed, a man who derived pleasure from his work. He stared at her. "Where you going to put everybody—where they all gonna go? All these paying visitors? In here? In that little office across the hall?"

"We'll set it up in the basement, Marcus. Terrence knows how we do things. It's where we hold graduation every year, and if Terrence had ever come here for anything, he'd have seen for himself. We move the vending machines and tables out and set up chairs. We can seat up to seventy-five people."

"*Up to* seventy-five people."

"We'll get seventy-five," Mrs. D'Allessandro said. "With Mitchell Brightman the speaker and Kennedy the subject, we'll get seventy-five."

"You'll need more than seventy-five. I'd say you need a couple of hundred paying customers for the evening to be a success."

"We can't get that many in here. The fire marshal would close us."

"You have a problem."

She thought a moment. "There's Saint Matthew's, down the street. Maybe they'll let us use *their* basement."

"Better get working on it."

"I'm sure they'll let us use it. They let us use it the year our pipes broke."

The toy man said nothing for a moment. Then he brought one hand out of his pocket and rubbed the back of his neck. "Mitchell Brightman's going to cost, isn't he?"

She indicated Marshall. "This young man is going to get him on a volunteer basis."

"If I can," Marshall hastened to add. And then, because the man scowled at him, he said, "I think I can, though."

"There," said Mrs. D'Allessandro.

After a brief pause, Marcus stirred. "I'll relay the information."

He crossed behind her and moved to the doorway. "Mr. Brace may have some ideas of his own, of course."

She stood. "You tell Terrence that what we do is not to be tampered with, if he wants his money." Then she gave the young man a look, as though she had unintentionally revealed more than she wanted to. He averted his eyes. "Do you hear me, Marcus?" she went on. "He's not to interfere."

"I'll tell him," Marcus said. Then he tore a piece of the bread from the sandwich and put it in his mouth. "Sourdough," he said. "Good."

When he was gone, she sat down and seemed to sag. Walter stayed where he was, just inside the door, looking first at the empty corridor where Marcus had gone, then at Mrs. D'Allessandro, who had buried her face in her hands. The street outside was in shade now, and the light had gone from the window. He thought of Natalie Bowman sitting there and then tried to imagine Alice as his wife, to send warm thoughts in her direction. Poor Alice, who had done nothing wrong and didn't deserve to have her bright expectations dashed.

Perhaps he had sighed, thinking about this. Mrs. D'Allessandro moved slowly, almost sleepily, lifting her head from her hands. When she looked at him, she seemed surprised to find him still there. "You haven't approached Mr. Brightman," she said.

"No, ma'am. But Alice's father can get him to do it. She's sure."

"But you won't know until the weekend?"

He nodded.

"Why don't you sit down," she said, running her hands through her hair. "You make me nervous hovering over me like that."

He was several feet away, in fact, but he would not contradict her. He took a chair at the end of the table.

"You want the rest of this?" she said, indicating the sandwich.

"No, thank you."

"My eyes were bigger than my stomach."

Marshall said nothing.

She smiled. "Don't know why I asked you to sit down. I don't have a bleeding thing to say."

After a pause, he said, "Is Mr. D'Allessandro—is he—"

She looked at him. "Still in hospital. He gets out tomorrow morning."

He waited.

"There will be class tomorrow evening, if that's what you're wondering."

"Yes, ma'am."

"You think I'm an old lady, don't you?"

"No, ma'am."

She was now rubbing her cheeks, slowly, eyes closed. "I know I said that to you before. Either that or I'm bloody well losing my mind."

He was quiet.

"How old are you?"

"Nineteen."

She muttered, "Nineteen. Was anybody ever that young? Jesus."

As had been his habit for some time now, out of the sense that he could make a prayer out of the profane use of the name, he said, Have mercy on us, to himself.

"I'm twenty-four years older than you are," she said.

"Yes, ma'am."

"Seems like a lot to you, doesn't it?"

"No, ma'am."

"Don't 'ma'am' me," she said. "I can do without that, thank you."

He said nothing.

She smiled at him, and seemed to laugh softly, then pushed the sandwich across to the other side of the table and buried her face in her hands again. "I know. You're at that awkward age. Everybody's a character in your bleeding flicker."

"No," he said.

"Of course they are. It's quite normal for a boy your age."

"I have to go," he told her.

"I'm not stopping you."

He stood, then hesitated, trying to come up with something else to say.

She hadn't raised her head, but when she spoke, her voice was a shade brighter. "I'll tell Lawrence it's all right, then."

"Yes, m—" He stopped himself in time.

Now she did laugh, pushing the hair back from the sides of her head and resting her chin on the palm of one hand to look at him. "You are so bloody polite. Your parents must be awfully proud."

"It's just my mother," he said.

"Oh, I'm sorry."

"No," he told her. "It's okay."

She smiled. "Lawrence says you've got talent, but that you've decided you're not going after Mitchell Brightman's job after all. Is that true?"

The reference to Brightman's job threw him briefly.

"You're not interested in a career in broadcasting."

"Oh," he said. "Yes. I mean no, I'm not."

"Such a funny boy," she said. "You're really very cute, aren't you? You've got those big, watery, dark-blue eyes, and such lovely, natural blond hair. I know several girls who would kill to have that hair."

"Thank you," he said.

"Do I make you nervous?"

"No, ma'am."

"Do you have any brothers or sisters?"

He shook his head.

"Just you. And your mother."

"Yes."

She looked at the other side of the room, then shook her head. "I have a brother."

"Just the one brother?" he asked her.

She nodded. "Lawrence, though, comes from a big family. He's got brothers and sisters by the bleeding truckload. His father was married four times, and he had children in each marriage, and in three of the marriages the wives had other children. You could fill D.C. stadium with his brothers and sisters and half-brothers and half-sisters and cousins and aunts and uncles and in-laws by marriage all over the world. And all of them together don't add up to the trouble the one brother on my side of the family—" She stopped herself, put her hands down on the table, and stood. "Do you want a ride to your bus stop?"

"No thank you," he said, perhaps too quickly.

"Well," she said. "I guess I'll choose not to take offense." She stood there, the tips of her fingers touching the table.

The door to the building opened, and Natalie stepped into the foyer, turned and looked in at them. She wore a light blue blouse and jeans, and seeing her, the recently affianced Walter Marshall faltered slightly on his feet.

"Hello," Mrs. D'Allessandro said. "I'm afraid I'm not quite ready yet. I have some things to do upstairs. Why don't you wait here and we'll take young Mr. Marshall to his bus stop. That is, if young Mr. Marshall has no objection."

"No, ma'am. I don't," Marshall said.

Mrs. D'Allessandro had moved around him and started up the stairs. "You okay? You look a bit green all of a sudden."

"Oh," he said. "I'm fine."

She looked at him, then at Natalie, then back at him. "I'll just be a minute."

Natalie walked into the library and sat down where Mrs. D'Allessandro had been sitting. "Whoops," she said. "The seat is warm."

He sat across from her. The submarine sandwich sent its odor of meat and olive oil and peppers and mayonnaise up at him. He tried to seem casual, perhaps a little depressed. He didn't know why this pose seemed the one he should take, but he couldn't quite help himself.

"Poor Walter," she said. "Not feeling well."

"I'm okay," he said.

"Mrs. D'Allessandro helps me, with langwege. I haf a langwege problem."

"You speak beautifully."

"I sound like a foreigner."

"My boss is German. You speak much better than he does."

"Your boss is Mr. Wolfschmidt."

He looked at her.

"You told me about him."

"I did?"

"Oh," she said, laughing softly to herself. "That's like me. I don't remember from one day to the next. I'm always losing my mind." She sighed, remembering. "I vas little girl from Berlin when I came here. Year vas 1951. Did I tell you that?"

"I knew you were a child."

"Yes. Not like now. An old lady." Like Alice, she was older than he was.

"You're—twenty-five?"

"In a few days, I'll be twenty-six." She smiled. "When I came here I vas only thirteen, and so frightened, you know. From the terrible bombing in Berlin. And there vas the camps for refugees. I lived in one for a year ven I was very little. I vas little girl, four and five and six years old when it all happened, and then I come to America and grow up, and in America I have seen incredible things and been to places I never dreamed—places no one ever could dream in a million years—if I told you—vell—" she stopped and seemed to catch herself up. Some memory had gone through her. "My own life is almost inconceivable to me, Walter. I have a lot of trouble believing it sometimes."

For a moment they both listened to the creaking in the ceiling, someone moving around above them.

She looked at the folded paper with the submarine sandwich lying in it. "You people in America. The way you all waste food. It's a sin to do this. A big sin. When I vas small, I see people eating out of tresh, in the debris of bombed buildings. Little babies, like me."

"You went through that," Marshall said.

"Once I eat a piece of bread I took from a rat. Moldy, bugs in it. A piece of garbage on the street."

"I'm so sorry," he said. "I hate to think that you went through a thing like that."

"Planes flying over, dropping bombs."

He shook his head.

"And look at how you waste food."

"Oh," Marshall said, "this isn't mine." He pushed it aside.

She seemed to consider a moment. "I haven't eaten."

"Why don't you eat it?" he said. "You're welcome to it."

She took it and began to eat, taking big bites, so that her lovely cheeks bulged.

"I try never to waste anything," he said.

But she had gone on to something else. "I am not American citizen yet," she said, chewing. "Maybe I'll never be. But I feel like one. I think in English, mostly. And people still talk loud to me, you know—as if I can't understand better. I have been where most

Americans can never go—" She paused, looked at the open door-way, then seemed to lose the thread of what she had been saying.

"You've been where most Americans can never go," he said, trying to help her.

"If you only knew," she murmured.

Yes, he wanted to say, and I'm in love with you. Briefly, it was as if he had spoken the words aloud. She shifted in her chair and seemed a bit embarrassed.

"I am a chatterbox today, yes?" She took another bite of the sandwich.

"It's fine," he said. "You know I like talking to you."

She licked one finger, swallowing. "You are a nice friend."

He drew in a breath to ask if she would like to go have some-thing to drink with him, and then he remembered Alice again. She stood out in his mind like an accusation.

"Where are you going to go, Walter? What will you do with your life?"

"I'm thinking of going into politics."

"Politics," Natalie said, putting her hand to her mouth and sti-fling a laugh. "Oh, no."

"I am," he told her.

This had the effect of making her nearly hysterical. "Politics. He is going into politics."

"Well—"

"Maybe you will run for office." She kept laughing. "Maybe you'll grow up to be a powerful man. Politics. I don't believe it—"

He said, "What's wrong with that? John Kennedy called it the 'honorable profession.'"

She kept laughing, trying to get her breath. "Oh, Walter. Ah. I'm sorry. Forgive—forgive me. I'm a magnet. I must have done something in another life—"

"What?"

"Nothing." She was still laughing. "It's not funny, I know." She held both hands over her mouth and seemed about to choke. "Please. Oh. It's not the least—I'm so—ah-hah." She breathed, then cleared her throat. "You must forgive me."

"I don't see why it's such a subject for hilarity," he said.

"Don't be mad, Walter."

"I'm not mad."

"It's nothing to do with you, really."

"Can you tell me what it is?"

"No." She took a breath, then started quietly to laugh again. "I can't help it."

"Well, I'm glad you're happy."

"Oh," she said, "now his feelings is hurt."

"No," he insisted. "I just would like to know what's so funny."

She put her head down on her arms and seemed in the grip of a kind of seizure, laughing so deeply that the table shook. He watched her. When she sat straight again, her shining black hair was mussed and hung about her face. She threw her head back and ran her hands over it to smooth it, sighing. "Ah. My goodness. I'm so sorry, Walter, but you see the world is such an ironical place, really." And she went on laughing into her hands.

When at last she subsided, she reached over rather tentatively and patted him on the shoulder. "I vas thinking of someone else," she said. "Really. You don't want to know."

"I think every citizen ought to want to have some impact on the problems we face," he said, mouthing the words of the late president.

"Please," she said, trying not to laugh. "Let's talk of something else. Okay?"

"Is it because you're German?" he asked. "I mean, we all know the Germans aren't great at politics. Not democratic politics."

"No, they aren't."

"Is that it?"

She tilted her head to one side. "No, I don't think so." And she began to laugh again.

"I don't understand you," he said. Again he was sitting there helplessly watching her struggle with herself.

She sighed, gingerly touching the corners of her eyes. "Please," she said. "Never mind."

"Okay," he said quietly.

"No, Walter. I am sorry. You must please forgive me."

"There's nothing to forgive."

"I don't mean to hurt your feelings."

"My feelings aren't hurt," he said.

She was taking some trouble to compose herself. She brought out a handkerchief and blew her nose. "I feel as if I have been running."

He left this alone. He was thinking that, anyway, he was going to marry Alice. He had asked her, and she had accepted, and that was that.

"You are not here to study?" Natalie wanted to know.

"I had to see Mrs. D'Allessandro about something."

She raised one eyebrow at this, but said nothing. He had the suspicion that she might be toying with him. After all, she was from another world, the world of grown-ups. The world of the memory of war, before he was born. It was ridiculous to think of her as he *had* been thinking of her, if it was not a sin.

"You are not disillusioned, I hope," she said.

"Pardon?"

Now she seemed to be ruminating alone. She stared at the table surface. "Americans haf such a slow capacity to learn. They do. And they have such a big capacity to imagine. They are like little children."

"*You're* an American," he said. "Now."

She looked at him. "Well—not yet."

Mrs. D'Allessandro came laboring down the stairs with a box of papers and notebooks. Natalie hurried out to help her, and the two of them said their good-byes to Marshall, the older woman apparently having forgotten that she had offered him a ride to his bus stop. He stood on the landing and watched them pull away in Mrs. D'Allessandro's beat-up car.

Chapter

1

*A*lice called him twice that evening to discuss plans. Her engagement had set something free inside her, it seemed, and she felt the necessary confidence to pursue matters that she might only have daydreamed about before. She told him this, and she told him how she had faced her father down about living her life as she felt she must. She was a grown person with her own opinions and values and she would behave accordingly. "I never thought I'd have the nerve," she told Marshall, laughing softly. There was a note her voice struck in laughter, a lovely trill, of which she was unaware. She seemed, indeed, to be trying to stifle herself, holding back. She even apologized.

"I'm just giddy," she said.

She had been in touch with Albert Waple, and had invited him and Emma to her birthday party, but then had decided it would be good to meet them both for dinner tomorrow, before Albert and Walter's class. It was a perfect idea, but she wanted to be sure it was all right with Walter. He hadn't made any other plans, had he?

"No," he said.

"I'm so excited, Walter. The whole thing has a kind of—symmetry, doesn't it? It's perfect. It fits perfectly. I know, maybe we could have a double wedding."

"Well," he began.

"Are they Catholic?" she wanted to know.

"I don't think so," he said.

"Will I see you tomorrow for lunch?"

"I have to eat lunch in the mailroom tomorrow. Mr. Wolfschmidt has a shipment of forms that have to be collated and sent out."

"What if I come to the mailroom and eat with you there?"

"I don't think that's such a great idea," he said. "You know how Wolfschmidt is."

His mother sat at the kitchen table, watching him talk. She seemed to study him. And when he hung up the phone she said, "Alice?"

"Yes."

"There's no light in your face, son."

"Pardon?"

"When you talk to her. I don't see any light in your face."

"I'm not a lamp, Mother." He was surprised at the irritability he felt.

She put her cool hand on his forehead. "No fever."

"I'm all right, really."

He helped her with the dinner dishes and then sat in the living room with her while she watched television and drank cordials with her tea. The news showed Negroes running under a barrage of water from fire hoses. It was a report about the trouble in Alabama, two years ago, and resistance to the new Civil Rights law. She sipped her tea slowly, watching this without seeming particularly interested in it. The television, she had often said, was company. She seemed unaware of her son's presence. He read from the book of President Kennedy's speeches.

> *Ladies and gentlemen of this Assembly, the decision is ours. Never have the nations of the world had so much to lose, or so much to gain. Together we shall save our planet, or together we shall perish in its flames. Save it we can—and save it we must—and then shall we earn the eternal thanks of mankind and, as peacemakers, the eternal blessing of God.*

Reading these lines, the young man was abruptly assailed by the possibility that the world might somehow find a way to resolve its problems before he got the chance to be the person saying such things. And he had a moment of recognizing, with dismay, the prodigious solecism of the thought. He could not have expressed this in words, but he knew it was selfish and sinful, and he tried to put his attention on something else, after murmuring a prayer—against the urges of his secret heart—that the nuclear nightmare would end.

How he hated these spirals his mind led him in, more and more.

He understood that he was inclined to be overscrupulous, but there were times when he couldn't help himself. His thinking tended in all cases to flow back to his faults: If he did something kind on the walk to Saint Matthew's—stopping to talk with someone who looked to be in need, giving money to one of the men who lined the street across from Lafayette Park—afterward he would catch himself feeling generous and good-hearted for the kindness, feeling a kind of pride; and so then he would murmer the prayer of communion:

Lord, I am not worthy that thou shouldst come under my roof, but only say the word and my soul shall be healed,

and in the words as he gave them utterance came the sense of his own journey toward sanctity, like a healthy, bracing walk through rarified air. He would bask in the pleasure of this feeling until the thought struck him that the enjoyment itself could be construed as a form of hedonism, a kind of spiritual gluttony for the delectation of his own piety. This was followed by a heavy sensation of hopelessness about being able to truly purify his thoughts, and an attendant shock of realizing that *now*, after everything else, he was close to the sin of despair, the worst sin and the one for which there is, of course, no forgiveness.

One evening, when Mr. D'Allessandro was late, and Albert Maples, Joe Baker, and Marshall were sitting in the basement by the vending machines talking about nuclear fallout and the end of the world, Joe Baker changed the subject by telling a joke about a young woman studying to be a nun:

As she's coming out of the church, she hits her foot on a rock, see. She says, "Oh, shit." Then she says, "Oh, God, I said 'shit.'" Then she says, "Oh, shit, I said 'God.'" Then she says "Oh, fuck it. I was going to be an airline stewardess anyway."

As he laughed with the others, worrying about the words, the young man had a guilty moment of sensing that the joke was a rather painfully accurate portrayal of the kinds of mental tangles he was contending with, all the time. It was discouraging, and it distracted him now, trying to read Kennedy's speech to the United Nations.

"Stop fidgeting," his mother said, pouring from the crème de menthe bottle.

He went to bed early, and lay awake, hearing the rattle and tumult of the television, on into the night. It was still playing when at last he drifted off, trying to pray, his mind turning on the vague, unbidden hope that the world's problems would wait for him, and presenting him with random images of the day he had just been through. He wished fervently that he was forty-five years old. Established. Questions answered, mind made up. All the necessary knowledge acquired.

On the edge of unconsciousness, he had a brief sexual dream of Natalie, which woke him and left him trying again to pray, waiting, humiliated, for the effects of the dream to wear off.

When he did sleep, he wandered through the other rooms of the house, and Natalie, all mixed up with his mother and Alice, was there with him in various states of undress. He kept shying away, and then running after them, and something in his soul—something that in his sleep felt as though it were the soul's trembling, unappeasable center—acceded to everything, and wanted more. He came to himself in the early morning, sitting up in the bed breathing as if from long exertion, the sheets moist with the turmoil of what he had been through in the hours of fitful dreaming. He found his mother asleep in her chair, in much the same position as the evening before, though the television was off and the room had been straightened. The tea and the crème de menthe were put away. She had dusted and polished the furniture—you could still smell the polish—and placed his book on a small shelf above the television, where she kept her own books.

He decided not to wake her, since it was clear that she had been through another of her restless nights. From the time he was small, she had been periodically subject to these episodes of sleepless energy, and he had awakened on some nights to find her in the middle of arduous and complicated tasks, which she defended with the assertion that she did not like wasting time, and wouldn't permit herself to do so. In her mind, there could be nothing more useless than a wakeful, healthy person lying in bed. The hours of her day were therefore various and changeable, and he had long ago become accustomed to organizing his own life around hers.

This morning, as on many other mornings, he brought a blanket in from her bedroom and put it over her. Then he got himself ready for work, and quietly made toast, which he left on a plate in the middle of the kitchen table with a note:

School tonight. Don't wait up if you're sleepy. Love, Me.

The bus into town coughed and sputtered. It would be another muggy, warm day. People sat quietly reading or looking out at the still-green trees lining Old Chain Bridge Road. The route took them through McLean, past Hickory Hill, where the former attorney general and his large family still lived, though Kennedy was now running for senator of New York. Marshall looked at the big house behind a wrought-iron gate. There were several black cars parked in front, and a big, oxblood-colored dog lay in the sparse dry grass of the lawn. At this stop, a nervous, wiry man always got on, having hurried down from one of the smaller houses on the other side of the road. Everything this man did was imbued with a kind of haste and worry: His thinning hair stood on end; his coat was missing a button or was frayed at the sleeves; his tie was always partly undone. He carried a newspaper rolled under one arm, and a thermos from which he poured himself coffee each morning, spilling it onto his fingers and into his skinny lap as the bus jarred over the uneven surface of the road. Marshall found that he couldn't quite keep from attending to the various signs of distress the man showed, spilling the coffee or trying to get the paper unfolded so he could read it. Occasionally, he was late enough that the bus driver would have to wait for him, and on these mornings he could be seen turning briefly to face the little house from which he had come, waving at the very round woman standing in the doorway there, surrounded by many children of indiscriminate ages—they looked out from under her robe, from over her shoulders, from beneath her arms—all waving and calling to him.

On the bus, he sat with coffee spattered on his coat, reading the paper, and Marshall would watch him, thinking about the sad-sack characters of the movies and television: Buster Keaton, and Jackie Gleason's "Poor Soul." There seemed something sorrowing in the face, a timid expectation of harm coming from some unforeseen quarter. Marshall resolved inwardly to find a way never to be this poor little rabbit of a man. Except that the man himself seemed quite content in his rushed, half-desperate condition, so that Marshall's feelings were of a kind similar to the dread of nameless diseases, the unhappy fate that might befall a person unawares, that might reduce him into thinking that such an existence was a happy one, an end to be desired.

This morning he saw not the little man, but himself hurrying down the black driveway from the little house, and it was Alice standing in the doorway, in the midst of all those children, waving to him, saying for him to hurry home. He thought he could feel how it must be to know that each day, every day into the years, would end with coming back to that house. Shivering, he looked at what was gliding by the window as if it might provide some avenue of escape, a way out of his own future.

At work, Mr. Wolfschmidt was dour and distracted. Thousands of letters had to go out to field representatives, and it all had to be done before the end of the day. Several of the boys from the stockroom had been drafted to help, and in the steady drudgery of the work, Marshall lost all sense of time. It seemed that not more than an hour had gone by before Alice was waving to him from the hall. He wondered why she had come down to bother him now, since Mr. Wolfschmidt was in such a bad humor and would surely have something to say. It was Mr. Wolfschmidt who brought him to the understanding that the day was over.

"We don't pay overtime," he said, tapping his wristwatch with one forefinger and looking at Marshall with a censorious scowl. "Go home with your nice little girl."

"Yes, sir," said Marshall. "I didn't know it was so late."

"Time goes quickly when you're having fun, *ja*?"

Alice took his arm as he passed out into the hall. "I waited for you downstairs. For a while there I thought you'd left without me."

"Don't be ridiculous," he said.

"I didn't bring my car, so we're going to have to walk."

When they got out into the street, and had gone a few blocks, she took his hands and pulled him toward a little alleyway between two buildings. They had just crossed in front of the Lafayette Hotel.

"What is it?" he said. "Alice."

Out of view of the passersby, she let go of him and stood against the soot-colored brick wall. "You can kiss me now," she said.

"Now?" he said.

"You want me, don't you?" She reached for him. "Don't hide it."

"Wait," he said.

"Open your mouth," she murmured.

He took a step back. "I don't think we should."

"Why not? We're engaged, Walter. Come *on*."

"I don't think this is the time—" he began.

"Oh, please," she said, breathing, moving her hands along her thighs. "Kiss me like you mean it. I love you."

Again he put his mouth on hers, and her lips seemed to spread over the whole surface of his lower face. "Walter," she said, pulling away. "I want you to really kiss me."

He did as she asked, and tasted the gum she had been chewing, the minty sweetness of it. Her breath was faintly sour, and he wondered about his own, which he was holding as best he could, tightening his arms around her and feeling wrong for the roaring in his nerves, even as he remembered that he had decided to go ahead with it all and that this was part of it. An image of Natalie shuddered through him, and then he thought of sex in general. The idea of it swept over him. This was finally happening, this alluring, true thing his body had turned on in the feverish nights. The world was offering it to him. He tried to think about Alice, who moaned and moved against him. He told himself he loved her.

"Oh," she said when they had separated. "We can't wait until June, can we? My lips are burning."

"Well, they're not actually *burning*," he said.

"Oh, Walter."

He gathered himself, breathed out slowly.

"Walter?"

"Well, guess we better go," he said in the voice of someone try-ing to put a cheerful face on things. The ingratiating tone of it filled him with chagrin.

Her face for the moment was blank, expressionless. Then she put the back of her head against the brick wall and seemed to toss back and forth, like someone in the grip of dreaming. "Walter, don't."

"Don't *what*?"

"You're doing this to torture me."

"No," he said. "Come on. Don't be silly. Don't do this now."

"Kiss me," she murmured.

He did so. They tottered for a moment, so that he had to reach over her shoulder to support himself on the wall.

"I'm on fire," she said. "I'm so hot. Are you hot?"

"We probably ought to go," he managed.

"What's the matter with you?"

"Nothing, really—" He shivered. "It's getting cold."

"It's eighty degrees out."

He said, "I'm a little chilly."

"I want you."

"I know, but Albert'll be waiting—"

"Don't you want me?"

"What?"

"*Walter*."

"What?" he said. "What, what, what?"

"Don't you want me."

He said, "I do, really. I can't talk about it." The blood was thun-dering through the veins of his neck and up the back of his head.

She looked at him. "Have you ever done it, Walter?"

"I don't think we should be late—" he got out, and then realized what she had asked him. "Pardon?"

"You know," she said. "Have you?"

"I—" he began. The nerves that controlled speech seemed to have short-circuited and left him with nothing but a sort of low, muttering whine. He looked down the alleyway to the open space of the street. "No," he told her. "I haven't. Come on, Alice. I'm only nineteen. And I—I don't believe we should—we don't—I—we—"

"It's the religion," she said. "It's against your religion. Right?"

"Well," he said. "Really, I—"

"Love is against your religion."

"Love?" he said. For a moment he didn't believe he knew the word. "No. Love is okay. Beautiful. Within—the—in marriage—but sex—" He took a step back, and realized that he was nodding vehemently, so that *she* was nodding, following his eyes with her own. "Outside marriage—sex outside—"

"I know, I know," she said impatiently. "What's wrong with you. Where's your brain? But when you love someone, you want them that way."

"That, too," he said, and his own voice sounded to him like a whimper.

She put her arms around his neck and pulled him to her against the wall. It was a kiss that nearly went beyond his capacity to hold his breath. The muscles of his chest and abdomen were beginning to quiver, as were those of his back. Finally, she drew back and looked at him.

"You're not breathing, are you."

"It's fine," he said, gasping. "Really." He was standing slightly bent over.

She looked down at him. "You're hot, aren't you. I can see."

He moved to the wall and folded his arms on it, then rested his head on his arms.

"Do you love me, Walter?"

He nodded against his arms, without looking at her.

She gave forth an exasperated sigh, "Please say it."

"I—" His voice caught. "L-love you."

"That's the best you can do? Look at me."

He did so. "I love you."

"You don't say it with much feeling."

"I do, too," he said. "For heaven's sake, Alice. Come on. Please. I'd love to—I—this whole thing is not allowed. I mean, I'm committing a mortal sin just standing here."

"Say you love me like you mean it."

"I do," he said. "I love you."

"Have you ever done it with anyone?"

"I don't want to talk about this."

"Well, have you?"

"Alice, I'm nineteen years old. I live with my mother. Who would I have done it with?"

She caressed the nape of his neck. "You probably won't believe it from the way I've been acting. But really—I've never—done it, either." It was as if she were admitting a failure.

"Well," he said. "Me, too. I mean, I understand."

"There's nothing to understand. What the hell—you *understand*? I tell you I've never done it with anyone and you say you understand?"

"I mean—I *know*. I can't think straight."

"It doesn't mean no one's *tried*."

"Not at all," he said.

"And it doesn't mean I haven't wanted to sometimes."

"Well, me, too." The muscles of his lower back were tightening, so that a sharp pain was stitching its way around his middle.

"Do you think about it a lot?"

"So-sometimes," he stammered, believing that she would never understand the truth. "It's—you know—can't—the—" He breathed. "Entertaining these—these thoughts—occasions of sin."

"It's a sin to think about it?"

"Mortal sin," he said too loudly.

She was quiet for a moment. Then, "I'm tempting you, huh."

"Well," he said, unable to return her gaze.

"We're going to be married, Walter."

"That's—" he got out, then had to swallow suddenly.

"Eventually, we're going to have sex," she said.

He nodded, feeling his diaphragm seize up. He couldn't breathe out.

"Don't you want to do it now?"

"You mean, right now?" he said.

"Not *here*." Her voice was full of teasing exasperation. "Jeez."

"Oh, ah—just a minute—"

"The thing is," Alice said, "I don't know if I can wait till June. I want you, Walter. I want you inside me."

He felt his knees buckle. And once again there was the cramping sensation in his lower abdomen. The ground seemed to shift under his feet.

"I know," she said. "Okay—the religion."

"Yes." The word had come out of him like a chirp. He cleared his throat, succeeded in pushing the air from his lungs, still feeling the squeezing of his diaphragm. When he tried to say the word again, his throat caught, so that the one syllable didn't escape before he coughed.

"Oh, why do these things have to come between us?" said Alice, folding her arms under her breasts and looking toward the street as though whatever it was that stood between them was waiting there. "It'll be so nice when we're married and we don't have to let anything get in the way."

He was trying to inhale, and something was impeding him. He had the sense that his air passages were closing off, and he turned from her again, trying to breathe in, making a high, squealing sound.

"Are you okay?" she said. "Lord Almighty."

He could make only the nearly inhuman yelping noise of trying to get air. His lungs seemed to have filled with fluid. While she slapped him above the shoulder blades and said his name in a fluttery panic, he put both hands on the wall, like a man about to be searched by the police, and continued helplessly to make the sound.

"Wait here," Alice said. "I'll get somebody."

He tried to signal her, shaking his head and waving his hands, wanting her to please be quiet, and trying desperately to pull in enough air to keep from—he was certain of this—dying. Finally, after a good deal of coughing and throat-clearing, he was able to draw enough breath to say, "I'm okay."

"My Lord," she said. "What happened? A little making out and you almost die choking."

"Something just went down the wrong way."

"We haven't been *eating*, Walter."

"No," he said through the rasp of having nearly choked. "That's true."

They started out of the alley, and she took his arm again. "I make you nervous now, don't I." She seemed almost pleased.

This stung him. "No," he told her.

She hadn't really heard him, was already talking. "Oh, Walter, I know we'll find some way to get through everything and be together. I can feel it in my bones."

They met Albert at the bus stop down from the school, where he was waiting for Emma's bus. He hugged Alice, who looked at Marshall as if to say that this was how one unselfconsciously and guiltlessly showed affection. "You're such a lovable old bear," she said to Albert, who seemed a little puzzled about the description. He had been reading, standing in the light of the bus stop with the book held so close to his face that he looked like a man hiding his eyes. Now he put the book in the back pocket of his jeans and rocked on his heels, staring myopically at the street. "Bus is late," he said. He seemed a little worried.

"Won't it be nice when we're all married?" Alice said. "We can go over to each other's houses for dinner, and go out to movies together."

"I can't see movies too well," Albert said, smiling. "And Emma can't see them at all."

"Oh, no," Alice said, glancing at Marshall with a horrified expression. "Actually, I didn't mean movies per se—"

Albert reached over and touched her shoulder. "It's okay."

"I have such a stupid ability to put my foot in my mouth."

"Stop it. You didn't do any such thing. We will go over to each other's houses, and have dinners together."

"I can't wait," Alice said, taking hold of Marshall's arm and squeezing.

Albert said, "Here's the bus." It was a block away, just slowing to let a passenger out. "I heard the brakes," he said, standing a little taller.

Alice looked as though she might begin to cry. Marshall put his arm around her and addressed Albert. "You sure it's her bus?"

"No," Albert said simply.

They waited. The bus labored toward them and slowed, and Emma did get off, aided by the driver. She wore a soft, red blouse, with a pink skirt, and looked almost glamorous with her dark glasses. She held the knot of her scarf with one too pale hand while the driver took her other hand and ushered her into Albert's waiting embrace as though she were a child. "Thank you," she said, not quite turning. The driver smiled, but said nothing, climbing back into the bus. As he pulled away, she waved at the surging sound of the engine. "Nice man," she said.

"Emma, this is Alice."

Emma reached out her hand. Alice stepped quickly around to take it. "So wonderful to meet you," she said in the exact instant that Emma said almost the same thing. They laughed, and Alice hugged her. "I just know we're going to be the greatest friends."

They all went together down Eighteenth Street to a little Italian restaurant, Vittorio's. It was almost empty, and there was a sign on a podium: PLEASE SEAT YOURSELF.

"Pretty waitress," Alice said, low, as they moved through the room.

Marshall saw that it was Natalie. She wore an apron over a black dress, and a small white cap, and her hair was arranged in coiled braids on either side of her head. She had stopped to wait on a couple sitting along the wall, and Marshall watched her, unable to take his eyes away, or to hear much of what was said to him. The talk near him seemed to be taking place on another plane of existence, somehow, until Alice pinched him on the arm.

"Ow!" he said, turning angrily and rubbing the place. "What're you doing?" he said.

"Albert was talking to you. Why're you standing there? Come on."

"Is everything all right?" Emma wanted to know.

"My future husband is so daydreamy sometimes."

"Don't pinch me again," Marshall told her. "I don't like to be pinched."

"It wasn't supposed to be fun."

"Well, don't do it again. I mean it."

"Poor baby," she said. But her eyes were abruptly troubled.

There was a supplicating look on her face. "Albert was telling you something."

"I heard you," he said, realizing the harsh note of irritation in his voice, looking beyond her at Albert, whose heroically ugly features seemed almost aghast, the mouth open and fixed, the eyes frowning deep into the hollows of the bony cheeks. "Sorry," Marshall said in a much softer tone. "But that hurt."

"I wasn't saying much," Albert said, "really."

He led the way to the other end of the room, and they waited while he helped Emma into her seat. Natalie hurried over with menus, and ran a damp cloth across the polished surface of the table. She glanced at them, and then stood up straight and smiled at Marshall.

He said, "Hey."

She answered, "Hello," without any inflection.

"Shakespeare tonight?" he said.

"Yes. Better than yesterday. Yesterday vas English history."

He sat down. Alice stared at him. Albert coughed and cleared his throat, watching Emma, who folded her hands on the table and said, "Someone has very nice perfume."

Natalie breezed away, into the kitchen, and for a time no one had anything to say. Albert cleared his throat again, and touched Emma's wrist. "The waitress, dear," he said.

"Where do you know her from?" Alice asked Marshall.

"She wears nice perfume," Emma said. "Is she pretty?"

They all seemed to be waiting for Marshall to answer.

"She's beautiful," said Alice. "Where do you know her from?"

"School. She's a friend from school."

"She's going to radio school?"

"No, the night college."

Again, they were all quiet.

"Albert wanted to know if Mr. D'Allessandro is going to raise tuition," Alice said. "He asked you about it and you saw your beautiful friend and got distracted."

Marshall ignored her tone, and related what he could recall of his conversations with the D'Allessandros, and described what he had witnessed between Mrs. D'Allessandro and the little man. Albert shook his head, sitting there with his hand on Emma's wrist.

"I can't afford any more tuition," he said finally. "So if he raises it, I guess I'm out."

"I'll help you pay," Emma told him.

"I wouldn't be able to let you do that," said Albert.

Natalie came out of the kitchen with glasses of water on a little tray. Marshall sought an opportunity to smile at her, but, perhaps purposely, she wasn't noticing anyone. She set the water glasses down, then put the tray on another table and took a pad of paper and a pencil out of the big pocket in the front of the apron. She stood, waiting for them to order.

"You go to the D'Allessandro School, don't you?" Emma asked her. "At least, you were there the other night."

"Yes, I go," said Natalie. "I don't think I see you there."

Emma leaned toward Albert, as if to confide something, but she spoke clearly, in a normal tone. "I recognized her by her walk, and her perfume." Then she faced Natalie. "These gentlemen go to the broadcasting school. I was visiting them the other night and you walked by us. In the library."

Natalie's eyes drifted past Albert and settled for a mere second on Marshall, whose tardy smile she just missed. She had brought her lovely attention back to Emma, though she said nothing.

"Nice perfume," Emma said.

"This is Natalie," Marshall said.

"I am happy to meet everyone," said Natalie.

Alice extended her hand and said her name. "And this is Albert, and Emma."

"You have a wonderful friend," Natalie said to Albert. "With her vay of knowing people from the sound and smell."

"She's my teacher," said Albert.

"You are very lucky." The note she struck now was dimly insincere.

Emma held a hand up and waved the fingers. "Hello," she said, then smiled.

"Hello," Natalie said. "What would you nice people like to eat?"

"I'd like a Caesar salad," Alice said. "The mushroom cap, and lobster bisque. Some cheese sticks. Some spaghetti. And an order of gnocchi. Asparagus. And a Coke. And cottage cheese. Am I going too fast?"

"No."

"And a milkshake. Chocolate."

"Yes," Natalie said, writing. She turned the page of the pad and kept on.

"And a slice of Boston cream pie."

"Are you ordering for the table?" Albert asked.

They all laughed.

Natalie wrote the order out. "We must keep up our strength," she said.

In that moment, five young Negro men walked into the place and moved in a slow but deliberate procession to a pair of empty tables along the wall, where they sat together, looking nervous and determined. They arranged themselves, hands clasped before them, and waited. Several people left quickly, walking away from plates of food. No one spoke. A woman with several packages gathered her coat and bundled herself off, so that now that side of the room was empty.

"It got so quiet," Emma said.

"Don't say anything," said Albert. "There's a situation."

"Situation?"

Natalie had gone into the kitchen, and in a moment she returned, accompanied by a heavyset, dark-haired man in shirtsleeves with a large, squarish jaw and a scar running along one side of his face. The man stepped to the table opposite the Negroes and put his hands down, regarding them with a kind of tolerant incredulity.

"Here?" he said. "Here? There's no problem here."

The Negroes said nothing, yet they seemed to attend to him with courtesy. One looked straight at the man and simply waited.

"Well?" the man said.

"May we please have menus?" the one said to him.

"That's all you want?"

"We want to eat, sir."

The menus were in a small rack on the wall. Natalie took some from there and handed them around the table.

The man straightened and put his hands on his hips. "I don't want trouble. Okay?"

"No trouble, sir," one said. He appeared to be the leader. He had large, brilliantly black eyes, and a wide, flattened nose. His skin was the color of deepest night.

"Hell," the man said. "You want trouble. That's exactly what you want."

"No, sir," said the leader, quietly. "We want dinner."

The man turned and gestured to Natalie. "Take their orders. We'll see how long it takes for me to get dinner. We're very busy." He looked around the room, and his eyes settled on Marshall's table. "Ain't we very busy, folks?"

Albert said, "No."

The man seemed not to have heard. "Very busy," he said. "But we're in compliance with the law. We'll try. You'll get no trouble from us."

"We're glad to hear you say that," the leader told him. "Friends of ours told us it was inclined to be slow in here, regarding service. We disagreed, of course. We said we were sure that there was no problem here."

"No problem," the man said bitterly.

"Very good, sir."

"Understand, it might be a while."

"And by 'a while,' what did you have in mind, sir?"

"That'd be hard to say. We're *very* busy tonight."

"Well, we're *very* patient, I think you'll find."

Natalie kept her head down. The proprietor walked back into the kitchen and storage area, and she came over to where Marshall and the others were sitting. Her face showed no emotion at all.

"What's going on?" Emma said.

"Should I order for you, dear?" Albert said.

"I thought Alice was ordering for us."

He smiled. "I'll do it. " Then he turned to Natalie and ordered pizza and Coke. Marshall ordered a Coke.

Natalie wrote everything down without looking up from the pad. Then she went to take the orders of the young black men. She did so, Marshall saw, with the same impassive expression. She kept her gaze averted from everyone. A moment later, two women entered, and headed for a table, only to pause suddenly, seeing the young men, and turn around to leave.

Alice said, "I don't see how people can be so stupid about skin color."

"Albert, why is everything—" Emma said. Then she seemed to realize. "Oh," she said.

"I swear," said Alice. "The stupidest thing."

The five young men talked quietly among themselves, and waited for the food that wouldn't come for a long time, if at all.

Alice went on about it all the way to the school—telling about a friend of her father's from the war, an Apache Indian, who had been refused medical help in Arizona last year and had nearly died of an infected cut on his one thigh. The other leg, she said, was lost at Normandy, defending the freedom of the very people who refused to help him. This brave man had fought the worst prejudice in history and, in the bargain, had given up a normal life for it; he came home and couldn't get medical treatment because he was an Apache. "It makes me sick," she said. "And then I think of those three poor young men in Mississippi and it makes me mad, too."

"I've got some Indian blood," Albert said. "Way back."

"I felt so awful eating in front of them."

"There wasn't anything we could do," Emma said.

Alice said, "We should've supported them somehow."

"We could've given them our food," said Marshall.

"They wouldn't have taken it, Walter. That's not the point, anyway."

"But this is Washington, D.C."

"I've joined a group here," Alice continued. "WSO. We Shall Overcome. Actually, so far, it's made up mostly of concerned white people, but we're going down to Charles County this Saturday."

"You are?" Marshall said, looking at her.

She nodded. "I'm driving. I'm going to be at a sit-in."

Marshall stared.

She turned to Albert. Apparently she meant this as a kind of dismissal of Marshall. "Want to go to a sit-in?"

"Listen," he said, smiling. "My high school friends still call me Abe."

"I think people ought to stay with their own kind," Emma said abruptly.

They were all stopped by this.

"You don't mean that, honey," Albert said.

"Sure I do. After all, I come from a long line of Southerners. It's just custom. It doesn't have anything to do with people not wanting other people to be free. It's just keeping folks with their own, that's all. We don't think people ought to go where they're not wanted."

There was a silence that seemed to draw out. They had come to the front of the school.

"I don't have anything against Negroes," Emma said. "But I keep to myself and my own kind and I expect them to do the same."

"Well," Albert said. "But—that's not really what's the matter—"

"I don't care," Emma said. "That's how I feel."

"But you don't . . ." Albert began. Then he seemed to think better of it. "I wonder if Mr. D'Allessandro will be here—"

"Don't skip over it," Emma said angrily. "It won't go away, you know. What does that stuff mean—we shall overcome? They keep singing that. Overcome. Well, I don't plan on being overcome by anybody, and that's just that."

"I don't think it's meant quite that way," Albert said gently.

"I don't know what else they mean," said Emma. "Do *they* know what they mean? I swear, sometimes I don't think the coloreds know what they want. They didn't come from any civilization. Did they? If it wasn't for us, wouldn't they still be uncivilized?"

"Honey—what do you mean—uncivilized?"

"They'd still be savages. Killing people for food and sacrifice and all the rest of it."

"How civilized, Emma, were the Nazis? Listening to Mozart while the corpses of the thousands of people they murdered were burning."

"That's not what I mean," she said. "And you know it. The coloreds just aren't like us."

Alice put one hand to her mouth and stifled something, a cough, or a groan. She turned from the others and started up the stairs.

"I'm sorry if that makes you mad at me," Emma said.

"No," said Albert. "Not mad." He took her by the arm. "Let's talk about something else, though."

"You're not going to change my mind," Emma said.

They filed into the building, and up the stairs to the glass doors, in a silence that seemed to grow thicker with each passing second. All the others were there, including Mr. D'Allessandro, who looked a trifle less florid but seemed himself. He greeted Alice with a special excitement, shaking her hand and smiling that wide, tight-skinned, grimace-smile. Then he rattled the keys on his belt, opening the supply cabinet where all the tape cartridges were stored, and proceeded with the evening's work as though nothing at all had taken place. It took a little while for Marshall to realize that Mr. D'Allessandro was putting on the best face for Alice, addressing all his talk to her. He talked about integrity, and being faithful to the trust of one's audience, being truthful. This made for an odd evening, since the night's format was top-forty music. Mrs. Gordon read the news off the wire, and Ricky Dalmas read a commercial he had written about Christmas:

> It's a rotten thing to open a gift on Christmas morning and realize it's not what you wanted. That you can't keep from making a face, that you'll never be able to convince anyone that you'll get used to it. It just makes you sick to your stomach, doesn't it? Do you want your kids to feel that way on Christmas morning? Do you want your kids making faces and getting nauseous and questioning that there's really a Santa?

All through the evening, Marshall watched Emma and Albert, who sat side by side at the console in the studio while Albert played disk jockey and tried to be glib and quick, as he apparently supposed a top-forty deejay ought to be. Mr. D'Allessandro stayed close to Alice, and hurried through each stage of the class, his keys rattling on his belt. Toward the end of the session, a Negro strolled in and stepped to the wall, arms folded, watching the proceedings. He wore a beige trench coat and a suit and tie. His black shoes were shined bright. He looked vaguely amused by everything, watching Mr. D'Allessandro conduct the class. When it ended, Mr. D'Allessandro gathered everyone and announced that he had managed to get permission to broadcast the Mitchell Brightman evening locally on December twentieth, using a small station in Falls Church.

He had accomplished this by promising that Brightman would lead a discussion of the news and President Kennedy. He looked at Walter Marshall as he said this, and then bowed to Alice. "This is in great part due to the help of Miss Alice here."

Alice nodded and seemed confused, her face flushed in big patches on her cheeks.

"Now, I have accepted a new student, as of tonight. And I want you all to meet him. He's got some experience in broadcasting, and he'll be a wonderful addition to our group. Everyone, this is Wilbur Soames. Wilbur?"

The Negro pushed away from the wall. "Hello." His smile was startling; it changed his whole face. He raised one hand slightly, then leaned against the wall again.

"We're almost halfway through the fall term of the second year," Mrs. Gordon said.

Mr. D'Allessandro nodded. "As I say, Wilbur has some experience already."

"Doing what?"

"Broadcasting experience, Mrs. Gordon."

"Doing what?" she persisted.

"Little of everything," Wilbur Soames said. "I'd like to get back into it."

"Mr. Soames worked at a radio station in Vermont, back in the early fifties. He can add a great deal to this class," said Mr. D'Allessandro, grimacing or smiling.

Marshall stepped across the small space between them and, offering his hand to the new man, introduced himself. Soames's hand was leathery, and soft. He smiled, tipping his head back a little. The others introduced themselves. Joe Baker gripped his hand and spoke too loudly about how happy he was. "Not all us folks from Alabama are benighted fools," he said.

"I'm happy to know that," said Mr. Soames, still smiling.

"I was with the guard," Baker went on. "I fought off the mobs when it all came apart in Montgomery."

"Glad to know you," Mr. Soames said. "Really."

When Mrs. Gordon gave him her hand, he held it between his thumb and index finger. "Very happy to meet you also," he said.

She nodded, looking too serious.

Ricky Dalmas moved a little to one side as he shook hands, as if to size up the new man. He kept his pipe in his mouth and said nothing.

"Pleased to meet you," Soames said to him.

Dalmas responded with an overweening dignity. "Likewise, I'm sure." He continued to watch as Martin Alvarez leaned in and said his name, smiling, looking straight at the new student with the open trusting expression of a man who believes others will like him. Finally, Albert stepped up. "Very glad to have you here," he said simply.

Mr. Soames's smile changed slightly. And then he glanced away.

"This is my fiancée," Albert said, ushering Emma into the circle.

"Happy to meet you," said Soames, extending his hand.

Albert took Emma's hand and put it into the other's.

Soames looked at them both with an expression of extreme study, as though he were worried about being wrong concerning what was politely expected.

"You have nice, gentle hands," Emma said.

Alice looked at Marshall and smirked, then quickly caught herself, glancing at Albert.

"Well," said Mr. D'Allessandro, obviously relieved and happy to have gotten through this, "see you all next week."

And the class broke up.

On the stairs going down, Albert asked if they could get something to drink from the machines in the basement, and Marshall followed him down. The two women waited in the foyer, looking nervous and faintly sorry to be stuck together.

"Well?" Albert said as Marshall watched him get a Coke out of the machine.

"Well, what?"

"I guess Emma kind of had some surprises for us tonight."

"You didn't know she felt that way?"

Albert shook his head. His features were so sorrowful that Marshall felt the need to look away. It appeared that Albert might cry in a moment. "I guess it was wrong to do that to her just now. And it wasn't very kind to Mr. Soames, either. But I knew—it was clear she couldn't tell from his voice that he's—well."

"You're sure she couldn't?"

Albert shrugged. "Maybe not."

"Look," Marshall told him. "It's not that important, is it? A lot of people feel the way she does. It's just going to take time, that's all. She'll learn."

"It changes everything," Albert said. "Surely you can see that it changes everything."

"Not necessarily," said Marshall. "Come on."

"Never would've believed it. Soft-spoken, kindly hearted Emma."

"It's nothing, Albert. To tell you the truth, I was a little worried about that 'overcome' business myself, at the beginning. My mother wanted me to go to Philadelphia with her the weekend of the march on Washington because she was afraid there'd be violence or something."

"Did you go to the march?" Albert asked him.

"Yes," he lied. He had watched the whole thing on television, and felt wrong for not going once it was clear that there would be no bloodshed. He had told himself that he must obey his mother's wishes, for her peace of mind, but there had been, he knew, a small, cowardly part of himself that kept him at home. He could not look back at Albert, who stood there waiting for him to say something else.

"I was there, too," Albert said finally. "And I'm sure I talked about it when I first knew Emma, and she didn't react at all—never let on that she was against it."

"She didn't say she was against it," Marshall said. "She said people ought to stick to their own kind. She can learn to feel another way about it."

"I wish she'd never brought it up."

"Come on," said Marshall. "Let's go."

"So discouraging," Albert said. He hadn't moved.

"They're going to wonder what happened to us," Marshall told him, pulling at his arm. "Come on, you can change her mind, can't you?"

Again, Albert shook his head, and now one hand went up to scratch it. "It's just such a big surprise." He took a step, then paused and seemed to peer at Marshall. "I grew up here, Walter. I went to places where they wouldn't let colored people in, and I sort of took it all for granted. You know? I accepted it like it was the right thing—all those years. I never questioned it."

"Me, too," Marshall said.

"Well—and I've been trying to make up for all that—just with myself. Quietly. Just with me. These killings in Mississippi—it—that kind of thing happens because something in the way things get said all around us—something in the air from the time we're babies—something must convince these people that it's all right to do such things. Kill people because they have dark skin, or they're trying to help people with dark skin. Something makes people think they have the right to do a thing like that. That something they think they're defending is worth doing a terrible thing like that. And then Emma—Emma winds up—well, it's very depressing—"

"You can work on changing the way she feels about it," Marshall said.

"I have a weak heart," Albert said matter-of-factly. He opened the Coke and drank most of it down in a gulp. "I probably won't live much past thirty-five. I'll be lucky to get that far."

"Don't talk like that."

He gave Marshall an almost impatient look. "It's what they told me."

Marshall simply stood there.

"Emma is so stubborn."

"She'll come around," Marshall said.

Albert raised one steep eyebrow. "I wasn't talking about that anymore."

Upstairs, the two women were quietly waiting, watching the street. They did not seem particularly uncomfortable, and Alice immediately embarrassed Marshall by throwing her arms around him. "Thank you for a lovely time," she said.

They went out onto the front stoop. Albert helped Emma down the stairs. "Well," he said, then paused, looking up and down the street as though uncertain of which direction to take. Marshall thought his face was sad, and felt an ache for him. Emma held out her hand to say good-bye. Alice took it, then embraced her.

"I know we're going to be such good friends," she said.

Albert looked helpless. He started guiding Emma down toward the bus stop on the corner. Alice took Marshall's arm, and they followed. There was a slight chill in the air, but there wasn't any wind, now. The stars were bright above the black edges of the city's rooftops, and a sliver of moon put off more light than seemed possible. At Emma's stop, they all said good-bye. For those few seconds everyone seemed as before. But then they had started away, and Alice walked back and embraced Emma and Albert again, and things were abruptly very awkward.

"'Bye," Emma said pleasantly. "Nice meeting you."

"Such pals," Alice said over her.

"Congratulations," Albert said.

At last, Marshall and Alice headed toward K Street and the bus to Arlington. He looked back once and saw that the other two were standing a little apart, Emma facing the street and Albert looking away. They did not even look like a couple.

At the stop on K Street, Alice said, "I hope everything's all right with them."

There was a screeching of tires somewhere off in the confusion and bustle of the city, and Marshall thought of Mrs. D'Allessandro.

Their bus came, and they got on. They held hands until her stop. She rang the bell, then turned and kissed him. "I'd love to see you tomorrow, but I have to help my father get ready for this, um, party." She smiled. The garish light of the inside of the bus discolored her skin and gave it a blotchy look. She shouldered her purse, and made her way, lurching, to the rear exit. Braced there, she looked across the heads of the other passengers and made a kissing motion with her lips.

Chapter

8

Thursday, Mr. Atwater came to dinner. A slight, pear-shaped man with a small, violet mouth and a feminine, dimpled chin, a little potbelly, and bowed legs, he had a way of walking that made you think of penguins. It wasn't quite a waddle, but there was something fussy about it, almost mincing. He wore brown gabardine slacks with white socks, and his button-down shirt was a strange, off shade of yellow. Marshall could not imagine what his mother saw in Mr. Atwater, whose pants legs often rode up on his calves, showing droopy socks and white ankles with blue, forking veins in them, and whose strangely doll-like mouth was set in a permanent smirk. Loretta seemed not to have noticed these very glaring details about him and, in fact, seemed at times to enjoy his company. Though on occasion she also appeared simply to be humoring him for the company he provided.

Over the months, Marshall had become accustomed to having him at the periphery of life with his mother. But he was faintly surprised to see them sitting together on the couch in the living room when he arrived home from work.

"Hi," his mother said, almost meekly.

"The hero returns from the field of conflict," said Mr. Atwater.

He was not possessed of the sort of cleverness that made for badinage. He wore glasses, bifocals, which magnified his eyes and gave him a look of being perpetually startled. The eyes were the color of river water—deep green, like that, without facets or shades of any other hue. Marshall had always felt, in a detached sort of way, without malice, that there was something ferretlike about him.

"Have a seat," Loretta said.

They were watching the news—Mitchell Brightman was talking about the FBI's ongoing investigation of the murders of the three Civil Rights workers in Mississippi.

"We're having roast," Loretta said. "It's almost done."

"Quiet," said Mr. Atwater.

Loretta had set up three TV trays. Marshall saw this, but excused himself and went into his room, closing the door. In a moment, his mother knocked and entered. "Sweet pea," she said. "Don't be unsociable."

"I'm not."

"Will you come out and sit with us?"

"I thought you might want to be alone," he said, feeling crowded.

"No." She stood there, waiting.

In the small living room, Mr. Atwater had put his feet up on the coffee table and was smoking a cigarette. He stared at the television. "They'll never get a guilty verdict," he said about the Mississippi story. "Even if they get to the bottom of it and arrest some folks. Not in a million years. Not so it'll stick. Not the way things are down there."

"I think the whole thing is dreadful," said Loretta. "When you can't even trust the law itself not to kill you."

"It's complicated, L'retta. These riots, you know—the trouble in places like Harlem and Philadelphia last summer. That kind of thing gets people wondering."

"Those three boys weren't rioting, Clark."

"Yes, but now—the way the folks in Mississippi see it, it's a bunch of outside agitators. Some people are saying they got what was coming to them."

"I know you don't mean that."

Atwater took a long, satisfied draw on his cigarette, then talked the smoke out. "Oh, I'm not saying it. Of course I don't mean it for myself. I'm just saying a lot of people feel that way, though. That's all. Whole country's crazy, and that's the truth."

"I think it's terrible," Loretta said. "These poor Negroes don't even hit back."

"Some'd say it's stupid not to." Mr. Atwater took another draw on the cigarette, then sighed loudly and adjusted his weight, recrossing his legs at the ankles. "It's a battle, though. And, in fact, a strategy. That tactic goes all the way back to Tolstoy, and Thoreau."

"I'm going to have some tea," Loretta said. "Anyone want some tea?"

"Not me." Mr. Atwater appeared proud of it. He looked at Marshall. "How 'bout you, cowboy?"

"No," Marshall said.

"How's the radio career coming?"

"Oh," Loretta said, heading into the kitchen. "Didn't I tell you? Walter's not really interested in a radio career anymore." She opened the refrigerator.

"No?" Atwater watched as the young man moved to the other side of the room and sat down. His mother had set a cup for tea, and a glass, on the TV tray. She walked over and filled the glass with milk, then went back toward the kitchen.

"He's thinking about a career in politics."

"That so." Atwater sat up and put his feet on the floor. He held his cigarette between his index finger and thumb, with his hand turned toward his chest as though he wanted to keep the smoke from drifting away from his body. Then, looking at Marshall above the frames of his glasses, he put his head down and drew on the cigarette again. "A politician, huh?" It was as if something sly had passed between them. "You've got a slight drawback, son."

Loretta was in the kitchen, making her tea. "What?" she called.

"I was talking to the boy, here."

Mr. Atwater sat smoking, watching Marshall, who took a magazine from the rack by his chair and opened it on his lap. Here was a photograph of President Johnson waving to an enormous crowd of people in the stormy weather of some campaign stop. Farmland stretched far beyond him, roofed by rough-edged dark clouds. "Know what your drawback is?"

Marshall said, "No, sir." He took a drink of the milk.

"You have to be a millionaire to run for office."

Marshall shook his head.

"Sure you do." Atwater stared at him. "You think this is a free country?"

"No, sir. Not completely. Not for everybody."

"You're talking about the colored people."

"Yes."

"Well, and you're a very idealistic young fellow, I can see that all right. Those are fine sentiments. They're true. True, indeed. Some people have it rough."

"It's not just sentiment, sir. It's the facts."

"And I'll bet you're going to change things. I'd be willing to bet on your generation."

"I'd like to try. I think we should all try, don't you?"

"Admirable." Mr. Atwater crushed his cigarette out. "You underscore my faith in the youth of America," he said.

Marshall was silent.

"L'retta, what're you putting in the tea?"

"Galliano," she called. "Want some?"

"No thanks. How much of it are you having?"

"Just a little."

Marshall turned the pages of the magazine.

"First thing to learn," said Mr. Atwater, "is that this is not by any stretch of the imagination a free country." He spoke almost jauntily, lighting another cigarette, and smiling. "Hasn't been for a long time. And I'm not just talking about ni—about colored people."

Marshall felt abruptly as if he had come upon the older man performing some privy act. It was exactly the same feeling. He had an image of Atwater standing with a pointer in front of a classroom, teaching social studies and civics.

"No," Atwater went on, "it's not the—the colored people I'm talking about. Because God knows they do have it rough in the South. Hell, all over, when you really look at it. The thing is, we're not all that much better off when it comes to life, liberty, and the pursuit, you know? There's income tax, social security tax, state tax, and property tax—it's all mandatory, it all goes overseas to help foreigners, and it's aimed at controlling things and people."

Loretta came into the room with her tea. She set it down on her TV tray and took her place next to Mr. Atwater.

"Then there's the draft, of course. And the welfare business, and everything you've got to do to own anything—you see what I'm getting at?"

"Let's not talk about politics," said Loretta. "It never leads anywhere."

Mr. Atwater went on as though he had not heard her. He was still addressing Marshall. "What sort of politics were you thinking you might like to get into, son?"

"I don't know. Politics."

"You must have some idea—ward politician? City councilman? Mayor? A legislature sort? Board of supervisors? Congress?"

"He wants to be president," Loretta said, sipping the tea. Marshall, who had told her nothing of his secret hopes, was for the moment too astonished to speak.

"President," said Mr. Atwater. "President of what?"

"I never said that," the boy managed.

"President of these United States?"

"I never said *that*."

"Well," his mother said. "But of course that's what you want. You wouldn't want to be one of these congressmen or senators. Why go into it if you aren't going to aim for the top? Besides, Alice said you told her as much."

"You've talked to Alice?"

"She called again today to invite me to her party. She was very nice."

Mr. Atwater laughed. "That's wonderful. Truly wonderful. President of these United States." He laughed again.

Marshall felt that the laugh was at his expense. He put the magazine back in its place and stood.

"Where're you going?" said Mr. Atwater. "Boy, you can't leave us now. Not after a revelation like this. Sit down, sit down, come on. Finish your milk. We got a roast coming."

Marshall's mother gave him a pleading look, and he sat down.

"There," Mr. Atwater said, rubbing his hands together. "President, huh? Am I correct in assuming you mean the president of these United States?"

"Of course," Loretta said.

Mr. Atwater considered a moment. "Let's see—when will you be eligible? I'd like to live to see this, and I think I might just be able to manage it." He was straining to control his own amusement. "What party will you join?"

"We're Democrats, here," said Loretta.

"Please," said Marshall. "I never said I wanted anything more than to be in politics—and that was just maybe—"

"Oh, but your mother's exactly right. You ought to aim for the top."

"I don't have any plans like that," the boy lied.

Mr. Atwater went on. "You'll have to get through some dangers, of course—there's some chance of war. I'm sorry to say it out so plainly, Loretta, but the way things are set up in the world, there's always a chance of a detour for us men. It can actually be an advantage, though, for a presidential candidate—having a good war record. Kennedy had PT 109, remember. And since we've got wars breaking out all the time all around, there might be an opportunity before you know it. And these days you never know when the situation at home will get down to shooting. You don't have any plans to head south, do you? You're not going to be a big Civil Rightser, I hope? Not like those boys—that Chaney and the others. That sort of thing makes nice newspaper copy but it won't get you the votes you need. And you can't get elected if you're buried in an earthen dam in Mississippi, right? But you have to start establishing your record right now, of course. And then you've simply got to find a way to make a whole lot of money—millions, kiddo. Millions."

"That's not so," Loretta said. "Plenty of people . . ." She stopped. She seemed to have lost the train of the discussion.

"I never said I was going to run for president," Marshall told them.

Mr. Atwater blew smoke at the ceiling. "I knew he was a kid outlined for something special, L'retta. I could've predicted it. When I had him in civics, I could see it. Born to be a leader of men—that's what I said to myself."

Loretta had stood, and was moving into the kitchen to tend to the dinner. He watched her go, then turned to Marshall and smiled. "Then there's this little difficulty in Southeast Asia."

Marshall nodded.

"What would you do about it—if you were president."

"I'd . . ." He halted. He had almost said something about a measured response. But that was the phrase President Johnson had used.

"Take your time," Atwater said, smiling at him.

"I'd do about what the president did, I think."

"Good answer," Atwater said. "Made me glad to be part of a powerful nation that could decide a thing like that. They try that funny stuff on the high seas with us, so we sting them good, and now they'll think twice about messing with us. Made me proud when we bombed the little bastards. It make you proud?"

"Yes," Marshall admitted. He had felt exactly as Atwater described it, and the knowledge of this troubled him.

Mr. Atwater said, "Sure it did. You're an American."

Marshall felt the other man's blank stare. Atwater seemed to be waiting for something.

"Sure it did."

"I have to mash the potatoes," Loretta said from the kitchen. "Bring me a cigarette, will you, somebody?"

Marshall took it in to her. She grasped his wrist and murmured, "Be nice," then smiled, leaned over, and kissed his cheek.

In the other room, Atwater was waiting. He stared for a few awkward seconds, then ran the flat of his hands across his scalp and sighed. "Of course, all that pride is nice, but if I know my history, that little situation's gonna be a lot worse soon enough. A lot worse. Yes, sir, this could be a land war in Asia. And we were warned about them, you know? I think it was Ike, warned about them. And there's all that unstable mess in the Congo. I'd say you better get yourself in college and stay there, if you can. Trade school just won't do. You know what I mean?"

"I'm supposed to start college," Marshall said rather pointlessly. The other man was crushing out the second cigarette, talking on as though no answer had been given.

"And, of course, if it's not in Asia or Africa, it'll be in the Middle East, or even Europe again. Probably it'll be in Africa, though. The Congo. Or Algeria, or maybe the Middle East. There's lots of places, of course. The pattern seems to be every twenty years, see, and it's been twenty years."

"I'm not afraid to fight for my country," Marshall said to him.

Atwater nodded, and the magnified green of his eyes seemed to shift a tiny increment. "Admirable," he said. "I feel that way, too. But one life to lay down for my country."

"I swear," said Loretta from the kitchen. "Can't you boys ever talk about anything else?"

This was embarrassing, since they had never spoken about anything of the kind until now. Mr. Atwater shook his head a little, then gave Marshall a look that invited a collusion between them about her, as if she were the object of a joke they shared.

"When Walter filled out the forms to register for the draft, he wrote that he'd be proud to serve his country."

"Ask not what your country can do for you," Mr. Atwater said, smiling out of one side of his mouth. "Right?"

Marshall said, "I don't understand what you mean."

"I mean, I think it's admirable."

"Well," Loretta said, "I know women have stood for it and were brave and all that, but I don't know that I want to give up a child to the state, for any reason."

"You might not be able to help yourself," Mr. Atwater said. "When the time comes."

"I'm not a child," Marshall said.

"Of course you're not."

Loretta brought their plates in and put them on the trays. She had sliced the roast beef, and put carrots and mashed potatoes and biscuits on the plates. She refilled Marshall's milk glass, and poured ice water for Mr. Atwater, who sat forward and breathed in the aromas rising from his plate, making a big show about how hungry he was and how good everything looked. Then they were eating quietly in front of the television, with its small, washed-out, snowy screen. The news was still on—local weather. Marshall saw that his mother was growing uneasy. She kept glancing at Atwater, as if to monitor his reaction to the food or to the company. When her eye caught her son's, she frowned, and seemed to be trying to signal him.

"Is something wrong?" Mr. Atwater asked.

"Lord, no," she said, laughing nervously. "I think I'll have more tea."

When she was in the kitchen again, Atwater said, "She likes her tea."

Marshall nodded, in spite of himself.

"Likes what she puts in it, too, doesn't she?"

Loretta came back, and sat down, taking some time to arrange herself. She sipped the tea and then wiped her lips gingerly with the napkin. "There."

"Didn't you hear me say I wanted some?" Mr. Atwater said.

"Oh, no. Forgive me." She rose, seemed faintly hesitant, then made her way back into the kitchen.

Atwater returned Marshall's look with placid calm. "Did you say something?"

"No, sir."

"What's on your mind, son?"

"Nothing."

Loretta came back with the bottle of Galliano and the tea.

"I'd like mine with ice in it," Atwater said.

Loretta turned to her son, and then to Atwater again. "All right," she said doubtfully, moving away.

Atwater smiled. "Talk to me," he said to Marshall.

"Why don't you get your own ice?" the young man said.

"Now stop that," Loretta protested from the kitchen. "I'm getting it."

"So," Mr. Atwater said. "Say something to me, boy."

Marshall said, "What do you want me to say?"

"Well, tell me about getting married." The eyes were like saucers, staring. The little, feminine mouth twisted back in another smile.

Loretta hurried into the room with the ice tray from the freezer. "I told Clark about it," she said quickly. "I was—excited for you, Walter—"

"You were worried. Come on, L'retta—you can tell the truth to the boy. The truth won't hurt him. The truth never hurt anybody. The truth shall set you free, remember? Besides, the boy'll do what he wants to do anyway, won't he?" Atwater leaned across his tray toward Walter. "She was worried. Which anyone can understand, of course."

"Maybe a little worried," Loretta said, settling into her chair.

There was a helpless look of apology on her face. She fussed with her napkin, then poured more tea for herself, watching her son with obvious apprehension.

"Actually, you know, your mother and I have been talking about getting married, too," Mr. Atwater said.

Marshall stopped eating.

"Isn't that right, L'retta?" said Atwater.

"I'm not sure this is the time," Loretta said, looking from one to the other of them.

"What better time than now? Here we are, the three of us together."

She spoke under her breath. ". . . said if I would, yet," Marshall heard.

Atwater was staring at him. "What would you think about that, son?"

"That's between you-all."

Loretta gave him another sorrowing, apologetic look.

"That's what I've been trying to tell your mother."

"Please, Clark."

"Just the facts, ma'am," Atwater said. It was one of his traits to quote the TV shows he liked, and he was a *Dragnet* fan. "The indication seems to be that young Walter, here, is a stumbling block of sorts, and so I just thought I'd see if I couldn't clear the air a little. Ma'am."

"I'm not a stumbling block to anybody," Marshall said.

Mr. Atwater wasn't listening. He was concentrating on Loretta now, with that sidelong smile. "The thing is, you know, it seems quite strange that at this time you'd be going off to some party with a lot of bigwigs without me. That just seems to me to be the strange thing, here, ma'am."

"I explained it to you," Loretta said.

"I know you explained it. I just don't get the explanation. That's the thing."

"You don't owe anybody any explanations," Marshall said to his mother.

"Stop it," Loretta said. She made a fluttering motion with her hands. "Both of you. My goodness, don't make a federal case out of it."

Mr. Atwater leaned back in his chair and folded his arms, gazing at her out of the glassy exaggeration of those impassive eyes.

Loretta seemed about to cry. "I wouldn't lie to you," she said to her son. "I was a little worried. Alice is older than you are."

"I told your mother to look who the girl's related to," Atwater said. "There's no sense turning your nose up at a good thing. I just wondered why no effort was made to include me."

"I explained it to you," Loretta said. "Please drop it and let's eat."

"You obviously haven't kept Walter, here, very well informed," said Atwater. Then he shook his head. "Women."

They were quiet for a few moments. On the television was a special report about South Vietnam, the failing civilian government. Mr. Atwater watched this, chewing. Then there was a commercial for Alka-Seltzer, a little animated stick figure dancing and singing about relief. "I'm going to get a color television set," Mr. Atwater said. "I think I'll give it to myself for Christmas."

No one answered him.

"Imagine getting the Sunday night movie in living color. Be like sitting in the theater."

Loretta poured more tea and Galliano.

"Baseball, too," Mr. Atwater said, regarding her.

"Did you want some?" she said.

"Sure do." His tone was expansive and generous.

"Well." She poured him some, then sipped her own, and seemed not to know what to look at, where to let her gaze fall.

"Good?" he said. "Like it?"

She said, "Yes."

"I do, too. Very good, very good."

They drank.

"I like to see you happy." He reached over and touched her arm.

"I guess we're going out to a movie," she said to her son.

"He can come along if he wants to," Atwater said.

"Do you want to?" she asked, almost hopefully.

"No, thank you."

"It's really all right," she said.

"L'retta, he said no. Didn't you hear him?" Mr. Atwater deliv-

ered these words with a kind of cheeriness, like a joke. "This is a
wonderful meal, L'retta. You've outdone yourself."

"Thank you," she said, staring at her son as if to explain.

Their life had been suffused with a tenderness born of the fact that
they had been abandoned. They never voiced this, never used the
word in connection with the fact; they simply lived in it, and went
on in their peculiarly considerate, and nearly shy way. To others,
they might have seemed to be guarding some mutually shared
infirmity: There were times when they seemed a little too protective of each other, a shade more solicitous than normal. During the
missile crisis, they had walked together the mile and a half to Saint
John's Church to go to confession. There was a line all the way
around the inside of the church, perhaps a hundred people.
Marshall and his mother waited an hour, then gave up and walked
back home.

"I'm not afraid," she said. "If it's the end of the world, I'm ready."

"Me, too."

"I hope it isn't, though."

It was a clear, starry night, with a bright moon providing a
glow above the houses along the street. The stars seemed connected by strands of pure, white energy, out there across the
unthinkable distances.

"Imagine, talking about such a thing," she said. "The end of
the world."

In the yard of one of the houses, a boy was handing boxes into
the lighted space of the entrance to what looked like a storm shelter.

"Look," Marshall's mother said.

They paused, and watched for a time. The boy kept disappearing into the house, and then coming back with another box, which
he handed into the shelter. Finally, a man looked out from the
entrance. "Move along, folks. We don't have any room."

"Is that a fallout shelter?" Loretta asked him. "I've never actually seen one."

"Just move along."

The two of them went on down to the end of the block, and
across the street, before she spoke again. "Do you suppose we
ought to find someplace like that?"

"I don't know," Marshall told her.

The shelter had affected her, as though the sight of it had convinced her of the magnitude of their peril. In the apartment, under the light of her reading lamp, they knelt and said a rosary, and then they simply waited together for the sunrise. He thought about all the drills at school, filing out into the hallways and getting down next to the lockers, hands clasped behind the head, in the giggling and talking, no one believing it was actually possible, and the words of the adults, describing how there would be a white flash and then the shock. The adults talked about surviving the attack, and kids passed around a little yellow card,

> *What to do in the event of a nuclear attack: 1. Remove all sharp objects from your pockets; 2. Remove all jewelry and all eyeglasses; 3. Seat yourself in a chair away from windows; 4. Bend over and put your head between your legs; 5. Kiss your ass good-bye.*

"They say at school there'll be a blinding flash first," he said to her. "I know," she said. "Let's not talk about it." But she didn't want them to go to bed. She would hate to be surprised in her sleep, she told him. "I used to think I wanted to be surprised, Walter. I don't. It turns out I really don't."

Neither of them said very much, after this. They both dozed a little. But she would say, "Awake?" And, startled, he would say, "Yes." And she would apologize. He would say, "It's okay." Then silence, and the whole process of waiting, and drifting off, would start again. When the sun began to redden the sky to the east, she turned on the television. The news was hopeful for the first time in days. There had been a release of tension, the newscaster said, and negotiations were continuing. She turned it off with a quick motion, as if she were afraid to give the newsman the time to recant, and then she started cleaning the house—running the vacuum, dusting the furniture, waxing the tabletops, getting rid of the week's accumulated clutter.

"I guess we're going to be all right," she said after an interval of rather furious work. "Either that or they had their war and we didn't hear it."

"I don't think they had it," Marshall said, lying down on the sofa.

She was standing on the other side of the living room, a stack of old newspapers in her arms, when she suddenly dropped them at her feet, crossed to where he was, knelt, and put her arms around him. "I love you," she said, crying. "I love you, my dear boy."

"I love you, too," Marshall said. "I love you, too, Mom."

Then she was backing away, wiping her eyes with the backs of her hands. "I guess I was more worried than I realized," she said. "Lord, I'm a mess, aren't I?"

He said, "You're perfect."

She walked over and began to pick up the fallen newspapers. "You know—I kept thinking all night that I wished I could've been better than I was, somehow. I feel like—well, like starting over. Don't you?"

He did not feel this. Indeed, he didn't quite know what he felt. He was numb. It was hard to imagine what the rest of life might hold.

Several times, during the course of his growing up, Loretta had come close to marrying again. There had been Mr. Raymond Sykes, the hi-fi and TV salesman, who wore a black toupee and looked, Loretta said, like someone who might wear a black toupee. He was a big, apple-shaped man with dark, Mediterranean skin and large, bulbous brown eyes, whose speech, when it was not incomprehensible and weirdly self-referential, was overly elaborate and stagy, as if he were bending his spoken sentences in order to use words he had just culled from a dictionary. But he seemed like a nice man. He made a friendly presence. He had showered gifts on them, and though the gifts were always too practical and in some cases too personal to be quite acceptable, they were also clearly the result of his innocent affection; he gave everything with an almost childlike timidness and hope. He bought a pair of special hosiery for Loretta, designed to be used by women with varicose veins, thinking that because it was expensive, it must be the best, and he wanted, he said, nothing but the best for her. He bought Marshall a car coat, with big barrel buttons on it, and a hat with earflaps; it was the style among men his age. He had the tires changed on the car, and paid for a tune-up. He bought Loretta a hair dryer, and a vacuum cleaner, and an iron. He wanted her to have every convenience. When Loretta gently refused his offer of marriage, using the excuse that he wasn't Catholic, he immediately began taking instruction in the faith, and she had to tell him finally that this would not change her mind. "You mean," he said, "all this that I've been putting myself through is going to be unavailing?"

Loretta said, "I'm afraid so."

He looked stricken. And kept on taking the instruction anyway. They started seeing him at Mass on Sundays. And he kept calling, kept doing favors for them. "In the name of our disinterested friendship," he told Loretta. "And because it's a do unto."

"I'm sorry?" Loretta said.

"Do unto others," he said, smiling. "I'm keeping to it."

One Saturday morning they found him waxing the car. Another time he left a bag of groceries outside the apartment door. Finally, Loretta asked him to stop. None of it was going to be of any use, she told him. She just didn't feel that way about him. She related the whole story to Marshall the day Mr. Sykes took the tires, all four of them, off the car.

"You're quite adamant," he'd said.

"I'm sorry," said Loretta.

"I see," he said. "Well, I told you these were do untos."

"I am sorry," she said. "It's the most flattering thing in the world, but really I . . ." She halted.

"No," he said. "Really. Do unto others as you would have them—you remember. I'm just making my mansion. Storing up my treasures." He pointed at the sky.

They found the car on its four hubs. And when they made their way by bus across Arlington to the television and hi-fi store where he had worked, they were told that he had been fired from the job weeks earlier, for stealing from the cash register. They never saw Raymond Sykes again.

And before him there had been others, less vivid in the boy's memory.

There had been Tim Dreen, who coached the junior college basketball team in Bethesda, and had two daughters by a first wife.

He had a habit of mussing Marshall's hair—the boy hated it—and he often talked about how Marshall could be the son he'd wanted, but hadn't been fortunate enough to have. He thought he would make an athlete out of the boy, and began trying to teach him the necessary discipline. This involved several instances of rough treatment when Loretta wasn't around, and once when he had grabbed Marshall by the upper arms and was shaking him for failing to understand some fine point of the pugilistic art, Loretta came in on them unexpectedly and ended the lesson by means of a sharp, short blow with an iron skillet across the back of Tim Dreen's skull. When he came to, whimpering and wanting to know what he had done to be treated so badly, she used the threat of more of the same to send him on his way.

The kindest friend she had had over the years was Father Soberg, as far as her son was concerned. He had seemed the one man she was most comfortable with, including her present companion, Mr. Atwater, whose tendency to vacillate between irritable familiarity and jovial, yet faintly hostile, expansiveness left Marshall feeling confused and more than a little worried, since his mother seemed determined to tolerate it—and to require that Marshall do the same. There was a willingness on her part to do Atwater's bidding, and this did not seem to arise out of particular affection for him.

When she returned from the movie, she told Marshall that it would be necessary for Atwater to accompany her to Alice's party.

"She wants you to meet her father," Marshall said.

"I can't help that," his mother said, moving away from him, into the kitchen, where she poured Galliano into a juice glass and drank it down.

"Mom," the boy said.

"I told him he could come, and that's that. If he can't go, I can't go."

Marshall watched her pour more of the yellow liqueur.

"I can't help it," she said, not looking at him. She drank, slowly this time. Then she seemed to come to herself. "Is there any tea made?"

"No."

She shrugged. "You have to understand, Walter. I work for him. He's—he's my boss. Do you understand? I can't very well tell him to get himself lost, even if I wanted to, which I don't."

"But why don't you?" Marshall said, to his own surprise. A torrent of ill-feeling toward Atwater went through him, and he stood straighter, bracing himself inwardly, wanting to hold back.

"You don't know anything about him, really," she said. "It's not your business."

"I know I don't like the way he talks to you."

She drank, turning from him. "Go to bed, Walter. I'm telling you, you don't know anything about it. Just—tell Alice we'll have Clark with us."

Chapter

9

riday evening was cool, clear, and calm. Mr. Atwater arrived late at the Marshalls' apartment house, and then insisted on driving. Marshall and his mother piled into the big car—the boy in the softness of the wide backseat, with a wrapped gift for Alice on his skinny lap, his mother in the bucket seat in front. The present was a pair of fluffy slippers that Loretta had helped him pick out, and now he wondered if they were the right gift for a fiancée. It was too late now to do anything about it, of course.

Atwater got in behind the wheel, and headed out in the wrong direction, saying he knew Arlington well and had spent time in the house of friends who lived near Alice. He drove with both hands tight on the wheel, sitting forward, shoulders hunched. He was heading toward McLean.

Marshall said, "It's the other way, sir."

"No. Sixteen hundred block—it's got to be south."

"It's behind us," Marshall told him.

Atwater drove on for a few more seconds, then slowed, and turned down a side street. "This'll come out on Lee Highway."

"It's a dead end," the boy told him.

"He's been driving the Lark all over," Loretta said. "You know."

"Well, that's nice," Mr. Atwater said. "But I've been driving these streets since I was a kid fresh out of the army. 1946, Loretta."

When they came to the dead end, he stopped the car. "Used to be a road through here," he said. "I swear to God."

No one spoke for a space. There was just the sound of the big car idling. Atwater backed up, looking beyond the young man. "Okay," he said. "Maybe our putative presidential candidate will guide me."

Marshall said nothing.

"Well?"

"Just—the other way from the way we went."

"Wonderful."

A moment later, Loretta said, "Aren't you going a little fast?"

Atwater said nothing, but slowed the car a little. He held the wheel with both hands, the knuckles showing white. His shoulders were hunched. Loretta put the radio on, listened to the weather for a moment, then turned it off.

"Nothing like spending time with the rich and famous," Mr. Atwater said as they pulled onto Alice's street.

"I have to meet Albert and Emma at the bus stop on the corner."

Atwater said nothing, but pulled the car over as they approached the stop. Albert and Emma had met there, coming from opposite directions. They were waiting, holding hands. Marshall gave Atwater the number of Alice's house, and got out. "We'll walk up," he told his mother.

"There's room for everybody," Mr. Atwater said.

Marshall shut the door and stepped up onto the sidewalk, holding his wrapped gift. Emma reached for him, and he put his free hand in hers. "Hello, Walter."

"I'm fine," Marshall said, realizing that the question had not been asked. "Hello to you."

The car pulled away with a small screech of the tires.

"I was starting to wonder if you'd forgotten us," Albert said, watching it go. His own gift for Alice was in his jacket pocket.

"Somebody's angry," said Emma, turning in the direction of the car speeding away.

"What did you get her?" Marshall asked.

"He got her a book," Emma said. "Aristotle."

"It's a very nice bound book, with ribbons to mark your place."

"I don't think Aristotle makes a good birthday gift."

"Emma wanted to get her these stupid, fluffy slippers."

"They were very nice. With fur around the ankles."

"What did you get her?" Albert wanted to know.

"Stupid, fluffy slippers," Marshall said, and after a moment's hesitation, they laughed.

"Really?" Albert said. "You're not pulling my leg?"

"Fur around the ankles," Marshall said. He led them up the street, to Alice's door. Mr. Atwater had parked on the grass, and was in the open, lighted doorway, his arm around Loretta's middle. Loretta looked over her shoulder at her son, then was ushered inside. Other people were coming out, two men and a woman. One of the men, the taller of the two, was smoking a big cigar, and when he spoke, Marshall recognized the raspy voice of a local radio weatherman named Hinckham, whose identifying tag line was "Don't let it rain in your heart." Clark Atwater had paused in the doorway and he said, "Mr. Hinckham, what's the weather?" Hinckham turned to indicate the inside of the house. "It's not raining in there."

Atwater laughed, too loudly.

"Zero chance of rain," Hinckham said. He glanced at Marshall, not quite seeing him, going by, and spoke to the woman. "Who were those two?"

Marshall knew he was talking about Loretta and the social studies teacher.

"Such a lot of people," said Emma, holding tight to Albert's arm.

They moved into the foyer, where a very dignified, diminutive, elderly colored man in a dark suit was taking coats. Albert was so much taller than everyone, and Marshall could see that people were looking at him. Albert gave his jacket to the colored man, carefully removing his gift from the pocket, and helped Emma out of her coat. Then he turned in a small half circle, his hand up to his birdlike face, and started toward the arched doorway to his right. He looked curious, almost bemused. The colored man watched him with wide, staring eyes. In his long life, clearly, he had never seen anything like Albert. The crowd seemed to be carrying him away, now, with Emma in tow. Marshall edged toward them, breathing cigarette smoke and the fumes of alcohol. A woman with wine on her breath said "Wait" to another woman, shouldering her way through the crowd toward the front entrance. Behind her was a man whose face Marshall recognized immediately as that of Mitch Brightman. "Tell that idiot I won't wait," Brightman said, speaking to the receding two women. "I mean it." He looked at Marshall. "Yes, are you with the birthday girl?"

"It's an honor to meet you," the young man said.

"Oh," said Brightman. "Well, all right. Certainly. How do." He pushed on past.

Marshall made his way to the living room, where Alice hurried forward to greet him. There was a pile of gifts in one corner, near the fireplace, and she took his from him and stepped over to put it with the others. She wore a blue gown that showed her shoulders to wonderful advantage, and her hair was arranged in a French twist, so that she looked really quite pretty. There was a bright, almost a desperate sparkle about her. "Where are Albert and Emma?"

"Here somewhere," Marshall said. "I thought they were in front of me. There's their gift to you—that book."

"It's a book?"

"Sorry," Marshall said.

"Well, I don't know what book, yet, do I."

"Remind me to tell you what happened when I asked Albert what it was."

"What can I get you to drink?"

It dawned on him that she smelled of wine, too. "Coke?"

"Come on." She pulled him through the throng, into another room, on the other side of which he saw Albert, still with that expression of mild curiosity on his face. "Have you met anyone yet?" Alice wanted to know.

"Not really."

"Mitch Brightman's agreed to visit your school."

"Already?"

Alice was delighted. "I told you it was no problem. My father got it done in less than a minute." She stepped to the table and asked another colored man—this one much younger-looking and much less interested in everyone—for two Cokes. "My father's over there with other people from the station, talking about some kidnapping in Venezuela. Have you been following it?"

"No." Marshall watched the man pour the Coke into clear glass cups. Alice took them and handed one to Marshall, then leaned close and murmured, "Do you believe all these people?"

"No."

"A birthday party for little old me." She drank the Coke. She was searching the crowd. "Come here." She led him across this room and through another archway to a closed porch and a little knot of young people, in the center of which stood another young colored man whose dusky skin was pitted around the jaw. "This is Stephen James." Next to Stephen James was Wilbur Soames, the new student Mr. D'Allessandro had brought in.

"How're you doing," Soames said.

"Hello," Marshall said.

"Stephen's with WSO. We're all with WSO. Except Wilbur, here."

"Nice to meet you," Marshall said to Stephen James.

"We're talking about tomorrow," said one of the others, a woman with braids on either side of her face and rounded features, like a series of circles someone might have drawn. Even her makeup appeared to have been drawn by a hand interested in arcs, the eyebrows bowed like half-finished circles, the rouge applied in two equal, round smudges on the cheeks, the lipstick inscribing a small oriental red circle when the mouth was closed. "I hope it doesn't get cold."

"This is my father's youngest sister and my aunt, who is exactly two months older than I am," Alice said.

The woman inclined her round head slightly and said, "Diane."

"Oh, didn't I say your name, Diane? I guess I didn't."

"We were talking about tomorrow," Diane went on. "I thought we'd ride down in the back of Stephen's old truck. If it's not too cold."

"It's supposed to be in the seventies," Stephen said. "But I have some friends coming, too, so I don't think the truck is such a good idea." His pitted jaw seemed to flex when he smiled, as though the expression had not begun as a smile. His deep black eyes bulged slightly. There was a space between his teeth on one side. He sipped his drink and looked around the room.

"Well, the more the merrier," said Alice. "I can't get Wilbur to say he'll come."

"You know," said Soames. "Other commitments."

"I'd like to come, too," Marshall said to her. "And I'll bet Albert would."

"Will that be all right?" Alice asked.

"The more the merrier," said Diane.

Alice turned to Wilbur Soames. "Well?" she said.

"I'll pass," he said, smiling. "Like I said, I'm busy tomorrow."

"Can we all fit in the truck?" Diane asked. "We could take my car."

"It's a big old pickup truck. From my daddy's farm in Virginia," said Stephen. "I just don't think it's the right vehicle."

"Your dad has a farm?" Marshall said.

The dark eyes took him in. "Sharecropper."

"Oh."

"He died last year."

"I'm sorry."

Stephen said, "He was almost ninety. Had me when he was sixty-six years old."

"Stephen is one of nineteen children. The second youngest."

"My father's gone, too," Marshall said.

"Was he a sharecropper?"

"Oh," Marshall said. "No."

"There's Mitch," Alice said. "Come on."

"Shouldn't I wait until your father introduces me?"

She seemed momentarily puzzled. "I'm going to introduce you."

"We already spoke, briefly."

"Come on," Alice said, taking him by the wrist again.

On their way across the room, they came upon Emma, standing alone, holding a drink with both hands and muttering something. "I'm counting," she said. "Albert said he'd be back in sixty seconds."

Soon after this, Albert was there, towering over them. Something about the low ceiling in the room made him appear even taller than he was. "Been looking for you guys," he said.

They all wended their way to the next room, a book-lined study in the center of which Mitchell Brightman stood talking, a lighted cigarette in one hand and a glass of whiskey in the other. He looked very tan and healthy, though there was a certain puffiness in the cheeks, a suggestion of thyroid trouble, Loretta had said, watching him deliver the news on TV. Up close, he looked as though he were still in makeup. His skin was surprisingly smooth for his age and his dark brown hair was thick and combed straight back, without a part. He might have been a man in his young thirties. Several people, including Mr. Atwater and Marshall's mother, had crowded around to listen to him. He was talking about the Civil Rights movement. "The real trouble, the next few years, is going to be in the North. That business in Philadelphia and Harlem this past summer, that was no fluke thing. The big cities— Chicago and Detroit and New York. Washington, D.C." He nodded as a small stir went through his listeners. "Mark my words. Powder kegs, the lot of them. There's a kind of prejudice that's unexpressed, tacit, quiet. In some important ways that's worse than the kind that's out in the open. At least the Southern kind of bigotry is clear and blunt and in front of you and you know something about how to deal with it. I'm gonna tell you, there's a lot of discontent and rage and hopelessness in the cities of the North. Seen it in my travels. Ingredients in a recipe for trouble. James Baldwin is right. *The Fire Next Time*." He waved the cigarette, seeming to watch the drifting line of smoke from it. Then he took a deep drag and blew the smoke at the ceiling.

"Mr. Brightman," Atwater said, "what was Jack Kennedy really like?"

Brightman did not respond at first. The question seemed to have put him off, somehow. Then he burst out. "Tremendous charm!" And took a drink.

The others waited.

He looked around, and again his eyes settled momentarily on Marshall before passing on over the other faces. "The most wonderful fun to be around—something about him." He took another drink. "Ah. Uh—a great president, too. In my opinion. All the way—blazing talent. Had the best memory of any man I ever knew, bar none. And I've known some pretty important men." He held the glass up and seemed about to propose a toast. But then he shook his head, and tears came to his eyes. "Some misfit ex-marine son of a bitch . . ."

Everyone was quiet.

"Don't like to talk about it. But let me tell you about—cooperation—"

Alice's father pushed through the crowd and murmured something in Brightman's ear. Brightman's face changed and showed interest. It looked as though Alice's father was telling him something funny.

"That's right," he said and nodded, taking another drag on the cigarette. "Happy to serve in any capacity, Patrick." He held the glass up. "Battle of good and evil."

"I think Daddy's going to announce our engagement," Alice said.

Brightman looked around at everyone again. "Where was I?"

"Kennedy," said Atwater. "Cooperation." He was leaning in, avid, one arm around Loretta, the other around some woman, his sport coat pulled back so that it looked like the button that held it closed might come loose.

"Oh, yeah. Unspoken agreements, see—" He halted, looked around him. Then he shifted his weight and seemed to throw something off. "Never mind about unspoken agreements. I don't want to talk about it."

"You were talking about President Kennedy," one of the others said.

"Kennedy," Brightman said. "Right. Kennedy came back from Palm Beach one time, you might've seen this, and announced that he'd been with the people and talking with the people, building it up, right, and then he says, 'And I've come back to Washington and I'm against my entire program.' We all fell apart, one of the biggest laughs I ever heard in that room. Great wit. And great timing. We used to love it when he'd call on May Craig at the press conferences. And he'd do it knowing there'd be something funny in it. Wonderful wit. And great recall. Did I say that? Faces, names. History—May Craig . . ." Brightman paused and seemed to consider. "History," he said again, a man expressing exasperation with something. It was as though Mr. Brightman were talking about a personal friend, and this had its effect on the others. "Tell you what," he said, raising his voice a little, "we're in for some awful times, folks. Little wars, firestorms all over the globe. South America, Africa, Eastern Europe, India, China, Southeast Asia. That's what they've set out to do—beat us down with little police actions like Korea. One after the other. Keep us running from hot spot to hot spot until the till's empty, then move right in. Walk right in. Hell, they won't even need any bombs."

"What should we do?" a woman in a feathered hat asked.

Brightman looked at her and smiled. "Pardon?" he said. Then he reached over and took the end of the feather in his fingers. "Can you write with this?" He let go and gave a small bow. "Madam, that's a most ridiculous hat."

"I asked what should we do."

"What would you *like* to do? I'm open to suggestions."

"He's lit," said the woman, moving away.

"Come on," Alice said to Marshall, "I'll introduce you."

"The strategy," Brightman said, to the room, "is to get women with big feathers in their hats to think you're tanked . . ." He paused. "That may save us in the end."

"Mitch," Alice said, "this is my fiancé, Walter Marshall."

Brightman smiled at her, gave another little courtly bow, and then turned his attention to the young man. He stared, slowly extended the hand with the cigarette in it, paused and remembered the cigarette, put it in his mouth, and reached again. His hand was moist, and utterly limp at first. But when Marshall squeezed as his mother had taught him to do, Brightman squeezed back. "Walter Marshall," he said. "I knew a Walter Marshall once."

"My father," Marshall told him, trying to suppress his excitement.

"Good for you," said Brightman, letting go of his hand. "Where's he living now?"

"He died two years ago in Arizona, sir."

"You from Arizona?"

"No, sir."

Brightman tottered a little, taking the cigarette from his mouth and blowing smoke, nodding, blinking. "Died? Did you say died?"

"He always liked your reporting, though."

The hand with the cigarette in it waved this away. "Showbiz."

"He said you have integrity."

"He didn't know me that well."

"No," Marshall said. "I know. He told me that—"

"Sorry for it," Brightman said. "You must miss him."

"I do, but I didn't really know him. He left us when I was small."

"He said all this about me when you were small?" Brightman seemed pleased at the prospect.

"No, sir. He came back here for a few days, the summer before he passed away."

Brightman stared. "Trying to undo old wrongs."

"I don't really know, sir. He wanted to see us again."

"It's Walter's school that you're going to visit," Alice put in.

Brightman smiled. "We'll do some good."

"Y-yes—yes, sir."

He started out of the room, and the people around him moved to let him through. Mr. Atwater stepped in at his side, pulling Loretta with him. "This is the boy's mother," Atwater said, indicating Loretta. "I'm with her. I teach social studies and I'm principal out here at Fairlington Heights. I'm Clark Atwater, sir. I introduced myself to you earlier."

Brightman gave them a vague acknowledging expression. "Atwatersir?"

"No." Atwater's head dipped and then tilted. He straightened, seemed to be trying to stand taller. "Atwater." He spelled the name.

"Good," said Brightman. "Good for you." He took a drag of the cigarette, paused as if trying to absorb the information, then went on, with Atwater talking loudly, following him. "Social studies, civics, and history, that's me. I was just telling them the same things about the little wars. I know exactly what you mean. The continent of Asia—" They went on into the next room and along the hallway, and a moment later they were at the far end of the stairwell, near the front door. Atwater had Brightman's ear now, and Marshall's mother was leaning in, listening to the two of them, looking interested.

"Somehow I want to introduce your mother to my father," Alice said. "If I could get her away from that awful little man."

"I'm sorry about it," Marshall told her. "There wasn't anything she could do to get out of it. She's thinking about marrying him. I'm afraid she might."

"You can't like him."

"I don't want him as a stepfather."

"Do you like my party?" Alice said suddenly.

"It's great," he said.

"You're not sorry you came?"

He looked at her.

"You don't wish you were with that pretty German girl?"

"What?"

"Wait here," she said and then moved off.

A moment later, a man walking on his hands came through from the hall, followed by another who was scuttling along like a crab, on all fours. There was a loud bump, and a roar of laughter from the next room, and the man walking on his hands came back through, followed by a woman who carried a drink in either hand and looked annoyed. Marshall followed them into the small side porch, where a woman with an absurd hive of sparkling red hair sat reading palms. She looked at Marshall, and without warning reached over and took him by the wrist, turning his hand ceiling-ward. "A short life line," she said. "Not necessarily tragic." The man standing next to her looked down at Marshall's hand.

"I don't see it."

"What month were you born in," the woman asked Marshall. It was spoken in the tone of a command.

"April," he said.

She looked at his palm again. "You have ambition," she said.

He was pleased. "Yes."

She studied the palm, then smiled up at him. "Do you want children?"

"Someday," he said.

Again, she looked at his palm, traced something with a red fin-gernail, a thin thread of ticklishness along the inside of his hand, at the base of the fingers. "You want to rise up in the world and do important things."

Marshall glanced at the man, then nodded at her.

"Did you ask to have your palm read?" the man wanted to know. He seemed vaguely agitated; a face full of bumps and tufts of hair, jaws that seemed puffed with something unpleasant.

The woman let go of Marshall's hand while speaking to the man. "Don't lose it, Fred. It's a party, for God's sake."

"You're making an idiot of yourself, Margaret."

Marshall backed out of there, into the room where Alice had asked him to wait. People crowded past him, some carrying little plates of finger food and glasses of wine.

Across the room, Albert stood, holding a mug of beer. Emma had her hands wrapped around his elbow, and seemed to be listening raptly to everything around her. Marshall went over to them, and Albert shook hands—as though they had not come in together in the first place. Emma said, "Get him to talk, Walter. He's so quiet tonight."

"Alice looks beautiful," Albert said.

"Do you know what just happened here?" Marshall asked him.

"No."

"Some guy went through there walking on his hands. I followed him in there and a lady read my palm."

"I didn't see," Albert said. "What did she say?"

"I have a short life line." Marshall looked at his own palm, then dismissed the thought as a temptation. "I don't believe in that stuff, of course."

"Of course not," Albert said.

They were quiet, watching the swirl of faces.

Emma said, "Usually he talks my ear off. Especially in a gathering like this. He likes to tell me what he sees. What everyone looks like and what's on the walls. But not tonight."

"To tell the truth," Albert said, "I'm feeling a bit tired."

"Here they are," said Alice, leading her father into the group. He had his shirtsleeves rolled up, exposing thick, muscular forearms covered with dark hair. He was a big man, with heavy shoulders and a hulking way of standing, as if he were carrying some invisible weight. "Daddy, these are some dear friends of mine. Albert and Emma."

Her father's greeting was somewhat perfunctory, and there was a slight hesitation when he offered his hand to Emma. Then, evidently realizing the situation, he reached down and took Emma's hand briefly. "Very nice to meet you," he said.

"And you remember Walter."

"I do. I suppose congratulations are in order," Patrick Kane said, shaking hands. His grip was almost painful. Alice put her arm over his shoulders, and kissed the side of his face. He wiped the kiss off without appearing to be aware that he had done so, and she kissed him once more. "Well," he said to them, rubbing the side of his face again. "I understand your mother's here."

"Yes, sir."

"Good." This seemed to have satisfied him. "Well, you people enjoy yourselves."

"You have to meet Walter's mother. She's here somewhere."

"Well, then, suppose you go and get her," Mr. Kane said simply.

"Don't move." Alice walked off through the crowd, and in a second two men edged in to speak to Mr. Kane. One of them Marshall recognized as the man on all fours who had been following the hand walker. He and Mr. Kane and the other man were apparently golf partners. They made their way to the other side of the room so Mr. Kane could get another drink.

When they had gone, Albert wondered aloud if there might be a place nearby to sit down, and Marshall led him and Emma down a corridor of entrances to other crowded rooms, until they came out into a brightly lighted space that turned out to be the kitchen, where the bottles of liquor were laid out and the dinner buffet was being prepared.

Everyone here was colored. They were all busy keeping things going. Marshall watched them, not sitting down. Emma had taken a chair at the table, and had her hands folded in her lap. Albert looked at her, and then he looked at Marshall.

"Crowds can get her down a little, sometimes," he murmured.

The head person in the kitchen was a big woman with upper arms the size of barrels, and small, delicate-looking, bony wrists. Her skin was a deep, smooth brown, and her hair was in a tight ring around her face. She held out a cookie to Albert. "For the young lady."

"Thank you, ma'am," Albert said.

She shooed this away. "Look lak she feelin' this mess."

"Yes, ma'am."

"Big mess o' people. Makes me nervous, too."

Albert nodded.

"She's pale as a ghost. Honey, you wont some wata? Sonthin' warm?"

"No," Emma said, smiling. "I'm fine, thank you."

"Look lak a li'l slip of a ghost. Prutty as a June day, tho."

"She's always a little pale," Albert said.

"I can shore see that, honey."

The others laughed.

"But ain't you prutty, tho," she said to Emma, who smiled.

"Yes, ma'am," Albert said.

"An' ain't you a tall, hansome young man, suh."

"I think you need some glasses," Albert said to her. "I'm tall, all right."

"You a good man, I can see that."

"Well," Albert said, "I'm good and ugly."

She laughed. "Honey, Minnie don' mean nothin'. You know that."

"Yes, ma'am," Albert said, smiling.

"You as tall as I'm big aroun', honey." Her laugh was high and loud, and it made the others laugh, too, though Albert's joke about eyesight had made Marshall uneasy.

"Y'all just set, an make yourself comfy," the colored woman said. Then she turned and began speaking to one of the other kitchen workers. There were trays of drinks to be carried into the next room. "Git on wid yuh. Do like I say, na. You ain't gwine spend the evenin' settin' roun' lak de whorl owes you no livin'."

"Alice certainly has a lot of friends," Emma said when Albert had given her the cookie. She sat there chewing contentedly, holding it between her index finger and thumb as though it were as delicate as a soap bubble. A few crumbs had broken off and fallen into her lap.

When Alice came back, she casually reached down and brushed the crumbs away as Emma put the last of the cookie in her mouth. "Thank you," Emma said.

"My father's going to announce us," Alice said to Marshall. "Hurry."

Emma stood, and Albert took her by the arm.

"You certainly have a lot of friends," she said.

But Alice had moved off, was already partway across the next room, waving at them, gesturing for them to hurry. In another room, the one beyond this one off the kitchen, one voice was speaking. Alice parted the backs in the doorway, pushing through with small pleadings for tolerance. Marshall was being pulled along now, and he felt exposed, rushed, the object of all these staring eyes. The engagement would really be out in the open now, and it was as though he had to steel himself to the idea all over again, master all over again the sense that the whole thing was a kind of playacting, a fraud. He looked back and saw that Albert and Emma were left behind. "Alice," he said, "hold it." When Alice realized what had happened, she stopped and hurried back to where Albert and Emma waited. Albert looked confused now, his deep-set eyes glazed over with indecision. His hand had come to the bony cheek under one eye, and he seemed to be picking at something there.

"I don't suppose there's anything—" he began.

"Oh, Albert," said Alice, taking his wrist. "Come on."

They all pushed through the throng, holding hands, led by Alice, with Marshall holding Emma's hand now. At the center of this large room, under the bright ceiling light, Mitchell Brightman stood talking. He had one hand in his pocket and was wavering a little, managing to hold his balance but slurring his speech. He was talking about a little baby girl toddling around a newsroom during the reporting on D day, the sixth of June 1944.

Through the small space between his crooked elbow and his rumpled sport coat, Marshall saw a face staring at him fixedly, and realized with a shock that it was the toy man, Marcus. He blinked, and looked again, and the face was gone.

"That man is here," he said to Albert.

"What?" Albert said, bending down. "What did you say?"

"The guy. The guy who was threatening Mrs. D'Allessandro. He's *here*."

Albert looked at Mitchell Brightman. "Where?"

"Shh," Alice said.

Marshall started toward the other side of the room, but she took hold of his wrist. "Come on," she said. "He's introduced us."

Everyone was applauding. People stepped aside to allow them to move into the center of the circle, and now a cheer arose. Alice held his hand up, a victory gesture, as though they had just been introduced at one of the political conventions, and the applause grew louder. Her father stepped close and poured a glass of champagne for her, then handed the bottle to Marshall, who searched the faces for that of the toy man, and saw instead Clark Atwater with his arm around Loretta's shoulder, kissing the side of her face. Someone was calling for a speech; it was Brightman, who held a glass of whiskey up as if to show its color under the light.

Alice stepped right into the role. "Well," she said, swinging Marshall's hand, "I'm so happy to be my father's girl, among all these friends."

There was another cheer.

"That's good," Mr. Kane said, applauding loudly. "Let's quit while you're ahead."

"I know my father thought I'd never do it," she said. And then repeated it, talking over him as he tried again to interrupt her. "I know he was getting tired of having a spinster for a daughter."

"Not true," Mr. Kane said.

"And I know he's happy for me because he knows I won't be under his feet anymore—"

Everyone applauded.

"But mostly he's worried because he knows I've picked a young man who reminds him of himself, thirty years ago."

Cheers and whistles, and everyone was looking at Marshall, who kept searching among the faces for the one face.

"I used to say that the worst thing any young man could do is remind me of myself at that age," said Mr. Kane, and then in the laughter that followed, he took a big swallow of the champagne.

"Where's Mrs. Marshall?" Alice said. "Mrs. Marshall—"

The young man saw Atwater force Loretta into the circle. Alice took her by the wrists and completed the motion, so that now the four of them were standing there while the others applauded and cheered. Loretta shook hands with Mr. Kane, who seemed anxious to remove himself, looking around at the crowd and drinking from his glass again. Alice asked for and was given a glass, into which she got Marshall to pour some of the champagne. She handed it to

Loretta, and then led everyone in another toast. "To the new family," she said. For a few seconds they were all lined up there—Marshall, Alice, Marshall's mother, and Alice's father. The people in the room applauded again.

Alice turned to her father and said something, smiling, and indicated Loretta, who also smiled. Mr. Kane gave the subtlest bow of his head, then patted Loretta's shoulder and headed away, across the room.

"Bless you all," Alice said.

There was more applause, but the moment had ended, people were wandering off into different groups. The line had started for the buffet. Several people were already eating, sitting with plates in their laps on chairs around the room. Marshall recognized the man who had been walking on his hands and pointed him out to Alice. "Who's that?"

"That's one of Everett Dirksen's speechwriters. Or he used to be."

"Everett Dirksen, the senator from Illinois? That Everett Dirksen?"

"Mmm-hmm. He quit because Dirksen tried to block the Civil Rights bill. And now it looks like he might go to work for CBS. I don't remember his name."

"He was—"

"I know," Alice said, interrupting him. "He's had too much whiskey."

Mitchell Brightman had dropped down on a couch near the windows looking out on the backyard, and Clark Atwater had seated himself at his side. Loretta stood before them, holding two drinks. When she saw Marshall, she smiled and indicated with a tilting of her head that he should kiss her cheek. He did so.

"What do you think?" he said.

"About what?"

"Alice's father."

"He's nice."

Marshall waited. "And?"

She shrugged. "We said hello. I had the feeling he might've preferred a more formal occasion for us to meet, before this kind of—festivity. It's hard to say much—" She broke off.

"India and China are the two to worry about now," Atwater was saying. "Because of the populations. Not Russia at all. Surely you've read Toynbee?"

Mitchell Brightman had his drink resting on his abdomen. He lifted his head and drank, then let his head fall back. "I'm hungry," he said.

"Toynbee sees this as the last living civilization."

"Yes. Interesting." The broadcaster's tone was not quite magisterial. He lifted his head and sipped his whiskey again, then looked at Marshall with eyes that did not take him in or appear to recognize him. What the eyes communicated was exasperation with this Atwater fellow, who had apparently been stalking him from the earliest part of the evening. A moment later, Mr. D'Allessandro stepped into the circle, edging Marshall to one side. "Excuse me," he said. He put cushions out of the way and got himself seated on the other side of Brightman. "Allow me to introduce myself," he began.

Brightman had turned toward Atwater. "Why is it," he said with a brittle smile, "that everywhere I turn at this festive occasion, with all these people, from all these different walks of life, why is it that everywhere I turn *you're* there, too. Are there six of you? One for every room?"

Atwater laughed too loudly, reaching up to take one of the drinks from Loretta, who leaned down and said, "Come on, Clark."

Mitchell Brightman seemed to be agitating somehow, as though he wanted to shake the couch out of its place, but then it was clear that he was trying to stand. When he gained his feet, he put one hand on Marshall's shoulder to support himself, then walked unsteadily away. Atwater had stood, too, and he leaned into the young man. "Follow him, boy. Your father knew him."

"Clark," said Marshall's mother, "can't we go now?"

Atwater looked at her. "We just got here, L'retta. We haven't even got our food yet. There's people here with a lot of influence, famous people, and you're not mixing with them."

She put her drink to her lips and turned a bit, someone trying to get out of a column of bad air. Stepping to the wall, she gazed back at her son. Mr. D'Allessandro hadn't moved from the couch, and he looked crestfallen. "Did I say something to offend?" he said.

"Mr. D'Allessandro," said Marshall, "Marcus is here, isn't he?"

D'Allessandro looked around. "Where?"

"I saw him."

"Is my wife here?" he said.

"I haven't seen your wife."

"I don't know," Mr. D'Allessandro said. "I shouldn't have come." He had gotten to his feet and started off in the direction of Alice's father, who was standing on the other side of the room listening to some woman talk. The woman spoke with sweeping hand gestures, somehow keeping her wine from spilling. Marshall watched them for a few seconds, then went through all the rooms, looking for the little man named Marcus and for Mrs. D'Allessandro. He saw Albert and Emma in a corner of one room, seeming to stare out. Emma was holding his hand, and he had the other, as usual, up to his face. He had that aghast look again. "Aren't you going to eat?" Marshall asked him.

"I'm waiting for cake," Albert said.

"Do you know the D'Allessandros are here?"

He nodded. "I saw."

"Did you see Mrs. D'Allessandro?"

"I saw him, not her."

In another room, Alice and Mitchell Brightman sat in a window seat. Alice was pouring wine for him. An elderly woman wearing bright, metal-framed half glasses introduced herself as Alice's great-aunt Arlene, cornering Marshall on the side porch. She began talking about Alice as a little girl. Always so precocious, she said, gazing above the lenses at Marshall's chest. It was as if she couldn't lift her head any higher. "We all thought she'd end up running off with a sheik or something."

"That's interesting," Marshall said and started to edge away from her.

"Wait. You have to tell me about yourself. Alice's father thinks you're delusional."

"I'm sorry?"

"I'm only partly joking," she said. "Tell me—do you have designs on the *presidency*?"

It was as if she had struck him in the stomach.

"Well," she said, smiling, so that the little eyes almost disappeared in skin, "*do* you?"

"I don't know what you're talking about," he said.

"I'm only partly joking when I say it, you know."

He waited for her to continue.

Alice walked over and put her thin arm through his. "Arlene, what're you asking my fiancé about?"

"I'm only partly joking," Arlene said again, as if this were the final point she wanted to make. She turned and walked away, looking back to offer her partly joking smile.

"Pay no attention to her," Alice said. "She hasn't had a kind word for anyone in years."

"I don't think your father likes me," Marshall said.

She shook her head and appeared to pout. "Aren't you going to wish me a happy birthday?"

"Of course," he said. "I didn't know you asked the D'Allessandros."

She had spoken through him.

"Pardon?" he said.

"Do I get a birthday kiss?"

"Here?"

She took a step closer. "You want to go upstairs?"

He took a breath and couldn't answer.

"You're so cute." She laughed and touched his cheek. "I'm so happy. I'm really happy tonight, Walter. Are you coming with us tomorrow? We're going to a funeral service first. A friend of Minnie's, and Stephen's. Well, she was sort of a figure, around here. With the people in the kitchen—Minnie and them. One hundred six years old."

He nodded. It was partly reflexive. "I saw that little man here. He must've come in with the D'Allessandros."

"Think of living a hundred and six years. She saw absolutely everything that happened in this century. All of it—the whole coming of the modern age, Walter. And Minnie says she could remember things about the Civil War. Imagine. She was born into slavery, here in Virginia."

He said, "Alice, did you invite the D'Allessandros?"

"I haven't seen them."

"Wait," he said. "Did you say we're going to a funeral tomorrow?"

"That's first. In the morning."

Her father appeared from the doorway and reached for her, pulling her away. "Okay, kid. Time to eat. Then cut the cake and open your gifts."

Marshall waited in line with them, and when they had filled their plates, he followed them out to the side porch. He had filled his plate with bread and butter. Alice wolfed down a big helping of pasta salad, talking all the while. She didn't really know the old woman whose funeral they would attend tomorrow; their going would be a gesture of togetherness. They would pay their respects, and then they would travel together to a restaurant in Maryland that Alice knew was still refusing service to colored people. The owner was using excuses to do it, but so far it had been discouragingly successful. The whole day was planned, and she was happy talking about it with Marshall, keeping her voice down through some of it so her father couldn't hear. Apparently, he was not interested in having his daughter involved in any protests.

Her father ate quietly, concentrating on his food, and now and then she would ask him if he was listening.

"I'm listening," he said.

"Good." She waited a moment. Then, "Walter and I are already sexually involved."

He kept eating, watching the others on the far side of the room.

"I'm expecting, in fact."

"Yeah?" her father said, chewing.

"Twins."

"Good."

"We've been swapping with another couple, of course, so we're not sure if these are actually Walter's twins or our Jamaican friend's."

He looked at her. "What're you talking about?"

"I said I always wished I'd had a twin."

"Oh." He went on eating.

She winked at Marshall, then went on talking, to Marshall now, about her happiness and being in love. Marshall kept searching the shifting crowd in the room, and found that he was unable to eat much. The D'Allessandros and their odd friend were nowhere to be seen.

"Okay," Mr. Kane said, rising. "Let's cut the cake and open the presents."

"I'm not finished eating," Alice told him. "I want some more pasta."

"You're gonna blow up like a balloon one day. I swear to God I never saw anybody eat like you do without gaining weight. Come on." He had taken hold of her elbow and was pulling her into the next room. From somewhere, the big woman from the kitchen, Minnie, glided past and took their plates as they passed through the hallway and into the living room.

All the birthday gifts were stacked next to an easy chair to the left of the fireplace, and straight-backed chairs from the dining room had been placed in a semicircle around it. The cake was on a portable table in the center of the room. Mitchell Brightman got the attention of the crowd and led them in singing "Happy Birthday." Alice held onto Marshall, resting her head on his shoulder as they sang. There was yet another cheer, and again she held Marshall's hand up, waving to everyone. Then she cut a few slices of the cake, and her father began passing them out. Finally, he called Minnie from the kitchen, and she took over. There was a lot of confusion and noise, and someone put a Beatles record on, "I Saw Her Standing There." Alice took Marshall's other hand and started dancing. There were more cheers, and others commenced dancing, too. Marshall saw Atwater and his mother doing the jitterbug, and now, to his relief, Mitchell Brightman cut in on him to dance jerkily, precariously, with Alice. The man who had written speeches for Everett Dirksen was standing on his hands again, in a corner of the room, but no one was paying any attention to him. When the music shifted into a soft ballad, the man dropped to his feet and lay down along the floorboards, his hands folded under the side of his head, apparently asleep. Across the room, Albert and Emma moved stiffly in a slow dance, rocking slowly back and forth, looking like statues coming loose at their moorings.

Finally, it was time for Alice to open her gifts. She sat in the chair, picked up one of the packages, and shook it. "It's so light," she said. Her father stood nearby, talking to another woman, low, stirring his drink with one finger. The woman had her hair in a bun on top of her head, and her glasses came to sharp points, which gave her very white face a cruel look. She nodded, leaning close to him while he went on. Alice said, "Should I read the card, Daddy?"

He hadn't heard her.

"Daddy?"

Now he seemed to come to himself. "What? Open the gifts."

"I'll read the card."

"Just get on with it, kid. You got a lot of loot there."

"The card says 'Happy Birthday, Love, Dad.'" She held it up and made a gesture as if to say "So much for fatherly love," then tossed it behind her and began tearing at the gift wrap. Marshall edged away, out of the circle and back toward the kitchen. There were several knots of people in each room, talking quietly, some of them still eating. He saw Atwater and Loretta sitting on a couch, sipping drinks and watching everyone else. Loretta lifted her hand and waved at him. In the kitchen, Emma was seated at the table, while Albert stood over her, drinking a glass of water. He had one hand on her shoulder.

"I think we'll be heading out soon," he said, not quite looking at Marshall. "It's a long haul back into town for me. And Emma's tired."

A moment later, Atwater walked in. "I thought I saw you come in here," he said to Marshall. Then he turned to Minnie, who was going over a silver cup with a soft cloth. "We need a kitchen towel," Atwater said. "We've had a spill."

"Yassuh."

"You don't have to 'sir' me," Atwater said. "I don't believe in any of that stuff. I'm all for tolerance. Integration now, that's me."

Minnie simply stared back at him. "Yassuh," she said. Then she produced a hand towel and took a step toward him. "Where is this mess you wont cleaned up?"

"Oh, I'll do it," Atwater said.

But she held the towel back from him. "Na, suh. This is my woik. Where is it?"

Atwater led the way out.

Emma stood. "Take me in to say good-bye to Alice."

"She's opening her gifts," Marshall said.

Emma reached for Albert's hand, and made a gentle slapping motion into the palm of it. Albert started out of the room with her. "We'll just say our good-byes," he said. "I'll see you tomorrow, I guess."

Marshall watched them go. And then he was alone. He looked at the windows, saw the light from an outbuilding on the far side of the yard. The light shone through the merest reflection of himself. A half-moon was sailing over the tops of the trees. Then, out there, in the cold yard, he saw Mr. D'Allessandro walk into view. Mr. D'Allessandro stood with his hands over his eyes, as though to shield them from blinding light. His shirt was pulled out, and the wind had picked his hair up. He looked hurt. He seemed to falter, his hands dropping to his sides. Marshall opened the door, pushed the screen out, and stepped down off the stoop. He looked back at the lighted windows of the house, the brightness there. By the time his eyes were accustomed to the dark, Mr. D'Allessandro was gone.

"Mr. D'Allessandro?" he said. "Sir?"

Silence. A little, chilly breeze stirring in the rustling branches. Down the driveway, through the hedge that bordered that end of the property, some people were getting into a car. He thought he heard a man's laughter.

"Hello?"

Car doors slammed. The engine caught, the car pulled away into the night.

Marshall went back in among the guests. Some people were out on the side porch, laughing and singing. Others had gone out to stand on the stoop and look at the sky. At one point, standing in the arched entryway to the porch, he came face-to-face with Alice's father, who took hold of his arm above the elbow, leaning close. "Listen. You want to marry my daughter?"

"Yes—yes, sir."

"You're not messing around?"

"No." The younger man's voice caught and struck the falsetto note. He faked a cough and said again, "No."

"It's not just so you can get Mitch for that school?"

"Oh," Marshall said. "Oh, no. *No*. No, sir. We'd already—I

asked Alice before that happened—before I knew about it—" Mr. Kane's grip was tightening on his arm. "I swear to you, sir. It's—I'm gonna marry her. Really."

"You love her."

Marshall nodded. He could not have spoken now if he wanted to.

"Okay, well, I want you to understand something. You listening good?"

Again, the young man nodded.

"I've killed better men than you," Mr. Kane said, also nodding. "You know what I'm saying, son? I've shot men dead. Tough, hardened soldiers with a history of brutal behavior. Germans. Veterans of war. And I shot them dead, or ran them through with a bayonet. It happened. You understand me? I don't want my little girl to get hurt." He smiled, as though what he had said were a witticism. Then he murmured, "Excuse me," and moved through to the other room.

Marshall went shakily back to the kitchen, where he encountered Minnie and the young man, Stephen, to whom he had been introduced earlier. They were sitting at the table drinking coffee.

"H'lo," Minnie said, rising. "You look lak you're a little green around the gills. Lemme git you sonthin'."

"No, ma'am," Marshall said. "I'm fine."

"You sho?"

He nodded.

She sat back down. There was a fluidity to her motions that seemed incongruous for someone as big as she was. She nodded at Stephen, who leaned toward her across the table and said something low, then sat back again. They smiled at the young man. The two of them seemed to be waiting for him to leave. He felt that things had gotten beyond him somehow, and he was bungling in trying to catch up. He said, "Quite a party," wanting to talk.

"Sho is," said Minnie without enthusiasm.

"Minnie's friend passed, recently," Stephen said. "It's her service, tomorrow."

"Oh," said Marshall. "I heard. I'm so sorry."

"She lived a full, long life," the other said in the tone of someone trying to ease a shock. "Eva was born into slavery, wasn't she, Miss Minnie?"

"Yes she was. One of the fus' things she evah remembuh is Yankees on the poach, when she lived in Winchester in 1864. Whud'n nothin' but six yeahs old at the time. She used to tell about that. How she got scared and run. She talked about that the day she passed. One hundred six yeahs old, too. Seem lak that mem'ry was clearuh than some things."

"She must've been a wonderful person," Marshall said.

Stephen put his cup down and stood. "Thanks for the coffee, Miss Minnie."

"Yassuh."

He looked at Marshall. "See you."

When he was gone, the big woman got to her feet and held onto the back of the chair for a moment. Then she moved briskly to the sink, and turned on the tap. Marshall stepped to her side. "Can I help?"

She stared at him.

"You wash and I'll dry."

"Ain't you the groom, honey?"

"Yes," he said, remembering.

"You betta git on out there, han't you?"

"Alice is opening her gifts," he said.

"This ain't no place for you, honey. You g'on, na. Don't be gittin' in Minnie's way."

He hesitated a moment.

"G'on, na." She stepped into his place and edged him aside with a massive elbow. And when she looked at him, her eyes were fierce, fixed on him out of a frown, a lowered brow. Her big nostrils flared. "Git. I got enough to worry about. You done found your way in enough as it is, all of you. Git on witchya, na."

He went out, chastened, still more flustered. He thought he might even be sick. He had been trying to be friendly, had been wrong about something, and he couldn't understand what it was. Surely he had not meant his gesture the way Atwater had meant *his*; he was accustomed to helping his mother in the kitchen. He had merely wanted the feel of ordinary work, to calm himself. And he had wanted to help if he could, with the grief over the lost friend, Eva.

Out in the other room, Alice was still tearing at packages. He waited by the doorway until she had opened the last one, his own.

He looked around for his mother, for Atwater. Albert and Emma had apparently gone home.

Later, Alice's father and another man helped Mitchell Brightman upstairs to bed. He was spending the night, Alice said in a low voice, because he was about to pass out anyway. The party was breaking up. She asked Marshall to wait for her, though Atwater and Loretta were in their coats and standing by the front door. She went upstairs, following her father and the two men, and she was gone several minutes. When she came back down, she put her arms around Marshall's neck and kissed him on the mouth. The force of her slight body suddenly pressing against him almost caused him to fall. He staggered back against the frame of the entryway, and put his arms around her. He was aware of all these others, including his mother, watching. When he thought of her father, he tightened his hold.

"I'll pick you up around ten," Alice murmured in his ear. "Dress up nice. Church nice, okay? A tie and jacket. Something dark. Black, if you have it. Albert's going, too."

"Walter," said his mother. "Please."

Alice walked over and hugged her. "I just know we're going to be great pals," she said.

Loretta smiled, but her eyes were troubled. Marshall knew the look.

"Good night," Alice said. "Mom."

"Call me Loretta."

"Good night, Loretta."

"Good night—" Marshall's mother paused. "Dear. Tell your father we said good night."

Out in the dark, walking to the car, Mr. Atwater said, "That Brightman's just a mouthpiece, if you ask me. I don't think he's read Toynbee."

The other two said nothing.

When they pulled in front of the apartment building, he said, "I'd like some coffee."

"Not tonight," Loretta said. She got out of the car, and held onto the door frame for a moment. The blinking neon on the roof illuminated her in a weird, red-and-yellow glow. Marshall walked around the car and took her arm at the elbow.

"Little dizzy," she said.

"That's my job," said Atwater, shouldering Marshall aside.

"Clark, I wish you'd go on home now," she said. "Please."

"I need some coffee, L'retta. I can't drive home like this."

She sighed. "Okay."

"Wait," Marshall said. "Just a minute."

His mother put one hand on his chest. And then the three of them moved a few feet along the sidewalk in front of the building. Atwater leaned on the boy, pushing him away. "This is goddamn ridiculous," he said. "Pardon my French."

"We're fine, Walter," said Loretta. "Go on in. We'll—I'll just be a minute."

"We're all going in," Atwater said.

"Go on, Walter."

He went on in to the lobby, and up the stairs, and when he entered the apartment he hurried to the window and looked out. He could see the car and the empty street, but nothing much else. They were standing too close to the building for him to be able to make them out. He could hear Atwater's voice, but couldn't distinguish words. There was anger in it, though, and a kind of smugness, too, as though this tone were not under any circumstances to be found wanting or inappropriate. He opened the window and called out, "Mom?"

Loretta stepped out and looked up. "I'll be right up, sweetie."

"If I hear any more yelling," Marshall said to her, "I'm coming down."

And now Atwater stepped out. "Just shut the goddamn window."

"I think I'll leave it open," Marshall told him. Atwater looked at Loretta, then walked to the car and opened the door.

"Come on and have some coffee if you want it," she said.

"Good night," said Atwater.

"I said, come on and have some coffee. Please."

"Please?"

Loretta repeated the word.

Marshall closed the window.

Chapter
10

*H*is dreams were all of the many faces, and the one face. The staring, small face, gliding in and out of scenes. And then he was laboring through some thickness of air, trying to reach his mother. In the morning, he found her asleep in her chair, wearing her robe and slippers, but with her stockings still on. She had spent at least part of the night cleaning; the dust mop was leaning against the wall by her chair. There was no sign of Atwater. As he moved through the room, into the kitchen to get himself some cereal, she woke and yawned, as if satisfied with her night's sleep. She came creakily into the kitchen and put coffee on. He watched her without speaking.

After a time, it seemed clear that she was avoiding the prospect of speech. She went into the other room while the coffee perked, and put the mop away. He heard her puttering around in her room. He ate the cereal, washed the bowl and spoon and put them away, then went to his own room and got into his dark blue blazer, black slacks, white shirt, and dark blue tie. When he was dressed, he stood for a minute in front of the mirror, assuming the poses of Kennedy at a news conference, pointing, choosing another questioner. He had the hair just about right now. He stood close and tried the smile. His teeth weren't quite straight enough, or big enough. He stepped back and pointed again, looking serious, presidential. It would be a picture the news services would circulate, perhaps, after he was assassinated. The thought brought him back to himself. It was embarrassing, like waking from an erotic dream. He went back into the kitchen and sat at the table again, restless, worried about this daydream side of him that could take him so far away. His mother came back in, having changed into her dark green dress, the back of which wasn't zipped. She stood at the counter and poured the coffee.

"Clark and I are going out today," she said without turning. "You look like you must have plans, too."

He decided against telling her what Alice and her friends were planning. He said, "Nothing special."

"You're all dressed up. You want to look nice for your lady love."

He said nothing.

"Does that embarrass you, son?"

"No."

"You seem—well, embarrassed about it all. I thought you looked that way last night at the party, too. Why should a young man be embarrassed about his engagement. It's not as if this is some game among children at school. Alice is a grown woman."

If there was anything to say in reply to these observations of hers, he didn't know what it might be.

A moment later, she said, "Zip me up?"

He stood, and did so, then sat down again at the table.

She turned and leaned on the counter, holding the saucer with her cup of coffee on it. "I had too much tea last night." She lifted the cup to her lips.

He said nothing.

And she paused. "Are you mad at me?"

"No," he said.

"You hate Clark."

"Hate is a mortal sin."

This seemed to irritate her. "Okay, you don't like him."

Marshall said nothing.

"Maybe he's not much," she said. "But I have to work for him."

"Does that mean you have to take his guff?" Marshall said.

She spoke before he had finished the question. "Yes!" Then she slapped the cup back into its saucer. "It does."

They were both quiet. Perhaps a minute passed. She sipped the coffee, and he sat staring at his hands on the table.

"Want some coffee?" she asked.

"No, thanks."

"He's not all bad sometimes, Walter. He has his moments."

"I don't like the way he talks to you."

"It's just his way. He doesn't mean it."

"It sounds terrible."

A moment later, she said, "His intentions are honorable."

"I don't want to talk about it," Marshall said.

"No," she said, looking at her hands. "I guess not."

A little later, Atwater honked for her, and she hurried out the door, leaving him with admonitions to be careful, to put away his dishes if he was eating lunch at home, and not to be out late. He went to the window and watched the car pull away from the curb. Then he went into his room and tried to pray, kneeling by his bed. It was too quiet. He felt obscurely guilty, as though he had done something in the night that he should be sorry for, only he couldn't decipher what it might be. He had tried to be faithful and honest. He was going to go ahead and marry Alice. Abruptly, he thought of sex, and of the fact that he was alone here. The room seemed to shift a fraction inward, as though the walls were closing in. If Alice came here now, she would want to do it.

It.

His blood told him this was true, and somehow he could feel the swiftness with which his spiritual resolve might crumble, given this perfect opportunity and his own huge curiosity and yearning. He got to his feet, backed away from the innocent, smoothly made bed as though it had suddenly burst into flames, and hurried out of the room. He was standing outside in the summery warmth when Alice pulled up in her baby blue, '51 Ford, with Stephen and Minnie in the back and Albert riding shotgun.

"Hurry up," she said. "We're late."

Albert scooted into the middle and Marshall got in next to him.

Albert smiled, sitting with his hands on his upraised knees. "I took the bus to Alice's this morning. She gave me breakfast."

"My father thinks I'm two-timing you," she said to Marshall.

He looked back and greeted the others. Minnie was taking up most of the backseat, her hands folded on her heavy lap.

Alice said, "It's Minnie's friend Eva."

"I know," Marshall told her.

Minnie wore a black suit and a small pillbox hat with a black veil. She stared out the window. Stephen reached over and took one of her gloved hands into his own dark fingers.

"You remember everyone," Alice said, pulling away from the curb.

The funeral was in Washington, at a small white church set back among big, spreading oaks whose leaves were starting to turn. The sun poured through the trees. There were many cars in the parking lot, and a line of people waiting to file into the church. Alice pulled into a space and they all got out, under the quiet gaze of those in line. Several of them recognized Minnie, and gestured hello. Others came a little toward them, offering hands. "Welcome," one of them said to Marshall. "Thank you for coming."

Inside the church, people were standing along the side aisles and in the back. There were no seats left. The dead woman lay in an open coffin at the front, a thin dark face bordered with white hair surrounded by light blue satin. The coffin seemed propped against an enormous escarpment of flowers. Someone played softly on an organ, and a slow procession of people moved past, saying their prayers and farewells. At the podium, a very heavy man stood, seeming to attend to everything. His dark face and close-set eyes seemed pinched with the effort to keep silent. Finally, he spoke. "Oh, Lord Jesus, receive your sistuh Eva unto your care today. She has lived the full life, the good life in your name, oh Lord."

"Amen," came from someone in the seats.

"Say it, Reverend," someone else uttered.

"Uh-huh," said someone else.

Marshall was astonished at the seeming disturbance, though he kept from showing it.

"Miss Eva lived a life of grace," the reverend said.

And again the voices rose separately from the congregation. "Amen, bruthuh."

"Bless his name."

"And she has gone to her blessed relief, in a chariot of angels. I said, she has gone to her relief, my friends, in a chariot of angels."

And the voices rose again. "Say it, Reverend."

"Praise be."

The reverend seemed to be gaining strength from these admonitions. He raised his voice now, and shook slightly, so that the flesh of his jaw trembled. "B-a-a-w-n in the dark night and degrada-shun of slavery, bruthuhs and sistuhs, b-a-a-w-n in the trial of fire and in the chains of o-preshun, I don't believe you heard me, bruthuhs and sistuhs."

There were several assenting voices, this time speaking at once. And almost instantly it was quiet again. Marshall felt himself being drawn into the silence.

"And made her way to freedom," the big man said quietly.

"Tell it, Reverend," a woman said.

"Mmm-hmm," said another.

"Made her way to freedom, bruthuhs and sistuhs, and demanded-a—"

"Amen."

"Demanded-a—"

"Yes, Lord."

"Demanded-a—"

"Praise God."

"Demanded-a—that she be free." Now the big man took a long breath and raised his eyes to heaven. "And was free."

"Amen."

"Lived free."

"Oh, yes."

"Raised her children free."

"Yes."

"Raised her grandchildren free."

"Praise God, yes."

"Raised her great-grandchildren and her great-great-grandchildren free."

"Yes, Lord."

"Lived a life of grace with her loved ones and her dear ones all around her unto that day when the angels descended-a. Halleluyuh. Lived her life of grace unto her one hundred sixth year, praise Jesus' name."

"Say it, Reverend."

"Amen."

"Amen, bruthuh," Minnie said.

". . . His name."

"Jesus."

"Came though hard times," the reverend went on, "with grace. Raised her sons Jeffrey and Joshua in grace. Helped raise her grandchildren and great-grandchildren and great-great-grandchildren in grace. Lived her life in grace." As he repeated the word, the congregation began to clap hands and cry out, so that the whole church was filled with the sound—everyone, Alice and Minnie and Stephen and Albert, too, calling "Amen" with the rest; and Walter came to know that his was the only silence now. The litany went on, growing deeper in intensity, and after each utterance of the word "grace," the heavy voice made a small in suck of air, like a gasp, which punctuated everything, almost as though this sound were beating time with the roar of the other voices.

"Taught her childrun to love, in grace. Ah. Taught her friends the meaning of love, in grace. Ah. Taught all her neighbors the meaning of charity, in grace. Ah. Bore her sorrows, in grace. Ah. Praised her joy, in grace. Ah. Spent her moanings, in grace. Ah. Spent her afternoons in grace. Ah. Spent her evenings in grace. Ah. In JEE-sus' name. Ah. And lived in the dignity of her faith, through the changes and the depredations and the sorrows. Ah. Through the fire and the tri-al. Ah. Lived in God's grace through the troubles and the inequities. Ah. Lawd, yes. Ah. And was in all her ways a pleasure unto the sight of Gawd. Ah. Praise JEE-zus. Ah. Praise JEE-zus. Ah. Praise his holy name. Ah. Amen. Ah. Amen. Ah. Amen. Ah."

And now it seemed that the voices made a chorus of encouraging cries, which led into something like a collective sigh, the many voices becoming a single voice, a rapturous din, slowing to the music of an organ, a hymn, singing.

What a friend we have in Jesus, all our sins and griefs to bear . . .

They sang four or five other songs, ending with "Amazing Grace." And then the family stood to carry Eva to her last rest. The coffin was closed, and the procession began, out onto the shady brown lawn, in the quiet morning. The coffin was put in the back of the black hearse, and the doors closed on it. People stood and exchanged hugs and handshakes and murmurous talk, then walked by the members of the family, who waited in a line at the end of the sidewalk. Two old men, four women ranging in age from very old to very young, and three small children.

"Thank you for coming," one woman said to Alice.

"I'm so sorry," Alice said.

"Nuthin' to be sorry fuh, young miss."

"A tri-umph," someone else said.

"Thank you," said one of the men.

"Beautiful ceremony," Albert said.

When they had all gotten back into the car, Stephen said, "Minnie's got to say something to Eva's granddaughter."

Marshall saw her on the other end of the lawn, making her way across the grass, helping what appeared to be a much older woman. Minnie's legs were muscular and heavy, like the legs of a big man. She walked on tiptoe, oddly like a dancer.

"How old is Minnie?" Marshall asked.

"Seventy-four," said Stephen and Alice in the same breath.

Marshall stared.

"I know," Alice said. "She doesn't look close to seventy-four."

"It was a beautiful ceremony," Albert said.

"I wish we'd gone to church when I was growing up," said Alice. "I think I've missed something." She squeezed Marshall's hand. "I'm planning to make up for it."

He repressed the urge to tell her that his church was nothing like this, not remotely like this. Even so, he was suffused by the sense that he had seen something awe-inspiring and wonderful. He felt oddly banked, held in. At the same time, he believed that what he had witnessed was primitive and strange, and he imagined what he might find to say to these people about the mysterious faith he practiced so assiduously. Their sincerity moved him, and troubled him.

"My daddy was a Methodist," Stephen said. "We went every

Sunday and listened to some preacher go on about hellfire and damnation. And nothing at all about the misery we were in all the time. I stopped going as soon as I was old enough to decide for myself. I'd go to Dr. King's church, though, if I could."

"I'd love to," Alice said. "Wouldn't that be wonderful?"

She had addressed Marshall, who hadn't quite understood her.

"Oh, wait. That's—you couldn't go into his church, could you? My father said, well . . . "

"What did your father say?"

"Well . . ." she said, and paused. "Well . . . but how did you do it today? Wasn't that a sin? Going into a Baptist church like that?"

"It was a funeral," Walter Marshall said. "I don't think . . ." But he wasn't certain. He could feel the color rising in his cheeks.

"Hey—have you committed a sin, here?"

"No," he said with too much emphasis. "It would have to be something I willed. And I wasn't even thinking about it. It was a funeral."

"Well, and actually we sort of dragooned you, didn't we?"

"No, you didn't, either," Marshall said.

"Okay."

They waited for Minnie to come to them.

The ride into Maryland was sober and quiet. There were logistical things to get established, and as they neared Pope's Creek, Stephen began going through them. "We do not answer taunts, or any name-calling. We're always polite, and show no anger, not even if we're hit or knocked around. If they manhandle you, go limp. Absolutely limp. Do not at any point encourage or incite them. What we want is polite and quiet determination. We go in and sit down and ask for menus, and then we wait—all afternoon, if it takes that long. And into the night. If people hit, you can duck away from it, but don't hit back. And when they grab hold, relax all your muscles and just become dead weight. We have to make ourselves wait for them to drag us out of the place, if that's what it comes to, and then we have to take whatever comes."

"They better not try draggin' me," Minnie said. "They're gonna hurt themselves."

"We have to let them do whatever they want to."

"What will they do?" Marshall asked. He had tried to keep the mounting apprehension out of his voice. He was beginning to wish secretly that he had found some way out of this.

"Mostly it's name-calling," said Alice. "Around here. I mean, the law's been signed. You know?"

"The police might come and take us away on some trumped-up charge. Disturbing the peace. That's what it was for the guys who went in there and tried to get served last week."

"They'd arrest us? Really? Here?"

"You ain't never been arrested, chile?"

"They didn't arrest them," Stephen said. "They took them to a high school gym and let them sit for a few hours and then let them go."

"Is it—just us?" Albert asked.

"Diane's going to meet us there with some friends."

"Do the people—the restaurant people—do they know we're coming?" Marshall asked.

"I wouldn't really know," said Stephen. Then he frowned. "If you're having second thoughts—"

"Oh, no," Marshall hurried to say. "Not at all." In his mind, he said a prayer, asking for courage. He would suffer whatever happened as an expiation for sin. Briefly, he felt almost elated by the prospect of it. But as he gazed out at the passing countryside, the fear came back.

"Would'n be messin' with this foolishness," Minnie said. She had evidently been speaking to herself. She looked out the window.

"You can stay in the car, Minnie. Nobody expects you to get in the way of trouble."

"You just mine your own bidness, na. I buried Eva today. I done made up my mind."

The sky was darkening out over the highway in the distance; they were in Maryland, heading out Route 5 toward Waldorf. When they pulled off the highway in the direction of Pope's Creek, Stephen said, "Get ready."

The restaurant was on the river, part of it jutting out over the water. There were many cars in the lot, and next to the building was a wooden pier on which several men stood talking. They wore T-shirts and jeans. Five or six big boats were moored to the pier, and electric wires ran from tall poles at either end. Across the water, a row of dark trees cast a jagged shadow along the edge of the sun- and cloud-reflected smoothness of the surface.

"Well," Stephen said, low. "Here we are."

For a time, no one moved. They were apparently waiting for others to show up. But then Stephen got out, and the others followed.

Marshall had eaten at this restaurant several times as a child, and he remembered walking in the door, seeing the sign: WHITE ONLY. At nine and ten years of age, he had felt something unfriendly in the thing, to have it fixed that way on the entrance of a place, though none of the adults he had been with seemed to notice it. It was the world he had lived in. There had been colored men working on the boats from time to time, and in his child's mind they had occupied the same place, oddly, as the boats themselves, a familiar part of the scenery.

Today, there was no sign on the door. But the outline of the place where it had been was visible in the wood.

"We're gonna have to go on in," Stephen said. "Somebody don't get here soon. Those men have seen me and Minnie."

"What men?" Albert wanted to know. He squinted in the direction of the pier. "Are those men? I can't see that far."

"Four of them," said Alice.

"They watchin' us, too," said Minnie.

"Just wait, please," said Stephen. "This has to be orderly."

The four men in the T-shirts seemed to be talking about what they could see of the people next to the '51 Ford—a black woman, a black man, a white woman and two white men, one of whom seemed to be making a face at them, standing there head and shoulders above the others with his hands clasped together at his hollow chest.

"Yep," Albert said. "They seem to be coming this way."

They moved a little in the direction of the doorway of the restaurant. The light had gone sunbright. The water of the river looked metallic and polished, now, and the wind rippled its surface.

"I guess nobody else is coming," Stephen said. "Let's go."

"What do we do?" Alice said.

"Just as I said. We go in and ask for menus. We're law-abiding citizens, within the law. Remember that. They will be the law-breakers now."

Another car pulled slowly into the lot. It was crowded with Negroes. It stopped a few feet from Alice's car, and all four doors opened. Alice's aunt Diane got out, with five young colored men. They were all dressed in their Sunday best, suits and ties and white shirts. Diane hugged Alice, and shook Albert's hand, then turned to Marshall and embraced him, too. "Isn't this a nice day to eat out?"

The four T-shirted men had begun walking over. They were young, grizzled, with the glazed eyes of too much alcohol. One of them had a pack of cigarettes folded up in his left sleeve.

"Howdy," the biggest of them said. He had fiery red hair and a red cap set back, showing a lot of forehead. "We was just wonderin' if you folks was lost or somethin'.".

"No, sir," said Stephen. "We're not lost."

"Well, then, we was wonderin' what you thought there was for you around here."

Minnie had struggled out of the Ford, and she took a step toward them. "What you got to know fuh," she said. "You git on about your bidness. Git on with yuh, na." She stepped toward them, making a shooing motion with her hands.

"Mammy, you ain't here to cause trouble, are you?"

"I ain't your mammy, and you best be glad a that, too."

"Now, just hold on there," another of the men said.

"Y'all git on about your bidness like I done tol' yuh."

"Minnie," said Stephen, taking her lightly by the wrist.

The other men had come to stand side by side, their hands in their jeans pockets. The two groups were facing each other.

"Are you men connected with the restaurant?" Stephen asked.

The big one smiled. "You might say we are."

"I see."

Minnie started toward them. Stephen said her name quietly, but then simply watched as she pushed herself through them and headed toward the entrance. The men had moved reluctantly—it had taken her physically pushing past them, moving them, and now they closed ranks again, seeming momentarily confused.

"Look, you people ain't wanted . . ." the big one began. But then he seemed to recognize the futility of saying anything, with

Minnie forging on, reaching the small stoop and marching up to the door and in. The door slammed behind her.

"Goddammit," the big, red-headed man said. "Go get her."

The other three started toward the door, but then Stephen made his way there, too, followed by all the others.

"Shit," the red-headed man said. "This is going to be some trouble." He moved to stand in front of Stephen.

"Excuse me," Stephen said, side-stepping him.

Marshall followed, with Alice and Albert close behind. All the others crowded in behind them. Inside, Minnie had already seated herself at a booth near the windows. Alice saw her and said, "She looks magnificent, doesn't she? Come on."

"Pardon me," a waitress said, getting in their way.

Alice said, low, "Just politely walk around them."

There were too many people for one waitress to stop, and soon they had all gathered in the three booths by the windows that overlooked the river. Albert, Alice, Diane, and a young man crowded into one; Marshall, Minnie, Stephen, and one other young man occupied the second; three more arranged themselves in the third booth. Alice turned to the young man next to her and introduced herself. He smiled and shook hands, and said his name was Reg. He introduced his friends—Ollie, Mike, and Cole, sitting in their booth, and Ty, sitting in Marshall's booth. For the moment, they were all occupied with greeting each other. Minnie told them all to be quiet, finally, and to sit up straight. Marshall saw that several whites had gotten up to leave, and he marked the angry looks of some of them.

The waitress walked over, carrying her notebook. It looked momentarily as though she were actually going to take their orders. But then she seemed to parade before them, evidently trying to decide which of them to address. She finally chose Stephen. "Look, we're awful busy here," she said. Her accent was decidedly Northern. "We're shorthanded in the kitchen."

"Could we please have menus?" asked Marshall.

Stephen looked at him and smiled, and so did Minnie. He felt marvelous.

"Okay," the waitress said. "You try to help some people." She stormed past the staring crowd of customers and through the swinging doors into the kitchen. The room was very quiet, now. Everyone simply stared. It was as if they were all waiting for an explosion. Alice and Albert began talking about steamed shrimp with Reg, who commented that in his family there was nothing prized as highly as steamed shrimp for lunch on a Saturday afternoon. Reg was from southside Virginia, near the ocean. So were Ollie and Mike. They were students at the University of Maryland. They talked on, animated, all brightness, but there was something a little agitated about it, as though they were trying to keep from being scared. The silence had begun to seem freighted with bad possibilities. More people were getting up to leave, muttering words, glaring.

"You don't expect to feel so exposed," Stephen said, low, to Marshall, whose throat closed with elation at the confidence.

"Be strong in yoursef," said Minnie quietly. "It's lonesome on the side of right."

They waited. It was a long time.

Some of the people who had cleared their things and left the restaurant were milling around outside. Soon a crowd was gathering, beginning to look like a mob. They stared through the windows on that end of the building, perhaps forty feet away. A young man walked over to the jukebox in the corner and put a coin in, leaning on the machine with both hands, going over the list of songs. When he glanced at the booths with the Negroes in them, he seemed almost to be smirking, as if to say that he was in on the joke. The first song began to play—Peter, Paul and Mary singing "If I Had a Hammer." The song played, and the young man stood there, reading down the list of songs.

But then a wiry, balding man came out of the kitchen and reached down and pulled the plug on the machine. The voices ground to a deep basso, and ceased. He turned and said something in a low voice to the man, who shrugged and held out one hand, apparently asking for his money back. The older man wore a cook's apron with food stains on it, and he reached under this to bring out a coin, which he dropped into the other's hand. Then he walked over to the three booths and stood with his arms folded, almost as if he had decided to stand a sort of guard over them.

"Aft'noon," Minnie said. "We just need some menus, suh."

"This establishment does not allow loud talk and disturbances," he said. "One of your number said something offensive to

my waitress. This is a private establishment, and we know our
rights." His jaw trembled. His voice shook with rage. But Marshall
saw that there was fear in it, too. "We reserve the right to refuse
service to anyone."

"You own this place?" Minnie asked him.

"I'm the manager."

"Yassuh. I see."

"We're short in the kitchen," he said as though he were recit-
ing it. "We can't serve this many people in a group. One of your
number was rude to my—"

Minnie began to hum, low, and quickly the others picked it up.
The manager's face whitened, and he marched across the room,
saying something to those few patrons who had remained at their
places. Marshall heard the word "niggers." And then someone at
the front windows shouted "Niggerlovers!"

Others took it up.

"Niggerlovers!"

"Niggers!"

"Go back where you came from!"

All this shouted across a space of empty tables, some with food
still on them. "Good thing we sat here," Ollie said. "Nice view on
this side." He looked out at the river.

"Go back where you came from!"

"Niggers!"

Minnie was singing now, and Marshall and the others joined in.

*Ain't gonna let nobody turn me round, turn me round, turn me
round. Ain't gonna let nobody turn me round, I'm gonna keep on a-
walkin', keep on a-talkin', marchin' down to freedom land. . . .*

Stephen had begun tapping the rhythm on the table with the
flat of his hands, and Marshall joined in, feeling exhilarated, clear
inside somehow, as if the complications of himself had been suddenly obliterated. The other voices rose around him, the shouts of
the crowd growing louder, too.

*Ain't gonna let segregation turn me round, turn me round, turn me
round . . .*

Outside, two police cars pulled in, and men got out, wearing flat-brimmed hats and carrying nightsticks. It was a lot of police—six or seven men. The wiry, balding man in the cook's apron rushed out to meet them. Marshall saw Stephen's eyes widen slightly. Stephen smiled, a small, pained smile showing the gap in his teeth. Then he nodded. He seemed to have acceded to something with the look. He kept singing, holding Minnie's hand now, as the policemen entered and crossed the room, approaching the three booths. The few remaining patrons were hurrying out of the place, looking like people executing a fire drill, and the waitress and two other women came from the kitchen, going out with the others.

Ain't gonna let no police turn me round. . . .

The oldest of the policemen, a tall, balding man with black tufts of hair over his ice-blue eyes approached the middle booth and seemed to know instinctively that Stephen and Minnie were the leaders. He only glanced at Marshall. "Okay, folks," he said, then waited, and when the singing went on, he said it again, holding up one hand. "Okay, folks."

Minnie stopped singing and held up her own hand. Everyone grew quiet.

The policeman looked at each of them, his hands on his hips now. The other policemen made an audience; they were ranged around the room in attitudes of calm vigilance. Two of them had gone outside to get the crowd under control. They were not doing a very good job. The shouted epithets kept coming.

"Get those niggers out of there!"

"Nigger-loving, Commie-Jew bastards!"

The policeman turned. "Now, hold on, out there. We have children present. Whoever that was, you watch your language."

"It's 'bastards' he objects to," Stephen said sadly.

"Now—what did you say, there, boy?"

"Nothing, sir. We mean no harm and no trouble. We're within our rights under the law. We only want something to eat."

"I don't know, singing in a restaurant. You're disturbing the other customers, wouldn't you say? I could run you all in for disturbing the peace."

"Niggerlovers!" someone shouted at the window.

The policeman turned his attention to Minnie. "Mammy," he said, "my name's Wyatt Barnes. How do you do?" He offered his hand.

Minnie looked at it, then touched the ends of the fingers.

"I didn't get your name?"

"Minnie."

"I got the feeling maybe I can reason with you, Minnie."

She looked at him. "I buried a friend today, suh. Moan a hundred yeahs old. And you know before she passed she done asked me why I ain't been out marching and I didn't have no answer when she did. You see?"

"But I can reason with you."

"It depends on whut you got to reason wif, I guess."

"Minnie, why d'you want to mess up my Saturday?"

"I got bettah things to do, too," Minnie said, looking at the backs of her beautiful hands, "than mince words wif you."

"I just wondered what you had in mind," he said.

She almost smiled at him. "Just tryin' to git lunch out the way."

"Maybe you can't read."

Her gaze was fierce. "Maybe you *can.*"

"Yeah, I can," he said. "I can. There's a law against disturbing the peace."

"I think singing is peaceful," Albert said, and Alice laughed.

Wyatt Barnes moved to that booth. "Miss, why don't you take your freak somewhere he belongs."

"That's me," Albert said, smiling, looking straight ahead.

Wyatt Barnes turned to Minnie again. "I ain't got a lot of patience left. You don't want a world of hurt, you'll leave peaceably. Otherwise, I won't be responsible for what happens."

"Sho you will, Mistuh Wyatt," Minnie said. "Ain't no need lying to me about it. I'm old, but I ain't no fool. You don't git old bein' no fool."

"I'm tellin' you, I won't be responsible."

Minnie said nothing.

"I could arrest the whole bunch of you, but I know that's just what you want."

No one answered.

"Id'n it?"

"What we want," Walter Marshall heard himself say, "is lunch."

The big man looked at him. "What you're gonna get is bloody."

"We will not raise a hand against anyone," Stephen said. "We're within our rights under the law."

"Naw. See, look over yonder. That sign above the cash register." Barnes read it aloud: "'We reserve the right to refuse service to anyone.' Well, Mr. McConnell taken a dislike to you-all for pushing in here and saying offensive things to his waitress, and within the earshot of the peaceful, law-abidin', God-fearing citizens of this town, and then singing that song and putting everybody in a bad mood. So he's insisting on his right to ask you-all to leave."

"We were singing," Stephen said, "to drown out the obscenities your peaceful, law-abiding, God-fearing citizens are throwing at us, sir. Even now."

"Look," said Barnes, "I'm tryin' to find a way out of this so nobody gets hurt."

"All we want, sir, is a little something to eat. Then we'll be on our way."

Barnes walked over to the entrance, where the man in the cook's apron stood, and muttered something to him. The aproned man muttered back. The crowd outside had gotten bigger, and the tumult of disapproval seemed to be growing with their number. Barnes came back to the table, and leaned down and looked at Minnie.

"Well, I'll tell you, Mammy—"

"Minnie."

"All right, dammit—Minnie. I'll tell you what's gonna happen. In about five minutes, we're gonna pick up and go. You understand me? We're gonna get back into those squad cars and head out to the highway and look for speeders, and whatever happens to you-all is just gonna happen."

"You gonna let them tear up this man's place a bidness? That just don't seem right, do it?"

The crowd was getting louder, and Marshall had begun to feel afraid. He could see that Stephen was afraid, too, and Minnie. The knowledge gave him a small, electric surging inside. It was fear, but it was mixed with something else, too, now—a fellow feeling that went beyond the fear. They were actually going to be able to draw on each other for strength. He had the thought, and then he looked at the screaming face of a blond boy, perhaps thirteen years old, the ugly twisting of the little mouth to utter the word "niggerlover," and he felt abruptly alone, and threatened, and extremely weakhearted. He wanted to slip out of sight of all these angry people and somehow make his way to safety. There were so many. Their anger had become personal, somehow. And a chanting had risen among them. "Niggers go home, niggers go home . . ." Grown people stood with their children, repeating this, the children chanting along with them. Grandmothers, women with babies. Little girls with braided hair and bobby sox and missing teeth.

Barnes said, "This is gonna be a riot and people are gonna get hurt."

"You got your mind made up," Minnie said. "Is you?"

"Now come on, you don't want to get killed. You didn't come here to get killed."

"Don't nobody do nothin," Minnie said, loud, not looking at him.

Out in the parking lot, something was burning. They had brought an oil can around from the pier and lighted a fire in it. Some men were making torches from it, using sticks and pieces of planks from the pier.

Barnes turned to one of his men. "Get out there and exercise some control, goddammit. I do not want a riot. You want a riot?" He turned to Minnie. "You want a riot? Look, you've made your point. I don't see the use of getting yourselves shot, or worse."

Marshall looked across the empty tables at the roiling in the windows, the angry faces. He saw men with sticks walking back and forth waving their arms, shouting. Other cars were pulling in, and more men got out, carrying shotguns.

"They've got shotguns," Alice said.

"Oh, Christ," said Barnes. "Not on my shift."

"Ain't you ashamed a your people, na," Minnie said. "Folks carrying on that way."

"Look," Barnes said to Stephen, "it ain't a matter of protest now. I'm gonna have all I can to get you folks outa this without some real harm comin' to you."

Out in the lot, a television crew had pulled in. Marshall saw the van, and the logo across its side panel, and he reached across the table to touch Stephen on the wrist. "Look."

Stephen leaned around Barnes and peered out, squinting. "What is it?"

"TV," Marshall said, remarking oddly to himself that Stephen was nearsighted.

Barnes had seen it, too. "Oh, well—that's just terrific." Even as he spoke, some of the men in the crowd began pushing and shaking the van. Someone—a woman in a leather coat—hit the windshield with a burning piece of wood.

Barnes had returned to the man in the cook's apron, and was arguing with him in the din. Finally he came back over and put his hands down on the table, waiting for the opportunity to speak. "Here's the story," he said to Minnie. "They got the TV people pinned in their own vehicle, and they are gonna hurt you people. I'm placing you all under arrest for your own safety. Understood?"

Minnie said, "You ain't got to protect me, young man."

"There's a couple of police vans coming. Understand? We have to wait."

"Ain't no need," Minnie said.

"We'll need the keys to your cars so our boys can get them out of here before the crowd figures out what's happening."

For a small space, no one answered him.

"Look, in a minute they're gonna be setting your cars ablaze. You see what we're up against here. I understand what you all want, but it's gone past that now, and I'm tellin' you something awful's gonna happen if we don't get you outa here quick. There's elements out there you don't want to mix with. And they ain't figures of authority or representatives of the civil courts, neither. You understand? You can't do anybody any good if you're dead. Or layin' in a burn unit somewhere."

Minnie turned to Stephen and said something, and he turned to speak to Alice in the other booth. Alice brought her keys out of her purse.

"Whore!" someone yelled from the windows. There was more breaking glass.

"Goddamn it," Barnes said. "Where the hell are they all coming from? There ain't this many people in the whole town."

Alice looked at Marshall and smiled—a perfectly serene expression, as though they were witnesses at some benign spectacle. The crowd now must have numbered close to a hundred people. They were brandishing sticks and clubs and shotguns. Someone hurled a bottle at the windows, and there was more shattering glass. The television van was burning. The crew had gotten out, somehow, and the mob had gathered around it; they were trying to overturn it. Others threw flaming pieces of wood or paper. Someone set off a band of firecrackers, and there was still more breaking glass.

Barnes signaled the other policemen to approach. "They're all under arrest." He turned to Minnie. "Will you walk out with us, or will we drag you out? If we have to drag you, I mean it, this crowd will take us all apart, and this riot will be a massacre."

Minnie looked at Stephen, who nodded.

"We'll walk," Minnie said. Then she indicated the man in the cook's apron. "But that man done vilated the law of the land, and we're gonna see he pays the price."

"Thank God for small favors," said Barnes.

They waited while the shouts from the crowd continued. Near the door, two of the policemen were trying to move a man out of the way. The man flailed and swung at them.

"Jesus Christ," Barnes said, wiping the back of his neck.

Marshall murmured the prayer, "Have mercy on us," and then realized the true import of the words. He said again, under his breath, "Have mercy on all of us."

"Where the hell're you all from?" Barnes asked Stephen.

"Here," Stephen said.

"Never saw you before in my damn life."

"Washington," Stephen said.

"You're a little ways from home, then, ain't you?"

"A little."

"This is our home," Alice said.

"Just thought you'd go out and cause some trouble in it."

"No, sir," she said. "We thought we would come in and have something to eat."

Barnes turned to Minnie. "Ain't you a little old to be getting yourself into this kind of foolishness?"

"Old," Minnie said. "And tired."

"Well, you see?"

"It's *whut* ah'm tired of," she told him. "You ain't got to guess." Her eyes moved, taking in the angry faces at the windows.

"You just gotta give people some time," Barnes said.

"Time. Whut they teaching these chirrun? Listen to 'em. Time. Look lak time is a luxury we ain't got."

The police vans pulled in, two of them, sirens going.

"Okay," Barnes said. "Let's do this right." He got his men to form a double file, on either side of the protestors, and they all made their slow way out into the parking lot, under the roar of the mob. There was a lot of jostling and pushing and shoving. Fights were going on a few feet away, and they seemed to be separate, somehow, like little fires burning around a larger one. In the distance, on a small rise opposite the pier, the television people were working to set up their cameras. Their truck continued to burn, sending up a big, many-layered column of black smoke. Someone spit at Minnie, and someone else threw a bottle, which hit Albert on the side of the face. Albert went down, sagged between the two files of policemen. They tried to hold him up, and the mob pressed in. Albert turned, bleeding, as if to confront the person who had hurt him. The men holding him lifted and pulled him along, the crowd pressing closer, shouting epithets, spitting. Albert was bleeding badly from the side of his face, and he looked very wobbly getting into one of the police vans. Alice got in with him, already attending to his wound, and Ty and Ollie followed them. Marshall was ushered into the first van, with Minnie, Stephen, Diane, and three others.

"Well," Diane said, sitting on the bench across from Marshall, "you ever see the inside of a jail?"

He shook his head no.

"You're about to."

The van doors were closed. The sudden dark was frightening. And then people began banging on the metal walls, the doors. The noise was incredible. Across from Marshall, next to Diane, Minnie sat with her hands folded in her lap, staring into space. She seemed not to hear the noise, now. Stephen was directly across from her, at Marshall's side. He leaned across the small space and took her hands. She looked up but didn't seem to see, and he let go. The three other young men were Reg, Cole, and Mike, each of whom Diane called by name, asking if the others had made it into the second van.

"Niggers, niggers, niggers . . ."

The roar went on and the van began to rock violently, the mob trying to push it over on its side. Through the small space looking into the front seat, they could see torches, fires burning.

Stephen began singing again, waving his hands like a conductor.

Ain't gonna let nobody turn me round, turn me round, turn me round . . .

They joined in, and the terrible clattering and rocking continued, but then there was a commotion in the front seat, people struggling, doors slamming, and curses, shouts. Two of the policemen were in the front, they had gotten in and closed the doors, and now gradually the van edged forward, still being rocked wildly, still in the din of fists and sticks beating against its sides.

The singing went on. It came from them with a force, like an element of some new spirit in their bodies, something given from somewhere so that they might withstand the storm of hatred outside. Marshall looked at the round, exhausted, singing face of the old woman, Minnie, who sat there clapping her small hands and shaking the enormous coffee-colored, flawlessly smooth flesh of her arms, and he found that he had the voice for this song, that it came flying out of him like a gust, the words and the breath rising with the others, drowning out the terrifying roar of the mob. He felt the strength flow through him from these others, and it seemed to him that no force could stop them, really, not now. Surely the rage outside would, in the end, have to give way to this fellow feeling, this rush of grace, this rightness. He looked at the faces ranged across from him, looked at the happiness in them, the courage, singing, and he had a wordless rush of knowing what a

beautiful country they would build together when at last the igno-
rant and frightened were made to see. The van was slowly gathering speed. Stones and sticks and bottles rattled against the doors, in
no rhythm anyone could use, though they used it anyway, clapping
and singing, and then they were free of it all, and there was only
the sound of their voices, the whir of motion, the van speeding
along the road, and on—out of the way of harm.

Chapter

11

*T*hey sang together for the hour it took to arrive. When
the van stopped, they grew quiet. For a moment, no one
spoke. There was a small wave of fear. The idling engine
ceased, and then there were footsteps on the gravel outside. The
doors swung open. Barnes stood there, and behind him was a dim
green tangle of trees and undergrowth, a field in a bath of sun
through the wall of clouds in a lowering sky. "All right," he said.
"Everybody out."

Stephen led the way, helping Minnie. When they were all out,
standing in the gravel in the iron-gray light, the van doors were
closed and the vans pulled away.

"Where are we," Diane said.

"You're in Howard County," said Barnes. Then he took a step
back and addressed them all. "Your vehicles are parked right over
there. You can take them and go home. Understand me? Or you
can drive the fifty miles back to the restaurant and we can do this
all again, or else just let the mob tear you limb from limb. Because,
folks—that's what they were gonna do to you this afternoon. Now,
you made your point. Call your damn lawyers and do whatever it is
you think you have to do. But I'd appreciate it if you took your

little protest somewhere else, and if you don't want a snootful of real bad trouble, that's what you'll do. I'm a good police officer, believe it or not. I'm hired to keep the peace and protect the citizenry, and that's just what I did today. I got you out of there with a minimum of bloodshed. Now, unless you want something else from me, I suggest you go on home where you belong."

"I can bring TV people with me," Alice said, low. "We can go back there tomorrow."

"It might surprise you-all to know that I'm on your side," Barnes said. "I'd like to see you Negroes get an even break. But I get paid to keep the peace—"

"You get paid to enforce the law of the land," Stephen said quietly.

Barnes stood there a moment. Then he muttered, "Some people don't know when they have it good."

"You said your say," Minnie told him gruffly. "Na git. Les' you gwine arrest us."

He shook his head, turned and walked over to his car, got in, and rode away. Minnie walked slowly, with Stephen's help, to Alice's car. They all gathered around Minnie—Diane, Albert, still bleeding from the side of his face, Ty and Reg, and the others.

"Y'all g'on home, na," Minnie said in a breathless voice. Diane hugged her, and then the others did, too, one at a time. She stood and accepted this homage with some small impatience. "G'on home, na," she said again as Marshall put his arms around her. "Say a prayer."

Marshall, Albert, and Stephen got into Alice's car.

"Ain't nothin'," Minnie said, getting in herself. She waved to Diane and the others, who were pulling out onto the road. Then their car stopped and Diane yelled from the passenger-side window, "Which damn way do we go?"

"That way," Stephen said, pointing.

"See you," Diane called.

Alice leaned across Marshall to wave at her.

They drove back toward Washington without saying much. As they crossed the bridge into Virginia, they could look to the right and see the Washington Monument shining on the gray sky, and Alice remarked that it looked as though it glowed from the inside.

About a mile on the other side of the river, Minnie began to experience chest pains. She held both delicate hands over her expansive chest and tried to breathe. The sound of it made everyone quiet. Minnie gasped for air, and seemed to cough, then leaned over onto Stephen's shoulder. He put his arm around her while Alice sped through lights and made the turns to get to Arlington Hospital—the emergency room, where the man at the registration desk seemed reluctant, a little cowed by the number of people with this patient, who seemed to be sagging from sheer discouragement and whose eyes now seemed to fix on everything that passed in front of them, as if searching for something they desperately needed in order to keep taking in light. At length, Minnie was wheeled into the corridors of the hospital, and the wait began. Albert called Emma to tell her he would not be over that evening. Marshall phoned his mother to say he wouldn't be home, but his mother didn't answer. Alice got in touch with her father, who didn't understand what she was doing with those people at that hour on a Saturday when she had been going out for a picnic with her fiancé. She did not trouble herself to explain it to him over the telephone. She hung up on him, then turned to Marshall and shrugged. He was thinking that she would make a good wife, and that he would definitely go ahead with it, now. From certain angles, she was almost beautiful. He had this thought, then tried to push it out of his mind. These strangely icy and detached moments made him uneasy, and shaky inside. He said a Hail Mary for Minnie, then fixed his attention on what Alice was telling him.

". . . I'm a grown woman, for God's sake. And he ought to have been there today. It's his goddamn job."

They all waited for news of Minnie. The man at the desk wanted to know what their connection to her was, and Alice said, "We're friends of hers, okay? All of us."

She turned to Marshall and said, "What in the world goes through people's minds, anyway." She seemed about to cry.

He put his hand on her shoulder, and felt abruptly as though it were the wrong thing to do. It felt too comradely, as though they were both men, and yet he couldn't position himself to do it differently. With his free hand, he took her hand and held it. She let her head rest on his shoulder. Across from them, Albert sat talking in low tones with Stephen. He was holding a handkerchief to his face. The bleeding had stopped, and he was developing a black eye. Several more people came in with their own injuries and problems, and the time drew on into evening and then night. Marshall called home again, and Clark Atwater answered.

"Where are you?" he said. "Your mother's frantic."

"I'm fine. I'm with Alice."

"Well, your mother's frantic."

"Could you please put her on?"

"She's using the bathroom."

"Tell her I'm fine, and I'll be home in a little while."

"What's that mean—a little while?"

"Mr. Atwater, I'll be home as soon as I can."

"I'll tell her. I don't know that it'll make her feel any better."

Alice and Stephen were sitting side by side in a far corner of the waiting room. Albert was sitting across from them, reading a magazine, the tip of his nose nearly touching the glossy page. There was no news. Marshall sat down on Alice's right, and she reached over and took his hand.

"We're going to be married," she told Stephen.

"Congratulations."

A nurse had given Albert an ice bag to put on the side of his face. He held it there, his face buried in the magazine.

"What a day this has been," Alice said.

They were quiet, then, for a long time. They watched others come and go—there had been an auto accident in the vicinity and several people were brought through on stretchers. Once Stephen went to the desk and inquired after Minnie, but there wasn't any news. Alice talked about her, about growing up under her stern, black, loving gaze. Stephen talked about how he had come to know Minnie through the old woman, Eva, whose funeral they had gone to in the morning. Eva had been a churchwoman, an important person in the church. It was very important to Minnie, and it had been to Eva, too. Minnie had been attending that church since she had lost her husband, some time shortly after the war started. Her husband had joined the army at the age of thirty-seven, and had died on a ship in the Pacific during the battle of Midway. She never got over that, Stephen said. She often talked about him to Eva.

"I never heard her talk about him at home," Alice said.

There was a small, awkward pause.

"She never wanted to talk about him. She wouldn't allow us to mention him."

"Well," Stephen said gently. "That's just Minnie."

They waited. Finally, a doctor came in to them and spoke to Alice. The patient was resting comfortably; there had been some worry about her heart, but she seemed all right in that respect. They would keep her overnight for observation, but apparently she had simply shut down from exhaustion.

She was asleep, and it was best to let her sleep through the night.

Alice thanked him. They all went out into the dark. Stephen and Albert would take a bus into town. Alice offered to drive them there, but they refused. It was just as easy to ride in on the bus. She and Albert embraced, and said their good-byes, and then she embraced Stephen. Stephen helped Albert along the walk, toward the bus stop. They looked odd, Albert was so much taller than the other, who seemed to lean into him, a bolster against gravity.

Marshall and Alice were alone, then. They got into the car, and she turned the ignition, crying softly.

"It's okay," he told her.

"I know. I just—those people—how could they say those horrible things in front of their children?" She sniffled. "Think about those people at home—the ones who were doing all the yelling and shouting and throwing things. They all love their families, don't they? They're all hard-working and loyal and good workers and religious, too, I'll bet. They teach their kids to be kind and considerate and loyal and mannerly, and they teach them this—this poison, too. I don't get it. I don't get it."

He said, "I don't get it, either." But it was reflexive, and he was ashamed of it.

She drove to the apartment house. It only took five minutes. When she stopped the car, she leaned across the seat and hugged him. "Well," she said, "kind of a tough date."

"Are you okay?" he asked.

"Yes." She seemed about to cry again. "I love you."

He said the words back. He was beginning to think they might be true. The fact was, he rather admired her after today. "Do you want to come in for a while?" he said.

"I think I'm already in trouble."

"Your father won't be mad at Minnie, will he?"

"He's mad at me. I'm sure he'll think I got her involved, though you know it was really the other way around."

"I'm glad she's okay," Marshall said.

"I was going to suggest that I go to church with you in the morning, but I think I better stay home and take care of things with Minnie." She leaned over and kissed him again. "'Bye, baby."

He stood on the sidewalk and watched the car pull out of sight at the end of the road. In the lighted window of the apartment, his mother stood. He went in and up the stairs, and she had opened the front door and come out on the landing.

"I was so worried."

"Is Mr. Atwater here?" he asked.

"Yes, of course. Where were you?"

"In Maryland. We went to a crab joint."

He made his way past her and into the apartment. Atwater was seated in front of a TV tray with a bowl of ice cream, watching *Have Gun, Will Travel*. "Where the hell have you been, boy? You had your mother in a state."

Chapter

12

*S*unday after Mass, he spoke to Alice on the phone. Minnie was no better, but she was stable. Alice had spent the morning with her, and there were other visitors, mostly members of Minnie's congregation. She didn't really have any family. "I'm her family," Alice said and started to cry.

"Do you want me to come over there?" he asked.

"I don't know how long I'll be here," she said. "Call me at home, later?"

He took the Lark and drove into Washington, to the school. At least partly, he wanted to check on Mr. D'Allessandro, having spent much of the night seeing his image, beset and vaguely aghast, mixed with the images of crowded rooms, a man walking on his hands, mobs of angry people and police. He was restless, and sick at heart: The violent hatred of the crowd—the weirdly automatic quality of it, as though the rage had been some social function long devoid of its actual purpose or meaning, a ceremony of empty faith practiced by people whose minds had stopped there, without questions or doubts or an idea of anything beyond it—all this had worked in his soul, undermining his earlier enthusiasm for what he had been through with the others.

Loretta was going to spend the afternoon watching football with Clark Atwater.

So he drove into town alone.

Mr. D'Allessandro usually did paperwork at the school on Sundays—Marshall had come in on other Sundays to record commercials for the Spanish radio show—but today the broadcasting school was closed. The night-school library was open, and he waited around for a little while, hoping D'Allessandro might show up. There was also the thought of Natalie, which he tried to suppress. Finally, he made his way east, the mile or so down New Hampshire Avenue, to the big old Victorian house where Albert Waple kept his small apartment. Loretta had a deep horror of imposing on people, and had taught her son that it was rude to call on someone without warning, so he stopped at the corner phone booth and called.

Albert seemed relieved to hear his voice. "Yes, of course. Please stop by. I talked to Alice earlier."

It was a sunny, chilly afternoon, with high, sculpted canyons of white, white cloud in a sky that seemed a darker blue somehow. A beautiful day, yet all the streets seemed deserted. The trees lining Albert's street threw shadows on the road's surface, on the cracked, weed-sprung sidewalk, the grass. There were some yellow leaves in the trees, now, and a few scattered traces of the burnished colors of autumn. But the houses looked stained by soot and coal dust, and in this light their dirtiness seemed somehow exaggerated, like a kind of insistence. There was no wind. The air smelled of coal and car exhaust. Albert's apartment was one of three in the house, and there were separate doors opening onto the porch; his was the right-hand door. Marshall rang the bell, and his friend came and peered out through the window. His thin face was badly swollen and discolored on the one side. He opened the door, smiling, and stepped back. "What a nice thing. I'm so happy you thought of us."

Emma was seated on the small sofa, holding a saucer with a steaming cup of tea on it. An Andy Williams album was playing on the hi-fi. "Hello," Emma said over the strains of "The Days of Wine and Roses."

Albert said, "Emma took the bus in. She's getting to be quite the navigator."

She smiled. "Alice isn't with you?"

"No."

"That was such a wonderful party."

Albert pointed to his face and then shook his head, frowning. "So," he said. "What brings you into town?"

Marshall explained that he'd come to the school.

"Albert never seems to go to the school unless he's got a class," Emma said.

"I go there sometimes," Albert said quietly. He really did look bad. The skin around his puffy, violet- and yellow-shaded eye was a sick, pale hue. He touched the place gingerly, and offered Marshall some tea. They sat quietly for a few moments. Marshall gazed at the pictures on the walls of Albert's parents, of nieces and nephews, the porch of a house Albert said was in Montgomery County, Maryland. He talked of watching thunderstorms from that porch, and being able to step straight off it onto drifted snow in the big storm of 1958. The apartment was furnished rather sparsely, and there were books everywhere, lining the stairs which went nowhere (they had obviously once led up to bedrooms in this house), stacked on the small end tables and the desk against the left wall, in piles next to the bed in the other room, which was visible through the opening into the book-lined hallway. There were even books on the kitchen table, the counter, tucked into the cabinets meant for dishes. Marshall let his eyes take all this in, sitting in the straight-backed chair opposite them on the couch, and then Emma began talking about Mr. D'Allessandro's plans to save the school. The record played: the pleasant, light baritone voice and violins, a chorus of female singers. Pouring the tea, Albert seemed sad and a little irritable.

"We're having a regular English afternoon, aren't we?" Emma said. "All we need is crumpets. I love the little sound of the cups clinking against the saucers. It's so—civilized, somehow. In my family, we have tea like this every day."

"My mother drinks tea," Marshall said. "She puts cordials in it sometimes."

"I've never had it with cordials. Is it good that way?"

"I only had it once. It's okay, I guess."

"But your mother likes it?"

"Yes."

"And she drinks a lot of tea."

"That would be my guess," Albert said with the slightest trace of sarcasm. Then he patted Emma's shoulder.

"Albert's been acting kind of depressed the last few days," she said. "I think he's worried about the school. He's so negative about everything lately."

"I don't know what good it is to worry about the school," Albert said to Marshall. "You're not interested in radio anymore, and I'm beginning to see that I'm not really cut out for it. And God only knows what some of the others—did you hear Ricky Dalmas's commercial about getting something you didn't want for Christmas?"

"See how negative?" Emma said.

"I'm being truthful with myself."

Emma addressed Marshall. "I think Albert has a very soothing voice and I think he's perfect for the radio. What about you, Walter?"

"Someone told me I had a voice for radio," Marshall said. He thought of Clark Atwater. "I don't know, though."

"I'm asking what you think of Albert's voice."

"Oh. I—I think he'd be fine." Marshall was unable to muster more enthusiasm with Albert's dour, myopic gaze on him.

"He'd be more than fine." Emma set her cup down on the saucer she held. The motion was so confident that it would have been difficult to convince an onlooker that she was blind. The cup made a decided clink, and she sat back, satisfied.

"Maybe I'm beginning to see that I don't want it anymore," Albert said.

"But you were so excited about it when we met," Emma said. "Broadcasting was all you wanted to talk about. And if you were really deciding against it, you wouldn't be so sad about it now."

Albert shook his head, but didn't speak.

They were all quiet again while the record played.

In a while it ended, and there was the little mechanical sound of the player arm automatically lifting and returning to its cradle. The quiet seemed to stretch out, a lengthening, embarrassed pause. "Do you like Andy Williams?" Emma asked.

"Sure," Marshall said.

Albert got up to turn the record over.

"I love that song, 'I Can't Get Used to Losing You.' Don't you?" Emma said.

Albert had set the record going. He returned slowly to his place next to Emma. He kept staring at the floor, the one hand gingerly moving over the bruise on the side of his face.

"Alice likes folk music," Marshall said.

"She's not a Beatles fan?" Albert wanted to know.

"I don't understand what the excitement's all about," said Emma. "They're not even cute." A moment later, as if to explain, she said, "My aunt Patty described them to me."

"They won't last," Albert said to her. "Remember Fabian?"

"Oh, I like Fabian."

"Well, yes—but you never hear about him now."

"I like him a lot. You don't like him, Albert?"

"I just meant he was a big teen idol, too, you know. Like Tommy Sands. Ricky Nelson and Frankie Avalon. Those guys. You don't hear about them so much anymore. The Beatles will be like them."

"I don't think the Beatles are as good as those guys," said Emma.

"No," Albert said quickly. "Me, too. I don't think they are, either." After another awkward pause, he said, "What about Elvis?"

"Remember when everyone was so upset because of his sideburns?" Emma sat forward as if to offer this to the room. "They'd love to go back to the sideburns now, wouldn't they?"

There was yet another silence.

"More tea, Emma?"

"Thank you, yes. It feels light."

Albert poured the tea.

"It certainly is nice to have company," Emma said. "Isn't it, Albert?"

"Yes, it is," Albert said.

Marshall wondered what they could've been talking about when he called. He felt the necessity to speak, and it made him dumb. His mind was a blank, with only the scrabbling for words, anything to say. "Well," he told them, "as a matter of fact, I can't stay very long at all."

"Busy man," Emma said.

"Are you heading back to Virginia?"

"Yes."

"Maybe you could give Emma a lift."

"Do you want me to leave now?" Emma said. "I have everything all planned out. I'm supposed to call Aunt Patty this evening."

"I just thought it might be easier for you," Albert said.

She seemed annoyed by the consideration. "Don't be ridiculous, Albert. I'm perfectly capable of getting home."

"I didn't say you weren't. I was only trying to save Aunt Patty the trouble."

"Well, you put Walter on the spot, I think. Walter, it's perfectly all right. Aunt Patty doesn't mind a bit. And I couldn't bear to leave my handsome prince this early in the afternoon."

Albert said, "I'll walk you out to your car."

"Did I say something wrong?" Emma wanted to know.

"Don't be silly, dear," said Albert. "I'll be right back."

Out on the porch, he said, "You believe a thing like yesterday? In Maryland, no less."

"How have you kept it from her?" Marshall asked him.

"She knows. We're just not talking about it. She's pretending it didn't happen. That's why we're drinking the tea. I have orders not to involve myself again, and she's upset with Alice. Nothing Alice will ever know about, of course. Because that's the way they do things in Emma's particular little Southern family of aunts and cousins, you see. If there's anything unpleasant, or any ill-feeling about something, well, we just won't talk about it. And we won't allow anybody else to talk about it."

They walked out to the car. The sun had gone behind a heavy-looking gray cloud. There wasn't anyone else in the street, but the sound of traffic came to them on the air.

"Wonder if Minnie's okay?"

"Alice said she was stable—" Marshall said.

"No, I know."

"I asked if she wanted me to come over there."

"Minnie doesn't want anybody but Alice, and her people—you know, from the church, right now."

"Did Alice tell you that?"

Albert nodded. "I offered to go there, too."

This was a lovely, sunny fall Sunday in the city. And now there were people out walking, bundled against the chill, and the complicated shapes of shade moved in the breezes. Albert had his long arms wrapped around himself, staring out at the street. "Wasn't that something? In Maryland. I don't understand why it wasn't on the news or in the paper. I read the paper from cover to cover this morning. Nothing."

"Maybe it'll be on this evening."

"You go along thinking life makes some kind of sense . . ." Albert shook his head. "Well—you talk yourself into believing there's some progress, you know? They pass a law, and you figure it's over now, settled."

"I dreamed about it all night," said Marshall. "I felt terrible this morning. For a little while, when we were in the vans—we were singing, and I thought—it made me feel that maybe something— like we could . . ."

Albert was gazing at him with his sad, too-deep-set eyes.

"I don't know," Marshall said. "Change it all. We'll make it a better country, won't we? I mean, our children won't—we won't teach that to our children, will we?"

"I saw a picture once, in a history book—one of those *Life* magazine–type picture books about history. It was about lynching—in the South. In this picture, Walter, you see all these people, a crowd standing around the hanged body of a colored man, some poor young man, maybe twenty years old. He's hanged, there. Dead. Not two feet off the ground. Just enough to kill him. The rope looks like it might cut his head off, it's that tight. And—and these people are all standing around, it's a party—a celebration. It's in their eyes, they're all bright and excited. Some of them are actually *laughing*, and—and—there's this little blond girl in the picture, in the middle of all these people—she's standing close to a woman—her mother, I guess. She's holding onto this woman's skirt and smiling, too, this angelic, pretty little girl's bright smile, right? This innocent little girl—enjoying the damn party, Walter. A Sunday picnic, and she's perfectly happy, staring at this dead man, this hanged man. But you see that little girl and then you see that there are other children in there, too, in the happy family circle— not as blond or as pretty as that little girl, not wearing white like she is, but kids—*kids*. And you realize that they can't be more than eight or nine years old—eight or nine, Walter."

Neither of them spoke for a moment. A young boy came by, walking a big German shepherd. They watched the dog strain at the leash, the boy leaning back, holding on, being pulled along to the corner and across the street.

"What does Emma say about it all?"

Albert waved this away. "I can't even bring myself to repeat what Emma has to say." He sighed. "My head hurts." He was shivering, standing there in the chill.

"You better go on back inside," Marshall told him.

Albert started back up to the apartment, then stopped and turned. "I thought Alice was great yesterday."

"Yes," Marshall said. "She was. So were you."

Albert seemed not to have heard this last. "You must be really proud," he said.

"Yes."

"I don't know what to do," Albert said, standing there with his hand up to his bruised face. "Everything's changed."

Driving by the school on his way out of town, Marshall saw that Mr. D'Allessandro's car was parked along the curb in front, so he pulled in behind it. There was a light on upstairs, where the studio was. Two young women were sitting at the big table in the little library. They had been laughing and trying to speak over each other, but they looked at him and fell silent as he came by the entrance. Then one of them called out to him, "Tell Mr. D'Allessandro we want to see him." Her voice was somehow tauntingly childlike. He nodded, then turned and climbed the inside stairs to Mr. D'Allessandro's office. The door was open, but no one was there. He went into the sound booth and found Mr. D'Allessandro sitting at the console with Mrs. Gordon on his lap, her arms resting lightly around his neck.

". . . but I don't like bacon," Mrs. Gordon was saying in that caressing voice. When she saw the young man, she came quickly to her feet, smoothing her dress, her motions exactly those of someone trying to brush insects from her clothes. She kept her eyes averted from him, and moved past him out into the corridor without saying anything. Mr. D'Allessandro had turned into the console, and was sitting there moving his head to the music that was coming from the speakers.

"Pay no attention," he said, not looking at Marshall.

The young man moved to the top of the steps in time to see Mrs. Gordon walk out. When he turned, Mr. D'Allessandro was staring at him. "Pay no attention—I—I was telling Mrs. Gordon a story. Something—" He breathed, grimacing, "that happened back when I was doing radio in the war."

Marshall was silent.

"Well—what're you doing here, anyway? Aren't you supposed to be reading commercials on that Spanish program?"

"He didn't need me this week," Marshall said.

"Well, what is it, lad?"

"The—two downstairs. Women. They said they were waiting to see you."

"What?" He rose, brushed at himself, adjusted his pants, moved past Marshall and down the stairs. Marshall stayed where he was, staring from this height at the empty foyer. In a little while, perhaps five minutes, Mr. D'Allessandro came back, climbed the stairs, and went into the booth. He put more music on and seemed to be listening for something inside it, some code or other. Now and again he nodded, as if he'd heard whatever it was and understood it. Minutes passed. Marshall thought perhaps he should just leave him there, but then the older man muttered a word that sounded like, "strudle."

"Pardon?" Marshall said.

Mr. D'Allessandro repeated it. "Strudle." He nodded, keeping a kind of time with the music. He was talking to himself. "I don't believe it. Walk in here with it."

When Marshall stepped into his line of sight, he sat up, suddenly straight—the chair squeaked—and gave forth a high, startled sound, like a whimper.

"I didn't mean to bother you, sir."

"*Bother* me. You scared the living shit out of me. I thought you'd gone—look, what the hell do you want?"

"I'm sorry."

D'Allessandro looked at him. "What're you doing here, anyway?"

Marshall had no answer.

"Did Marcus—does he know you're here?"

"No, sir. Is *he* here?"

"He came with two girls from God knows where. Strudle—you know what I mean? Not girls from home. He walked in my building and left them, without even saying anything—" D'Allessandro suddenly sat forward and reached for the young man's wrists. "He wasn't—look, when you came in here, what you saw, it wasn't what it must've looked like. Did you—did you see him—when—was he here when you got here?"

"There was just them—the girls," Marshall said. "Downstairs."

D'Allessandro's face had that drastic, grimacing look. He smiled briefly, then sat back and offered a chair. "Sit down, lad."

Marshall did so.

The older man stared at him. "You believe me, don't you?"

"Yes, sir," Marshall said.

He watched the older man adjust the volume on the music, and he saw the trembling in his hands.

"Well, things are shaping up, lad. I spoke to the pastor at Saint Matt's—a Father Malloy, a very nice old minister, and it looks like we'll have the use of the cathedral basement for our evening."

"We don't call them ministers," Marshall said.

"Priest. Well, all right. The two are fairly synonymous, I'd suppose."

"I know one of the priests at Saint Matthew's—Father Soberg," Marshall said. "He's been a friend of the family."

"Well, I wish I'd been privy to that information," Mr. D'Allessandro said. "You could've done the asking. My blood pressure goes sky high whenever I'm put in the unfortunate position of having to beg for something."

There was a motion in the doorway, and both of them turned to see Marcus standing there, working a toothpick in his small mouth. Marcus winked at the young man, and then indicated that Mr. D'Allessandro should go on with what he was saying. Mr. D'Allessandro leaned toward Marshall and said, "When the time comes for you to marry, lad—if and when that time comes—be sure to take the trouble of looking very closely and critically at the girl's *family*."

"Keep it up," Marcus said. "Mr. Brace likes these comments of yours. They're like a sort of ammunition."

Mr. D'Allessandro ignored this. "Word to the wise," he said, winking. But it was clear that he was quite frightened; the flesh around his mouth was leached of all color. In the tone of someone making an announcement, he went on, "I explained to Father Malloy that we'd had the same sort of arrangement with the previous pastor when our pipes burst before graduation a few years back, and he was very agreeable. We've decided to make it a panel discussion about broadcasting and politics, with a focus on the Kennedy years. It'll be in honor of our late president, of course."

"It'll be in honor of your pocketbook," Marcus said. "You never cared about anything else. Well, that's partly true." The little man paused. "Isn't it?"

"What do you think you mean?"

Marcus said nothing. He stood there working the toothpick in his mouth.

"Pay no attention to the dwarf in the doorway," said Mr. D'Allessandro.

Marcus came away from the door slowly, and walked over to stand at Mr. D'Allessandro's shoulder.

Mr. D'Allessandro addressed Marshall. "Do you know the music of Gustav Mahler?"

Marshall indicated that he did not.

"We're listening to the Sixth Symphony. 'The Tragic,' it's called. This is the adagio."

Marcus had taken out a nail file and was standing there, meticulously cleaning the nails of his left hand.

Mr. D'Allessandro's face had pulled back into its grimacing smile, but he went on talking. "They say beauty is only skin deep, lad, but when you're ugly, you know, it really does show. Top to bottom, it shows, and mind you, the distance between them is sometimes rather negligible—not top to bottom. I didn't mean the distance between top to bottom is often negligible, though of course it is, isn't it?" He glanced at Marcus, then fixed his gaze on Marshall again. "Of course, I meant the distance between ugliness and beauty. Winning and losing."

"Keeping a wife's loyalty and losing it," Marcus said.

Mr. D'Allessandro pulled at his collar. "It's getting close in here, don't you think?" he said, still addressing the young man.

"Living and dying," Marcus said.

"Very good." Mr. D'Allessandro's tone was that of a teacher with a slow pupil. "Being human and being freakish."

Marcus put the nail file away, and seemed to coil into himself. "I'm going to get such pleasure out of the end of all this. When it all fails, and Brace lets me have a free hand."

Mr. D'Allessandro cocked his head slightly; he was listening to the music. "I always loved this passage. It cries out for love and understanding and the acceptance of every monstrosity in nature." He was still addressing Marshall. "There's a good lad. Thanks for the visit."

Marcus had moved back to the doorway. "I'll be here again tomorrow," he said.

"Will you have strudle with you?"

The little man gave no answer. He went out and down the stairs, whistling.

"That's my name for the chippies," Mr. D'Allessandro said.

"Chippies."

"Whores."

"Those were—" Marshall started.

"Absolutely. Remember what I said about learning as much as you can about the girl's *family*." Abruptly, D'Allessandro got out of his chair and made his way into the little bathroom off his office. Marshall heard him being sick, retching and coughing and sputtering. It went on, and then there was the sound of water running, of the older man cleaning his teeth. Finally, he came back across to the booth and in, took his seat at the console, and slapped his hands down on his knees. "Now," he said, with that tight smile, "what can I do for you?"

"Me?"

Mr. D'Allessandro seemed impatient. "What did you come to see me for?"

"Oh—I—nothing, really. I saw you at Alice's party. You looked upset—"

"And you came in to see about me?"

They paused for a moment, hearing the girls laughing in the foyer downstairs.

"*Un*believable," said Mr. D'Allessandro. He looked for a second like he might have to go and be sick again.

"I was in the area," Marshall told him. "Visiting Albert. I saw your car."

"Well, you're very kind, lad. I'm—I'm kind of busy now, though."

"Yes, sir."

Downstairs, the girls had gone. The library was empty, a sunny room full of dust motes and shadows.

He drove up the street to Natalie's tall, dark-brick apartment house and sat with the car idling, watching the front door. It was getting late. The late-afternoon sun had gone behind the building. He leaned down in the seat to look up at what he remembered to be her windows. They were curtained, and no light shone in them. Other windows in the facade were lighted now, and twice he saw young men go into the building. He imagined that they had come to see her. But each time they came out with others—one with another young man and one with an elderly woman. Finally, he turned the car off, got out, and hurried in the increasing chill across the street, his heart pounding in all the veins along his neck and face. In the dim, echoing foyer, he looked over the blur of labels above the mailboxes for her name. And here it was, "Natalie Bowman." Some part of him watched from a kind of inner distance as his hand reached for the little bell and pushed it. Nothing. No sound. He waited. This was about the time that Alice would be expecting him to call her at home. He felt the weight of his promise. It was getting late. The wind moaned in the high, arched frame of the entrance, and it seemed that the whole building creaked. He pushed the button again and waited, shivering a little now.

When the outside door opened in a rush of air, he almost yelled. An elderly couple walked in. "Excuse us," the woman said. "Who did you want to see?"

"Natalie Bowman?"

"Fourth floor. She must not be in."

"Thank you," Marshall said and edged past them, out into the street.

And there Natalie was, at the corner, having just crossed. She wore a white scarf and a long, dark trench coat, and she walked slowly along the street, holding her purse over one shoulder, two fingers hooking the strap. She stopped before the young man and smiled. "You vere looking for me, Walter?"

"I thought I'd stop by," Marshall said.

"How sweet. I almost missed you. I went for a valk."

You are so beautiful, he wanted to say. There was a lovely, soft, rose flush in her cheeks; her hair shone against the white of the scarf.

"Are you going somewhere?" she said.

"No."

"We could go on a date, maybe." She smiled.

He had the decided impression that she was being sardonic with him. He said, "I just wanted to say hello."

She said, "Don't be glum." She reached over and touched his cheek. "Let's go to the Cafe Lounge. Can't we, hmm? It's right down there." She pointed to an area of open asphalt above the parking lot of the school. There was a row of buildings on the other side of this area—back entrances and an alleyway.

"Shall we?" she said.

He nodded. She took his hand as they walked, and he felt something begin to give way in the muscles along his spine. They crossed the open area and entered the alley, which led out onto Connecticut Avenue. The Cafe Lounge was up the street to the right. It was closed.

"I never know what day it is," Natalie said. "Today is not Saturday, but Sunday. And tomorrow is not Sunday, but Monday."

The drugstore at the circle was open, and they walked up there. The neon above the entrance looked brilliant against the pale sky. Inside, there were only a couple of women in nurses' uniforms at the counter. Natalie led him to a booth along the left wall, beyond the counter. She took her scarf off, and her coat, settling into the booth, and he took his place across from her, unable to believe this was happening yet feeling, too, in spite of all efforts to block out the thought, that it was precisely as he had hoped.

"So," she said, folding her hands on the table before her. "What vill you have?"

"Coke," he said.

"Nothing warm?"

The waiter came to them, a young, balding, red-haired man with long, thin arms and spidery, skinny, freckled fingers. "Something to drink?" he said. "The grill is down, so we only have cold sandwiches to eat."

"Ginger ale for me," Natalie said.

"That sounds good," said Marshall.

"Two of them," the waiter said, moving away.

Natalie sat, smiling at him. "How nice you came to see me."

"I was in the neighborhood."

"Lucky for me."

He said, "I almost missed you."

"And where are your other friends?"

"I haven't seen them."

"Do you ever drink vhiskey?"

"I've tasted it."

"I like it in my ginger ale. It warms you from inside."

He said nothing.

"We could go back to my apartment and have some, maybe."

"I don't think you can buy it on Sunday."

She leaned across the table and murmured, "I know. I have some at home. In the cabinet." She stood and moved to the counter, where she told the waiter that she would like the ginger ales to go.

Marshall watched her come back to the booth, marked the grace and curvature of her, and the nerves of his stomach tightened. All this was happening.

"You know, you don't look twenty-six," he managed when she sat down. "You look closer to *my* age." His voice had caught on the last word. He took a breath, swallowed involuntarily.

"Do you think a woman should go on a date with a younger man?" she said.

"Why not?" This came forth with a sound like a laugh mixed with a cough.

"You're so nervous. It's nice how nervous you are. Some men are so sure all the time. Cocksure, like roosters."

He looked around the room. There were big, glass-framed pictures on the walls, of city scenes—the Lincoln Memorial and the reflecting pool in the rosy light of evening, the tidal basin at dawn, the Capitol building bathed in brightness against a night sky. Briefly, he had no recognition of any of it. In the next booth, a very old woman sat drinking coffee alone. She had a newspaper open in front of her. Marshall hadn't seen her come in.

The waiter called to Natalie from the counter. She put her coat on and walked over to pay for the drinks. She insisted on paying for them, though Marshall protested. The drinks were in a white paper bag, which she handed to him. They walked back to Eighteenth Street and up to her building in the washed light of low sun. The air was very cold now, and she pulled her coat collar tight at her throat. On the elevator, she said, "If I go with you, it is less strange than you might think."

"Excuse me?" he said.

"I have been vith someone—vould be thought stranger for a partner than you."

"I don't understand."

"You are so young. That makes you strange for me."

He couldn't respond to this.

"But you're not strange." She smiled cryptically, then shook her head, seeming to pout. "Never mind."

His gorge was threatening to spasm. He held the bag with the drinks in it, and followed her down the dim hallway to the black door with a bronze number four on it. Here, there was an odor of wood and dust and several kinds of cooked food. She fumbled with the keys, talking about how tired she was. Marshall took a shallow, murmuring breath, shifting the bag to his other hand. Opening her door, she entered and turned to face him, gesturing with her lovely hand for him to pass through into the small kitchen. He did so, and she turned the light on behind him. Several roaches scurried out of sight along the wall and out of the sink. It was a tiny room, with a single lightbulb hanging from a wire at the center. A narrow, smudged window looked out on an alley, a brick wall. He walked to this window, then turned to see that she had remained behind, in the living room, so he joined her there. On the walls were pictures of horses, and a large portrait of her with a muscular, deeply tanned, dark-haired man wearing a flattop haircut. She walked around Marshall and back into the kitchen, and he followed. Other snapshots, also of her and this man, were taped to the refrigerator.

"Is this your—boyfriend?" he said.

She made a small, snickering sound. "That's my older brother. Max."

She removed her coat. "He is a policeman now. In Düsseldorf. No—the—the one I talk about—that is someone else. A big secret." She looked at him as if she expected him to ask her to reveal it. But then her expression changed. Something went through her, a pang, and then a form of resolution. It was there, in her amazingly lovely face. "No, you wouldn't like to know this. And anyway, it is over now. A long time."

"How long?"

She thought a moment. "Two years." Then she sighed. "Almost."

"I don't understand," he said.

"It makes no difference how long . . ."

He had set the bag on the rickety card table. She opened it and lifted the drinks out. "Go have a seat, please, Walter. I'll fix the refreshments."

He went into the living room, to the couch, and sat down. Behind him was the window, looking out on Eighteenth Street. He could see Connecticut Avenue, the backs of buildings through the trees. The sun and shade of the city looked almost geometrical from here.

"Not much of a view," she said, bringing the drinks in on a tray.

She sat next to him and put her drink to her lips, watching him. He took his own drink and sipped from it.

"Good?" she said.

"Very." He took another sip. He liked the taste, though it did nothing to warm him inside as she had said it would.

"You are very attractive young man, Walter. And I do—I wish you vas older sometimes."

"What difference—what difference does my age make?" he said.

She studied him. "You are always so nervous."

He almost choked on the drink. "I don't know."

"Do you know you are attractive?"

"No."

"People who know they're good-looking—I think they are not such nice people sometimes. Even when they are supposed to be." She drank. Then she leaned forward. "A toast. To us."

"To us," he said, and they clinked the glasses.

She swallowed. "Because I feel the same vay. I don't feel attractive."

"Oh," he said, "but you are." He drank.

"No," she said. "I look in a mirror and vhat do I see? A big nose too big for the face. And a long chin. I don't like my chin."

"You're beautiful," he said. The drink was tingling in his nerves, somehow. He took more of it.

She stared at him. "You would not disillusion me, I think."

"No," he said.

"To beauty," she said, holding her glass up. "And to all the beautiful people."

"That's us." He drank. He looked at the room with its tall bookcase and its television, its pictures of horses standing in grass fields under sunny skies. "You like horses," he said.

"Since I was little girl in Berlin. I told you. We went to the Catholic school and the sisters took us for walks out to the countryside."

"Have you ever ridden one?"

"Long ago. In Germany. I vas very small, before the bombing starts."

For a long moment, they were quiet.

"My father works at the embassy," she said. "He is not an important man, but a good man. He keeps the accounts—for all the services, you know? The butlers and the maids and the drivers. All that."

"Yes."

"A good man, to bring me here. He wants to make me a citizen. Always I try not to let him down."

"I'd like to meet him."

After another pause, she said, "I don't ride horses now. I only have pictures. You ride horses?"

"I did when I was ten. A Tennessee walking horse. You know what they are?"

"I think so."

"A very strange gait, the Tennessee walking horse. I rode it bareback."

"Bareback. How nice."

The ice rattled in the glasses. She finished hers and got up to pour more whiskey for herself. "It's good straight, too, you know."

"I've still got some ginger ale," he said.

She came back and took her place. "I like to sit in the dark." She crossed one leg over the other. Marshall realized that the light was almost gone from the room. "I do," she went on. "It makes me feel hidden."

"You're not afraid of the dark?"

"Only sometimes."

A moment later, she said, "I vonder, has somebody broken your heart?"

"No," he said.

"You must have hundreds of girlfriends."

"Oh, well—sure. I've dated all the runner-ups for Miss America. Since—1960." He shook his head and gave her a sardonic smile. "I'm swamped with them. Can't fight them all off."

"I'm serious."

"I don't have hundreds of girlfriends," he said.

"Nobody for funny Walter?"

He took a long drink. The whiskey seemed to be gathering behind his eyes. It was as if some pressure had begun there. But he felt good, too, and he was no longer so nervous.

"I'm sorry—I embarrass you."

"I think you're very beautiful," he said.

She put her glass down and sat forward. "In Germany, a man does not speak to a voman like this unless he has intentions."

"Yes," he said, unable to believe his own ears. "I have in—intentions. Right."

"You vould not run away if I said I liked you to stay?"

"Yes," he said. Then, "No."

"Some men think a woman is something for their fun."

"Not me," he told her. His mind was swimming.

She put her hands on either side of his face and gazed at him in the near dark. "If I kiss you, you von't think it's merely what you deserve?"

"No," he said. It was almost a shout.

"You would treat me so gentle and nice."

"Yes."

She sat back, put her hands together under her chin, half reclining there, only a shape in the bad light. "You would be unselfish."

"Excuse me?"

She made a dismissive gesture. "Drink."

He swallowed the last of the whiskey and ginger ale, and set the glass down on the table, next to hers. She was very still, and quiet, and he couldn't tell if she was looking at him.

"Natalie?" he said.

"No." She stirred, brought her legs up under her. "It's no use."

"What's no use."

"I'm silly," she said.

"Me, too," he told her.

"Drunk," she muttered.

"What should I do?" he asked, feeling that he would charge through flames if she asked him to.

"What do you mean?" she said.

"Tell me what you want me to do."

"You are such a young nice person. Don't be a bad man. Don't be a politician."

He waited.

"You would marry me and make everything all right. You would not worry about before. What happened before . . ." She stopped.

"Yes," he heard himself say.

She moved closer and put her head on his shoulder. He breathed the fragrance of her hair, turned his own face into it, and kissed her.

"Sweet boy," she said.

His own voice seemed to come from a distance. "Will you marry me?"

She shifted slightly to look at him, then lay her head down again.

He kept still.

"You only know me from the school."

"I know I want to marry you," he said.

She seemed to take this as a challenge. She sat up straight, and put her hands in her lap. "All right, then. If you vill have me, I'll marry you. People do it all the time."

"You—you'll marry me?" he said.

"Why not?" She looked at him. "You don't believe me?"

"No—I mean—yes—you're—you're not joking."

"I don't joke about such a thing."

He coughed, looking through the dirty window across the dimness at the scattered lights of the city at sunset.

"Just hold me now," she said, snuggling closer.

After what seemed a long time, he said her name. Silence. She had fallen asleep. The whiskey was swimming in his head, and he was anxious about his mother, the time, Alice, the falling darkness outside, but he remained very still, supporting her, while she fidgeted and sighed, for more than an hour. When she woke, it was with a start, and she sat up, running her hand through her shining hair.

"I'm so sorry. Can you please go now, darling, I think I'm going to be sick."

"I'll go," he said. She stood, unsteadily, and put her arms around him. And now she kissed him, slowly, with an almost leisurely softness.

"Sweet boy," she said. They walked to the door, and she opened it, then kissed him again. "Good-bye."

"So long," he said with an embarrassing flourish that he regretted immediately.

Her smile was faintly tolerant, somehow. She kissed him again, this time on the chin, and then stood back, holding the door. "My very dear young boyfriend."

"Good night," he said.

She touched her finger to her lips, then closed the door.

*H*e would have to tell Alice. He would have to find some way to say the words, to let her down as gently as possible, and, of course, there were no words. When she called, Sunday evening, to tell him that Minnie was going to remain in the hospital for another few days, he strove to think of the way to say it all to her, how he had never meant to hurt her, how it was just that he hadn't understood his own heart, how he liked and respected her, and had mistaken that for love. No, that wasn't exactly true, either.

Everything felt false to him.

"What's the matter?" she said—her small voice in the slight static of the phone.

"Nothing," he said. It couldn't be right to tell her over the phone. "I feel bad about what happened. I've never seen anything like that." This was at least true.

"Minnie's lived with it all her life," Alice said, sniffling. "I'm sorry. I can't seem to keep from crying all the time."

"No," he said. "I feel exactly the same way."

He would wait until he could explain, face-to-face. He would explain everything.

But on Monday morning, when he saw her, he couldn't bring himself to speak, couldn't bring the words out of himself to begin telling it all. Even so, she seemed strangely withdrawn and quiet, which made him worry that she had somehow read things in his face. They went to lunch together. She seemed so sad and vulnerable. Surely it couldn't be the right thing to say anything now. She would be spending a lot of time with Minnie, at the hospital. The next few days were going to be hard enough. She and her father had gone to visit with Minnie yesterday evening, she said. And while they were there, the two of them had argued: Her father did not want her involving herself in protests; he forbade it. He talked about the deaths of the three young Civil Rights workers—this and other things, other enormities, frightened him, and he was not reluctant to admit it. He said he had only one daughter and he refused to give her up to anyone's idea of social justice or to some misguided idealism of her own. He said all this with Minnie lying there staring at him.

"Misguided?" Minnie said. "Misguided?"

"You know what I mean," he told her, "and you know how I mean it. I don't mean it generally."

"You the one misguided," Minnie told him. "Ain't you shamed of yoursef, na."

She couldn't get out of the bed on her own, and they were running more tests. At the end of the visit, she refused to speak to Alice's father, and he was now angry at Alice for this fact.

"I told him I'm of age," Alice said. "He can't tell me what I can and can't do, and he can't stop me from going anywhere I want to go."

"I'm sorry you're having to go through this," Marshall said.

"It's not your fault. Although he thinks it is."

"Me?" Marshall said. "He blames me?"

She wiped tears from the corners of her eyes. "Oh, of course. He wouldn't give me credit for having the idea myself, you see."

He said, "Albert thought you were wonderful, Saturday."

This seemed to go through her like a pang. Her face appeared about to collapse, and the tears dropped down her cheeks. "You didn't?"

"Oh, no—we both did. We talked about it. We thought you were great. We did."

She said, "Sometimes I wonder if I'm not just—if I'm doing it all for some kind of approval—from somewhere. But then I look at Minnie. I love her. She's my mother, for God's sake—as much as anyone else has ever been. I never even knew my real mother. And the thing about her—Minnie—Minnie's so much in charge of herself. She's—herself. Complete—you know? She has an exact idea of where she leaves off and the rest of the world begins. I wish I had her strength."

"Is she . . ." He didn't know how to phrase the question. He wondered if, now that Minnie had openly defied Alice's father, she would be let go.

"They don't know," Alice said. "They can't get to the bottom of it. She's—she says she thinks her time is up, and her body's just going along with it. And I took her there. I put her in the way of it."

"No," he said. "Alice—listen."

But she wouldn't be consoled. He walked with her back to work, and she kissed him on the cheek. He had never seen her so quiet. It was as though she were suddenly sensitive to his unease about her. There was something so kindly in the way she looked at him. "I'm going to the hospital after work. Do you want to come with me?"

"I've got school," he said.

"Well," she said, and hesitated. "My father—I think he's—he's sort of calling that Brightman thing off."

"He's what?"

"He said he blames *you*, Walter. And I got defiant with him. I told him I didn't care what he thought, that I was going to do what *I* thought was right. Actually, I didn't bother to deny it when he guessed the whole thing was your idea. We were—we were yelling at each other, you know, and he—he sort of said we could forget the Mitchell Brightman thing."

"Well, can't—we can't—we have to talk to him. You have to talk to him."

She shook her head. "I'm not talking to him. I'm moving out. I'm getting a place of my own, Walter."

"I thought you wanted him to—I thought he and my mother—" He heard himself say these words, felt the lie in it.

"Oh, he was so ungracious," Alice said. "Your mother had to notice it."

"But what about the party—all those presents."

"But that wasn't for me, really," she said. "Was it? That was for him, so he could show everyone how *fatherly* he is. You don't understand, Walter, and I have to go now. I'm late." She walked away from him, brushing her eyes with both hands. The other women in her office looked at her with concern, and in a moment they were all standing around her. One of them gave him a look, as though to fix the responsibility squarely where it belonged.

"It's not that," Alice said. "Please." She turned and spoke to him. "I'll be home later tonight, Walter. Okay? I'll call you. You better not call, because you might get *him*. And there's no sense giving him any opportunities."

Chapter

14

orgive me, Father, for I have sinned. My last confession was two weeks ago. I indulged in pride five times, Father. I was vain a lot. And I committed the sin of drunkenness once. I had impure thoughts twenty times. And, oh, Father, I went to another church.

Did you go there to worship?

It was a funeral. The people I was with went, and I couldn't get out of it.

If you went to pay your respects to someone, I'm sure it's all right, son.

I didn't even know the person, Father.

I'm sure it's all right, though. You didn't go there to worship.

No, Father.

Go on.

Father, I'm—I'm engaged to be married, and I went to see another woman. And now I think I'm engaged to her, too.

Pardon me?

I went to see another woman, Father. Not my fiancée.

Did you have relations with this other woman?

Relations, Father?

Sexual relations.

Oh, NO, Father. But I was drunk.

Were you drunk when you went to see her?

No, I got drunk while I was seeing her.

Did you go to see her intending to have sexual relations with her?

I don't think so.

You don't think so. Well, son—did you or didn't you?

I think I just wanted to talk to her, Father. See—see her.

Did you feel that you were doing wrong?

I think so, Father.

Did you or didn't you?

I think I did.

Do you feel something for this woman?

YES—er, no—I don't know.

Perhaps you should speak to her about what you feel.

You mean my fiancée? The first one?

The first one—what do you mean—the—I don't understand, son.

I asked her to marry me, Father.

Who?

This woman.

Your fiancée?

Well, not my—not the real—the first fiancée—no.

I think you're going to have to explain this a little further, son.

I asked a woman other than my fiancée to marry me. And she said yes.

So now you're saying you have two fiancées?

Yes, Father.

Are these women Catholic?

One is.

Which one?

The second one. But the first says she'll convert.

Do they know of each other?

Oh, NO, Father.

How old are you, son?

Nineteen, Father.

I see. Excuse me—I have a—little—a cough. Wait. Aha. Hah. Excuse me. Go on.

I don't want to hurt anyone, Father.

Do you love your—er—ah. Hah. Agh. Uh—fiancée?

Which one?

Either one—any one. I don't know. Ah. Let's start with the first one.

I'm sorry, Father.

Well?

I don't know, Father. I know I like her.

And the second?

I think so.

You think so what—you think you like her?

No, love. I think I love her.

Son—what is this?

I don't know, Father.

You love her. The second one, I mean.

I think I do. I don't know, Father. It's all so confused.

Look, what exactly are you trying to confess here? Confusion is not a sin. At least as far as I can still tell.

I think I might've lied to the first one, Father. In a way. I kissed her, and it meant more to her than it did to me. I mean, I think I knew it meant more to her. No, I know it did.

You know what conditions have to obtain for something to be a sin, don't you?

Yes, Father.

Well, what did you intend in all this?

I didn't want to hurt anyone, Father.

Agh. Ah. Hah, hah. Excuse me. Interesting way to go about it.

Father?

Listen, son, just try to be as truthful and as charitable as possible with everyone. And try to remember that one thing you really can't do is marry both of these young women. And that you'll do much more harm if you marry any girl without loving her. You say you love this woman—

Which one, Father?

You know, I no longer have the slightest idea which one. Do you love either one?

I don't KNOW.

Well, then—is it your usual practice to go around asking girls to marry you?

No, Father.

You understand that people don't ask other people to marry them unless they're in love—usually, anyway, these—these days. Ah.

Yes, Father.

Well, so—did you love your fiancée when you asked her? The first one.

I don't know if I did. I like her. I didn't want to hurt her feelings.

Who—where did you learn that asking a person to marry you— that's how you protect somebody's feelings? Son, that isn't the way the Western world is set up, you know.

Yes, Father.

Let me get this straight—you asked one girl to marry you to spare her feelings, and now you've found you're interested in someone else. Is that an accurate description of the mess you're in?

Well, I don't even really know her that well, Father. But I think so, yes.

Is this other person interested in you?

She said she'd marry me.

Oh, yes. Quite. I don't know how I could've let that slip my mind.

I went to see this other person, Father, and I think about her a lot. And I know it would upset my—the first one.

Your initial—your fiancée.

Yes, Father.

Well, of course. That seems clear.

I'm sorry, Father. I wanted to tell her about it, but I couldn't. I just couldn't.

You didn't want to hurt any feelings.

She's counting on it, Father. She doesn't have any idea.

And you think it'll hurt her too much to deprive her of yourself.

No, Father—that isn't it. It's what she says. The expressions on her face—I do like her—

Look, do you have any time to figure this all out for yourself? When're you supposed to be married? You haven't—you haven't set dates for these marriages?

The date—there's no date set quite yet.

For either one?

Right.

Does anyone else know about these engagements?

My mother does about the first one. And her father does.

The first one's father?

Yes, Father. He threatened me.

He what?

Threatened me. About his daughter. I haven't let that affect me, though.

You haven't—agh. Hah. Uh—excuse me again.

It doesn't have anything to do with it, Father. I'm sorry. I just wanted to give you the whole picture—

Son—

Father?

Never mind. Hold on a second. I have this cough—ah. Listen. Ah, look—just try to be as charitable and truthful as you can in all your dealings with people, especially people you say you—ah—love. These sorts of problems can change overnight. Now, is there anything else you have to confess?

I don't like my mother's fiancé. I have uncharitable feelings about him.

Your mother has a fiancé, too?

Yes, Father. And I have bad feelings about him.

Do you act on those feelings?

I've been cool to him, yes.

Anything else?

No, Father.

Try to be charitable.

Yes, Father.

For your penance—

Should I keep telling my mother when I have these feelings, Father?

I don't think so. It wouldn't really do any good, would it?

But if she asks me. Should I lie to her? Wouldn't that be a sin?

Don't volunteer anything.

And if she asks?

Be honest but charitable. Perhaps you should examine your feelings toward this man.

I can't stand being around him, Father.

Maybe you should work on it, for your mother's sake.

Yes, Father. Should I tell my mother I'll work on it?

Not unless she asks. Now, for your penance say a rosary, and ask

*the Blessed Virgin for guidance. And try to be a little more cautious
about what you say to people.*

Alice didn't call Monday night. Tuesday and Wednesday she wasn't
at work. He spent the lunch hour Wednesday deciding to call her,
and then changing his mind about it; he did not want to risk getting her father on the line. So he waited for her to call, and when
she did, late that afternoon, she seemed angry with him.

"Don't you care what's going on?" she said.

"Alice, you said not to call you."

"I meant the other night."

Now, he was irritated. "Well, how was I supposed to know
that?" She was silent just long enough for him to feel sorry again.
"Alice," he said. "Look—"

"There's something wrong, isn't there?"

"No," he said quickly, with a sense of capitulation and cow-
ardice.

"I took time off to be with Minnie."

"How is she?"

"Oh," Alice said, "she's just the same." She began to cry again.

"I'll pray for her," he said.

"Walter?"

"Yes."

"I feel like everything's falling apart."

"It'll be all right," he told her.

Mr. Wolfschmidt would not let him go early, so it was growing
dark by the time he got off work, and headed up to the school. He
had no time to stop and eat, or to visit Saint Matthew's. He hurried past the stores with their pictures of Kennedy at work, and
the wind stung him. The very air seemed inimical, loaded with
judgment. Leaves swirled under the lamps and seemed to skitter,
as though alive, across the surface of the road. He breathed the
odor of diesel exhaust fumes and the raw dust of the city and
thought of the sulphurous air of hell. On one corner of Eighteenth
Street, a black man sat with a cup in one hand and a bundle of
clothes in another. He rattled the cup at Marshall and said,
"Caught short, sir."

Marshall had a ten and a twenty in his pocket. He gave the man the twenty.

"Thankee, sir."

He walked on a few paces, then had the thought that the money was a kind of payoff, a ransom to keep from having to deal with the man in any other way, in the way of a true Christian. He walked back, and the man impassively watched him come. Walter got down on his haunches and looked out at the street, the people hurrying by.

"Chilly night," he said.

"You wont it back?" the man said.

"Pardon me?"

"The fuck'n money. You wont it back?"

"Oh. No, sir."

"Well, it don't buy you the right to mess with me, either."

"No, sir," Marshall said. "I'm not going to mess with you at all."

"Well," the man said, "what you wont wid me, then?"

"Nothing," Marshall said. "Nothing at all. Just—passing the time."

"Well, pass it somewhere else," the man said. "I ain't in no talkin' mood. You did good, and you can leave it that way. You wont your money back?"

"No, sir."

"Then I thankee. Now go on."

Marshall stood.

"Git."

"Yes, sir." He walked on in the stinging wind, discouraged, fighting the sense of the futility of every hope and intention, filled with chagrin and confusion.

At the school, gloriously lighted in the window, the embodiment of his most selfish wish, Natalie Bowman sat with her big book on her lap—Shakespeare. Seeing him, she waved, saying something he couldn't hear through the glass, then came to the entrance of the little library to greet him.

"Your face is purple," she said.

"The first really cold night."

"You're late." She didn't wait for an answer, kissing him on the mouth, her arms resting softly on his shoulders. He put his arms around her and tried to keep from dropping to his knees.

She said, "An un-gentle man is never nervous."

"Natalie—" he breathed.

"I know," she said. "I cannot go for a drink after class because I have to study." She stepped back and folded her arms under her breasts and seemed to study him. "Maybe one drink."

"Okay," he said.

She gave a small, thrilling laugh. "Maybe I vill tell you my life story."

"We could do that."

"Have you told anyone about us?"

"Not yet—"

"I have told Mrs. D'Allessandro that we are going together."

"Okay," he said.

"She didn't look too happy."

He was at a loss.

"I'll be here." She smiled, then reached over and touched the tip of his nose. "I hope you get some other color in your face before then. You look embarrassed."

"It's the cold," he insisted.

"I know." She turned and started back into the room, her dark hair swinging across the middle of her back.

He had a strange, breathless sense of unreality, a kind of practical disbelief; he almost pinched himself. In the radio school, he found Mr. D'Allessandro's office door open, his coat hung across the desk chair. The others were already engaged in the evening's work. Albert was reading a commercial about a restaurant. Mrs. Gordon was sitting on a stool with a headset on, getting ready to do the news. She glanced at Marshall with a reprimanding expression, then returned to her work. Ricky Dalmas sat in a ladder-backed chair against the wall behind her. Joe Baker was in the engineering booth, working the console. The new student, Wilbur Soames, stood with Martin Alvarez behind Baker, quietly talking. When Marshall entered the sound booth, Baker said, "D'Allessandro wondered if you were going to skip tonight."

"Where is he?"

Baker shrugged.

Albert's voice was in the speakers. "I'm probably not pronouncing this right, but in a minute, after the news, we'll have some of the music of Pro-ko-feef."

Baker turned it down a little and put on earphones. "I understand we got the cathedral. This thing is shaping up to be some night."

Martin Alvarez said, "Congratulations, mun."

"I don't know," Marshall said.

"D'Allessandro's all excited," said Baker. "You'd think he'd landed Edward R. Murrow himself."

"D'Allessandro's learning about showbiz," Wilbur Soames said. He was leaning against the wall, his hands in his pockets. He wore a gray suit with no tie. His white shirt was open at the collar and the darker coils of hair on his dark chest showed. The whiteness of the shirt made his skin seem even blacker than it was. Nodding at Marshall, he said, "I hear you had some trouble."

"Did Albert tell you?"

He nodded. Then, "It was on the six o'clock news, man."

"It was? We were on television?"

Soames was amused. "They didn't get any footage of you, no."

"We almost got killed. Did you see Albert's face?"

Soames took his hands out of his pockets and folded his arms, leaning against the wall again. "Well, I guess it turns out the Civil Rights bill hasn't quite gone into effect in some places."

"You should've been there," Marshall told him.

"No, thanks. I said before, I'm all through with that."

"I don't understand how you can say such a thing."

Soames leaned toward him; it was almost aggressive. "*Easy.*"

Alvarez made a clicking noise with his mouth, shaking his head. "Right here in the capital, mun."

Dalmas had risen on the other side of the glass, and was holding up a piece of paper to indicate that he was ready to read his commercial.

"Oh, good," Baker said. "Wilbur, dig this." He put the switch on so Dalmas could hear. "Okay, Ricky, take it away."

Ricky said, "Ask not what your country can do for you, ask what you can do for your country. Now is the time for all good men to come to the aid of their country."

"What the hell're you doing?" Baker said.

"I'm helping you set my level."

"You're fine," Baker said. "Damn."

They waited. Baker flicked the switch, so Dalmas couldn't hear him. "Don't miss this, Wilbur," he said without looking back at Soames.

"I'm listening," Soames said.

"You want me to start?" Dalmas said.

"Yeah. Right now," said Baker, signaling him.

"Ladies and gentlemen, baldness happens to the best of us, and there's no reason to make bald jokes about it and laugh about people like that Buddy does to poor Mel Cooley on *The Dick Van Dyke Show*. There's no reason to call people 'baldy' or 'skinhead' or 'billiard ball.' But for those who do, there's something to make the whole thing easier on yourself. Call Don's Hair Salon, where bald people have been going for years . . . "

Soames laughed as Baker put his head down on his arms.

"You shouldn't laugh at him," said Marshall.

"You're feeling virtuous," Soames murmured. "That can be a bit intoxicating, I guess, huh? But it's unhealthy to be too serious about it, you know what I mean?"

"It's a very serious thing," Marshall said.

"This boy's religious," said Baker. "He was gonna be a priest for a while."

"A priest, huh. Well, that is pretty religious." Soames patted the young man on the back. "Just playing with you, there, Walter, boy."

Marshall looked at him.

"That's all right, man. Really, I understand."

"*I* don't understand *you*," Marshall said.

Soames laughed. "I'm not that complicated, believe me."

Baker had put music on.

"What an operation," Alvarez said, going out.

Soames nudged Marshall's arm and said, "You think I ought to be out there with those folks because I'm colored, don't you?"

"No," Marshall said.

"Hell—sure you do. It's okay if you do, man. But, listen, I don't do *anything* for that reason anymore. It doesn't follow that just because my mother made a habit of staying out in the sun I'm going to be there in the street getting the shit kicked out of me by the police. I'm Wilbur Soames, first. Me. You know? You ever read a book called *The Invisible Man*?"

"Sure," Marshall said.

"Not II. G. Wells," said Soames.

Marshall was silent.

"I'm talking about Ralph Ellison," Soames went on. "And, well, I've decided to demand that I have the luxury of my identity—without having to tie it to everybody else whose mother made a habit of staying out in the sun, and without having to live up to anybody else's *idea* of me and what my needs and interests are. You see? I don't feel it's all that healthy for me to have to spend my whole life according to anybody's *idea*. You understand?"

"I didn't say anything," Marshall told him.

"I can see it in your eyes," the other said.

Mr. D'Allessandro came in then, rattling his keys. "What're you doing, Wilbur? Are you indoctrinating young Marshall, here?" He gave Marshall a look, which he quickly glossed over with that rictus-like smile.

Soames also smiled. "In a manner of speaking. I don't think I'm enough of a nigger for his taste."

"That's not true," Marshall said, sensing that he was far out of his element, and feeling the color rise to his face. "How can you say a thing like that?"

Soames patted his shoulder. "Just messing with you, son. Your heart's in the right place, and, man, not everybody's is. Not everybody's is."

"Wilbur likes to get under your skin," Mr. D'Allessandro said. "So to speak. It's the way he operates."

"He's not a Freedom Rider," Joe Baker said.

"As a matter of unpleasant fact," said Mr. D'Allessandro, "he was there. And he has the scars to prove it."

Soames leaned against the wall again, his arms folded, regarding Joe Baker, who shrugged and said, "Small world."

"I know—you were there, too," Soames said. "You told me before. That was some bad time, and I remember thinking about how much I loved the guard. Man, I loved the guard that night."

Marshall broke in, addressing him. "You were part of it, then—you know." He had meant to indicate that the other man understood, but then he couldn't quite formulate for himself what the understanding was.

"Yeah, well," Soames said. "It was a while back."

"Is young Marshall trying to draft you into the movement?" D'Allessandro said.

"Yes, massuh."

They all laughed, and the young man had the feeling there was something they were referring to that he had not been allowed to know or hear. Now D'Allessandro seemed to remember himself, stirring into motion. He went across to his office, and Mrs. Gordon made her way there, too. He closed the office door, then opened it again almost immediately. Mrs. Gordon appeared agitated, wiping her forehead with a napkin, her purse dangling from the crook of her arm. She went into the studio and gathered her coat, and Mr. D'Allessandro walked with her down to the foyer, then out. For a few minutes, there was just the sound of the music Albert had put on. Marshall looked at the others' faces, wondering what they were thinking.

"We'll all be famous," Wilbur Soames said, laughing. Joe Baker had murmured something to him. A moment later, D'Allessandro came back upstairs, exhibiting the pointless breeziness of a man who has managed to put something unpleasant behind him.

"Mrs. Gordon hasn't been—feeling well," he said, not quite allowing himself to look at Marshall. "She's—gone home. So." He clapped his hands together. "We'll have to go on without her. Let's get cracking now. This is supposed to be a radio station."

The others took their places to continue the evening's practice. D'Allessandro supervised this, bustling from the studio to the sound booth and back, and when things were settled, Soames at the console now, Baker and Dalmas in the studio at the microphones, he went into his office. Marshall followed. There was a cigar crushed out in the ashtray.

"That's right," Mr. D'Allessandro said, seeing the expression on the younger man's face. "Marcus was here earlier this evening. He's gone now . . ."

Marshall looked around the room, on impulse.

"What is it, lad? I've got some paperwork to get out of the way."

"There's been a—sort of a—a hitch," he said. "I . . ." He had the sensation that Marcus was still in the room, would step out from behind one of the window curtains, or come up from behind the desk.

"You're not—I told you what you—Sunday was a mistake. There really wasn't anything."

"That's not what I meant," the young man said.

"Well—what, then?" said Mr. D'Allessandro. He was standing behind his desk.

Marshall started to explain about the events in Maryland on Saturday, Alice's father's displeasure. But the desperate look on the older man's face stopped him. Mr. D'Allessandro sat down slowly. "Did anyone get hurt?"

"Well, Alice's family maid and cook is in the hospital, with some sort of fatigue. They checked her heart—"

"Yes, but what's this got to do with the school?"

"Oh," Marshall said. Again, he had misunderstood everything. "Nothing."

"I've got a date set. December twentieth. Mitchell Brightman's office said December twentieth was acceptable. I left a message with his secretary. I tried to speak to him, but I couldn't get through." D'Allessandro stared. "What is it, lad? Something's the matter? Nothing's wrong, is there?"

"No, sir. Really."

"My wife is worried. I can't get her to tell me anything. There's nothing to worry about, eh?"

"Nothing," Marshall said. "I just wanted you to know that."

"You're a good lad," D'Allessandro said, wiping his forehead with a handkerchief. "A fine young gentleman. Let's—let's keep Alice happy. Okay? Just until December twentieth. Anything you've got in your mind to do, son—you know? After December twentieth, I don't care if you want to go to the moon. That's your business. But please—don't screw it up for me with *girls*, for God's sake. You know what I'm talking about, don't you? We're men of the world, eh?"

"I'll do my best, sir."

"Don't say that. Don't stand there and say that when the date is set. The hall is set. Everything's arranged."

"Yes, sir."

"I'm depending on you. The whole school's depending on you."

"I know, sir."

"Don't 'sir' me. That's what you say to people you can let down. You're not going to let me down, are you?"

"No, s—"

"That's a good lad," he said, wringing his hands, rising from behind the desk and then sitting back down again. "That's good."

Marshall backed out of the room, determined that, if need be, he would find some way to get through to Brightman on his own.

In the engineering room, Wilbur Soames was sitting at the console while Joe Baker stood behind him, his arms resting on the back of the chair. Alvarez had come back, along with Albert. They were in the studio with Ricky Dalmas, who read copy about college football scores. "Colgate, sixteen, Bucknell, seven; Miami, thirty-four, Tennesee State, thirty-one."

In a few minutes it would be Marshall's turn to take the console, and he waited, standing a little to the side of Wilbur Soames, who had earphones on, with one ear exposed so that he could talk to Joe Baker. They had apparently been telling jokes.

Soames said, "How about this one? A guy in Las Vegas walks up to this chorus girl and says, 'Tickle yer ass with a feather?' And she turns and says, 'What did you say to me, you creep?' And he says, 'Madam, I said, "typical nasty weather."'"

Baker coughed and sputtered.

The young man moved toward the door, aware that Soames was watching him.

"Wait," Soames said. "I'm not finished."

"I don't really like those kinds of stories."

"What kind, man? It's a joke. Nothing wrong with a joke. Listen. So this drunk sees the whole thing, hmmm? And he goes up to the guy and says, 'You mind tellin' me what tha fuck you're doin'?' And the guy says, 'Man, that's how I get a woman for the night. I go up to every woman I see and say, "Tickle yer ass with a feather." And if they act shocked, I say "typical nasty weather." And I don't get slapped, see. And if they don't act shocked, hey, I got me a lady for the night.' Well, the drunk thinks that's the best thing he ever heard of, and he staggers up to the first woman he sees and says, 'Hey! Shove a fucking feather up your ass?' And she says '*What* did you *say*?' And he says, 'Look at tha fucking sky.'"

Baker was bending down with his arms folded at his stomach, making the coughing sound, and Soames sat there watching him, smiling.

"Oh, man," Baker said. "Oh, my, my, my."

"It's good, isn't it?" Soames said. "Did you hear the one about Johnson flying in a helicopter over Mississippi, and he sees these two white boys driving a boat with this colored boy on water skis behind them? You know this one?"

"No," Baker said, laughing. "It's already funny."

"The president gets them to land the helicopter, and he tells these two guys that's the spirit he's looking for in America. And he pats them on the shoulder and waves to the colored boy out in the water, and then flies away. And the first white boy looks at the other and says, 'What do you suppose is the matter with him, anyway? Ain't he ever seen two guys trolling for alligators before?'"

At this, Baker began to slide down the wall. He sat with his legs out, choking and laughing. "Jesus Christ, Wilbur," he got out at last, trying to catch his breath.

Have mercy on us.

Soames looked at Marshall. "What did you say?"

"Nothing," Marshall said.

"You're standing there mumbling. Are you okay, kid?"

Baker was still laughing, but he had gotten to his feet. "Trolling for alligators," he said. "Lord, that's great." He went out into the hall and down the stairs.

Marshall turned to Soames. "I'm not going to work the console. I'm down for it, but I'm—cover for me. Mr. D'Allessandro will understand."

"You tell him, boy."

"I'll be back."

"Yes, massuh."

Marshall went down the stairs and past the library, where several people were quietly reading and working. Natalie was not there, nor was she in the break area in the basement. Someone had left the outside door open, and the room was several degrees colder than the rest of the building. Joe Baker had put money in the Coke machine, and it hadn't worked. He was slapping the side of it and shaking it. Finally, the bottle clattered into the tray. Orange soda. He opened it and drank most of its contents in a long gulping. Then he looked at Marshall. "Is there a wind in here?" He saw the door, and walked over and pulled it shut. "Anybody could walk in."

Absurdly, Marshall thought of Marcus and looked around the room.

"That Soames—he's funnier than hell."

"Alice's father said he's calling the whole thing off with Mitchell Brightman."

Baker seemed only mildly interested. "No kidding. Well, I guess that might be that, then. To tell you the truth, Walter, I'm a little past worrying about it."

They heard footsteps on the stairs, a slow progress, someone descending. It was Albert. "Hey," Albert said.

Baker finished the soda, set the bottle in the rack beside the machine, and put another nickle into the slot. This time there was no trouble. The bottle clattered into the tray. "Albert," he said, "you don't look too good."

Albert said, "I've got a bad headache."

"You ought to go home and get some rest, boy." Baker got his second bottle of soda, then moved to the stairs and started back up. "That Wilbur," he said. "Man. A heart attack on wheels." He went on.

"What did I miss?" Albert said. He stood there in the center of the room, so tall, with his hand held up to the side of his face.

"Oh," Marshall said to him, "Wilbur Soames was telling dirty jokes."

"I'm really depressed," Albert said.

He went on to explain that he and Emma had continued to argue over the sit-in, and his part in it, and that they had finally gotten down to how differently they saw the problem. Other things had come out. Apparently, Emma's closed-mindedness extended to other groups besides Negroes: She didn't like Jews, or Catholics— Papists, she called them—or Muslims. She claimed—and Albert was careful to say that it had been in the heat of an argument—that she didn't care what the rest of the world did with these groups of people as long as she didn't have to deal with them. There wasn't anything she as an individual could do about these problems, and so if people kept to themselves and let her keep to herself, she had no problem with them. Each to his own, she said; it was the way of the world. She was dead set against any kind of mixing, and nothing Albert said could dislodge her. He had ranted and railed at her, he said. He had reminded her of what the country had recently enough spent so much of itself to ward off—the Nazis were in the near distance, after all, not even twenty years ago. Her own father had given his life at Anzio. Surely she understood that Hitler had come from this thing. This wrong thinking alone. This, he said, and nothing more. Surely she could see that one had to learn how to process these feelings of suspicion and distrust of differentness, one had to work to make oneself see individuals, people, one by one, and not abstractions based on these suspicions and distrusts. But she wouldn't budge, she sat in his living room with her hands clenched in her lap, and her lower lip sticking out, a stubborn baby used to having her way.

And what was worse, she had decided this week that she could leave her aunt's house for good. She wanted to move in with Albert. She had already gotten so that she could navigate freely in the little apartment, and she was tired of having to depend on her aunt for everything. She wanted to go to Maryland on the bus, and get married by a justice of the peace, and have it over with. She had, in effect, presented Albert with an ultimatum, and he was certain that this stemmed from the fact that she was beginning to sense his unease with her. Emma was the sort who would not shrink from bad news if she thought it might be on its way; she would insist on facing it rather than putting herself through the anticipation of it. There were all sorts of admirable things about her, Albert said. She was strong. She was brave. She had a stubborn will to do for herself and to make her life her own. She was amazingly tender and sweet in those moments when they were being affectionate with each other. She would make him a good wife, and he loved her.

"I do love her," Albert said, and his voice broke. Then he almost laughed. "What a mess."

They were sitting opposite each other in one of the two booths under the basement window. Somewhere a fan began to whir—it was probably in the back of one of the soft-drink machines—and people had begun straggling down from the night college as well as the radio school. Mrs. D'Allessandro came in with two students, and behind them was Ricky Dalmas, carrying the paper bag with his dinner in it. He nodded at Marshall, and took a seat next to Albert.

"That's such an ugly bruise. I hope you put ice on it."

"Yes," Albert said. "I put ice on it."

"You look terrible." Dalmas opened the bag and brought out a thick ham and cheese sandwich. "I got beat up once at school," he said cheerfully. "When I was in high school. And, of course, I got beat up at home every day." He bit into the sandwich. It smelled of garlic and Italian spices. "The bruises take forever to clear up on your face."

"Excuse me," Albert said. "I'd better get back upstairs."

"Me, too," said Marshall.

"I'm used to eating alone," Dalmas said. "Go right ahead."

Mrs. D'Allessandro took Marshall by the arm, above the elbow. "How are you this evening?"

"Fine," he said, making way for Albert.

Her face registered her horror at Albert's face, but Albert didn't see this. He took her hand when Marshall introduced him and said, "Hello." Then he stepped into the hallway, and turned to wait.

"What happened to your friend?"

"An accident," Marshall said.

She had already left this behind. "I take it arrangements are proceeding?"

"Yes, ma'am."

"I think we need more time to get the word out about our gala occasion—but my husband wouldn't listen. So our work's definitely cut out for us."

He nodded—wanting, as always, to please.

"I understand you're going with Natalie, now. And do you want to tell me how you're reconciling this with your young friend Alice? Aren't you and Alice engaged or something?"

"Alice—" he began. "She—"

"And does Natalie know about her?"

"I don't know what anybody knows," he said, looking back at her.

"You be careful, young man—we can't have your Alice mad at you, can we?" She smiled—there was something brittle and unpleasant about it, almost as though she had made a face at him.

Albert had climbed to the first landing and was sitting on the top step, waiting, his head in his hands.

"Are you okay?" Marshall asked him.

"Headache." He stood. "I think I better go home. I feel bad, Walter."

"I'll walk you home," Marshall said.

Mrs. D'Allessandro stood on the stairs in front of the building with Natalie as the two young men came back down from the radio school. She took Natalie's arm and introduced her to Albert.

"Yes," Natalie said. "I have met him before."

"I'm taking Albert home," Marshall said. "He's not feeling well."

"Natalie and I could take him in my car," said Mrs. D'Allessandro.

"No," Marshall said. "That's all right. It's just down the street."

"I need the air," Albert said, almost under his breath.

"I'll come back," said Marshall.

"Natalie, don't you have something you have to do?" Mrs. D'Allessandro said.

Natalie seemed hesitant, then irritable. "I can't stay here," she said to Marshall. She looked at Mrs. D'Allessandro, then back at him. "I'll—I'll see you next time, maybe."

"Natalie?" he said.

"Is fine," she said. "Please?"

"She'll talk to you later," Mrs. D'Allessandro said. "You'd better go now. Your friend looks none too worse for wear."

Albert stood there, gazing myopically at one and then the other of them, the one bony hand up to the side of the deep-eyed face. Marshall took him by the elbow and started down the stairs. He looked back once, but the two women had gone back inside.

"What was that all about?" Albert asked.

"Nothing."

They walked on for a time in silence, and then Albert said, "You can tell me, you know."

Marshall stopped and looked at him.

"Mr. D'Allessandro said something about it to me," Albert said. "I—well, I guess he thought I knew."

"I don't know what to do," Marshall told him. "I've always been so scared of hurting anybody's feelings . . ."

They walked on.

"I like Alice," Albert said.

"So do I," said Marshall.

"You haven't said anything to her."

"Not yet."

"And I thought *I* had trouble."

At Albert's street, they paused again. It was a chilly night, without wind. The moon was bright, almost enclosed by an enormous bank of dark clouds, the foliate edges of which were intricately limned with silver.

"Some would say you're a lucky man," Albert said. "I'm okay now. You can go on if you want to. Unless you'd like to come on in for a while."

"I thought you had a headache," Marshall said.

Albert's smile was cryptic. "I do."

"Give my best to Emma," Marshall told him.

He took the bus home. There were several other passengers, each alone. One man read a newspaper; another held a book and nodded off. A black woman knitted something, counting low to herself. The lights of the city streets glided by, and there were sirens in the distance. The bus rattled and squeaked and shook as it traversed the unevennesses in the road, and Marshall thought about being in that closed van, singing with the others—the sense he had experienced of being part of some accidental glory, the beginning of the new country that would grow out of the old one. That had seemed true; and yet this was true, too—this clattering through dirty streets, past storefronts with iron gates over the facades, their pictures in the windows of a murdered president.

He got off at the stop in Arlington, and saw that Mr. Atwater's car was parked in front of the apartment house. He almost walked down the street to the doughnut shop in the next block, but then thought better of it: If he were any later, Loretta might begin to worry. Mr. Atwater was sitting in the kitchen, across the small table from her, smoking a cigar. The smell of it had filled the apartment.

"Oh, good," Loretta said. "You're home." She stood and put her arms around him. She smelled strongly of coffee. Her hair was pulled back, and she had on makeup, but she wore her dark blue bathrobe.

"We've got news," Mr. Atwater said.

"Let me tell him," said Loretta. "Please, Clark."

Atwater took a long drag of his cigar and blew the smoke at the ceiling. "Go," he said.

Chapter 15

*M*arshall managed for his mother's sake to feign surprise and gladness concerning the very unsurprising and unhappy news that Mr. Atwater had asked her to marry him. And somehow he hid his considerable displeasure upon hearing that she had accepted. "Isn't it wonderful?" she said, her eyes shining with an unnatural light. "We've only just now decided it."

"Wonderful," Marshall said. "When?"

"December seventeenth. Next year. December seventeenth, 1965. Maybe."

"That's my birthday," Mr. Atwater said.

"Don't you think that would be appropriate?" Loretta asked.

Marshall nodded, a bit dumbly, he felt. But there was nothing he could think of to tell them. Mr. Atwater offered him a black Cuban cigar, which he refused, and Loretta poured champagne for them. "A toast," she said.

Atwater stood, the cigar in one small, white hand, and, waving it slightly so that the smoke curled about him, said, "To the marriage of true minds."

"True minds," Loretta said.

They drank. Marshall watched his mother, and tried to see through the rather frenetic brightness with which she moved and spoke. It was like looking at a stranger—someone imitating Loretta Marshall.

"Things're gonna change," said Clark Atwater. "I do believe."

"Here's to change." Loretta drank.

Atwater was looking around the room. "We'll have to get rid of some of this stuff, of course."

"Well—" Loretta glanced at her son. "Let's go over that sort of thing later. This is supposed to be a celebration."

"That is kee-rect," Mr. Atwater said. "Don't know what the hell I'm thinking of."

They'd been waiting for the young man to come home so they could tell him the news and drink the champagne. They had several glasses of it, and Atwater talked about the plans for next year, managing to imply that there was something tentative about them even as he went on about what would change. It was as though he were speculating about it all, woolgathering. Loretta kept steering him back to the present, to a happy contemplation of what a good time they were having. Finally, Mr. Atwater allowed that it was getting late. He was tired. He said good night to the boy and took Loretta by the arm. "Walk me outside, honey."

"I'll be right back, Walter."

"She might not be right back," Atwater said.

"Clark—you stop that."

Atwater leaned in and kissed her on the side of the face, then burrowed into her neck. His glasses were pushed out of line, and it appeared for a moment that he might fall. But then he righted himself, and looked at her, blinking. "My sugar," he said. "My angel of the night."

"Please, Clark."

"I'm going to bed," Marshall told them. "Good night."

"I'll be back in one minute," said his mother.

Atwater was pulling her to the door. "If she's lucky," he said. Then he stepped back from her and took a long pull on the cigar. "Loretta," he said, the smoke pouring from him, "you look like a lady who's engaged to be married someday."

"That's me," she said. "Come on, now." She started out.

At the door, Mr. Atwater turned and held up the hand with the cigar in it. "Good night, sweet prince," he said.

"Clark, please."

He laughed—it was a high-pitched, glottal sound, like a kind of throat-clearing—and tramped clumsily out the door with Loretta holding his arm, bumping along at his side.

"Clark, maybe I should drive you."

"Don't be r'diclous. I'm fine . . ."

Marshall walked into his room and sat down on the bed. From the window came the muffled sounds of the city at night, and another, softer sound. Perhaps he had imagined it—that laugh, the small protesting voice talking through it. He did not look out the window.

Perhaps fifteen minutes later, he heard the door of the apartment open, and he went to the entrance of the living room just in time to see her drop down, with an exhausted sigh, onto the couch. She closed her eyes, and was still for a moment, her thin legs outstretched, her hands resting at her sides.

"I know you're there, Walter."

He entered the room and sat across from her.

"So, we're both engaged now," she said without opening her eyes.

"He's kind of indefinite about it."

"Well."

"You don't seem so happy," he told her.

"I'm tired."

They were quiet for a time. He was biting his nails, looking at the room, the furniture and pictures on the walls and knickknacks on the surfaces, wondering what among these familiar things Mr. Clark Atwater would want to get rid of or keep, and thinking how everything was indeed changing, how he and she were in the midst of the change that would propel him away from her, out into the world.

"Stop that," she said. "You're always fidgeting."

He put his hands in his lap.

She sat forward, and looked at him. "You look worn out, son. What's the matter with you, anyway? You've been brooding lately—"

"There's a girl at school—" he began.

"Alice?"

"No. That's the point, see—"

"Oh," his mother broke in. "I think I *do* see."

Again, they were quiet.

"I had a feeling. You just didn't seem very happy or relaxed about Alice."

"That's what I see now with you," he said, too quickly and with too much force. "You don't seem so happy about Atwater."

She put her head back. "Well, I'm not, I suppose. I'm past feeling like a teenager about it, you know?"

"But if you're not that happy about it, why are you doing it?"

"Go to bed, son."

"You won't even talk to me about it?"

She had closed her eyes again.

"It's because he's your boss, isn't it."

"Walter—please. I'm very tired."

"But that's it, isn't it."

She looked at him. "Not entirely. Okay? I'm almost forty-five years old, and—and it makes sense. He says he wants to marry me, and it makes sense."

"It doesn't make sense if you don't want to do it. Are you—it's—it can't be just to keep him happy. There are other jobs . . ."

After a silence, she said, "Anyway, it's far into the future. It's entirely possible he'll change his mind between now and then."

"Will he fire you, then?"

"Please go to bed, son. I'm really very tired, and I don't want to talk about it. I like him, okay? He's a bit of a jerk sometimes, but I like him, and he's—he says he wants me to be his wife. The way things are, he could've been a lot less nice than he's been."

"Yes, but you don't really feel anything for him. You're not going to do this to yourself—"

She stood and moved to the entrance of the kitchen, talking. "That's enough. This is nothing for you to concern yourself with. Now I want you to promise me you'll make no trouble about it." She turned in the frame of the doorway, and regarded him. "Promise me, please."

He said nothing. He couldn't look at her.

"Walter."

"Yes," he said. "I hear you."

"Well?"

"I promise."

"Good," she said. "Now, would you like some tea?"

"No, thanks."

After a brief pause, she said, "Go on to bed, son. Things'll look better in the morning."

He said nothing, still sitting there.

"You'll be leaving me, soon enough," she said, "and I don't want to live alone."

"Yes, ma'am."

"And you. What about you, Walter?"

He looked up.

"What're you going to do about your own situation, regarding Alice?"

"I don't know," he said. "I have to tell her, I guess."

"You *guess*."

He looked at her.

"You don't expect *me* to tell her."

"No, ma'am."

"What's the other girl's name?"

He told her.

"Is she pretty?"

"She's—she's beautiful."

"You've decided on the basis of that?"

"No."

"Does she feel the same way about you?"

"I think so, yes."

"You got yourself in a cute little mess."

"I know."

"Well—Alice is older than you are. She'll get over it. We don't really fit in with those people, anyway. For God's sake, there was some man walking on his hands at that party, and nobody even paid any attention to it. Alice is a grown woman and she knows the score, I'm sure."

"The other girl—Natalie—is older than Alice."

His mother received this information with apparent calm. She hesitated for only a second. "Well, I do wonder what is going on with these women."

"I don't have any idea," he told her. "I said I'd marry them both, though, and now no matter what I do, somebody gets hurt."

"In other words, you're having the time of your life."

"I hate it," he said. "And I hate myself."

"No you don't. You just think you do."

He shrugged. "I can't seem to be—well—natural with people."

"Meaning what?"

"I keep going in whatever direction they seem to want me to go. I keep trying to please everybody. It's like I'm all air inside. Like I have no opinions or principles when I'm talking to somebody. That's why I went to radio school, because Mr. Atwater said I should in that history class my junior year."

"And now you got yourself engaged to two women—older women at that."

"I think I'm in love with Natalie."

"That's nice."

"And I like Alice."

"That's nice, too."

"I'm serious," he said.

His mother left a pause. "I can't believe *they're* serious, to be truthful with you."

"And why is that?"

"You're still such a—such a kid, Walter."

"They're serious, all right."

"Well." She smiled at him. "You're a very nice boy, of course."

He shook his head. "No."

"Don't be modest. It makes you seem—I don't know. Priggish."

"I'm sorry."

"Look, Walter—this isn't the Middle Ages, or east Tennessee, either. It's 1964, and you don't have to marry anyone if you don't want to. Why don't you talk to Father Soberg about it?"

"I'm too embarrassed to talk about it. It was hard enough to confess it."

"You *confessed* it?"

"Well," he said, "yes."

Now she seemed about to laugh. "You're—you—what sin is this, exactly?"

"I lied to Alice. I've been lying to her."

"Because you didn't want to hurt her feelings."

"I—Yes. I don't know. I got her to fall in love with me—"

His mother put her hand to her mouth, and spoke through her fingers. "Son—do you have any idea how silly this sounds?"

He felt like sulking. "No."

"It's not a sin to decide you don't want to get married to some-one."

"It feels wrong," he said. "You don't know Alice. She's—her father—it would hurt her, that's all. And I can't bring myself to do it."

"So what're you going to do?"

"I don't know. The D'Allessandros want me to wait until after the thing with Mitchell Brightman before I do anything."

"And what about this—Natalie person. Your second fiancée. What will she do when she finds out you're already engaged?" His mother was trying not to laugh. Then she was laughing. "I'm sorry. You'll—you'll just have to forgive me. I had the thought of telling you—not to talk to any other women—at least until you've settled on what you're going to do with these two. I'm sorry."

"I'm glad you think it's funny," he said, striving to seem offended. But he was pleased in spite of himself.

"Go get your beauty rest," his mother said. "You'll feel better after you get some sleep."

He got up, walked over to her, and kissed her on the cheek. "Good night."

"Come here." She reached for him, wrapped her arms around him, and put the side of her face against his chest. "My very sweet young man," she murmured. "You've just got to stop taking everything so seriously."

In the morning, he found her sitting in the chair, her head back, mouth open, asleep. The vacuum had been run, and she had waxed the kitchen floor. He had heard none of it. He woke her, gently.

"Oh, God," she said. "I was dreaming about your father."

"Tell me," he said.

"Nothing to tell. He was standing in a room. We were in a room with a lot of people, and it was time to leave."

"Did you and he love each other when you got married?"

"Of course we did. How can you ask a question like that?"

He gave no answer to this.

"It's not the same, Walter."

"Isn't it?"

"Look—there were things about your father and me that—this is different, okay? And you'll just have to take my word for it."

"When he was here, when he visited that time—I think he wanted to tell me something, and then decided he couldn't."

She waited. "Well?"

"I wondered if you knew what it was."

"It couldn't possibly make any difference to you now, son. Whatever it was."

"Do you know what it was?"

She considered a moment. "No, I don't imagine I do. Your father—your father was a very disillusioned man. He desperately wanted you not to feel that way."

"What was he disillusioned about?"

"Don't you have to go to work?"

"Tell me," Marshall said. "You can tell me."

She sighed, then seemed to give in to something, lying back in the chair, her hands resting on the arms. "He thought the world was one way, and it turned out that it was another."

That time his father had come to see him, and they had gone to stand at the Treasury Building, looking down Pennsylvania Avenue, the old man talked about how seeing the flags on top of the buildings always gave him a sense of pride and hope. He was an old brown man walking carefully with a cane, and Marshall found himself unable to assimilate the fact that this was his father, the man who inhabited his one clear memory of a father—that figure in a green fatigue jacket, helping build the snowman. This man was gray-haired, and his bones were visible under the flesh of his face and neck. He had made a life for himself in Arizona, had taught history in a private school there. His failing heart had aged him.

They stood beneath the statue of Alexander Hamilton and gazed at the city: a humid, hazy, July night, the air cooling gradually from the heat of the day. Looking past the ornate facade of the Willard Hotel on the left, and the tall, square tower of the post office on the right, they saw the creamy solidness of the

Capitol building with its many columns, its fresh-washed look in the light, standing up out of the dark asphalt beyond the trees as though it were a painted backdrop—all that marble radiance, that majesty, at the end of the long, gray file of federal buildings and art galleries.

"When you think of the people who've walked down that old street. This is where they carried Lincoln, his funeral, right down Pennsylvania to the Capitol. It gives you quite a feeling, standing here, knowing that."

The young man thought his father might say more, and when he didn't, felt confused as to what was expected now, what one might ordinarily do under the circumstances.

"I'm sorry, Walter. Here I am being the history teacher again."

"No," the boy said. "Really. History's my favorite subject." Of course, history was not, and had not been, his favorite subject. He had spoken to spare his father's feelings.

The old man looked at him. "I guess we should be talking about where I've been for the past thirteen years."

"We don't have to talk about that."

"Well."

They gazed at the long, wide street, the scene that lay before them, radiating up into the dark as in a dream. All the bright lines of the Capitol building were blurring; the surfaces appeared to be melting into the damp air.

"This was all blacked out," the old man said. "All this light. Look at it. All dark. We thought planes would come over. People were scared. Pearl Harbor was a big shock. People—people do things when they're scared. We had guns on these roofs, and it wasn't for practice. We didn't know enough, couldn't be sure. And we took steps. That's how it happens sometimes."

"Yes, sir."

"It wasn't like it is today, Walter, where you see Jack and Jackie on television all the time. We rarely saw Roosevelt, except in photos from the chest up. We heard him on the radio. There wasn't anybody in this country who didn't know that voice—but if you didn't see the newsreels—everything was radio then. We'd gather around that thing in the evenings, the whole family, the way people used to sit by a fire. When you think about it, things have changed and developed so fast—that old feeling that we were all connected by the closeness of a voice talking, all in some enormous living room—that only lasted a few years. Television came in and that was the end of it. During the war, people depended on radio, every day. I was older, you know, and had trouble getting them to take me until later on—I was almost thirty, and had some limitations with my eyesight. But I got in. And I saw some of the war. I did my part. Whatever you may ever hear about me, son, I want you to know I loved this country."

"Yes, sir."

"Your mother says you were thinking about the priesthood for a time."

"I was going to the seminary, but I didn't get in. My grades."

"Too much clowning around in the classroom."

"Yes, sir," Marshall said.

All the way here they had talked in a painfully innocuous way, like strangers, men in the uncomfortable vicinity of each other—about the always last-place Senators and the Redskins and the Bay of Pigs and the missile crisis.

Now, they were quiet. Below them, a newer city bus came squealing to a stop, and two young women got out. They crossed toward the hotel. The bus pulled away, and turned down Pennsylvania. In the distance there was music, probably from a car radio. The old man cleared his throat. "She looks good. Your mother does. She looks very good."

The boy let this stand.

His father sighed. "I want to explain something to you, but I don't know quite how to start."

"Yes, sir?"

"People—people do things when they're scared. They do things—and when a whole country gets scared, things—things happen..." He stopped. "The bomb put such a scare into us, Walter. We had used it. We knew. We had an unhappy knowledge about what it could do. And this got us all on some level down deep. The whole country." Again, he stopped. "Well. Your mother thinks I've come here to settle something. I haven't. But I want you to understand me."

The brightness and shapeliness of the Capitol had grown insubstantial in the falling summer haze. Above it all was a bone-colored half-moon and strips of luminous cloud. The stars were bright, a vivacious milky glow fading into the distant sparkle of the skyline. Traffic went by, and from somewhere came the unreal wail of a siren. It died, and the traffic sounds seemed muted slightly, still backed by the strains of music in the distance. A couple walked past on the sidewalk below, arm in arm, talking softly. Colored people. They faltered momentarily over an uneven place in the sidewalk, then laughed, and the man put his hand in the middle of the woman's back as they reached the curb. She wore a corsage. He swung his arms at his sides, proud and confident of himself, walking toward the Willard. Their voices were soon gone, and the boy and his father were alone again.

"I always liked it, living here. I felt lucky. It's strange to see it now, after all these years."

The boy waited.

"When I finally left for overseas in 1943, your grandfather said one thing to me. I had gone into the street in front of the house, loading up this old '37 Ford—a friend of mine was carting me off to report for duty. We were going to Baltimore, I remember, to Fort Holabird. I stood in the street and waved good-bye, and my father came down off the porch and out to where I was standing. He walked up to me and stuck his finger in my chest and said, 'Do your duty.' And then he said, 'And write your mother.' Nothing else. Those words exactly. He turned around and went back up to the house and in, and it wasn't until later that I realized what it must've cost him to do that, and that what he wanted was for me to write him, as well."

"I wish I could've known him," the boy said.

But the old man was thinking about something else, already speaking again. "The only thing I asked for, through the whole mess of that war, was that I be allowed to come home and start a family. That's what I prayed for." He shook his head as if with frustration. "I did some things when I was a young man, see. Back in the thirties. When a man's young and idealistic, as I was—just a kid. Well." He wiped his mouth with a handkerchief, looking down. It was as if he had checked himself. "It's water under the bridge now. Too much water under the bridge. We can't ask for time back, can we?"

There was nothing Marshall could think of to tell him.

"Your mother and I—you know, it was best at the time that she stay here, with you. In fact, for quite a while there I couldn't afford to send for her anyway. And then—well, it was just too late. And you know, I never married again, either. Never got to where I was comfortable with anyone else, really."

"Mom, too," the boy said.

"I wish I could've been here for you, son. I'm proud of the way you turned out."

"Thank you, sir."

"Did your mother ever—she hasn't talked about me, then?"

"Not much, sir. Just that you were—you weren't coming home. I was so young. I just seemed to grow into knowing it."

"Well, that's all understandable."

The truth was that she would not talk about him at all, nor would she permit others to do so, even if it was to commiserate with her for having been left alone that way, with a small child and no money or job or hope of a job. Over the years, there had been several instances of her anger at people for talking about it, wanting to name what had been done to her. She told her son that it was as if they required it of her, this kind of talk, but finally, it was no one's business but hers.

"You know," his father went on, "we were all very upset and exhilarated and scared during those first days of the war. The whole country was. The war had started for us and we weren't ready for it. The first two months of my training was with a stick for a rifle. We were afraid and we were ill-equipped and we were paranoid. Remember that. And when the war was over, we got even more paranoid—because of the thing we finally did to win it, and because we could see how terrible it was, and what it might do in the wrong hands—it's the central frightening thing in the world now, and when you look at the faces of people, I believe you can still see the effects of it." He paused, then nodded as though acceding to something in himself. Then he took the cane and shifted a little, moving away from the statue. The boy followed, reached for his arm, and then thought better of it. They moved to the edge of the low stairs down to the sidewalk and the street. "It's understandable, that paranoia. Remember that. We all had it. A bad mistake—

but understandable. Nobody'd ever had a thing of that magnitude to think about before. It was the first time in all of human history—this frightening and awful thing—a weapon that could put an end to everyone. Could—stop history, and take away any hope of a future. You have to see it that way."

"Yes, sir."

"Whatever happens—whatever anyone does or says, Walter, remember that you and I stood here and looked at this city, and I told you something of how it was."

"I understand," Walter Marshall said, not quite understanding at all. "Here." He offered his arm.

"I'm fine. I can walk."

"Yes, sir."

The old man stopped and fixed him with a look. "And don't believe everything you hear, son. This country is a beautiful idea, a great idea—but men fail their ideas all the time and you can't believe everything you hear."

"Yes, sir."

"Now, help me get over to the car. I'm getting tired."

They made their slow progress down to the street, got into the car, and the boy drove his father back to the motel on the other side of the river, where they had a beer together, though Marshall was only seventeen. His father didn't speak of the past again during his stay. And then he was gone. And the young man knew he would never see him again.

He took the bus to work. Again, Alice wasn't there. She called him at midday to ask if he would come to the hospital that afternoon for a visit with Minnie. Stephen and a couple of the others were planning to stop by. She was working on smoothing things over with her father, who had begun to soften, considering the seriousness of Minnie's condition. He had even visited Minnie again last evening. That alone was an admission of a kind.

"Are you sure Minnie wouldn't mind my visiting?"

"I'm sure, Walter. I wouldn't ask if there was a problem."

When Mr. Wolfschmidt let him go, it was well past five o'clock. The bus into Arlington was packed, and he had to stand, pitching back and forth with the motion of it, in a tight crowd of older men, all of them in long overcoats and wearing hats. The day was mild, with the threat of rain—a gray, featureless sky fading quickly toward a starless night. When he arrived at the hospital room, Stephen and Diane were already there. Minnie lay with her hands folded on her big chest, eyes shut peacefully, while they stood around the bed. Alice kissed him on the mouth, and to his astonishment, Stephen walked over and hugged him. The gesture made him feel as though he had come home from a long journey.

Marshall said, "How's Minnie?" taking off his coat.

"Resting," said Alice.

Diane offered to shake hands across the bed. Marshall did so. "We just got here," she said. Her eyebrow pencil made two perfect arches above the natural line of her brows, and her round cheeks were too heavily rouged. Her hand felt cool and small and dry, and when Marshall let go of it she smiled and touched it to the lobe of her ear.

The room was very small and severe, painted a flat white, with one smudged, narrow window, below which stood a radiator covered with a metal hood. The radiator clanked with the rising steam. Somewhere behind the walls water ran through pipes. There was a painting on the wall opposite the window of a line of very slender, pale girls performing ballet exercises. On the table next to the bed were two glasses and a pitcher of water, a Bible, a pair of steel-framed spectacles, and a box of Kleenex.

Alice reached over, picked up Minnie's smooth, brown hand, and held it.

For a long time no one said anything, and there was only the slow, soft sound of Minnie's breathing.

"She used to hold my hand like this," Alice said, low. "When I was little and had a nightmare. I had a lot of nightmares one year and she'd sit up with me. Hours. I was nine years old. She'd stay the whole night, watching with me until the sun came up and it was light and I could sleep. We'd hear Daddy snoring down the hall. Sometimes I'd fall asleep, and when I'd wake up she'd still be there, still holding my hand."

"I didn't know her until Miss Eva introduced us," Stephen said. He turned to Marshall. "I was interviewing Miss Eva for my high school newspaper, and Minnie was there, watching over her."

"She watched over everyone," Alice said. Her voice broke on the last word. Stephen paused, ran one hand over his mouth. She swallowed, seemed to struggle with herself briefly, then said, "She was something on Saturday, wasn't she?"

"I was so proud of us all." Diane looked at each of them in turn, smiling.

"I felt—happy," Marshall said. "I was more happy than afraid—some of the time, anyway."

"Yes," Stephen said kindly. "That, too. It's like that, isn't it."

And Minnie opened her eyes. "Stephen." Her voice came in a whisper.

"I'm right here, Miss Minnie."

"You got work to do."

"Yes, ma'am."

"Why ain't you doin' it?"

"It's not going anywhere, Minnie. It'll be there when I go pick it up again."

"You gone pick up your cross," Minnie said with a small smile. Her teeth were extraordinarily straight and white.

"Yes," Stephen said. "Amen."

"I done carried mine," she said. "Aftah years a turning away and hiding."

"The Lord provides and understands in his mysterious ways."

"Amen. I believe in my bruthuh man."

"Praise Jesus," Stephen said.

She looked at Alice. "Girl."

"Yes, Minnie."

"Where's my kiss?"

Alice bent down and touched her lips to the wide cheek. Minnie closed her eyes, sighed, then opened them again.

"Where's Mistuh Patrick?"

"He'll be here in a little while," Alice said. "Minnie, when're you coming back home with us?"

Minnie smiled, and when she spoke it was with an inflection almost like singing. "Ho-o-m-e," she said, drawing the word out slightly. "Mmm-hmm."

"The doctors say there's nothing wrong with you. That it's up to you. All you have to do is get up and walk out of here."

"Child," Minnie said, patting Alice's wrist.

"It's true," said Alice. "Stephen, tell her it's true."

"That's what they say," Stephen said.

Minnie looked at Marshall now, and for a brief moment there was something like anger in her features. It took a beat for him to realize that she was struggling to recall his face. He nearly backed away. "Why, you're that nice young man," she said at last.

"He came to see you," Alice said. "We're going to be married."

"Yes," Minnie said, "I remembuh, na."

"Minnie, you wouldn't want to miss my wedding, would you?"

"Oh, how we used to talk about that."

"Remember?" Alice said.

The old eyes closed, and Minnie seemed to sleep. They waited for a few minutes, listening again to the quiet sound of her breathing. "Ah been waiting for that gret gittin' up moanin'," she said sleepily. "Praise his name."

Again, she was quiet. The minutes passed. No one said anything. Alice sniffled once, and Stephen put his hand on her shoulder, lightly, then took it away. When a doctor came to examine Minnie, they all walked together out to the nurses' station.

"That's the way she's been," Alice said. "Going on six days."

"She wakes up," Stephen said, "seems herself. But then she's gone again, and they can't find a thing wrong with her."

"Maybe they're not looking hard enough," Diane said.

"They've been very kind," said Stephen.

Alice said, "My father wouldn't let them be anything else."

A moment later, Diane said, "Stephen's going south, to join up with Dr. King's people."

"I plan to ask if they'll let me work for him," Stephen said.

"Tell Minnie," Alice said. "Oh, and I would love to go with you."

Marshall was ashamed to find himself seeing this as an opening; he almost urged Alice to go. He looked at Stephen, with his large, moist eyes and pitted cheeks, and felt somehow duplicitous, as though he had already cheated these friends. And they *were* friends. He thought of his mother's chiding about what he had confessed, and felt newly embarrassed by it: There were no expressions with which to confess the sins of prevarication and falseness he had committed in the last hour alone.

He walked with Alice to the entrance of Minnie's room. Minnie lay asleep, just as before, perfectly at peace, as still as a work of sculpture. The doctor, a very short, stocky man who wore an expensive suit under the white lab coat, was standing at the foot of the bed and writing something on a pad. His oxblood shoes were well polished, and shone in the light. He had thick, stubby fingers, and there was some sort of hitch in his breathing, as though he were about to cough or clear his throat. The smell of tobacco was all over him.

"Well?" Alice said to him.

"Nothing very specific to report, I'm afraid. And no change. Suppose we just try to consider the sleep as being restorative. This is a form of exhaustion, apparently. When she's ready to come out of it . . ." he trailed off.

"Is her heartbeat—"

"Everything seems normal enough. Look, I know I've said this, but it's—it really is hard to tell sometimes with the elderly. You have to allow for a few things."

When the doctor had gone, she put her head on Marshall's shoulder. "I'm so worried about her."

"I know."

She kissed his cheek. "Thanks for coming by."

"I wish there was something I could do," he told her.

Then Stephen and Diane were there, and they shook hands with him. This time an embrace seemed too much, though he would have liked one. He asked their forgiveness for having to leave, using the excuse of his mother being alone, and took himself on down the lonely corridor. Alice called after him, and then hurried to catch up. "I'll walk you out."

"You don't have to."

She seemed puzzled. "Of course I do."

In the little bus stand out front, she threw her arms around him and kissed him on the mouth. It was a long, distressing kiss. "Oh, how can we wait," she said, finally breaking away. He saw the pulsing in her neck, and felt the heat in her bones, pressing her to him and looking beyond her at the tall, dark building with its warm lights in the windows.

"Alice," he said. "I'm so sorry."

"No," she said. "It's all my fault." She stepped back, crossing her arms as if to ward off the chill. "Will you call me?"

"Yes," he told her.

"I love you," she said.

And he repeated the phrase.

She rushed back at him, pressed herself against him, but the kiss was just a brushing of her lips on his. "'Bye."

"'Bye," he said.

And she was running across the space between the building and this bus stand. "Call me," she yelled over her shoulder.

The bus was pulling in. She waved from the big entrance of the building and, looking back as he climbed onto the bus, he returned the wave.

Chapter

16

*T*hrough the rest of the week, and into the next, Minnie wavered between waking and sleeping, and Alice was at her side for most of it. She took vacation days from work, and Sunday, against her father's wishes, spent the night in Minnie's hospital room. But Alice's father had begun spending time there, too, as it began to seem apparent to everyone, including even the doctors now, that Minnie was dying. They could find nothing physically wrong with her. All her vital signs and all the tests showed her to be quite normal, even rather robust for a woman of her heavy build who was past seventy. But she remained in the hospital bed, from which she was evidently unable to move, and where Patrick Kane had said she would be suffered to remain as long as this was so, no matter what the tests showed, and no matter what the cost. She lay there, breathing shallowly, eyes closed, drifting in and out of sleep, and everyone was simply waiting for the end.

Marshall saw Albert at the school, informed him of this, and Albert wept. "I'm not very strong just now," he said. He went on to say that Emma had moved in with him, and was proving to be more trouble than he had anticipated. Her aunt Patty had disowned her, in a rage, for flaunting the family's strict religious beliefs: Emma was living in sin. "And she won't let me near her. Not until we *are* married. So I have all the disapproval and anger and shame of an illicit affair without any of the pleasure of one. I know that doesn't sound like me. Sometimes I get a little tired of being so damn nice all the time to everybody."

"That's what you should do," Marshall told him. "Get mad." But there was something reflexive in this, and he knew it. He almost apologized, watching his tall, gangly friend walk away.

Mr. D'Allessandro wasn't there, but he had left instructions with Wilbur Soames, who conducted things efficiently and with an edge of amusement. He and Baker were still telling jokes, back and forth, and they laughed at Ricky Dalmas reading his commercial for Gauss's Funeral Home.

You know, death is always inconvenient . . .

"A masterpiece," Soames said, laughing.

Baker sat at the console, watching as Ricky concentrated on his copy, reading it in that strange, unmusical way. Marshall left early, claiming a headache, and made his way up the street to Natalie's building. The city was disappearing in fog—a heavy, drifting haze settling from a dull sky. There was no light in her window. He waited for a few minutes, standing there almost invisible in the murk, while all around him sounded the rush and noise of the streets, lights moving nebulously through the thickness like aspects of the fog itself, a moving glow, a tattered scarf of light. She was nowhere, and she didn't come walking down the block this time. He kept giving her another few minutes, kept expecting that she would, indeed, come from somewhere out of the shrouded distance. Finally, he gave up and walked down to K Street and the bus home.

Alice had telephoned, wanting him to call her at home when he got in from school. She had spoken with his mother about Minnie, and in her sorrow had let it out about the sit-in, the violence, blaming herself for Minnie's condition. Apparently, she wasn't even aware that she had given anything away. Loretta felt injured, she told him, to have to hear this from Alice, realizing that the truth had been kept from her. "I thought we had something special," she said. "I thought we could always talk to each other." She sat at the small table in the kitchen, smoking a cigarette and looking disheveled, worried, and sleepless. "I thought I could trust you."

"Of course you can trust me," he said. "I didn't want to upset you, that's all."

"You have to promise me," she said abruptly. But then she stopped, coughed, looked away from him.

He sat down across from her. "Mom," he said. "It's fine. I didn't—I felt—it was such an amazing thing. I felt so close to everyone and—"

"Your father . . ." She stopped again. "You can't do these kinds of things, Walter. You can't go against the government or the police."

"It wasn't like that," he told her. "We were within the law all the time."

She shouted, "So was your father!"

He had been startled by her vehemence, and he simply sat there looking at his hands on the smooth surface of the tabletop.

"You have to listen to me, Walter. Your father did the same kind of thing. Exactly the same. He went against the government, son. Do you understand? He was very idealistic, like you, and he went against the government and they punished him for it. They came to that little two-bedroom house we lived in and they took him away. They took him away, Walter. You have to listen to me, now. They went through his books and his letters and tore the house apart looking for things. They kept him for almost a week, and it was for something he did when he was twenty-two years old. Do you see?" She got up and moved to the sink, poured a glass of water, and sat down again. "He belonged to a group of people, they used to meet on the weekends, and some weeknights, and it was all about justice and freedom. Everything was terrible all around. Nobody had any work, and he joined because the talk was about those things—food for the hungry and work for those who wanted to work. Good ideals like that. He went to a few meetings, and then he saw that they weren't really talking about the same kind of justice, and he stopped going. I didn't even know him then, son. It was before I met him, 1934, for God's sake. And when you were a baby, the—the government people—they came and took him away and kept him all that time, days, asking him questions, grilling him about this little group, this—these few meetings that meant nothing and that he'd mostly forgotten about. They kept asking him for names. Names of people he hadn't seen in almost twenty years. And, of course, he wouldn't give them any. He told me he couldn't remember the names even if he wanted to tell them. It was just these—these meetings he went to. Meetings, Walter, that was all they were." She began to cry. She got up and pulled a Kleenex from the box on the counter, blew her nose, and sat down again, with the box. "I'm sorry," she said. "Can you believe this? After all this time."

They were both quiet, then. Perhaps a full minute went by, while she sat there struggling to gain control of herself, and slowly succeeding.

"He tried to tell me about it," Marshall said, finally. "That time we went into town together."

She was wiping her eyes with the Kleenex. "I remember."

He thought about his father, imagined him young, saw again the memory of him in snow, wearing the dark green fatigue jacket.

"When he came home—after the questioning—he was so frightened. He couldn't sleep, couldn't relax anymore. He was afraid of the phone, the windows of the houses across our street. He couldn't stay here. People were turning each other in, denouncing each other to the police, and he had been involved. He was guilty of what that McCarthy and all of them had decided was a crime. Do you see?"

Marshall said, "He . . ." but nothing else came.

"He went out to Arizona to start over. He was going to send for us, but then he couldn't, son. He just—he couldn't do it. It wasn't in him anymore. He couldn't—couldn't bring himself to do it. He'd gotten so scared. And there were problems—other problems. This thing made them all that much worse. Some people pull together when things go wrong. This pulled us apart. It just did. And, anyway, I didn't want to leave here. Not pick up and start over in a place like Arizona, so far away. No matter how beautiful he said it was. We—the two of us came to understand it, my darling, without ever really saying much. There was never any rancor or bitterness. We just knew. And—and the time went on." She kept folding and refolding a piece of tissue, sniffling, daubing at the corners of her eyes.

After a pause, Marshall said, "Well, but this—what happened the other day in Maryland—it wasn't the same kind of thing."

"I know what you're going to say, son. That's what I'm trying to make you see. It wasn't illegal—what your father did—it wasn't really illegal, either, at the time. It was a thing that he got in trouble for years after the fact. That's the way it is in this country. Different times tolerate different things. What was understandable—what was even laudible in 1934—becomes the reason you're stripped of your job, your ability to earn a living, in 1951. You don't know which way the country will go, do you? You can't say that ten or fifteen years from now you won't be hauled out of whatever home you're in, wherever you are, and made to answer for this—this sit-in or whatever it was. You don't know how things might change."

"Maybe we'll change them," Marshall said.

"Don't you think your father felt that way?"

"This is different."

She stood. "Oh, for God's sake—haven't you been listening to me?"

"Well," he said. "It is different. This is about the right to be a full citizen. It's the law, now, and there are people trying to subvert it or ignore it. We're only applying pressure for people to obey the law."

"And when the law changes?" she said. "What then?"

"The law won't change."

She took another Kleenex from the box and moved to the sink. She stood there, her back to him, sniffling. "You have to promise me—" she said.

"I can't do that."

She turned, and she was angry with him now. "I wasn't finished."

He waited.

"Promise me you won't—do anything dangerous or foolish."

"I promise," he said.

"This is all Alice's doing, isn't it? Alice and her liberal father."

"Alice's father was unhappy about it, too."

She sniffled again, and poured more water. "I'm going to bed. I won't sleep, but I'm going to bed."

"There's nothing to worry about," he told her.

She kissed his cheek, and he rose and put his arms around her. Her arms came around his middle. For a time they stood there. "It isn't as if I'm not proud of you," she said.

"I know."

"Don't be up late," she said. "Get some sleep."

They went to their separate rooms, and he lay awake, thinking about how this small apartment would soon be empty of them both—other people would live here, where he had for the most part grown up, living in what others must have seen as a kind of poverty, though it had never felt that way. His mother hadn't owned a car until his thirteenth year. There had been times when she'd had to scrimp and save and had worried about things he came to know other households took for granted: There had been winter nights when they could use only one light in the apartment at a time; nights when they had eaten pancakes for dinner, or cereal, or bread and butter. Nights she had been up late, sitting at the kitchen table, working over the figures, trying to make the money stretch. Times he had lain awake and heard her pacing in the rooms, worrying. At some point in those years, she had developed the habit of cleaning house in those late hours. He could marvel now at this trait of hers, this abhorrence of idle time, as a manifestation of the hardships she had endured in the years after his father left. And it seemed to him that for all her worry and work, she was entitled to some happiness. How much he would do for her, in the world.

He did not see Natalie until that Wednesday. Alice was in Arlington with Minnie. He spoke with her on the telephone, and he visited once. Alice kept the vigil, alone, mostly, sitting at Minnie's side and holding her hand. When Marshall visited, Mr. Kane was there. Alice's father was gruff, and barely polite, and when the opportunity for them to be alone presented itself, Alice took it, leaving her father and Minnie with Diane and two members of Minnie's congregation. She walked with Marshall to the hospital cafeteria for a cup of coffee. "It's just his way," she told him. "You mustn't take it personally."

"It's hard not to," Marshall told her.

"Everything's so sad now," she said.

He took her hand. He wished something would come along and sweep him away, out of the bounds of what he must do. "Alice," he said.

She had turned to look at the clock above the door. "They're getting a little hard to deal with," she said. "The hospital people. They want her bed. They can't find anything wrong with her and there's nothing she wants them to do. She's just occupying the bed, you know? My father was arguing with them about it when you got here."

"Has she—" he began.

"She doesn't say anything now. She opens her eyes and looks at me and then closes them again. I can't get her to say anything."

He was quiet.

"They want to take her off the IV."

"What happens if they do?"

"She'll starve. That's the only way she's getting any nourishment."

They finished the coffee, and walked back up to the room. Patrick Kane was talking to Diane about the events in Maryland. It was a quiet, rueful conversation in which they were both agreeing that 1964 was far too late in history for such things to be happening so close to the seat of democracy. When Mr. Kane saw that his daughter had entered the room, his demeanor changed; he stood, cleared his throat, and muttered something about work piling up at the office. He nodded at Marshall as he left, and when he was gone, Diane said to Alice, "He's proud of you. No matter what he says."

"Well, that ain't what he says," Alice told her with a rueful shake of her head.

Marshall felt a surge of admiration for her. He watched as she took her place next to Minnie, and he saw the light in her eyes as Diane talked about Stephen and his journey south to join Dr. King's Southern Christian Leadership Conference. Stephen had promised to send them news of himself, and Alice hoped that a letter from him, perhaps with some small greeting from Dr. King himself, would be the medicine that Minnie needed. Marshall took his leave then, said good-bye to Diane and kissed Minnie's cheek, feeling false, walking through the lighted corridors with Alice on his arm, taking her confident kiss, holding her while she fretted about Minnie and about everything else that was worrying her— her difficult father, the missed time at work, her engagement that was not going as she had always dreamed it would. "We should be going out on dates," she said, barely able to control her voice.

"I know," he told her. "It's all right. Don't worry about it, really."

That Wednesday at school, when he saw Natalie, she was distant, almost standoffish. He had spent time dawdling in the stores leading to Eighteenth Street, looking at the paperback books in the racks, and he had stopped at Saint Matthew's to pray, to ask for help for Minnie, and for Alice, and to plead for exactly the sort of courage he had come to understand he lacked. It was a clear, cold sunset, and stars were already glittering on the edge of the sky. He met Natalie in the school library, where she had been studying, and when he spoke her name, she seemed startled.

"I didn't know it vas so late," she said.

"I have to tell you something," he offered.

"I know. You're already engaged."

"I'm—" he stopped.

"Mrs. D'Allessandro told me."

"I'm going to break it off," he said, and felt oddly as though he were lying. Something stirred in the flesh around his heart, and he felt sick.

"It doesn't matter," she said. "Maybe sometime we can go together and talk. Not now. If Mrs. D'Allessandro sees me talking to you—" She had put her coat on and was gathering her books. "I can't talk to you right now."

"Wait a minute," he said. "What about Mrs. D'Allessandro?" He took her by the arm to stop her. "Natalie—"

"No, please. This is not good."

He let go. "Then—you're not—we're not—"

Her response was a little like that of a teacher talking to an infatuated student. "This is all for a later time. We vill maybe see each other later, yes?"

"Later. When, later?"

"Just—later. Not tonight and not tomorrow, either. After—" She stopped, gave forth a small sigh of frustration, then seemed to decide something. "After the big radio thing, vith Brightman, okay? I'll see you sometime after that, and ve talk it all out. Now I have to leave. Please."

He watched her go down the stairs, into the darkening street and on, taking the opposite direction from the one that led to her apartment building. No doubt she was going to her job, yet he had the feeling she was walking out of his life forever. He hurried to the doorway, and called after her.

"What?" She had gotten almost to the end of the block, was only a slender shape there in the dimness. The light of the street-lamp there seemed to send down a solid wall of illumination at the edge of whose border she stood.

"You're coming back?" he said.

"Don't be silly, Walter."

"I take that as a definite yes."

She waved this away, then crossed the street, hurrying now, disappearing into the dark.

"Natalie," he called.

Nothing.

The D'Allessandro School of Broadcasting was in session, but Mr. D'Allessandro was not in his office. Marshall went back down to the night school and along the corridor of classrooms, looking for Mrs. D'Allessandro. She was standing at a blackboard, talking about *Beowulf* to a room full of drowsy-looking men and women. She saw him, excused herself, and came out into the hall, closing the door behind her.

"This better be important, young man."

"You told Natalie about Alice Kane," he said.

She nodded. "Frankly, I was amazed that you hadn't."

"I don't understand."

"We need Alice Kane to be happy with us, remember?"

"That doesn't have anything to do with this—"

"Of course it does. Now run along. I have a class to teach."

"Alice's father wants to call the thing off," Marshall told her.

"And it has nothing to do with Natalie and me. And I hope he does call it off."

She straightened a little, and all the color left her face. "What did you say?" Then she grabbed him by the arms and held him there, looking up and down the corridor. "This has gone far enough. He can't call it off. It's done."

"Stop," he said. "I have to go."

"Did you tell this to my husband?"

He thought of telling her what he had seen between her husband and Mrs. Gordon, and his mind reeled with the spitefulness of it. He said, "Look—it's not certain. I was going to see Mr. Brightman myself, and try to fix things."

"*You're going to see him.*"

"I was going to try to fix it," he told her. "I just don't understand why you had to ruin things with Natalie like that."

She was looking down the hall, still gripping his arms. Then she looked straight at him. "You're not ruined. Trust me. Natalie is just—there's a situation with Natalie." Now she stepped back from him, her hands dropping to her sides. "Natalie has some things to tell you, too. Can't it wait? That's all. Just let it wait until Alice Kane's father delivers Mr. Brightman to us. Nothing can upset that. Do you understand? Or we'll lose everything."

"I understand," Marshall said.

There was the sound of footsteps on the stairs, steady but slow, and Albert crossed the hall, heading for the basement. He looked at them, seemed to squint, held one hand over his eyes like someone peering through bright sunlight, then gave up and went on his way down. They listened to his descent.

"Why does Kane want to call it off?" Mrs. D'Allessandro said.

"It's a long story. But it has nothing to do with Natalie."

"The date's set. We put an ad in the paper. We've already got orders for the bleeding tickets. He won't call it off, surely."

"It's not up to him now, anyway, is it?"

"But if he said he's calling it off—what in bleeding hell does that mean, then?"

"I don't know."

"We're depending on you," she said.

"Yes, ma'am."

She shook her head as if she couldn't believe her own words. Then she sighed. "Oh, God, I hate it here."

Released from her, he went down into the basement to look for Albert. There were three students from the night school standing at the Coke machine, and one was seated in a booth smoking a cigarette. They were apparently on a break in the middle of an exam, because they were talking about the questions, all of which had to do with ancient Greece. The downstairs door was open. Outside, in that little, cold, concrete space, surrounded by a tall wrought-iron fence and a cement wall, amid scraps of paper and soaked pieces of cardboard and the smell of garbage, Albert stood, hands deep in his pockets, head turned upward, gaze set skyward, past the sheer, towering shapes of the buildings rising into the starry dark. Albert blew breath, like smoke, then looked at his friend. "Hey."

"Hey," Marshall said.

"Was that you in the hallway?"

"Yeah."

"I thought so. Thought I heard your voice. Mrs. D'Allessandro, too?"

"Yes."

"She seemed upset. Her voice."

"Well," Marshall said, "that's her problem."

Albert looked at him and smiled, then took a step toward the wall, stretched his arms up and breathed a deep sigh that sounded like a sigh of satisfaction. Then he put his hands in his pockets and turned to his friend again.

"What're you doing out here, Albert?"

"Minnie's gone home."

Marshall stepped close. "She—died?"

"No," Albert told him. "Went home. Today. This afternoon. Not three hours ago. She got up out of bed, dressed herself, and went home. Alice couldn't get ahold of you, so she called me."

Marshall stared at him.

Albert breathed another slow, deep, satisfied sigh. "I was just standing here thinking about how good it is to be alive, Walter."

Chapter

11

Alice's father wanted to celebrate Minnie's return. In what Alice described as the new, expansive mood of gratitude that had taken possession of him, he had conceived of the idea of a dinner in Minnie's honor, at which Minnie would, of course, not have to lift a finger, or give one order, and to which she could invite anyone she chose. Minnie said she wanted Alice, any members of her congregation who could come, Diane, Stephen, and young Walter Marshall. Diane and Stephen had gone south, and were traveling in Alabama with some members of the Southern Christian Leadership Conference. When she was given this information, she left things up to Alice. She was only doing it, she said, to satisfy Mr. Kane. "In other words," Alice told Marshall over the telephone, "she's accepting my dad's peace offer."

"It's a miracle," said Marshall.

"I've asked Mitch Brightman, too," She said. "He's known Minnie a long time. And I want you and your mother, of course, and her friend, if he insists."

"They're going to be married," Marshall told her. "I don't think there's any way to avoid it."

"The marriage, or him coming to the dinner?"

"Both."

"They really are going to get married?"

"Yes, they really are, Alice."

"Poor boy."

He said nothing.

"I'm asking Albert and Emma, too."

"Do you think that's the best idea? I mean—with Emma—"

"Albert doesn't think she'll come."

"And if she does?"

"She's a polite Southern girl."

Alice had been alone in the room when Minnie came to herself. That was the way she put it when she told him about it. Minnie came to herself. Opened her eyes and looked at Alice, sitting there by the bed, holding her hand. It was growing dark at the windows, the afternoon visiting hours were ending. There were people walking along the hallway outside the room. Minnie looked over Alice's shoulder at the commotion, and Alice realized that this was a new development, this interest in what was going on outside the room. "Girl," Minnie said to her.

"Yes, Minnie."

"What you crying fuh?"

She squeezed Minnie's hand, but couldn't bring herself to speak.

"What time is it gittin' to be?"

"It's almost five," Alice told her.

"Well," Minnie said, "stop crying, na." And then she worked her way to a sitting position in the bed, reached over, and pulled the IV tape off the back of her hand. Alice, fearing that she might harm herself, stepped away from the bed and began to call for a nurse or a doctor. Minnie moved in the bed, brought her amazingly smooth, muscular, rounded legs over the side and stood, the IV still dangling from her arm, the apparatus rocking slightly with the pull of it. "Git somebody," Minnie said. "Go on, child. I'm fixing to go home, na."

Alice told Marshall that she ran down the corridor of that hospital, so excited and happy that she forgot where she was. "God knows what sort of a bizarre spectacle I made, running and yelling for somebody like that, so happy and scared at the same time. I mean a part of me thought maybe she was—you know—delirious

or something. The last mirage, you know, before dying. I thought
she might be dying. Or part of me did. I was afraid to think anything at all, really. But there she was, so big, pulling at the IV thing
and demanding that I get somebody because it was time she went
home. And yes, I think it is a miracle. I think I'm going to start
going to church with you."

"Alice," he said.

"What?"

"Nothing."

"I love you."

"Listen," he said.

"Walter?"

"Nothing. I—I love you, too."

He saw her at work on Tuesday, and they went to lunch together.
She was as bright as the sun-glorious, fall-crisp day, full of plans.
Stephen was going from Alabama to Chicago in the middle of the
week, with Reg and Ollie and Diane, to join Dr. King. There was a
lot of excitement about it. They had offered to stop in Arlington, for
Minnie's party, but Minnie wouldn't hear of anyone putting off such
an honor merely to celebrate the fact that she had been wrong about
her time. That was how she put it, Alice said, sitting in the window
of the sandwich shop, eating a big submarine sandwich and watching
the people hurry by on the sunny walk outside.

"And Walter—the best thing," she went on. "My father's not
going to call off the Mitch Brightman deal, at the school. It can go
ahead as planned."

He couldn't refrain from expressing some relief over this, and
even so he felt as if he were lying to her, using her. "Alice," he said.

She interrupted him. "Mitchell came to see Minnie, you know,
in the hospital."

He hadn't known.

"Aren't you hungry?" she said.

He took a bite of his sandwich. Outside, a couple walked by,
arm in arm. They looked utterly natural and comfortable together.
"Alice," he said.

"What?"

Looking into her clear eyes, her happiness, he thought of the distant future, and took another bite of the sandwich. Somewhere in the unimaginable distance, there were men his age tramping through jungles, more of them all the time.

"What?" she said again, smiling. "I've got food on my lips, right?" She put a napkin to her mouth.

"No," he said.

"Well, what, then?"

He hesitated. The words were there to tell her. He could back down slowly, gradually:

Alice, maybe we ought to think about seeing other people now and then. Just to be sure of ourselves.

No.

Alice, I'm in love with Natalie Bowman. I think.

"Walter?"

"Nothing," he said. "I don't know anything. My mother's getting married."

She reached across and took him by one wrist. "You told me."

"I hate it," he said. "It's depressing."

"That horrible little man."

He nodded.

"What'll we do?"

"There's nothing we can do."

She thought a moment. "Surely she doesn't love him. Actually, I can tell a thing like that. I've got a sixth sense or something. I mean it. I can sense it. I can always tell when the people I'm with— if they love each other. Married couples, and people going together. My father brings them over and they're not in the room five minutes and I know. There are signs, of course. But I think it's a sixth sense with me. I'm sure she doesn't love him."

He kept his eyes from hers.

"Don't you think?" she said.

"I don't know. It doesn't seem like it to me."

"Well, what's she doing it for?"

He shrugged. "You got me."

Again, she considered, holding the sandwich to her mouth, looking out the window. "God," she said at last.

They walked back to work, and she held his hand, kissed him at the elevator, and again while they were in the elevator. Anyone who saw them would have said that they were what they seemed to be—a young couple in love, in thrall to each other. He observed all the public forms of affection with her, and when she had gone her way he was sick with himself, walking down the long corridor to the mailroom, nothing resolved, nothing changed.

He worked the hours of the afternoon in a sort of torpor, going from one task to another without thought, speaking only when spoken to. And at the end of the day, she came down to meet him. They walked out together, arm in arm. Lovers.

"I think your mother just doesn't want to be alone," she said. "You'll be leaving and she doesn't like the idea of being by herself. It's understandable."

Autumn was in full blazing color in the streets of the city. They took the bus across the river into Arlington, and when her stop came, she asked if he wanted to come home with her for a time.

"I've got so much schoolwork to do," he said.

"Okay," she said simply. She kissed him, then made her way to the doorway. The bus slowed, and she stepped down, was out, the bus pulling away, rushing away from the rising dust and grit of the curb. She was small in the distance, walking toward her street, a young woman strolling in the failing sun of a fall day crossed with flying leaves and deep shadows.

Forgive me, Father, for I have sinned. It has been two weeks since my last confession. I failed to do what you asked me to do in my last confession, Father. I'm the one who got engaged to the two women?

Oh, yes. How could I forget?

Well, I couldn't tell the first one, Father. And she still thinks we're in love.

Well, she would.

I don't know how to do it, Father.

You say, We're not getting married. Those words, son. Politely, gently, evenly, honestly. We're not getting married. Like that.

I'll—I'll try.

You do more than try, son. You do.

Yes, Father. I'm confused, though—it's because I like her so much that I don't want to hurt her.

What have you said to the—uh—the second one?

She knows.

She knows about the first one?

Yes, Father. But I didn't tell her. I was going to, and she already knew.

The plot thickens.

Father?

No, never mind me, son. Hold on a minute. Aha. Uh—I take it the second one is none too happy with you.

Yes, Father.

Well, you see. I—ah. You have to take care of these things—some of these things on your own. You're really talking about something that has to do with manners. And—and honor. I guess. There's no sin here. At least not yet. You—that is, if you haven't had relations. You haven't had relations, have you?

No, Father.

Son, I can't help asking about the families of these two young women—

I've only met the first one's father.

I see.

They're both older than I am, Father.

Who? The parents—I'd think the parents—

No, Father. My—the fiancées.

The—the young ladies.

Yes, Father.

And how much older are they?

The first one's more than four years older and the second one's seven years older.

The one you think you want to marry is seven years—

Yes, Father.

She hasn't been married before?

No, Father.

I suppose that's good. Well—aha. Now, are there any sins you want to confess?

I lied all week, Father.

I see, yes.

I had impure thoughts. Several times.

Did you indulge in them?

I tried not to.

Anything else?

I let my first—the first one—fiancée—I let her kiss me, until I got aroused.

Do you mean to keep from letting that happen again?

Yes, Father.

Because I don't see why you bring this in here if you're just going to let that sort of thing go on. If this girl—this woman is not the woman you intend to marry, you have to avoid these occasions of sin.

Yes, Father.

Anything else?

No, Father.

Well, thank heaven for that.

In the apartment that evening, Clark Atwater dozed in front of the television set while Loretta drank tea, sitting at the end of the couch with a TV tray in front of her. Marshall kept to his room, mostly, coming through only to take the plate he'd had toast on back into the kitchen. Loretta smiled at him, passing through. Clark Atwater snored and made little sighing sounds, and the television rattled on—a movie about a couple separated during the war who are changed by it and come back together as different people. Marshall had seen the movie before; they each assume, to great comic effect, that the other is the same quiet, unassuming, timid person of the days before they were separated. He went into his room and tried to pray, and finally he lay in the dark, hearing his mother and Atwater moving around in the living room. He had drifted off, was lost for a time, and then he came to himself, sat upright, peering wide-eyed and dazed into the dark. There had been the sound of a scuffle in the other room. Or had it been a sound at all? He listened. Silence.

But then as he lay back down, he heard it again—a rattle and shiver, something thudding to the floor. He got up, pulled the blanket around himself, and opened the bedroom door. "Mom?" he called.

Nothing.

"Hello?"

A faint suspirance, like a breath—someone whispering. He stepped back into the room, dropped the blanket, and reached for his pants. He was certain he could hear it now, an urgent sibilance, a hissing. He got the pants on and started out, down the hall.

"Walter." His mother's voice, distressed, tearful. "Go back to bed."

"Mom?" he said, heading toward the living room.

"No," she said. "Please. Go back to bed."

He stopped.

"Do you hear me, son? Go back to bed."

"Are you all right?" he said. "Who's there?"

Atwater's voice came. "Who the hell do you think is here?"

"What're you doing?"

"Nothing," his mother said. "Please, Walter. I'm saying good night to Clark, and we got to teasing."

But he could hear that she had been crying.

"Mom," he said, "are you all right?"

"I'm fine. Please go to bed."

He went to the end of the hall, and looked into the room where she was, but it was too dark to see much. Her face turned to him from an angle of the couch, and she said, "Please, Walter. Leave me alone."

"Yes, ma'am."

He had not been able to make out where Atwater was. He went slowly back to his room, stood in his doorway, and looked back down the hall. "I'm not sleeping," he said.

"Well, go to sleep," came Atwater's voice.

"No, sir," Marshall said. "Not until you leave."

More whispering. Then his mother's voice. "Good night, son."

He couldn't sleep. He lay listening for the sounds, and the silence grew rickety with buried noises; perhaps he imagined more whispering. Nights when he was much younger, he had heard music in the whir and rush of the world outside his window, and he had understood that it was not really music at all, but something supplied by the nerves of his inner ear.

Daylight woke him, morning streaming in the window. His mother was in the shower. He made coffee for her, put the dishes away that had been stacked in the drainer next to the sink. She came into the kitchen wearing her bathrobe, smelling of the fragrances she used, her hair still wet. "I got a late start," she said.

He kissed her cheek, then moved past her to use the bathroom himself. As she turned from him, he saw a dark place on the ridge of her left eyebrow. "What's that?" he said.

"What—this? Oh, nothing."

"No, wait," he said, taking her by the shoulders.

"It's nothing, son—really. Clark and I were teasing around, you know—"

"It's a bruise."

"It's nothing. Go take your shower."

"He hit you."

"Don't be ridiculous. We were playing. It was an accident." She moved to the refrigerator and opened it. "Do you want some eggs for breakfast?"

"No," he said. "Thanks."

"Better hurry, you'll be late for work."

He paused a moment longer. "Yes, ma'am."

"You've got school tonight, right?" She reached into the refrigerator and brought out a grapefruit. "Clark wants to go see *Goldfinger.*"

"I've got school," he said.

She moved to the table, put the grapefruit down, then looked at him. "Honey, please don't."

"There's other jobs—" he began.

She waved this away. "Don't be ridiculous. I can't imagine what you're talking about. I like the job I have. Now please—"

He felt rooted to the spot.

"Walter, you're gonna be late. And you're gonna make me late. Please, son."

He worked the collator all morning while Mr. Wolfschmidt went over some drawings, lovely, delicate, brown-shaded pictures of cathedral spires and buttresses and statuary that his small, gray, architect father had brought in. The drawings were done on large pieces of heavy paper the size of posters. The old man stood by, proudly watching, as Mr. Wolfschmidt lifted each unwieldy page and put it gingerly facedown, revealing the next page, the next drawing. They were as exact as pale photographs; even the texture of the carved stone had been rendered with meticulous care. The old man wanted to mail them, and he was evidently asking for his son's expertise. Mr. Wolfschmidt began preparing the drawings for mailing overseas, using materials from the shelves, and occasionally sending to the stockroom for more. This became a daylong project, since the old man wanted the drawings sent flat, not rolled, as he must have sent all his drawings in the past. Before the workday was over, everyone in the mailroom had contributed to the project—offering advice, fetching tape and cardboard to brace things, holding the ends of the packages while Mr. Wolfschmidt taped them.

Alice hadn't come to work again, and there was no answer when Marshall tried to call her, shortly after noon. He left work early—Mr. Wolfschmidt and the old man had taken the clumsy packages on to the post office building, and there wasn't anything else to do, really. He made his way gradually to Pennsylvania Avenue, stopping to look in the windows of the travel bureaus—there were four of them within two blocks along Fifteenth Street—with their life-sized, vivid pictures of faraway places, exotic destinations whose commonest link, other than the overly bright colors, seemed to be the beauty and youth of the people doing the traveling. The lithe, bathing-suited bodies of the tanned women in these pictures provided an allure that weakened his resolve, finally, and caused him no small amount of discomfort. Yet he couldn't keep from pausing to stare at these lush, extravagant portrayals of *distance . . .*

He was beginning to think of how it might answer things to remove himself for a time.

He walked across Lafayette Square, with its spotted, colorful shade in the late sun, its drifting yellow and burned red leaves, strolling couples, and lone, hurrying passersby. He thought about the night he had walked there with Alice, the night he had gotten his pocket picked by some indigent named Walter Winchell, and had asked her to marry him. It seemed an age ago, and it wasn't even three weeks. At the edge of the park, he turned and looked at the White House, in its vivid green surround, and had a moment's faltering sense of just how farfetched his own plans were—that he could ever live there, or find anything to do there, really.

The city was alive with sirens. Bells. Horns. He walked up Sixteenth, past the AFL-CIO and the Lafayette Hotel, and at K Street he saw four big fire engines go by, heading toward the sunny west. The sun was blinding in the windows of the buildings there. He went on up K Street, to Eighteenth, and turned north, toward Wheaton's. He was hungry. A camera shop on the corner had placed a new picture of Kennedy in the window: It was a formal portrait, bordered in black, and beneath it were the words of his inaugural address.

Let the word go forth, from this time and place, to friend and foe alike, that the torch has been passed to a new generation of Americans

He might've read the whole speech again, gone back to the beginning and read it through, playing the voice in his head, but the commotion of the engines in the street behind him brought him to himself. A hook and ladder came blaring to Eighteenth and roared past him, heading north. He had gone only a few paces when he saw, beyond the trees lining the street ahead, a billowing cloud of black smoke. The whole sky there was being swallowed by it, the black edges crowding upward, spreading, hurrying on, a prodigious rushing away of dark folds. People were running along the sidewalk, and he fell in with them, realizing as he came past the corner with the dark-red, massive shape of Saint Matthew's to his right that it was the D'Allessandro School building that was the source of the alarm and the smoke. He had been running, but now he slowed, moving through the throng of onlookers to stand on the other side of the street from the building, with its library window and its staircase, its gray, stern look, pouring smoke from the roof and the upstairs windows. Two engines had already started sending their wide, solid spray of water at the fiercest part of the blaze, just above the front entrance. There were more sirens, and police.

The young man moved amid the crowd, looking for a recognizable face. He found Ricky Dalmas, Joe Baker, and Wilbur

Soames standing near the bus stop on the corner. Albert Waple was just beyond them, watching the building, squinting at it, one hand visored over his eyes. Marshall walked up to him. Albert turned to him and shrugged.

"How long have you been here?" Marshall asked him.

"A while."

They moved back a little, and Albert leaned against a black wrought-iron fence that lined the sidewalk.

"Was anybody in the building?" Marshall asked.

"There's nobody."

Joe Baker saw them and sidled over. "Well, that's that, I guess."

"Anybody know how it happened?" Albert wanted to know.

"Bet money on it—D'Allessandro started it."

Wilbur Soames and Ricky Dalmas stepped close, having heard this last. "You really think so?" Soames said.

"It makes perfect sense to me. I bet the building's insured for a ton of money."

They watched as the cascading spray of water seemed to disappear without effect into the flaming creases of smoke. A moment later, the D'Allessandros' battered little car pulled up. Mr. D'Allessandro got out on the passenger side, and ran into the middle of the fire engines and firemen, waving his arms and shouting something. Mrs. D'Allessandro got out of the car and simply watched.

"He doesn't look like he knew about it," Wilbur Soames said.

"What're you-all looking at?" said Albert.

Mrs. D'Allessandro had seen them now, and had left the car, walking toward them while still attending to the burning building. She looked pale, shaken. Her eyes were very wide.

"Did you—" she began, talking to Marshall.

"I just got here," he said.

She turned and watched it with them for a time. No one said anything. There were shouts among the firemen, and inside the building something big collapsed, with a tremendous shuddering groan. Flames licked out of the windows of the lower floors. Mr. D'Allessandro came limping out of the circle of engines, heading toward the car. He saw his wife standing on the other side of the street, and made his way to her, his face fixed in its grimace, not smiling now. He turned at her side, and she put one arm around his middle. "I don't understand," he said. He had to shout to be heard over the sound of more sirens, and so Marshall heard it, too. "I had it all worked out. He knew I had it worked out."

She said something to him that was lost in the noise, and he glanced over her shoulder at Marshall and the others. He signaled for Marshall to approach.

"Yes, sir."

"Nothing's changed."

"I'm sorry?"

"We've got the church," Mr. D'Allessandro said. "We can still do it. Brightman can still come do his program."

"Yes, sir."

"This doesn't change anything."

His wife turned and leaned in to speak to him. "Lawrence, it's over. They've done it to you anyway, don't you see?"

"It is not over," he said angrily.

She glanced at Marshall, then turned away.

"Keep it in mind," Mr. D'Allessandro said.

"What about us, sir?" Ricky Dalmas said.

Mr. D'Allessandro looked at him. Daylight was failing now, though there was a smoldering illumination and haze coming from the fire. "We'll finish the year in the church basement if we have to."

His wife said, "What'll you do for equipment?"

"We'll work something out," Mr. D'Allessandro said.

"That's what you always say," she told him. Then she stepped out into the street and peered along the wall of people; she had seen someone. She went a few paces in that direction, then turned and came back, facing her husband. "I don't even have to ask it, do I? How long ago did you do it?"

"Esther, please."

"I saw him, Lawrence! I saw Marcus just now."

"That's enough," Mr. D'Allessandro said.

But she shook him. "You gave it to him, didn't you? Terrence—you deeded it over to him. What did they have over you to make you let them have the deed?"

He took her by the elbow, and guided her back across the street. The light there was ghostly, a strange mixture of flame-glow and failing sun. They argued, or she railed and he tried to calm her.

"What was that all about?" Albert asked, putting one hand on Marshall's shoulder.

"I think Mr. D'Allessandro made some arrangements of his own," Marshall said.

The others—Baker and Soames and Dalmas—were a few feet away, talking to Martin Alvarez, who had just arrived. "Well," Joe Baker said, looking around at everyone, "I guess school is really out, now."

Marshall thought of walking up to Natalie's building, and he looked for her among the many faces gathered in the unreal glow of the flames. At last he walked with Albert to his apartment, thinking about getting on a bus home. The fire, the harsh, obliterating crackle and roar of it, had upset him, and made him strangely aware of the ongoing pathology of the city. He wanted to get home, and Albert very much wanted him to stay for a drink.

"How're things with Emma?" Marshall asked him.

"Swimming."

Marshall didn't pursue this. They came to Albert's building, and turned to look at the awful light beyond the trees.

"I wasn't cut out for radio," Albert said.

"What'll you do now?"

"I don't know." Albert sighed. "Go blind, I guess." This was spoken in a tone of surrender.

"I mean—for a career."

"I've got a job. I'll just keep it. Till I can't see anymore."

"I'm sorry," Marshall said.

"Come on," said Albert.

They went up the walk, onto the little porch. Emma was sitting with her back to them in the lighted window. Albert's entry startled her. She stood. "What is it?"

Albert told her what had happened, and she began to cry. She put her arms around him, sobbing.

"I heard all the sirens and smelled the smoke, too. I'm so sorry, Albert."

He said, "I've got Walter with me."

"No one was hurt or anything?"

"No."

"I heard the sirens. I'm so sorry, Albert. I know how much it meant to you."

He gave Marshall a look, as if to ask for his tolerance.

"I mean I know you were discouraged . . ." She halted. There didn't seem to be anything else to say.

"I should go," Marshall said gently.

But they wouldn't hear of it. They wanted to talk about the school, the fire, the things Albert had heard Mrs. D'Allessandro say. Marshall decided against saying what he thought he knew, that Marcus had used something of D'Allessandro's complications with Mrs. Gordon to convince him to give the school to Mr. Brace, or Terrence, or whatever his name was. It would be gossip to say anything, but it seemed perfectly clear as an assumption.

Albert made tea, and they listened to the news on his little transistor radio, the reedy, singsong voice of a disk jockey reporting that the fire had burned out of control for two hours now, and that the building was lost. No one had been inside; there were no serious injuries. Two firemen had been overcome by smoke, and one had suffered a minor abrasion from falling debris. Albert turned the radio off, and after a silence, Emma said, "He didn't sound a bit better than you do, Albert."

Albert sipped his tea and seemed to ruminate.

"Well," Emma muttered, "he didn't."

It was a strange hour. And when at last Marshall could extricate himself, Emma insisted on walking out to the street with them. "I smell the smoke," she said. In the dim light her pale eyes looked like drops of clear water, and there was an almost childlike aspect to her face, turned toward the sound of the fire engines four blocks away. Marshall's heart went out to her, for the fear and uncertainty he saw in her face.

"It's going to be all right," she said. "I just know it is."

Albert put his arm around her, and squeezed gently, held her to him. "I guess we'll both see you tomorrow night," he said. "At Alice's."

"'Bye," Marshall said.

At the end of the block, he looked back; they were just turning to go up to the open doorway of the building. They walked arm in arm, and seemed to be leaning on each other for comfort.

Chapter

18

*N*ever let anyone underestimate," Mitchell Brightman said, standing at his end of the table, "the power of the human species for cooperation."

"Sit down, Mitch," said Alice's father. "You've had too much wine."

"Wait," Mitchell Brightman said, "I'm serious. Defoliate a forest. Build a road. Cure a disease. Elect a president. Fight a goddamn war. Make a whole country change itself almost overnight—it all stems from one thing. Cooperation. An insignificant Negro woman decides she's tired of sitting in the back of the bus, and that gets it started. In six weeks there's a boycott of all the forms of transportation in the city, and an entire system is rocked to its very foundation. And how does this happen? Cooperation. That's our triumph, and our tragedy."

"Mitch, for God's sake."

"Let me finish, Patrick. I'm going somewhere with this—"

"That's what I'm afraid of."

"No, really now. Think of it. I ask you all, humbly, to think of the possibilities for goodness and evil in that one shining fact. You think Hitler could've succeeded without the cooperation of a whole lot of well-meaning people, good ol' day-to-day, work-a-daddy Germans just doing their jobs, trying not to make trouble for themselves or their loved ones, concentrating on the goal without ever really thinking about what the goal was? Think the Civil War could've happened? Think Lincoln could've freed the slaves? It's all part of the human habit of, and need for, cooperation. You think we could drop those bombs on Hanoi Harbor without cooperation? Think of those Russian technicians in Cuba, working like hell together for life and family, building those missiles, and all the cooperation that went into discovering they were there and then getting them out of there, everybody cooperating. Think of building a bomb that could blow up the whole damn world. We did that. Human beings did that. But we also cured polio, and smallpox, and diphtheria. We built this city. And the roads, and Hoover Dam, and we put a man into space."

"Very good, Mitch. Thank you. That's enough, now."

"Excuse me a second," Mr. Brightman said and hurried out of the room.

"I'm afraid I need your tolerance," Alice's father said, looking down the table. "My—uh—colleague's a bit under the weather." No one answered him. Things had been discomfiting for a time now, since the serving of the food was delayed: some problem in the kitchen, and Minnie had wanted to go in there to see what she could do. Mr. Kane wouldn't let her, and called for more wine. A mistake. They had all watched Mitchell Brightman emptying his glass and filling it and emptying it again. There was very little talk, and then Alice's father stood and gave a speech about being thankful for the return to health of his dear friend and employee, Minnie Jackson (it had struck Marshall as odd that this was the first time he'd heard Minnie's last name). Minnie sat at the other end of the table, opposite Mr. Kane. She wore a white blouse with frills down the front, and a lovely corsage that Alice had bought her. She had gone to the beauty parlor and gotten her hair done in a tight perm, and she looked, Alice said, so much younger. It was true. She seemed almost girlish. And until the trouble developed in the kitchen, she accepted all the service offered her by the other employees of Patrick Kane as though it were the most natural thing in the world. Alice, who had expressed the worry that the novelty of the situation might make Minnie nervous or uncomfortable, was very pleased.

She sat to her father's right, just down from the head of the table, across from Mitchell Brightman. Ranged opposite each other, going down the table, were Marshall and his mother, Albert and Clark Atwater, Emma and a member of Minnie's church—Mrs. Westerbrook, who was eighty-one and as small and dark as the window, with wide, watery black eyes and a high, soft, lovely laugh that issued forth nervously at nearly everything. After Mr. Kane's speech, the sense of relief seemed almost palpable in the room. Everyone began chattering at once. Mrs. Westerbrook and Albert talked quite good-naturedly to each other about their failing eyesight. Emma, following them, was animated, going on about learning Braille and how it had opened up the world to her. Mr. Kane and Alice talked about Woody Guthrie while Mitchell Brightman, lost in some contemplative reverie, drank still more wine. The fragrances from the kitchen wafted in to them all. Bread was served, and bowls of fruit, a plate of crackers and cheese. Brightman kept pouring wine for himself, and then asking for more, and then he and Alice's father were carrying on a heated discussion about tactics the Johnson campaign was using against Goldwater—a commercial in which a little girl picking flowers and singing softly to herself is interrupted by a nuclear explosion. "It's perfect," Mr. Kane said. "It gets the point across without the use of a single word."

"It's reprehensible," said Brightman, drinking the wine, "and you know it."

Alice agreed with this, and her father gave her a look. "Yes," he said. "Well, it's going to get Johnson elected."

"Fear, then, is what will work. Is that it?" Brightman said.

"You're not afraid of Goldwater?"

"He's a decent man," Brightman said. "And he's no more likely to blow us up than Johnson is."

"I don't think Madison Avenue ought to be deciding presidential elections," Alice said. "In any case. We're not buying a vacuum cleaner, we're trying to elect a president. You watch—if it keeps up, we'll end up with an actor or somebody like that in the White House."

Marshall had a moment of sensing that Alice was far ahead of him in her knowledge of the world. He watched her as she looked back and forth between her father and Brightman. The bottomless darks of her eyes seemed even darker.

Mrs. Westerbrook laughed at something Emma had said about Albert's first lessons in Braille.

Because Marshall was in the middle of the table, he could listen to the talk at both ends of it, and he found himself slightly adrift, neither part of the one nor of the other. Across from him, Loretta and Mr. Atwater were divided, attending to opposite ends, turned from each other, Loretta listening to Mrs. Westerbrook and Atwater leaning toward Mitchell Brightman, who began telling Alice about something that had happened on *Air Force One* back in the first months of the Thousand Days, or Camelot, as *Life* magazine had it. A miscommunication that had resulted in a presidential tirade, Kennedy standing in a sleeveless undershirt in the entrance to the presidential sleeping quarters, upbraiding a member of the White House staff. Marshall listened to this with deep fascination, of course—what he could hear of it: The details were lost in the general hum, as Albert caused Mrs. Westerbrook and Minnie to laugh, describing the way he had stumbled over himself, trying to tell Emma's aunt Patty that he wanted Emma's hand.

It was then that Mitchell gulped down the last of his seventh or eighth glass of wine, and stood to make his speech.

Now everyone seemed to be waiting for his return, even the two servers, young Negro men who stood on either side of the closed kitchen door with their hands clasped behind them, looking like guards waiting for some royal entry. One of them, the taller of the two, had a glazed left eye, partly dragged down in a faint scar, which reached to that side of the mouth. The scar was a bluish color, a shade darker than the rest of the face, whose skin was a perfect, flawless, dark brown the texture of polished mahogany.

It was this man that Mitchell Brightman leaned on, coming back through from the hallway. "Clarence," he said.

"Yes, sir, Mr. Mitchell, sir."

Brightman brought out a handkerchief and blew his nose, still being supported by the server with the scarred face. He sighed, swaying a bit, folding the handkerchief neatly and placing it in his suit-coat pocket. "There," he said, perhaps to himself. He looked at everyone. "Folks, this here is Clarence. Everybody know Clarence? Say hello, Clarence."

Clarence said, "Hello."

Brightman turned a little, and held up one hand as if to reach for the younger man, but then he seemed to forget all about him, lurching away, moving clumsily to the table, where he plopped down, staring at his plate. He picked up a fork and tapped it against the edge. "A toast," he said. He smiled and sat back. No one spoke. "Guess I ought to knock off on the wine."

"I'll have some more wine," said Emma, holding her glass up.

The server named Clarence hurried to pour some for her.

"Me, too," said Brightman. "Clarence?"

The other server, who was thin and sharp-featured and looked too young to be pouring wine, stepped up with his carafe.

"I don't want it from you," Brightman said. "Want it from my pal, Clarence."

Alice's father said, "Mitch, for God's sake."

The wine was poured. Alice had more, as did Loretta, Clark Atwater, Albert, and Alice's father. Mrs. Westerbrook and Minnie declined, as did Walter.

Clark Atwater began talking about India and China as the future repositories of world power and domination because of their uncontrolled population growth, the wars that would result from these factors. He spoke loudly and rather hurriedly, as though he were afraid someone might step in and wrest the group's attention from him. Had anyone at the table read Toynbee? None of this was in Toynbee, particularly, but reading Toynbee's great twelve-volume work, *A Study of History*, had given Mr. Atwater the means to arriving at these conclusions about the future. Western civilization was on the decline, of course. India and China, with their vestiges of civilizations and their burgeoning numbers of people, would change everything. This would all take place sometime in the 1980s, if not sooner. And the last of the world's civilizations was at stake.

Mitchell Brightman looked across the table at Marshall. "Tell us about the fire at your school," he said.

Marshall glanced at Mr. Atwater, who had clearly not finished talking and was visibly unhappy at the interruption.

"Come on," Brightman said. "Tell me."

Marshall began describing the scene at the D'Allessandro School as he had arrived last evening—the fire trucks, the police, the confusion. Alice's father broke in to say that he had sent a film crew to the scene, and mentioned the fact that the police were suspicious about the cause.

"Somebody torched it," Brightman said. "Right?"

"Could be."

"I was trying to make a point, here," Atwater said.

"Clark," said Marshall's mother. "Nobody wants to talk about world history."

"These are newspeople—and you're telling me nobody wants to hear about it?" He pointed down the table at Brightman. "What was *he* saying about cooperation? Wasn't that about world history?"

"I had a call," Brightman said to Marshall. "From that Mr. D'Allessandro. Apparently, my talk is still on?"

"Yes, sir," Marshall said.

"Maybe I'll talk about cooperation."

"See?" Mr. Atwater said. "This is the subject. Well, I'm on the subject." He leaned toward Brightman. "Have you read Arnold J. Toynbee?"

Brightman took a swallow of wine. "Twice a year."

"You have read him."

"I said. Twice a year."

"All twelve volumes?" Atwater seemed impressed.

Brightman nodded. "I read it through once in regular print, and then again in Braille."

"I read Braille," Albert said from down the table. He indicated Emma. "And this is my teacher."

"Yes," said Brightman, obviously embarrassed. "I remember."

Atwater was staring at him. "You've never really read Toynbee."

"Clark, stop it," Loretta said.

He turned to her. "Don't order me around."

"I'm sure Toynbee has a lot to tell us," Mitchell Brightman said. "At least twelve volumes' worth. Here's a toast to old Mr. Toynbee."

"I think I know when I'm being patronized," said Atwater.

"Nobody's patronizing anybody," Alice said crisply. She stood and poured more wine into Atwater's glass. "Have some more wine, why don't you?"

Atwater stared at her for a moment, then lifted the glass and drank.

"Think about a fire in a building in Washington, D.C.," Mitchell Brightman said. "Four alarms, four different fire companies arrive to fight this fire. Cooperation. And somebody started the fire. That prob'ly took cooperation, too. Isn't that right, Patrick?"

"Come on, Mitchell."

"Well, Patrick—it's true. I'm interested in the truth. Think about cooperation, I ask all of you. I'd like to make a toast to cooperation. Or did I do that already?"

"I think one toast is enough," said Mr. Kane.

"I'd like to toast Mr. Brightman," Clark Atwater said. He held his glass toward Brightman. "To you, sir. For your fine work on the news pretending to know what you're—"

"I have a toast," Brightman said with insistence, talking over the other man.

"—talking about."

"A toast," Brightman said, standing again. There was no slur in his speech. He held his stance straight, seemed completely in charge of himself. His voice was clear and his diction exact. He looked down the table at Minnie and smiled, then loosened his tie. "Minnie, you don't mind, do you?"

"Miss Jackson to you," Minnie said.

He smiled, then laughed lowly to himself. "You know the Billie Holiday song, 'Miss Brown to You,' Min—I mean, Miss Jackson?"

Minnie smiled, nodding.

"Bet you could sing it, right now."

"You'd lose all your money," Minnie said to him.

"Anyway," Brightman said, "I want all of us to toast the beautiful and tragic human capacity for cooperation. The source of all our joy and all our woe."

"I'd rather toast Miss Jackson again," Emma said, and she held her glass out in the faith that someone would follow suit. Alice hurried to do just that, standing and reaching across Marshall.

"Good, Emma," she said. "To Miss Jackson."

"Amen," Albert said. "That's right, Emma."

"I second it," said Patrick Kane.

And they all clinked glasses. Brightman drank his glass empty, and then poured more. "Okay, now that we've toasted Miss Jackson, I insist that we toast—" he stopped, looked down the table, and then back at Alice's father. "I can't remember what I wanted to toast."

"You were talking about cooperation," Loretta said.

"I was?"

"You wanted to toast cooperation," said Alice. "I think we've all been brought to an appreciation of it, though."

"Cooperation."

"That's what it was," Albert said.

"Cooperation," Brightman repeated. "What an odd thing to toast. I wonder what I could've been thinking about?" He sat down.

Mr. Atwater reached for the bread, and knocked over his own wineglass. There was nothing in it, but it made a clatter that silenced everyone for a moment.

Then Brightman stood again. "Oh, that's right. Cooperation."

And now Alice's father got up and took him by the arms. "Mitch, there's some things we need to talk about."

"I want to tell them about it, Patrick."

"Let's just—can you come with me for a minute?"

Brightman looked at the others. "He needs help in the powder room." Then he turned to Mr. Atwater and said, almost aggressively, "You had something to say?"

"I wanted to toast you, sir."

"Where do I know you from?"

Atwater reached down and picked up his overturned wineglass. "A toast," he said. "To newscasters."

"I don't have any more wine," said Brightman. "And neither do you." He turned to Alice's father. "This guy needs more wine."

"In one minute, Mitch."

Alice's father guided him to the doorway, and out, and for a few seconds they were arguing, in whispers, in the hall. The whispers faded, and then there was silence.

Alice turned to Marshall and laid her head on his shoulder, a gesture of weariness more than anything else. She sat up straight and sipped her wine. Mr. Atwater was watching her. "They'll be back soon," she said to him.

"That's immaterial to me," he said.

Loretta slapped him on the fleshy part of his upper arm. "Clark."

He turned on her. "Don't ever do that again," he said.

"Well, come on," she told him.

"You are not in a position to talk to me that way."

"I'd rather you didn't talk to *her* the way you are," Marshall said.

"Honor thy father and thy mother," said Mrs. Westerbrook.

This was followed by what felt like a protracted silence. Alice took Marshall's hand and held it in her lap. He was aware of his mother's eyes on him, and after a few seconds he gently took his hand away, using the pretext of pouring himself more water.

Mitchell Brightman came back into the room, followed by Alice's father, who looked at her and made a signal as if to say that he had tried his best, and that his best had ended in failure. Brightman sat down and brought a pint bottle of whiskey out of the side pocket of his suit coat. He opened it and poured a swallow into the empty wineglass at his elbow. "Anybody else?" he said.

"Nobody else," Alice's father said.

"Medicinal purposes," said Brightman. "You-all go on talking."

For a little while no one seemed willing to say anything. But finally there were a few soft murmurings—about the fire at the school, the lateness of the hour. Minnie and her friend Mrs. Westerbrook were discussing the difficulty Mrs. Westerbrook's son was having in his job as a driver for one of the members of the executive council of the AFL-CIO. The gentleman, a close associate of George Meany himself, was experiencing personal troubles with his wife, and was taking it all out on Mrs. Westerbrook's son.

"I work there," Albert said. "Is your son Jerry Westerbrook?"

"Yes, suh."

"I know him. I've had lunch with him a few times."

"Well," Minnie said. "Ain't it a small world."

"Jerry's a nice old guy," said Albert. But in the next instant his face registered some sort of distress. He looked over at Marshall, then lowered his gaze.

"Ah'm very proud of him," Mrs. Westerbrook said. "He turned sixty years old this week."

"Sixty years old," Albert said. "He—he doesn't look sixty."

"You got to git him when he ain't in that unifahm."

"Yes, ma'am."

"Sixty years old and working as a driver," Brightman said.

Emma said, "It's such a small world sometimes."

"Small world," said Mr. Atwater. "I'll give you small world. How about this—I was this boy's teacher." He indicated Marshall. "I told him to go to radio school. He wouldn't know anybody here—except his mother—if I hadn't said he ought to go to radio school and learn how to be an announcer. Think of that for a while."

For a little time, no one said anything.

Finally, Loretta murmured, "Clark, we have all understood your importance."

He glared at her. "I was merely pointing out a fact."

"About cooperation," Mitchell Brightman said, working his way to his feet again. "Consider the president of the United States."

"Mitch, that's enough, now."

"The president of the United States is a man who has in all cases having to do with the personal conduct of his life the cooperation of the American press. Would you say that's an accurate reflection of the situation, Patrick?"

After a pause, Mr. Kane said, "It's accurate."

"Consider the case of our dead hero president." Brightman looked directly at Marshall. "Now here's a young man with presidential aspirations."

Alice said, "Please, Uncle Mitch. Shut up."

Brightman swayed a little, then sat down again. "Where was I?"

"You were through," said Mr. Kane. Then he called for the main course to be served. The two servers made passes back and forth from the kitchen, carrying the food: a platter of steaming slices of roast beef and ham, a roast turkey, plates of hot green beans, bowls of salad, and cornmeal muffins, more glasses of wine, and iced tea.

"I wondered what you thought of Toynbee's theories about

civilizations dying as it relates to our civilization?" Atwater asked Mitchell Brightman.

"Forgive me," said Brightman, "but I don't—" He belched low, under his breath. "Have the—" And he belched again. "Slightest— idea who the—hell I'm talking to."

Atwater stood. "You people—" he began.

Loretta held him by the wrist. "Clark—please."

"You think you know everything—you think your lives are more important than other people's—"

"Excuse me?" Brightman said.

The other man made a sweeping gesture toward Minnie and Mrs. Westerbrook without taking his eyes from Brightman. "This dinner is supposed to be in honor of your host's maid. And you sit there talking. People like you are the ones who really keep these Negroes down. You don't care about anything but your own pres- tige—"

Minnie said, "Ah don't need you to defend me, mistuh."

"I think we should go," Loretta said, rising.

"I haven't had my say yet," said Mr. Atwater. "This has nothing to do with you."

"Clarence," said Alice's father. "Would you and John see this gentleman out?"

"Wait," Brightman said. "Let the man speak."

But Mr. Atwater appeared to have run out of steam. He sat down, his hands resting in his lap.

There was a long silence. No one moved.

Brightman hiccoughed loudly, then offered Mr. Atwater a drink of whiskey.

"No thank you," Atwater said.

"I've seen you somewhere before," said Brightman. "It's the damnedest thing. I can't remember where. You don't work at the D.C. drunk tank."

"I teach school."

"Great profession," Brightman said. "Future of the country. I'll drink to it. Takes a lot of cooperation to run a school."

"I run it, too," Atwater said.

"I bet you do. Everybody reading Toynbee?"

"No."

"It's forbidden?"

"No, it's not forbidden—"

"I can't understand what you're here for. You belong to some-body?"

"I'm leaving," said Atwater. And he turned to Marshall's mother. "Loretta?"

She had begun a nervous conversation with Minnie about mak-ing cornmeal muffins. She was trying to gloss over everything, and her son understood this with a pang. He looked across the table at Clark Atwater and said, "Why don't you eat a little something first?"

Atwater ignored him. "Loretta."

She paused. "Just a minute, Clark."

"I'm leaving now. You can come or you can stay."

She looked at him. "All right."

"We'll give you a ride home," Alice said.

Her father put his hand on her shoulder, and she moved to dis-place herself, shifting toward Marshall.

Mr. Atwater looked at everyone, his face beginning to whiten with rage. "You better get yourself out of that chair," he said to Loretta.

"What's the trouble, bunky?" Brightman said. "Why don't you sit down and shut the hell up?"

Minnie stood at her end of the table. "Ah won't have this unpleasantness, na. Ah'm the guest of honuh. Let's all sit down and have us a nice meal." She gathered her skirt and took her place again, her attitude final, as though there could be no further dis-cussion or conflict now that she had spoken.

"Amen," said Mrs. Westerbrook. "A nice meal."

"I'd rather read Toynbee," Brightman said.

"He's making fun of me," Atwater said to Loretta. "You're all making fun of me."

"Well, I'll tell you," Brightman said. "I don't know who the hell you are. That's for sure. If I did, I'd make fun of you, too."

"Mr. Atwater," Alice's father said quickly. "Surely you can see that Mitch is under the weather. I asked your tolerance, sir."

Atwater sat down again, slowly, muttering. "That's the trouble with people like him. People like us tolerate their behavior."

"Oh," Alice said. "His behavior hasn't been that bad."

"Could we say grace?" Mrs. Westerbrook wanted to know.

The rest of the meal went smoothly enough, though Mr. Atwater's ruffled feelings were still quite visibly ruffled. And Brightman kept saying things to needle him, kept asking him who he was and remarking that he had a familiar face.

"I was talking to you at Alice's birthday party," Atwater said.

Brightman looked puzzled. "I wasn't at Alice's birthday party."

"Yes, you were."

"No. Haven't been to one of those in at least a decade."

"You were there." Atwater turned his attention to Alice's father. "He was there. Tell him."

"Matter of fact," Brightman said before anyone else could speak, "I was there. I don't remember *you* being there."

"I was at that birthday party. Tell him, Loretta."

"Clark, can't you see you're being teased?"

"Well, goddammit, I *was* there."

It was a very strange, almost pathological evening, with the two Negro women sitting at one end of the table, and Alice's father and Mitchell Brightman at the other, and the talk that bore no relation, Marshall came to realize, to the reason they were all gathered in the first place. He offered a toast to their friends Stephen and Diane and the people they were traveling with. Minnie approved of this, and again the table grew quiet.

"Oh, I had something else to say," Mitchell Brightman said. "I'm gonna to do an article called the duplicitous press corps. You can all be in it." He indicated Clark Atwater. "Except that person."

Atwater had been talking to Loretta and hadn't heard him. He sat up straight, chewing. "What?"

"He's deaf," said Brightman. "And I don't know who he is."

Alice's father said, "He's with my daughter's fiancé, Mitch."

Brightman smiled. "Well, he's perfectly welcome." He leaned toward Atwater's end of the table. "And your name is Toynbee?"

There was a moment of an alarming sort of silence, and then Atwater simply nodded. "That's right, sir. Toynbee."

"Good. We got that established, at least."

After the meal, Alice's father had everyone gather in the little side porch where, Marshall recalled, the strange red-haired lady had read his palm. There were couches ranged along the left and back walls, and everyone took a seat. They were reflected in the blackness of the windows, so that the effect was of two rooms, side by side. Mitchell Brightman wanted to talk about the press corps, and cooperation. Minnie and Mrs. Westerbrook remained only a polite minute or so, then asked if they might make their way home. Alice's father drove them, leaving Alice to tend to Brightman. It was clear to Marshall that Loretta wanted to go, too, now, but Atwater was interested, trying to draw Brightman out about John Kennedy. Brightman kept calling him Toynbee, and it didn't seem to bother him.

Albert and Emma sat together on the opposite side of the room, near a small aquarium. Albert was whispering to her, describing the colors and shapes he saw in the lighted water.

"I have to go," Loretta said finally. "I can't stay awake another minute."

"I'll take you," Marshall offered.

"Wait a damn minute," Atwater said. "This is my girl. I'll take her." He stood, wavered, reached to the wall for support.

"Watch it there, Mr. Toynbee," Brightman said. "This stuff'll kill you."

"It's Atwater," the other said, a little too drunk to be indignant.

"No, it's whiskey."

"Whatever you say, there, Mitch," Atwater said. "You're the *expert*." The emphasis was disdainful.

"Hail and farewell," said Brightman.

Alice kissed Loretta on the cheek, and walked with them to the door. Albert and Emma stood and apologized for leaving early, too. They all moved to the living room, saying their good-byes. The air in the open space of the entrance was cold and moist-feeling. Marshall had hugged his mother and promised not to stay too late, then he shook hands with Albert as Albert was starting out. There was a lot of confusion: Clark Atwater sniping at Loretta about the cold and wanting to drive the car; Emma and Alice talking in the open doorway. The young man walked back through the house, to the side porch, where Mitchell Brightman was sitting on the couch under the black windows, staring into space. Marshall stopped and was about to leave the room.

"Sit down," Brightman said.

"Sir?"

"Sit down, son."

Marshall did so. They were facing each other from the farthest ends of a right angle, at opposite sides of the couch.

"You afraid of me?"

"No, sir."

"You want to be president."

Marshall said nothing.

"Alice told me all about you."

"Sir, I don't know about the presidency—"

The older man began to laugh. It started low, almost under his breath, but soon he was lying back, really laughing. Finally, he subsided. He sat forward. "Sorry."

"Nothing to be sorry about," Marshall said. Then, "Sir." He felt uncomfortably as if the other had put him in a category with Clark Atwater.

"Sure there is," Brightman said. "There's always something to be sorry for. Never forget that, kid."

A moment later, he cleared his throat and seemed to consider something, going over it in his mind. "I'm gonna tell you something."

"Yes, sir?"

"You're a nice kid. You have a sense of—ah—shit. Never mind. I'm gonna tell you something. Alice says Kennedy's your hero— and hell, it's obvious from your hairstyle."

Marshall ran both hands through his hair.

Brightman looked at him. "Look, kid. It's all a show. You had it right doing the radio school bit. During the war—men're dying all around us, you know? Thousands of lives ending, and the whole country's hurting. But that didn't stop it from being a show. Old Walter Winchell, you understand? H. V. Kaltenborn. All of them. Show guys, really. Bringing everybody the show. Winchell hunching over the microphone, waiting for show time, for the signal to start talking in that heavy, portentous voice. 'Good evening, ladies and gentleman, and all the ships out on the sea.' Like that. High drama. But showbiz. You understand? It's in everything. Kennedy—that New Frontier crap. A show. Hell, they put that flag up at Iwo six or seven times so the guy could get a good film of it. For the folks back home. So much of it is just show business."

Marshall simply stared at him.

"In twenty years, that's *all* any of it will be. And it's just not what you think it is, kid. None of it. Kennedy wasn't interested in anything but politics and skirts. You know how many women he screwed? He had them coming in all hours of the day and night. And we all knew it, every one of us. We knew it and we looked the other way. See? Because it wasn't part of the show."

The boy said, "Kennedy . . ." He couldn't finish.

"That's right. A skirt hound. Sometimes two at a time. Girls. Hollywood starlets, walk-ons. He was a skirt chaser from the first, like his old man. We had a couple of them around the White House—hell, we didn't even give them names. Called them fiddle and faddle. The guy screwed everything in sight. He used to say if he didn't get laid every day he'd get migraines. And he got laid every day. Sometimes more than every day and sometimes with more than one woman."

Marshall said, "That's—that's not true." He felt sick to his stomach. Something in him wanted to strike the man sitting there on the other side of the room. "That's just not—not true."

"Of course it's true. Why would I make that up? I was there, kid. I knew the guy. He was a regular poon hound. He was smart, and he liked talk, and he had one subject. Politics. Period. He wasn't this—prince they're making him out to be, that's all. There were things about him you had to overlook. Big things. Especially if, like me, you didn't think it was particularly a good thing for the president of the United States to be screwing whores in the White House by the goddamn numbers."

Alice came back, then, carrying Brightman's coat. "Time to go, Mitch," she said.

"Really?"

She stood over him, holding the coat out.

Brightman looked at Marshall. "Marilyn Monroe, kid. You remember her singing to him at Madison Square Garden? Know what happened later on that night?"

"Mitch," Alice said. "Home, come on."

"Not fit to drive," he said. "I'm telling this boy something of what he needs to know if he's going to take up the art of politics."

"You're wallowing in a lot of dirt and my father has told you about this."

Brightman got to his feet, and let her put the coat on him, turning a little to put his arms in the sleeves. She patted him on the back, then guided him out, and for a few minutes Marshall was left alone, in the quiet room reflected there in the windows, and in the lighted green-glowing glass of the aquarium with its tropical fish moving in their peristaltic slowness.

Alice came back through and sat down next to him, breathless, her hair smelling of the outside. "He's never going to make it home," she said. "I feel guilty. I had to pour him into the car."

Marshall said, "I've never seen anybody so drunk."

"Oh, it's been far worse. Tonight was mild."

"That—what he was saying—"

"Look," she said. "Don't pay any attention to him. That's a kick he gets on when he's had too much to drink. He played around on his wife and she died and he's always felt so low about it. Don't pay any attention to him, really."

"But why would he make up something so—evil—why would he make that up?"

"It's just the booze talking, Walter. Forget it."

"It's a lie, though."

She answered with a kind of sigh. "What difference does it make, really? Of course it's a lie." She put her arms around him. "Here's what's true, Walter." She kissed the side of his face. "We're alone."

"What about Clarence and the other guy?"

"They're in the kitchen."

"The kitchen's right through there."

"Forget about it," she told him. "Look, I know it's against your religion and all that, but something must happen sometimes in your church or there wouldn't be so many big Catholic families. Kiss me."

"Alice," he said. "I'm so sorry. I like you so much—"

"*Like* me."

"Please," he said. "Let me finish."

She sat back and regarded him, folding her arms under her breasts. "Go right ahead."

Across the way, his little reflected shape in the aquarium glass made his nausea grow worse. "I—I think we ought to slow down a little—"

"Slow down?" she said. "Jesus. The Ice Age was faster."

"I just don't think we ought to rush into anything."

"Fine." She stood. "I'm really tired, now, Walter. And I think I'll just go on upstairs and go to bed."

"Alice," he said.

"No, really. You don't have to say another thing. In fact, I'd rather you didn't say one more goddamn thing."

They both heard movement in the next room, then. Her father was home—had been home. He spoke to someone in the other room—Clarence, probably. There were the sounds of dishes clattering, water running. Mr. Kane appeared in the doorway and said, "Did you put him in the car?"

"Yes," Alice said.

"Alice, what're you thinking of?"

"I wanted him to leave."

"He drove straight up onto the Grantham's lawn. I don't know how I saw him. He got out and laid down on the grass. He could've frozen to death."

She said nothing.

"I put him in the car and Clarence is driving him home."

"Good night," she said and walked quickly out of the room.

Marshall stood. For a tense few seconds, the older man simply stared at him.

"She's upset," Mr. Kane said.

"She—she says she's—tired, sir."

"Your mother—she works for that guy?"

Marshall was momentarily stunned. "Pardon?"

"Does your mother work for that Atwater fellow?"

"Yes, sir. He's the principal at the high school."

"They going to be married?"

"I guess so, sir."

"Your mother's happy about that?"

Marshall shook his head. "I don't know, sir."

Mr. Kane nodded. "He's a bit of an asshole, isn't he?"

Marshall said nothing.

"I've been talking to Alice about it, son. It's no secret, is it?"

"No, sir."

"Your mother types for him—secretarial kinds of things?"

"Yes, sir."

"Tell her I've got a job for her if she wants it. I'll pay her more than the State of Virginia's paying her, too. Tell her that. Or do you want me to tell her?"

"I could tell her."

"Whichever you like."

"Yes, sir."

Mr. Kane scratched his ear, looking down. "I heard some of that—what you and Alice talked about."

Marshall waited.

"I think that's the mature thing. To go slow. I'm impressed with your maturity. And I agree with you."

"Yes, sir." Marshall swallowed the last word, then repeated it, barely missing the falsetto. "S-Sir."

"You got a car?"

"Yes. My mother's car."

"Good night, son." The older man turned and was gone.

Marshall heard him on the stairs, heard the noises in the kitchen. He made his way quickly to the front door, listening for Alice's voice amid the other sounds of the house. Her father was talking, and the tone was of a kind of badgering. It seemed to the young man that this was often enough the note Mr. Kane struck when talking to his daughter. He let himself out, crossed through the cold shade of moon-lighted trees on the lawn, aware of his own shadow, moving away, like a fugitive skulking from the scene of a crime.

Chapter

19

For days he carried inside himself the knowledge—no, the suspicion—like a wound under the heart, that all of what Mitchell Brightman had told him was true. At times, his mind presented him with the possibility that it was more than true, that Brightman had been giving him only the surface of what must have been a much larger story. At Saint Matthew's Cathedral, he knelt and tried to pray, thinking of a prince of the Church saying the words of the Mass over this man struck down in the sunlight, when he least expected it, taken before he could confess his sins or ask for pardon, and by the tenets of this faith, Kennedy's own faith, such a sudden blow made the state of his soul all the more terrible to think about, if all that Brightman had said was true. Marshall saw again the cardinal with the tall mitre, saying the Mass for the dead:

We ask your blessing on the wonderful man we bury here today.

Did the cardinal know? Did all of them know?

He couldn't pray. The words rode through his mind and left no trace, and he repeated them, to no avail.

There were practical matters to attend to. He had received a notice from Mr. D'Allessandro that there would be a meeting at his home concerning the unfinished school year. There was also the matter of trying to appease his mother in her anger with him for interfering about Clark Atwater.

"I just might marry him, Walter. Even if I take this—better job in Mr. Kane's office. And you'll just have to get used to it."

"But you don't have to marry him now."

"I never did have to. This is not your business. Clark has his foibles, but we get along. Do you understand me? We get along. He is not like—that man you saw at the party. He feels everyone's disapproval and it makes him nervous."

"He makes everyone disapprove."

"Walter, this is my business. I don't have to do anything for a year. I'm going to think about it. I have fun with him, believe it or not."

"But he hit you."

"No, he did *not*. That was just what I said it was, and you're going to have to start learning to accept that what somebody tells you is the truth and just leave it at that."

He went through that week, and then the next week, sleepless, filled with an increasing sense of failure, and haunted by fears that everything was true—the worst imaginings. They bordered on impure thoughts. Kennedy in a bed with two women, like the two women he had seen in the little parlorlike library of the now defunct D'Allessandro School. He had dreams about it, and lay awake at night remembering phrases from the speeches.

> *With a good conscience our only sure reward, with history the final judge of our deeds, let us go forth to lead the land we love, asking his blessing and his help, but knowing that here on earth, God's work must truly be our own.*

God's work. Had this been a lie? If what Brightman had said was true, then *wasn't* it a lie? Didn't that fact make it all a lie?

An anger was rising in him.

On a night when there would have been school if there had

been a school to go to, he went into a barbershop and asked the man to cut off all his hair.

"Whadda ya want, kid? A flattop?" The barber was from New York, a middle-aged man with thick, black eyebrows and thick hair, dark Italian skin. What did he believe?

"What did you think of Kennedy?" Marshall asked him.

"That's a funny question, kid. You just trying to make conversation with the barber?"

"No—I want to know."

"Well, to tell you the troot, I never gave him much thought. Till he got shot. Then—I dunno. I guess he was okay. So how do you want this?"

"Take it all," Marshall told him. "A crew cut all the way."

"Not even sideburns, like Elvis dere?"

"No sideburns."

At home, his mother stared at him in disbelief. "What in the world?"

"I just got tired of worrying about it," he said.

"Are you all right, son?"

"What do you mean?"

"Okay," she said. "Forget it."

He had gone that first Monday after the fire to Natalie's building, only to find that she had moved out. No one seemed to know where. When he spoke to Mrs. D'Allessandro over the telephone, she indicated that Natalie would be within reach soon enough— she used that phrase. He wanted to see her. He told Mrs. D'Allessandro this, and asked her to please relay the message. "Brightman is going ahead with the show," he told her. "It won't mess anything up to let me see Natalie." He was amazed at his own harshness, speaking to her.

"She doesn't want to see anyone just now, all right?"

He went to work each day, doing everything by a kind of rote, looking at everyone and wondering what they actually knew or believed. He kept to himself mostly, and in any case, Alice seemed to be avoiding him. At least during the first few days. What surprised him was that nothing, really, seemed to have changed. He walked the streets of the city and everything looked the same, people treated him basically the same, after remarking on the haircut, of course. But the world went on as before, and he himself ended up daydreaming about the presidency, about Kennedy, about the misty future. He took the comments of the others in the mailroom about his hair, and Mr. Wolfschmidt's teasing. Mr. Wolfschmidt said he looked like those pictures of people in the freshly liberated concentration camps.

When Alice did finally speak to him, she asked if this new look was the result of some religious feeling, some lacerating sense of penance for his sins, whatever they might be. She began to speculate, half teasingly, about this, and he cut her short.

"I got a haircut," he said. "I don't want to talk about it."

"Fine," she said, and turned to walk away.

"Wait," he said.

They had been standing in the doorway of the mailroom. She had come down to deliver something for a mailing to the field representatives of the bureau.

"Alice," he said, "can't we be like we were before?"

"And how's that?"

"I don't know—like it always was—"

Her eyes were swimming. "You know, you look funny like that."

He said nothing.

"Actually, it's like there's some aspect of self-mutilation about it. What's with you, anyway, Walter?"

"Nothing's *with* me."

"I've decided something, Walter. I'm leaving here. I don't know what I'm going to do yet, but I'm quitting. Maybe I'll join the others—Stephen and Diane. There'll be things for me to do. I'm going to make something good with my life. No matter what you or my father or anyone else says."

"Alice," he said.

"I've got work to do." She turned and walked away.

He followed her up the hall to the bank of elevators. She had pushed the UP button and was waiting, tapping her left foot, arms folded tight.

"Alice," he said. "I don't want to lose you—" He stopped. He'd meant to go on and say "as a friend," and had paused with the abrupt sensation that this was the most insulting thing he could say.

She turned to him, and put one hand, gently, on his shoulder. "I feel the same, darling. Even with the haircut—I mean, I think it's cute."

"No," he said. "Not that. I didn't mean *that*."

"Well, what then?" She stepped back. "Christ!"

"I don't think I'm ready to be married yet."

She let her arms drop to her sides.

"Alice, look—"

The elevator door opened with its dull metallic ding. She turned and got on. "I'm busy," she said. "Really."

The doors closed.

Later, out on the wintry streets of the city, he stopped in a recruitment office, a little cubicle on the same block with several travel agencies and savings banks, all in a row, as if there were some connection between them. The recruitment office was small and close, too well heated. There were pictures on the left wall of men in uniform—marines, sailors, airmen, soldiers. To the right were photos of ships in the middle of the ocean, the tremendous shimmer of the water under bright sun. The recruitment sergeant sat at a small metal desk with a portable fan on it, the fan rotating in a faltering, drunken nodding, troubling the air without quite stirring it enough to cause a breeze. The door into the back room, where other desks were ranged like a small schoolroom, was propped open with a big book. He pointed at it when Marshall sat down.

"Know what that is?"

"No, sir."

"That's the *Oxford English Dictionary*."

"Really." The young man looked at it. "Interesting."

"I do crossword puzzles. You do crossword puzzles?"

"No, sir."

"I read books. Fifty a year. I keep track. Write them all down. Title and author. People think the services are dumb. It's not so. I know career army guys who've read Shakespeare. You can *act* Shakespeare on army bases. Saw a very good production at Fort Myer not too long ago. You know Shakespeare, right? You look like an intelligent young man."

"I read *Macbeth*, in high school."

"Good, huh?"

"Yes, sir."

"I know that play, see. And the others, too. Well, some of them." The sergeant was thin, balding, with green eyes and a reddish cast to his skin. He had magazines and newspapers in a stack on one side of the desk, and books on a shelf behind him. On the wall there, set on either side of the shelf, were photographs of John Kennedy and Lyndon Johnson. The photo of Kennedy was draped in black cloth. "So," the sergeant said. "What can we do for you?"

Marshall had walked in here on an impulse. He said, "What does a person have to do to enlist in the army?"

"That's easy as pie. Have you ever been convicted of a felony?"

"No, sir."

The sergeant smiled. "Nothing to it." Then he laughed. "Hell, you won't even have to get the haircut. You're halfway there."

"Thank you," Marshall said and got up to leave.

"Hey, where you going?"

"I'm not sure."

"Want some literature?"

Marshall hesitated a moment. "Not now," he said. "Maybe later."

It was a dry, windless, cold afternoon. He went up to Saint Matthew's, and in, walked to the communion rail and knelt down. The smell of votive candles came to him, agitated in their blue cups with every current in the air. He looked at the crucifix and tried hard to pray, but the words simply wouldn't attach themselves to their own meanings. Finally, he walked around to the rectory to see if he could talk to Father Soberg, but Father Soberg was gone, had left earlier in the week for Southeast Asia. A young curate said this, and asked if Marshall wanted to write down the name of the place where Father Soberg would be. Marshall said he would remember it. "All right," the curate told him, apparently annoyed with him for not wanting to write it down, "His new assignment is in a place called Saigon. In French Indochina, though I think it has another name now."

"Vietnam," Marshall told him.

"I try to avoid the news when I can. I'm so out of touch with all that sort of thing."

"Thank you," Marshall said.

At the end of the week, when he drove into town for the appointment with the D'Allessandros, he half expected to find Natalie there. He stopped at Albert's building, and went through Albert's simple astonishment at his appearance. "Is this—religious or something?"

"No, Albert, it's not religious."

"I'm sorry."

"What is it?" Emma said.

"You should see Walter's hair."

She moved confidently in the room, like a sighted person, crossing to where Marshall stood. With the same confidence, she raised her arms and put her hands on top of his head. "Ohh!"

"Something, isn't it?" Albert said.

"My, my." She brought her hands down, but remained where she was. "What happened to you?"

"I got a haircut," Marshall said. "That's all."

"Well, didn't you indeed."

"Look, I'd rather not talk about it, if it's all the same to you."

"Okay." She went back to where she had been sitting, and took her place, reaching for the tea she'd been drinking.

"I don't know how long we'll be," Albert said to her.

"Okay."

They went out into the windy dusk. The sky was red in the west, with flaming shards of cloud in it, and to the north the moon, white and flat as a button, had risen above the level of the trees. Most of the leaves were gone now, and the wind kicked them up from the sidewalk and the street.

"Emma seems—happy," Marshall said.

"We're happy enough."

They got into the Lark. Albert had to put his knees against the dashboard. "The thing is," he said, "you have to get on with living, you know?"

Marshall started the car and pulled out toward Connecticut Avenue.

"We went on over to Maryland and got married, last Tuesday."

"You did?"

Albert was staring out the window. "I guess, finally, it doesn't really matter what she thinks. She doesn't have any political power, you know? She's a nice person. She'll learn. She wants to do well. I thought she did fine at that dinner for Minnie. Maybe we've all got to start trying to forgive each other a little."

"That Mitchell Brightman—he's—bad," Marshall said. "Bad."

"Well. Just seemed like a guy with a booze problem to me. He sure gave poor Atwater hell. Or Toynbee."

They both laughed, and Marshall felt the surprise of having allowed himself the luxury. "I've been really messed up lately," he said.

"I guess so."

"I don't mean about Alice and Natalie."

Albert looked at him. "There's something else?"

"Never mind," Marshall told him.

"No, tell me."

"He—he said some things about Kennedy."

"I thought they were friends."

"I don't want to talk about it, Albert."

The D'Allessandros' house was on Porter Street, just down from Wisconsin Avenue, tucked in among automobile-sized shrubs and tall hedges, shaded by old oaks and massive willows. The house was a big, dark Victorian with a wide front porch and awninged windows. Ricky Dalmas and Joe Baker were already going up the steps; Wilbur Soames was waiting for them, saying something with a smile that Joe Baker laughed at. Marshall parked the car, and then he and Albert made their way across the sidewalk and the lawn, walking slowly because Albert was having trouble seeing the ground. Marshall looked at the windows, for Natalie. The thought of her was strangely divorced from him, like a memory he couldn't be certain of.

"Alice is quitting her job," he told Albert. "Going away."

"So the marriage is off?"

"It's off, all right."

"What about the other girl—Natalie?"

"I guess it's off with her, too."

"So you're a free man again."

They were almost to the porch steps, and Wilbur Soames had

heard this last. "Man," he said, smiling broadly. "How's it feel to be a free man?"

Marshall gave no answer to this. In the doorway of the house, Natalie stood, wearing jeans and a sweatshirt. Her hair was pulled back in a French twist, and her skin was several shades darker. He had never seen any woman—not in magazines or movies or television or in all the streets he had ever walked—so beautiful. She offered him her hand, palm down, as though she expected him to kiss it. He took it and stepped through the doorway, into the brown foyer of the D'Allessandros' house.

"I had a vacation," she told him, and though she did not whisper, there was something confiding about it; she was talking only to him. "Key West."

He was speechless. He thought of her on a beach, in sunlight, at the edge of the sea.

"And you," she said, taking a step back to gaze at him. "You had a fanatical barber, didn't you?"

"Are you living here now?" he asked.

"What did you do with your hair?"

"I don't want to talk about that."

The others were all gathering in the living room, which was to the right of the foyer—a small room crowded with overstuffed chairs, potted plants, and tables stacked with books. There were bookcases lining the walls and flanking the fireplace, where a small plume of fire danced atop a single log. In the room were the D'Allessandros, Albert, Ricky Dalmas, Wilbur Soames, Joe Baker, Martin Alvarez, and Mrs. Gordon, who was watching Marshall, keeping herself back in among the shadows in that corner of the room.

"We're going to see if we can't continue the school," Mr. D'Allessandro said. "It's worth a try, anyway." He looked at Marshall, and then looked again. Marshall thought it was his hair, but then there was movement behind him and he turned to see Marcus, in a white trench coat and wearing a white hat, entering the foyer. Behind him was a big man with heavy features—thick, drooping jaws, swollen-looking brows, a bulbous red nose, and a pursed, full-lipped mouth. The man looked at each of the people in the living room, edging Marcus aside to enter. The expression on his face was pinched somehow, as though there were something sour on his tongue.

"This," said Mrs. D'Allessandro, "is Terrence."

"Mr. Brace to you," Marcus said.

The big man, without turning to him, said, "Shut up, Marcus."

"Yes, sir."

"Shut that up, too." The big man crossed the room and turned at the mantel, where he took a cigarette case out of his coat, opened it, extracted a cigarette, then snapped it closed. It shone in the light there, gold; clearly it was something he liked people to see. He took his time putting it back, then brought out a lighter of the same gold hue and lighted the cigarette. Mr. D'Allessandro was watching him, his face pulled back in that grimacing smile.

"What's he doing here, then?" The big man gestured at Wilbur. His accent was a tiny increment less pronounced than Mrs. D'Allessandro's.

"He's a student," she said. "Like the others."

He blew smoke, then turned to her. "Really."

"Yes, really."

He drew on the cigarette. "Well, we're an advanced sort, aren't we?"

No one said anything.

Natalie stood a little closer to Marshall; it was almost a cowering. Marshall reached over and took her hand, but she gently removed it.

"We were meeting to discuss continuing the school," said Mr. D'Allessandro.

"Shut up, Lawrence. You're a brother-in-law, not a partner."

Marcus said, "It's time for a little justice."

The big man pointed at him. "*You* shut up, Marcus."

"Yes, sir."

"You always have to get the last word in. Shut *up*." He smoked the cigarette, looking at them one by one. "There's been some talk about the fire. I want everybody to understand the fire was an accident."

"That's the official ruling on it," Marcus said. "From the police."

The big man took a step toward Marcus. "Go outside and wait on the porch."

"It's cold, Mr. Brace."

"You, with the haircut," Terrence said, indicating Marshall. "If he says another bleeding word, you have my humble permission to strike him over the head."

"Oh, Terrence," said Mrs. D'Allessandro. "Do get on with it."

He took another long draw on the cigarette, blew the smoke, then stepped back to the mantel. "We've decided that the school should be kept going—the radio school, anyway—and since the insurance money from the fire will more than cover outstanding debts, we shall be investing in new equipment and a new place. Mr. D'Allessandro will administer the classes only. Only that." He bowed in Mr. D'Allessandro's direction. "And we'll handle the—finances. There will be no return of tuition because classes will resume within the next week or two. The program involving Mr. Brightman will go on as planned. We'll start back a week earlier in January, and graduation will be in July rather than June. Are there any questions?"

"I won't be continuing," Albert said kindly.

"You won't get your tuition back," said Terrence.

"I understand that."

Marshall, to his own surprise, spoke up, too. "I won't be continuing, either."

"What is this?" Mr. D'Allessandro said. "You went through all that trouble to help us." He turned to his wife. "Kid went through all that trouble to help us—"

Terrence said, "Shut up, Lawrence." He was staring at Albert and at Marshall.

"If they want to quit," Mrs. Gordon said, low, "it's up to them."

Terrence turned to her and pointed. "You shut up."

She sank back against the wall.

Terrence stared at D'Allessandro, drawing on the cigarette, apparently thinking something over. Presently, he turned to Walter Marshall and Albert Waple. "What is it with you two, then?" He looked around at the others. "Is this an odd pair?"

"I'm sorry," Albert said to Mr. D'Allessandro. "I thank you for your help."

"I'm going to finish, and graduate," Ricky Dalmas said.

"Me, too," said Mrs. Gordon.

Terrence turned to her again. "Pardon me, I didn't hear you."

"I—" she glanced at D'Allessandro, who was staring fixedly straight ahead. "I—I said I was not going to continue."

"Why should that matter to you?" Mrs. D'Allessandro said to Terrence. "I don't understand."

"I couldn't hear what she said, Esther."

Joe Baker and Wilbur Soames stepped up. "We'll finish."

"I weel, too," said Martin Alvarez.

There was a general sense of relief. Mrs. D'Allessandro spoke of opening a bottle of wine. But no one moved. Terrence crushed his cigarette out, and produced some papers for everyone to sign. Mrs. Gordon signed, then walked out, her coat wrapped tightly around her. She spoke to no one.

Marshall stepped into the foyer, and Natalie went with him.

"Want to go for a valk?" she said.

"I've got Albert with me."

"I'll wait here for you," Albert said from the entrance to the room.

"Let me get my coat," Natalie said.

They went up the block, into the bath of light from a streetlamp there. The sky was almost completely dark. Along the street, lights were going on in all the houses.

"I haven't been honest with you," she said. "Walter."

He said, "I want to marry you."

"No. It would be wrong."

"Why?" he said.

She was staring. "What's the matter with you, that you can't see how wrong it would be? I'm older, I don't have your innocence, do you understand?"

"Innocence," he said. "I'm not innocent. You know what I found out recently? I found out that Kennedy wasn't what they're making him out to—"

"Who told you this?"

"Never mind," he said. "It doesn't have anything to do with us. Besides, I don't believe it. It was just some drunk talking—"

"No, Walter," she said. "It was me. Don't you understand?"

He waited.

"Me," she went on. "I vas one of those—the—I was with him,

Walter. That way. I was one of the girls he had, and now do you see? Do you see how I really am?" She turned away from him. She walked a few paces, out of the lamp's illumination.

Here, the night sky showed angry clouds high up, torn shapes sailing past the thinnest glow, a sourceless shimmer.

He moved to look into her face. "Natalie?"

She turned away again, then sighed. "Someone from the embassy came to me and asked if I would like to meet the president in person."

"You—" He halted. She had moved another step away from him.

"You're such a nice boy, you see. And you stand there looking at me with your god—damn—innocent—face. But you don't know anything. You don't know."

He simply remained where he was.

"Was the president of the country, and I thought maybe I love him. I am only twenty-three at the time."

"God," Marshall heard himself say. "My—God."

The wind blew and caught a wisp of her hair, which shone as if bordered by a thread of fire. Her dark eyes were too bright now. She turned from him once more. He moved to face her again, his hands on her arms. "Anyway," she said, "I need to go home. I'm going back to Germany."

"Natalie," he said. "I don't—"

She kissed his forehead. "You are so kind."

"No," he said.

She removed herself from him, and started back down to the D'Allessandros' house. He followed, then caught up.

"Natalie?" he said.

And she stopped again. "Oh, don't you understand? I'm not your girlfriend, Walter. It was a bad game I played with myself. You must please forgive me. It vas selfish and stupid, and I'm sorry."

"We could still be friends," he said, feeling the absurdity of it.

She sighed, then reached out and touched his face. "You sweet, true, young man. Don't be a politician, Walter." She put her arms around him then, and kissed him on the mouth—a slow, soft, heart-quickening kiss. "There," she said, smiling. "Good-bye, Walter."

He watched her go on up the walk, and the porch steps, into the lighted entrance, where Albert stood. Albert stepped aside for her, murmured a good-bye, then came out and made his way carefully down the steps.

"Guess it didn't work out," he said to Marshall.

"No."

They got into the car, and Marshall pulled out slowly.

"What're you gonna do?"

"I don't know," Marshall said. But he thought he did know. "What about you?" he asked.

"It's like I said—I make a pretty good salary right where I am. I can stay as long as my sight holds out. And Emma can teach Braille. There's plenty to do."

They were quiet for a time, moving through the cold streets behind the gray fan of the headlights.

"I hope we won't lose touch," Albert said.

"We won't," said Marshall, feeling as though he were lying. Against the feeling, somehow flying in the face of it, he repeated the phrase. "We won't."

He drove Albert home, and went into the apartment to say good-bye to Emma, who stood with Albert at the doorway and waved as he drove away.

He would go back to the recruitment office in the morning. His mother was probably getting married; Albert and Emma were already married; Natalie was going home, to the country she had been born in; Minnie was home; Alice was set to go out into the troubled world where her compatriots had gone. Well, he would go there, too. There must still be places where concern for what was right mattered, and people were what they seemed to be. Tomorrow he would enlist in the army, he would give his oath, his word, which he hoped had some value, for all his recent failures, and he would travel far from these endless confusions—to the fight whose outcome mattered most; to the center of the action. He would ask to be sent to that place, Saigon, where the war was being fought for freedom, and where the conflict was definite, the enemy clear. Yes, he would go there; he would seek the truth.

Broad Run, Virginia
1993–1996